Second Chances

Anne Dunphy

TRAFFORD

Canada • England • Ireland • United States of America

© Copyright 2004 Anne Dunphy. All rights reserved.

No part of this publication may be reproduced, stored in a retrieval system, or transmitted, in any form or by any means, electronic, mechanical, photocopying, recording, or otherwise, without the written prior permission of the author.

Printed in Victoria, Canada

Note for Librarians: a cataloguing record for this book that includes Dewey Classification and US Library of Congress numbers is available from the National Library of Canada. The complete cataloguing record can be obtained from the National Library's online database at: www.nlc-bnc.ca/amicus/index-e.html
ISBN 1-4120-1386-0

TRAFFORD

This book was published on-demand in cooperation with Trafford Publishing.
On-demand publishing is a unique process and service of making a book available for retail sale to the public taking advantage of on-demand manufacturing and Internet marketing. On-demand publishing includes promotions, retail sales, manufacturing, order fulfilment, accounting and collecting royalties on behalf of the author.

Suite 6E, 2333 Government St., Victoria, B.C. V8T 4P4, CANADA
Phone   250-383-6864   Toll-free 1-888-232-4444 (Canada & US)
Fax   250-383-6804   E-mail   sales@trafford.com
Web site www.trafford.com   TRAFFORD PUBLISHING IS A DIVISION OF TRAFFORD HOLDINGS LTD.
Trafford Catalogue #03-1764   www.trafford.com/robots/03-1764.html
10   9   8   7

PART ONE

COMING OF AGE

CHAPTER 1

It was Marian Year 1954 and to celebrate we were having a procession in Kilmanogue. The nuns had warned us to wear our Communion veils and to keep to our side of the road, but I wanted to be with Tommy and the boys, so every time Sister Dympna's back was turned, I slipped across.

"Look out, Dumpy's coming," warned Tommy, as the high-pitched warbling approached. I darted back to the girls' side and took my place behind Anna.

"*Bring flowers of the rarest. Bring blossoms the fairest.*" Sister Dympna came closer. "What have you done with your veil Maggie Brown? It looks like a dish cloth."

"The cat had kittens on it Sister," Anna cut in before I had time to answer. One of the boys tittered. Tommy gave him a kick in the backside. Dumpy whirled around but was too late to catch him in the act.

"Move along there boys, no dawdling," she said crossly, and turned to Anna. "Pity your sister isn't more like you, dear. That veil is lovely and crisp."

Anna smiled back, tossing her head so that the veil billowed out around her blonde curls. Frowning her disapproval at me, Dumpy moved on up towards the head of the procession. "*Our full hearts are swelling, our glad voices telling ...*"

Tommy grinned over as I stuck out my tongue at her receding back.

"Why aren't you singing Maggie?"

"Cos it's boring."

"Doesn't have to be."

Curious to see what the boys were up to, I moved across again to listen. "*...of the rarest. Bring blossoms the fairest in garden and woodland in bollocks and blaze.*" Anna waved frantically at me to come back before I was caught again.

"What does bollocks mean?" I whispered, slipping back to my spot behind her.

"Dunno."

"Thought you were supposed to be the brainbox?" I gave her veil a tug.

"Keep those dirty hands to yourself, Maggie Brown," she retorted, and moved on ahead out of my reach.

Later that evening we were helping with the washing up. "Bags dry," I said, grabbing the towel before Anna. "By the way Ma, what does bollocks mean?" A plate slipped from her hand and cracked against the side of the sink.

"What was that you said?"

"Just wondering what bollocks meant. Come on." I leaned across her and took another plate out of the basin. "You're falling behind."

"Where did you hear that word?"

"At the procession. Hurry up. We don't want to miss the Archers."

"At the procession?" Her face had turned bright pink.

"Yes. We were singing hymns."

She lashed out at me. Her ring grazed my ear. "Don't tell lies. Your father would be ashamed if he heard you using that sort of language." She pulled the tea towel out of my hand. "Now get out of my sight this minute. Up to your room, and don't dare come down again 'til you've made a full Act of Contrition."

"What did I do?" I wailed, full of indignation but she just shook her head, eyes closed as if in pain.

"Was it bollocks?" Anna demanded. Ma flinched. "She only wants to know what it means." Ma shook her head again.

"I wasn't the only one singing anyway," I added sulkily. "Tommy O'Connor and the boys were too, so there." Ma's eyes widened in disbelief. "Oh yes they were. I'll show you. *Bring flowers of the rarest. Bring blossoms the fairest, from garden and woodland and bollocks and bl...* ouch." I shrieked, as I caught another stinging blow. "'Snot fair. Sister Dympna was singing too. If you don't believe me, ask Anna."

"She's right Ma. Honest. We all were."

Anna moved closer. Together we stared mutinously up at Ma who remained frozen to the spot, a dinner plate in her hand, the suds dripping off it unheeded onto the floor.

"Don't you ever let me hear you saying that word again."

"But why? What's it mean?"

"Never mind what it means."

"You have to tell her, Ma. Otherwise she'll keep using it."

"You too Anna."

"But that doesn't make se ..." Anna faltered, as Ma's expression hardened.

"It's only a stupid word anyway," I muttered. "Don't know what all the fuss is about."

"It's a terrible word." Then Ma's expression softened. "Girls, ye'll just have to trust me on this."

Anna looked at her suspiciously. "Why can't you tell us?"

"I just can't."

"Okay so. We'll ask Dad."

The blood drained from Ma's face. "Mother of God, if you say a word about this to your father, I'll… I'll…" We stood open-mouthed as our mother struggled for words, our mother who was never ever stuck for words!

"If you tell us what it means we'll promise not to use it again," Anna offered graciously. "Ah go on, Ma. If you or Dad won't, we'll only have to find someone else who…"

"Ye'll do no such thing."

"But we have to know what it means."

"No you don't."

"Yes we do. Dumpy makes us look up all new words in the dictionary."

"You won't find this in any dictionary."

"Course we will."

"No you won't."

"Yes we will."

"No you won't."

"Why not?"

"Because I say so."

"That's not a reason."

"And I'm your mother."

But Anna wasn't ready to give up yet. "I know! We'll go next door and ask Auntie Nell or Uncle Pat. They've lots of books, they're bound to know."

Ma swayed against the sink. The forgotten plate slipped from her grasp and smashed in two pieces on the floor. Anna and I looked down anxiously. It was one of our good ones, but Ma didn't seem to notice. "Look, girls," she said with a note of desperation, "this is all my fault. Forget the word. I shouldn't have made such a fuss." I rubbed my ear pointedly. "And I'm sorry I hit you, love." She leaned down and kissed me.

"'Twas the shock, that's all. Promise you won't use that word again and we'll forget it. Okay?"

"Sure all I wanted was to…"

"Thanks love. Anna?"

"But Ma why don't you just…"

Ma put her fingers to her lips. "Good girl. Now in ye go to the Archers."

"Don't worry," Anna whispered as we walked into the sitting room, "Dumpy will tell me."

"'Cos you're her little pet." I pinched her arm and ran to the wireless.

"What was that?"

"Nothing, Ma," we chorused.

"Good girls."

The sound of Walter Gabriel's agricultural tones filled the room. "And by the way Maggie," Ma sat down and picked up her knitting, "you're not to play with Tommy O'Connor again."

"Why not?"

"Because I'm telling you. Anyway, you'd be better off playing with girls."

"I would not."

"MAGGIE"

Ma had that closed look on her face again, so I slouched down beside Anna on the sofa, wearing my best martyr expression.

A few minutes later Ma had to go out to the kitchen for more wool.

"Don't worry," Anna whispered reassuringly. "I'll find out. Nuns know everything."

I was always sorry I hadn't any brothers. There was only Anna and me, you see, apart from Ma and Dad. Boys seemed to have much more freedom. That's why I liked playing with them. Of all the families in Kilmanogue I liked the O'Connors best. Five boys and their sulky sister Mary. They lived at the crossroads and were forever in trouble. Ma said they were a wild family. Every week or so Paddy O'Brien's bike would be seen lying against the wall of their house. Paddy was the local Sergeant. Mr. O'Connor even had to go away to prison a few times. Tommy called it being *in the nick*. "Dad's in the nick again," he'd announce proudly, as I'd join him in our favourite field beside the crossroads for another session of mud balls.

"That's great Tommy," I'd mumble, never quite sure what my response should be. Some of the drivers didn't seem to mind as the missiles landed on the bonnet of their car but others did. They'd even get out of the car and chase us but we always got away because we knew a shortcut over the field to the beach. We'd race up the sand, dodging in and out of the waves if the tide was in, and lie flat on our backs in the sand dunes to recover. The odd plane would pass overhead cutting a white path through the blue. Tommy knew all the different makes. He was going to be a pilot when he grew up. But I wanted more. I was going to be an astronaut, the first woman in space.

CHAPTER 2

I hated when summer was over and we had to go back to school. Most of the classes in St. Angela's were so boring; all that stuff about saints, commandments, hymns and silly poems. Our classroom was on the top floor, overlooking St. Mary's Secondary School. Anna and I sat by the window. During the more boring classes, I used to watch the older girls playing tennis, and listen to the laughing and screaming as they chased all over the court. I couldn't wait to join them.

One day I was watching a girl serving. She stretched up very tall, threw the ball up and..."Margaret Brown!" The ball slammed over the net. "MARGARET BROWN!" Reluctantly I dragged my gaze from the window.

"Yes Miss Power?"

"Stand up this minute."

"Yes, Miss Power." I pushed my chair back and stood up. The entire class was looking over at me, beaming their gratitude for the interruption.

"What have I been talking about Margaret?" Miss Power was the only person who called me Margaret. We called her Droopy Drawers. Nobody knew why.

I glanced sideways. Anna tilted up her book and pointed to a heading at the top of the page. "The Immaculate Conception, Miss Power," I smirked.

"And are you so smart you don't need to listen?"

"I was listening, Miss Power."

"Glad to hear it, Miss Brown." This was greeted by a titter. "What was I saying?"

I glanced downwards. Anna's finger was hovering over the word *mystery*.

"You were saying how it was all a bit of a mystery, Miss Power." There was another titter.

"Sit down at once and pay attention, or I'll send you home."

Unfortunately she was far more likely to keep me back late, so I sat down and kicked Anna under the desk to say thanks, as Droopy Drawers rambled on. After a decent interval, I resumed watching the tennis.

Tennis was the rage in Kilmanogue that summer. For our class it was the end of our stay in St. Angela's. We had to sit exams to move on to St. Mary's. We were told our results were satisfactory. Miss Power looked at me particularly when she used the word *satisfactory*. She made it sound like an insult, but I didn't mind. Next year we'd be in St. Mary's. We'd be able to play on their courts; much better than the public court. Satisfactory indeed. Still, words could be important. We'd never managed to find out what bollocks meant. The new word for us kids that summer was *bloody*. Everything was *bloody* this and *bloody* that.

As soon as school was over, Anna and I played tennis every chance we got. One Saturday we took on the Tobin boys and managed to beat them. The next morning we couldn't get up out of the beds.

"Come on lads," Ma called, walking into our room, "we'll be late for Mass if ye don't get a move on." Her Sunday hat perched on her head, she looked around and sighed. "God bless us, but ye don't half make a pigsty out of a room. Ye can tidy up while I'm getting the breakfast. Now come on. Move yourselves or we'll be the talk of the town." And Ma didn't like us to be the talk of the town.

After Mass we tidied the bedroom, while the smell of rashers and sausages drifted up the stairs. Anna lined our books into a neat row on the shelf, while I put everything I could find into the laundry basket, and brought it down to the kitchen.

"There's not much badness in ye, really," Ma smiled as she doled out the rashers, "I'll do an inspection later."

After breakfast, Anna and I went up to the court to see who was playing. The other girls couldn't believe it when we told them we'd beaten the Tobin boys the previous day. It was the third time we'd played them. The other times we'd lost.

Sunday lunch was always on the table at one sharp, but this day there was no sign of it. The table wasn't even laid. Dad was reading his paper in the sitting room. Ma was in the kitchen with Auntie Nell. They stopped talking as soon as we walked in. Auntie Nell disappeared out the back door.

"What's wrong with Auntie Nell?" I asked.

"Nothing," Ma mumbled, wiping her hand in a tea towel. "Could ye sit down a minute?" She went to the laundry basket and pulled out my nightdress. "Is this yours, Maggie?" she asked tensely.

"Yes but …"

"There's blood on it. Did you hurt yourself?"

"I must have cut my leg at the match. Remember I was telling you we won? You should have seen the look on Tom Tobin's face…"

"Forget the tennis," she waved her hand impatiently. "There's something I've been meaning to talk to ye about."

"Something bad?"

"Are you not well?" The questions tumbled out of us.

"Is it Dad?" Anna's face was white with anxiety.

"No, no, thank God. It's nothing like that."

"Why are you so cross then?"

"And when are we having lunch?" I looked over at the cooker. Smoke was curling around the oven-door. "I think that meat's done Ma."

She jumped up and turned off the oven. "You're right, love. We can talk later. I'll get your Auntie Nell in to help me."

"Why can't you tell us?" Anna asked, but Ma just shook her head, and concentrated on lifting the chicken onto the table.

I handed her the carving knife. "Come on. I'm starving. You can tell us over lunch."

Ma's face went crimson. "In front of your father? Don't be ridiculous, Maggie. Go wash your hands while l carve."

Anna and I ran to the bathroom. We tussled with each other, scrabbling for the same towel.

Even Dad was showing signs of impatience as we finally walked in with our dinner plates.

"At last! My stomach thought my throat was cut." Ma frowned at him. "Sorry dear," he looked at her penitently. "Where do ye want to go for the walk, girls?"

"The beach," Anna replied.

"The harbour," I said, knowing the beach would be crowded.

"Which is it to be, Rose?" he asked.

"I'm not going with ye today."

We gaped at her. "But you always come with us on Sundays, Ma."

"I have to talk to Auntie Nell about something." She bent down to her plate. Anna and I looked at each other and got on with our meal.

"Why don't you just tell us whatever it is and get it over with?" I asked spearing another potato.

"I…er…I'll go and get my boots." Dad jumped up from the table and left the room.

"Auntie Nell will talk to you both at teatime. Now go for your walk and don't be annoying me."

"What have we done this time?"

"Maggie, for once in your life, do what I ask, like a good girl. Go on. I'll finish up here." She waved away our attempts to clear the table.

Dad was pacing up and down with his walking-cane outside the front door. "It wouldn't take this long for a regiment to get ready. Well, girls which is it, beach or harbour?"

"The harbour."

"Okay then. Let's go."

He marched off singing in time to his steps. *"Left right left. I had a good job and I left, left."* We had to walk briskly to keep up with him. We always started our walks this way, my father swinging his cane back and forward. "Heads up, backs straight, remember," he smiled. "We don't want curved backs in our family. *Left right left, I had a good job and I left left …left right left.*"

We joined in the song for a few minutes to humour him. Dad had had a brief sojourn in the army. He said the only useful thing he learned was how to walk properly. There'd be no slouching in his family, not if he could help it.

The road took us up towards the cliff and off along the narrow headland. Usually fairly windy up there, on that afternoon there wasn't even a breeze. The hot August sun shone down on us. By the time we reached the harbour, the tide was full in.

"Pity we didn't bring our togs." Dad looked wistfully at the water spilling over the pier. "It looks lovely and warm. We'll paddle anyway, but mind the rocks," he warned, tucking his trouser legs up. He tiptoed over to the steps and stepped down into the water. "Ooh, it's gorr…rrgeous!"

We tucked our skirts into our knickers and followed him.

Anna and I messed around happily in the water for ages while he sat on the pier smoking his pipe, looking out to sea, a half smile on his face. Every so often he looked down to see what we were up to. After a couple of hours he suggested it was time to head back. He was always anxious to get home when she wasn't with us, almost as if he hadn't the right to enjoy himself too long without her.

"Do you know what she wants to talk to us about Dad?" I asked him on the way home.

"I… I … no…" he stammered.

I looked at Anna. She shook her head at me. We walked on in silence.

"Come on girls ye can do better than that. *Left right left.*" He quickened his pace and pulled out in front of us. We had to run to keep up. "Wonder what we're having for tea?" he said, slowing down as we turned into our road. "I hope it's griddle cake."

"I'd prefer scones," I said.

"I don't mind which. I love them all," Anna said breathlessly as she caught up with us. Dad turned and put his arms around us.

"And I love my two little girls. But ye're not little girls any more, are ye?"

I looked at him. "Is it because we're starting secondary school Dad?"

"What is?"

"All this talk, the whispering, the funny looks between Ma and Auntie Nell?"

He seemed about to say something then shook his head. "Your mother will have to deal with this." He smiled down at our serious faces. "I'm only a man." He poked me in the ribs. "Come on Long Legs. Race you to the house."

I ran off after him. Anna followed more slowly.

Tea was over, table cleared, dishes put away before I was at last sent next door to get Auntie Nell. "Ma says you're to come in now Auntie Nell." She looked up from the Sunday paper, as I walked in through their back door.

"Okay Maggie. I'll just put on my cardigan."

"Is Uncle Pat coming home soon from hospital?"

"I hope so. You'd miss him around the place wouldn't you?"

I nodded politely. Uncle Pat was so quiet I doubted anyone would miss him. All I ever saw him do was sit in the chair reading the paper. It was Auntie Nell who did all the moving in that house. She was always fussing about something. There was never a cushion out of place. Things weren't thrown together like in our house. But then, as Ma said, she didn't have us to look after.

"Will I do Maggie?" she asked, tidying her hair.

"Of course. It's only us."

"Are you sure?"

"What's all the fuss about anyway?" I smiled up at her. "Come on. Tell me."

"More than my life is worth, sweetheart."

We made our way through their garden. Neat rows of vegetables bordered by even neater fruit bushes and shrubs. Unlike our garden, which was a wilderness of scutch grass and thistles. A single wild rosebush grew around our coal shed. Occasionally one rose would sprout from the wilderness. Ma would pick it carefully and put it in a glass of water in the centre of the table. But Anna and I loved our garden, weeds and all. It was our garden all the kids wanted to play in. It was our long grass that kept us cool in the summer. Ours was the favourite for tents too. And for treasure hunts.

"You're very good to help, Nell," Ma said, wiping her hands on the tea towel. "We'll go into the sitting room. Come on girls." Daddy looked up from his paper as the four of us marched in. "Sorry, John." Ma brought the procession to a sudden halt. "I forgot you were here."

He jumped up apologetically. "Will I go for another walk?"

"No, you need your rest." Ma backed out the door again. "I'll take them into our bedroom." Anna looked at me nervously. We hardly ever went into their bedroom.

We all trooped upstairs. Auntie Nell sat down on the bed. Ma looked at her nervously. "Auntie Nell has something to tell you girls."

"Why can't you tell us?"

"Because Auntie Nell.. er..is… Auntie Nell is …Auntie Nell was a nurse."

Auntie Nell's brows shot up but she said nothing.

"You never told us that!"

"So I'll leave you to it Nell," Ma said firmly, backing towards the door. "Ye won't give her any trouble, sure ye won't?" We shook our heads and she left.

Auntie Nell held her hands together on her lap and took a deep breath.

"Do ye know where babies come from, girls?"

"Is that all?" I said scornfully.

"Course we do," Anna said, "we were told in school"

"Were ye indeed? That's a relief. When were ye told?"

"On the feast of the Immaculate Conception."

Auntie Nell bit her lip. "Oh I see. And what exactly were ye told?"

I deferred to Anna, my expert on all school matters.

"Our Lady had Baby Jesus by a mystery. Some of the older girls asked where ordinary babies come from, and Miss Power said that it needs a father and a mother to make a baby. Lots of us had our hands up to know more, but she said we had to ask at home if we wanted to know anything else."

"I see." The relief faded from Auntie Nell's face.

"Is that it, Auntie Nell?" I turned towards the door. "Come on Anna. We have time for another walk before dark."

"Hold on Maggie. Didn't she tell you anything else?"

"About what?"

"About the difference between men and women?"

"You mean about men having a willy? What's the big mystery in that?"

"Ye're obviously very well educated young women." She gave a little cough. "But there is something else ye need to know."

"So tell us." I was getting bored. Auntie Nell gave another cough.

"Ye must promise to let me finish before ye interrupt." Anna and I nodded. She took a deep breath. "Having babies is a very important job, girls. The woman has them. Yes, yes I know." She put up her hand to stop me. "I know the man has something to do with it as well but it's mainly the woman's job." She paused.

I looked out the window. The tide would be in again by now. "I don't think I'll have any babies Auntie Nell. Could we leave this 'til later? Come on Anna."

Auntie Nell looked at me crossly. "You're not listening, Maggie."

"I am so. You're telling us how to have babies, but I don't want any so it doesn't matter."

"Your mother says I have to tell you, so you're going to listen whether you like it or not."

My mouth dropped open. I'd never heard her speak like that before. "Sorry Auntie Nell. Go on."

"It's a woman's job to have babies, so our bodies have to be made ready."

"But what if we don't want to?"

Auntie Nell took my hand. "Maggie love. You're quite right. Not every woman is lucky enough to have babies or…" her voice sank to a whisper, "or to keep them when they have them." She sighed. "But whether or not we're going to, every woman has to be able to have them and God in His wisdom has designed a way that prepares us and this starts while we're still young."

"How young?"

"Twelve or thirteen."

Anna's eyes widened. "Twelve or thirteen?"

"Yes, love."

"Who'd want babies at our age?" I asked scornfully.

"What about school?" Anna added.

"More important, what about tennis and swimming?" I demanded. "Why would anyone in their right mind want to have to stay home minding babies when they could be out playing tennis?"

Auntie Nell put up her hand again for silence. "I asked ye to let me finish girls. Whether or not they want to have babies, girls of that age…" she looked at both of us, "of *your* age find that their bodies begin to change."

"In what way?" I was getting an uneasy sinking feeling.

"Every month from now on you may notice a little blood on your clothes." She looked directly at me. I could feel my face going hot.

"That was only because I cut myself at tennis."

"There was blood on your nightie too, Mags," Anna said accusingly.

"Where does this stupid blood come from?" I asked crossly.

"From inside your body, where babies are made."

"Is it just a drop or two?" I was thinking of the white tennis shorts Ma had bought us for St. Mary's.

"No. It's more than that love. In fact it lasts for a few days." I looked at her shocked. "A few days … … .every month."

"Every month?" My eyes opened wide. She nodded apologetically.

"How long does it go on for?" Anna asked, ashen-faced.

"A good while."

"A year?" Auntie Nell nodded.

"More than a year?" She nodded again. Anna and I looked at each other.
"For years and years?" Again the nod.
"Until we're grown up?"
This time Auntie Nell shook her head.
"I'm sorry girls. But it'll go on a bit longer than that."

Suddenly, I could see our lives stretching ahead of us like a horrible nightmare, months and months full of bloodstained shorts, dirty nighties and crying babies.

I shook my head firmly. "I'm not having that, thank you very much. Someone else can do it." Auntie Nell laughed.

"It's not as bad as it sounds love. You'll get used to it."

"Who organised this bloody system anyway?"

"God, I suppose." She smiled. "He decided in His wisdom that women should have the honour of bringing babies into the world. And it is an honour, girls. Lots of men would love to be able to have babies."

"They can have mine so," I snapped.

She sighed, and turned to Anna. "What do you think Anna?"

Anna had a faraway look in her eye. "I still don't understand, Auntie Nell. Do we bleed when we piddle, is that it?" I envied her her calm in moments of crisis. We both looked at Auntie Nell, but she was shaking her head again.

"I wish I could say yes to that question. Things would be so much simpler. But I'm afraid the blood comes from somewhere else. The fact is we bleed for a few days every month."

"You mean we.. we've no … no control over it…" The words tumbled out of me. "We're going to *leak blood* for a few days? *Leak*, not even piddle?" Auntie Nell nodded and hung her head. No wonder she was ashamed. "And how many years will this bloody *leaking* go on for?" She shifted uncomfortably on the bed and said nothing. "Come on. How long? 'Til we're seventeen?" She shook her head. "Eighteen?" She shook her head again. "Twenty-one?" She cleared her throat nervously.

"Until ye're… until ye're about fifty."

"FIFTY" I yelped.

Anna collapsed onto the bed. "But that's the end of our lives, Auntie Nell. That can't be right." Auntie Nell hung her head again. So well she might!

"Well I'm not doing it and that's that. Come on Anna." I flounced out of the room nearly knocking Ma down. She was standing outside the door, a guilty look on her face. She put her arm out to stop me running down the stairs.

"Maggie I know it's a shock but it's not as bad as it sounds."

I looked at her. "Surely all the women in Ireland don't put up with this?"

"Of course they do."

"I bet the Americans don't," I retorted. Molly Dillon in our class was born in America. She was always telling us how much more freedom women had over there.

"Even American women have periods, love." Ma smiled and drew me back into the room and sat down beside Auntie Nell on the bed.

"Well it's not fair. Ye don't think it's fair, do ye?" I searched their faces for some sign of protest.

Ma shook her head and laughed. "Of course we don't. But life's not fair, not all the time anyway."

"And what has Dad got to say about all this?"

"Glory be to God." Ma put her hands up to her face. "You must never talk to men about this. Ye can talk to Auntie Nell or me any time, but you must never bother your father or Uncle Pat. The only men who know about this are doctors."

"Why can't men do the bleeding?" Anna asked suddenly.

Auntie Nell's shoulders started to shake. Ma smiled at her.

"You're no help Nell. Stop it."

"I don't know what's so bloody funny," I said angrily. "I'm not going to do it and that's that." I flounced out of the room again. "Come on, Anna. The tide's in."

I ranted and raved all the way down to the beach. The angrier I got, the faster I walked. "So that's what all the whispering was about. Bloody Hell, Anna! What are we going to do?" I waited for her to catch up with me. "We can't let babies ruin our lives. I don't want to be *leaking* all over the place for the next hundred years, do you?"

"Slow down," she panted.

"The Tobins will laugh themselves stupid when they hear about this."

"Ma said we can't tell any boys."

"But they're getting away with murder. And don't forget we have to carry the stupid things in our tummies for months as well. Men don't have to stay home washing dirty nappies or minding them either. It's us women who have to do everything. It's not fair, and I, for one, am not going to put up with it."

"What can we do, Mags?" Anna asked. "Even the American women have babies."

We'd arrived at the promenade by then. The moon was bright. The tide was full in, the sea calm as a milk pond, the earth covered in a silver carpet as far as the eye could see, but for once I barely noticed.

"We'll find someone to help us."

"It'll have to be a woman or a doctor. Nobody else knows."

"That's it." I grabbed her arm. "We'll talk to Dr. Tobin."

"We can't."

"D'you have a better idea?" She shook her head. "Right. We'll go up tomorrow after tennis."

My parents were listening to *Any Questions* when we got home. Ma looked up all smiles. "I'll put on the cocoa girls. Get into your nighties. I've some nice fresh scones."

"She's trying to make up to us," I whispered to Anna as Ma hurried out to the kitchen. Dad picked up the paper and buried his head into it.

"It's not her fault," Anna said as we went upstairs.

"It is so," I retorted, "they've given in far too easily over the years. Makes it harder for us to say no."

My bad humour didn't last long however. Having supper downstairs in our nighties was usually only permitted when someone was sick. Mind you, after what we'd just learnt, we were entitled.

The next day we met the Tobins for tennis as usual. Following their defeat there was a new look of respect in Tom's eyes. We switched partners twice. Everyone played well.

"Ask them about their father," Anna whispered as we came off court.

"Oh yes," I turned to Jack. "Anna and I want to see your father."

"Surgery's on Tuesday Wednesday and Friday."

"That's no good. We have to see him today."

"What about?"

"Women's things."

Tom shifted uncomfortably. "Come on so," he said, picking up his racquet.

The Tobins had a big house at the top of the town. The boys led us past the side door marked Surgery and around the back. Dr Tobin was digging the garden. He looked up as we arrived.

"What's this, a deputation?" he asked and held out his hand.

"I'm Maggie Brown, and this is my sister Anna."

"Ah the tennis champions. Congratulations, girls." He smiled. "That should put manners on the lads for a while."

"We have to see you in private." I looked pointedly at Tom and his brother.

"In that case we'll go inside. Haven't you boys some tidying to do? Remember what your mother said." The boys nodded. The doctor led us through the kitchen and in through another door on the left. "We won't be disturbed in here. Would ye like to sit down?" He pointed to a couch. Anna sat, but I remained standing. "Something to drink, orange or milk?" We shook our heads. "Okay girls," he smiled encouragingly, "what can I do for you?"

"Tell us how to stop this monthly business, because we're not going to have babies," I said crisply.

"Not for the moment anyway," Anna added.

"Ahha… So that's the way it is, is it?" He sat down at the far side of the big desk and started to fiddle with a pen. We waited anxiously as he scribbled on the blotter. "… mmm… well.…. "

"We knew you'd be the best person to help us, being a doctor and all that."

He nodded gravely.

There was a long pause.

"You do know about the leaking?"

"Leaking? Oh I see what you mean. I do, Maggie. I must admit I do."

"Good." We sat back and waited.

He cleared his throat a few times. "And why would you girls want to stop the…er…leaking?"

"'Cos we don't want to have babies, like I said."

"It's the leaking part we don't like, Doctor," Anna added. She was always more polite than me. "We might want babies at some stage, but we don't want to bother with the leaking at the moment. We play tennis you see, and we swim, and we have these lovely new shorts…" He looked at her and kept nodding his head.

"And we don't see why we should have to do all the work and the boys get away with everything," I said, cutting to the chase.

"I can certainly see where you're coming from." He shifted uneasily in his chair. "It might seem awkward at this stage but it's not so bad really. You'll get used to it."

"We don't want to get used to it, Doctor." Even Anna was beginning to lose patience.

"It's not all that bad, is it?" he said with a smile.

It was the smile that did it. "How would you like to leak into your knickers every month?" I snapped.

Something must have caught in his throat because he started coughing. "I'm sorry. I suppose I wouldn't." He looked down apologetically at his desk.

"Good, so you'll give us something to stop it?"

He shook his head. "I can't do anything for you girls. I'm sorry. But don't worry. There's nothing to be afraid of. It's quite natural."

"Natural? It's a disgrace. That's what it is, a bloody disgrace," I added, copying one of Sister Dympna's phrases and adding my favourite adjective.

"I'm fed up hearing we'll get used to it. Why should we? Would men get used to it?" His eyebrow arched. "'Course they wouldn't. If they had to do it, there'd be a cure long ago."

"I'm sorry if you feel medicine has let you down girls," he said, after I'd stopped for breath.

"So you should be. Come on, Anna."

"Thanks for seeing us, Doctor Tobin." The ever-polite Anna held out her hand.

I turned back, ashamed. "I'm sorry Doctor. It's not *all* your fault, I suppose. But as a doctor you *do* have to take most of the responsibility."

He took my hand gravely. "I do, Maggie. Indeed I do. But cheer up. They're talking about sending men up in space. Who knows what will happen in the next fifty years? I suppose what we need are more women scientists."

It was the first sensible thing I'd heard since this leaking business had started.

The following week Ma bought us pads to use on what we should call our *special days*. They didn't feel special to me, but she said it was a kind of code so boys wouldn't know what we were talking about.

CHAPTER 3

Two weeks later we started in St. Mary's. The first morning, we were called into the assembly hall. Great wooden doors were pulled open so that the three classes made up one big hall. At least a dozen nuns were lined up on the stage at the end. There was one man. He stood at the end of the front row.

"I wish we were back in St. Angela's with Dumpy and Droopy Drawers," Anna whispered nervously, as we took our places in the front row with the new girls. I looked back at a sea of white blouses, brown tunics and orange ties. The new material felt rough around my neck.

"We'll be fine," I whispered, "aren't we just as good as any of them? You'll beat them at lessons and I'll beat them at tennis so what's there to be nervous about?" Anna glowed at praise from such an unexpected quarter. The nuns' headdresses were higher and stiffer than the nuns' uniform at St. Angela's.

"Don't they look like a bunch of penguins?" I nodded my head up and down, imitating their movements. Anna giggled. One of the nuns looked down at her and frowned. Anna went scarlet. The same nun shook a brass bell for silence. Everyone stopped talking, and straightened up like soldiers standing to attention.

"Most of you girls know me only too well." The tall nun looked around smiling. "But, perhaps for the benefit of the new girls, my name is Mother Maria. I'm the Reverend Mother here in St. Mary's. This morning we want to say a special welcome to the new girls who have joined us from St. Angela's." There was a faint hooting from the back of the hall. She raised her arm. The hooting stopped as quickly as it had started. "If I catch anyone, I repeat anyone, attempting to make the new girls feel unwelcome they'll be severely punished. Is that clear?" There was silence. "IS THAT CLEAR?"

"Yes Mother." A chorus of voices echoed around the hall.

"Now before you go to your classrooms, I'd like to call for God's blessing on the School Year. In the name of the Father and the Son and the Holy Ghost…"

"See that man teacher?" I whispered to Anna. "I'd say he's Science. That's what I'm going to do."

"Science?" Anna snorted. "Since when?"

"I'm going to be the first woman on the moon."

"Have you told them you're coming?"

"Shut up Smarty Pants."

"And what would you know about Science?"

"Nothing yet. But that's what I'm going to do."

"Really?"

"Either that or a doctor."

"I thought you were going to be a tennis coach?"

"That was before this bloody leaking business."

"What has that got to do with anything?"

"Someone has to find a way to fix it."

"How?"

"Don't know yet. That's why I'm going to do Science, stupid."

"Who're you calling stupid?"

"You can help if you like," I offered. "Think how proud they'll be at home. *The Brown Sisters Discover a Cure for Women Leaking.*" She broke into a fit of giggles. "It's not funny," I whispered fiercely. "I'm not going to spend the rest of my life bleeding into my knickers. You can if you like but I'm not."

A sudden hush made us look up. Mother Maria was glaring down at us. There were a few stifled giggles from the older girls. Some of the nuns' faces had gone red. Others were holding their Rosary beads, eyes closed, lips moving in prayer. I put on my most innocent expression, and looked around as if to see where the problem was. This had always worked in St. Angela's.

"You girls, yes you… what's your name?" Mother Maria glowered down at me, two bright patches of pink in her cheeks.

"Who? Me?" I pointed to my chest and raised my eyebrows.

"Yes, you."

"I'm Maggie Brown."

"Maggie Brown what?"

"Maggie Brown… er…" I paused unsure what other information she wanted. "Maggie Brown from Kilmanogue?"

Laughter broke out in the back rows. It was instantly quelled by a glare from Mother Maria. "Well, Miss Brown. It seems they didn't teach you any manners in St. Angela's."

"Oh yes they did," I retorted loyally, "Sister Dympna would kill you if she heard you say that." There were more giggles. She quelled them with another glare.

"You were obviously not her star pupil."

"No, I certainly wasn't. But Anna was. This is my sis…"

Her hand went up to silence me. "It may interest you to know Margaret Brown, that in St. Mary's, we address the nuns as Mother. Is that clear?"

"Yes."

"Yes what?"

"Yes …… er… Mother?"

"Ah the penny drops at last." More giggles. I scowled back at the culprits.

"And you? What's your name?" Her gaze fixed on the scarlet-faced Anna.

"I'm…I'm Anna B… Brown, Mother."

"You two come to my office. The rest of you go to your classes. AT ONCE."

She turned on her heels and strode off the platform. Her headdress swept behind her, and almost took the eye out of the man, who had to jump back to let her pass.

Anna was trembling. "If we're thrown out on our first day Ma will kill us."

"Don't worry. I'll tell the penguin it was my fault."

"It was."

Somebody pulled my sleeve. A tall redheaded girl stood there grinning, with two other girls. "Ye could be expelled for that sort of talk."

"What sort of talk?"

She smiled and held out her hand, "I'm Angela, this is Mona and Orla. Welcome to St. Mary's."

"Thanks. I'm Maggie and this is my sister Anna."

"I know, the famous Brown sisters," she laughed.

"God Almighty, how much did ye hear?" I asked, trying to remember what I'd said.

"Just about bleeding into your knickers for the rest of your life. We don't use words like that."

"What are we supposed to call them?"

"We're not supposed to be talking about them at all."

There was obviously a lot we had to learn, if we were to survive in St. Mary's. I grabbed Anna. "Come on. We'd better go and get it over with."

"Her office is at the end of the corridor, the one with the statue outside it."

"Thanks."

Our Lady's blue eyes bored into us, as I knocked on the door.

"Come."

At the terse command, Anna went pale. Mother Maria was standing in front of the window, her back to us. She swirled around as we entered. "Why have you kept me waiting?" We stood nervously in the centre of the room. "Door, please." Her voice had an edge to it.

"S…sorry." Anna turned to close the door but it didn't catch. She pushed it again but it clicked open. I went over and gave it a hard shove. This time, it stayed closed. I turned back satisfied.

There was a furious expression on Mother Maria's face. "Rough in gesture as well as words, Margaret Brown. I can see we have our work cut out for us. Stand up straight while I'm talking to you."

We straightened up. She swayed up and down on her heels as she examined us. Through the window over her shoulder I could see the tennis court. Nobody on it. What a waste.

"What were you doing at assembly just now?" She looked coldly at me.

"Nothing, Mother."

"Looking for notice, I suppose?"

"No, Mother."

"We don't use language like that here in St. Mary's."

"Language like what?"

"You know yourself, child. Don't pretend you don't."

"But I didn't use any bad language. Did I Anna?"

"Don't try to involve your sister. You have a dirty tongue on you, and it won't be tolerated in this school."

"But I didn't say anything that was dirty."

"Don't contradict me, child." She moved towards her desk. My gaze drifted out the window again. I was beginning to doubt we'd be here long enough to use the court.

"Look at me when I'm speaking to you," she barked.

"Sorry" I dragged my gaze back to her face.

"Sorry what?"

"Sorry, Mother."

"For your punishment write out the Hail Mary ten times. I want it on my desk first thing tomorrow. Is that clear?" I gasped. That would take all night. "IS THAT CLEAR?"

"Yes, but…"

"Yes what?"

"Yes, Mother."

"And you." She turned to the quaking Anna. "I realise you weren't entirely to blame, but you mustn't encourage your sister. Write it out five times. Now get out of my sight the two of you."

"Can we do them in class?" I ventured.

Mother Maria turned on me, her eyes glinting dangerously.

"You'll do them at home. Close the door on the way out. And I said *close*, not bang."

"May I ask a question, please?"

She looked at me as if she couldn't believe her ears, then nodded.

"Which word did you think was dirty? Was it knickers, Mother?" The way the colour rose in her face was answer enough. "But what should we call them?" I looked her straight in the eye. She glared back at me. I nudged Anna for support.

"She's right Mother. We're bound to discuss knickers at some stage. What do you call them in St. Mary's?"

"Get out of this office at once," she bellowed. "I don't want to see or hear either of you again for the rest of the term."

"Does that mean we don't have to do the lines?"

"OUT" she roared, "or you'll do twice the amount."

I pulled the door behind us. It didn't close properly so I pulled it really hard. It shut but the handle came away in my hand. Anna tried to put it back on the steel rod but the best she could do was hang it on. One push and it would be off again. As we backed away nervously I looked up at the statue. The blue eyes stared coldly back.

"I don't see what's wrong with knickers anyway," I muttered. "Everyone wears them, even Our Lady." I tugged at the blue plaster skirt.

Anna slapped my hand away. "One of these days, you'll be excommunicated Maggie Brown. Anyway, saints are different."

I gasped, as a new thought struck me. "Hey, nuns don't have babies, sure they don't? They must know how to stop the leaking. Come on. Let's go back and ask her."

"For God's sake, Mags!" she said, dragging me away from the door.

From that day on I was known as Knickers Brown, but I didn't mind, because for the first time in my life I'd found some purpose in school. Thanks to Mr Reid, I'd discovered the wonders of Science. I loved the Chemistry experiments. He'd split the class into pairs. He'd move from one pair to the other, making sure we knew what we were doing and why. He'd clap his hands in delight when the experiment turned out correctly. When it didn't, instead of being cross, he'd smile. "Either you girls have just broken the laws of Chemistry, or ye didn't prepare everything like I told you."

"But we did, Mr Reid."

"No. Ye didn't. Go back to the beginning and check each step again."

Inevitably we'd find something that we'd done wrong.

"See?" he'd smile at us. "Learn by your mistakes, girls. Some of the greatest discoveries have been made when scientists make mistakes, and that's a fact."

Mr Reid was always saying *'and that's a fact'*. Physics was more difficult. It was like a new language, but once I got used to it, I enjoyed learning about molecules and atoms and the vast internal world, which up to that I hadn't realised existed.

Anna had chosen cookery instead of Science. Every week she'd bring home something she'd made in class.

"I hope you're hungry," Ma said, one evening when I came in late from school. "Anna's made chocolate éclairs. We kept some for you."

"Split the atom yet, Mags?" Dad smiled up at me.

"Not yet, Dad. What are these like?"

"Delicious," he replied, smacking his lips. "I had two."

Afterwards I went up to the bedroom to study. We were having a test the following week. Anna looked up from her book. "What did you think of the éclairs?"

"Yummy"

"Mother Maria said I didn't use enough eggs."

"Don't mind her. They were gorgeous."

"What did you do in Chemistry?"

"We proved that you need water and air to make nails rust," I said, delighted she was interested. "We had to do three separate experiments."

"Why don't ye learn something useful?"

"That was useful."

"But you can't actually use rust, can you?"

"Mr. Reid said he might let us make soap next term, if we work hard."

"Great. And when are you off to the moon, the term after?"

"Shut up."

CHAPTER 4

Uncle Pat was the first person we knew who died. We didn't know what to say the morning Ma sat on the edge of Anna's bed and told us. "One minute they thought he was getting better. Then he went unconscious, and an hour or so later 'twas all over. But at least Auntie Nell was with him at the time. They had the priest too, so it was a nice death, very peaceful. Just the sort of death your Uncle Pat deserved."

"What's all this talk about nice?" I said crossly. "He's not coming back, is he?" Ma shook her head and said nothing.

"Course not, stupid," Anna said, "he's dead."

Ma looked at us wearily. "Now I don't want any squabbling between you two. And you're to be especially nice to Auntie Nell."

"Okay Ma."

"Good girls. I knew ye wouldn't let me down."

The next few days brought a constant stream of visitors. Auntie Nell had to talk to them all. Anna and I made sandwiches 'til we were blue in the face, plates and plates of them. We no sooner had them made than they were gone. We kept running up the town to get more ham and bread.

Ma decided we shouldn't see Uncle Pat laid out. "Better to remember him the way he was," she said. We didn't get to the graveyard either, because we had to go home to make the tea. His two brothers arrived from England with their families. Most of the others were from Wexford, and had worked with Uncle Pat. We heard all sorts of stories about him, and what he did at work. To us, Uncle Pat never seemed to do much of anything, so we were surprised that people thought so highly of him. Nobody stayed long, but they always said yes when they were offered tea. Tea meant sandwiches, so Anna and I were run off our feet.

Suddenly the excitement was over. Auntie Nell went back next-door, and our house became our own again. Anna and I had been so busy we hardly realised that Uncle Pat was gone. We thought at any moment he might pull up in his car outside and give the usual rat-tat on our door. But one look at Auntie Nell's empty face told us he wouldn't be coming back. The light had gone from her eye, the spring from her step.

On Saturday morning, Anna and I went next door and rang the bell. She came out, still in her dressing gown, even though it was almost eleven. "Yes, girls?"

"We're going to do the garden for you, Auntie Nell."

She looked at us uneasily. "That's very nice of you but…"

"We'll do it right, don't worry. We'll keep the rows straight, not like our own."

"And we'll do the weeding too if you tell us which is which," Anna added.

"Ye're very good, really, but I don't think…"

"Is there anything else we can do for you?" Anna looked around. "Sweep, clean or …"

Auntie Nell's eyes filled with tears. "If ye could just come in to see me now and again? I don't know how I'm going to get used to being on my own. Would ye like tea?"

"Any Boudoirs?" I asked quickly. We never had any in our house. Ma said they were too delicate for us.

"I don't know, love. Come on in and we'll see." She ran her hand wearily over her forehead.

Their house looked different without Uncle Pat. It even smelt different.

It was several months before the spark came back into Auntie Nell's eyes. By then, she'd become one of the family. She spent every weekend with us. After lunch on Sundays, she'd sit talking with Ma, while Dad took Anna and me for our walk.

One Sunday afternoon we returned to find the two of them laughing and giggling together on the sofa.

"What are you women up to now?" Dad asked, as he hung his cane on the hallstand.

"Great news," Ma said, "Nell's after landing a job."

"Congratulations!" Dad gave her a big kiss. "Where?"

"In Flavin's, the drapers."

"Great. You'll be able to get us something off the dresses."

"Give her a chance, Anna," Dad laughed. "This calls for a celebration." He opened the door of the drinks cabinet and took out a bottle of whiskey.

Ma frowned. "We haven't had tea yet, John."

"Never mind your tea. Sure won't we be dead long enough?"

Ma gasped, and put a hand to her mouth. But Auntie Nell only laughed.

"Pat would be delighted for me to have whiskey with you, John. Didn't he enjoy many a one with you himself?" Dad looked relieved.

Anna and I had lemonade.

"To Auntie Nell and her new job," Dad said, raising his glass. "They're lucky to get her."

"To Pat, God rest him," Auntie Nell raised hers.

"May he watch over us all," Ma said, smiling.

I liked the idea that Uncle Pat might be up there somewhere looking after us.

"I'm so lucky," Auntie Nell said. "I'd be lost without ye."

"We're the lucky ones, Nell."

"Yes Ma, after all, we could have the O'Connors beside us, couldn't we?" I looked over my glass at her.

"You may well jeer young lady, but look what's happened to him."

I pulled a face but said nothing. Tommy had been in trouble with the Guards. He'd been sent off to reform school, so we couldn't even write to each other now. Mr O'Connor was in the nick yet again. The rest of the family had left Kilmanogue and gone to England.

Later that night, in bed, I thought about Tommy. We'd lost touch since I'd taken up tennis. I fell asleep wondering what reform school was like. I dreamt that he and I were robbing a bank. We'd been caught and locked in jail. Uncle Pat was given the key and he was in heaven so we'd never be let out again. I was trying to persuade him to drop me down the key when I woke up.

CHAPTER 5

Anna and I sat mock tests at Christmas, to prepare for the Intermediate Cert the following summer. Anna did well in Domestic and English. I did well in Science and Bookkeeping. The Tobin boys told us they were planning to go to university. There had to be more to life than getting married and having babies so I raised the subject with Anna on the way home that evening.

"Who do you think we are, millionaires?" came the scornful reply. "You'll work in a shop or an office, get married and have babies like everyone else."

"What if I don't want to?"

"Doesn't matter what you want."

"I'm not going to do it just because everyone else does."

"Course you will Lumpy."

"Why should I?"

"Because that's what girls do."

The new nickname had replaced Knickers. I'd put on weight since going to St. Mary's, probably from eating Anna's baking. Because of the studying I was playing less tennis too. Anna was lucky. Her weight never changed.

A few weeks later, I raised the subject again. I was in bed and Anna was brushing her hair. " I think I'll go to UCD," I said, watching her reaction in the mirror.

"You'll what?" The brush was poised over her head.

"If Dad can afford it, and he will, if I ask him," I added and pretended to yawn.

"You go to college! You haven't a hope."

"Mr. Reid says I have. I'll be taking Physics and Chemistry in Fifth year."

"What has that got to do with it?"

"I'm going to do Science."

She burst out laughing. "Who do you think you are, Marie Curie?"

"Why shouldn't I?"

"Cause you're a girl, Stupid!" We glared at each other. "Anyway, I'm the eldest."

I hadn't thought of that. She could have a point. There were eleven months between us. It had never counted up to now. It would be just like her to spoil my chances.

"I hope my girls aren't fighting again," Dad called up the stairs.

"Dad, did you know that Maggie wants to go to university?" she shouted back.

I jumped out of bed and pulled her hair. "I told you not to say anything."

She slapped me and ran downstairs. "Lumpy thinks she's going to college. You can't afford to send us, Dad, sure you can't? Anyway, I'm the eldest so I'd have first call, isn't that right?"

Dad looked at us and frowned. "I certainly wouldn't manage both of you, whatever about one."

"I knew it." I could hear the glee in Anna's voice as she hurried back to bed.

If only I'd kept my big mouth shut. I followed her up and threw myself on the bed. The door opened again. It was Ma.

"You want to go to college, Maggie?" I nodded. "Are you sure that's what you want?" I nodded again, not trusting myself to speak. "But you do realise Anna would have to get first choice?"

"She'd never even thought about it 'til I said it," I shouted, "dirty little spoil sport!"

"Let's wait and see, eh?" Ma said soothingly. "Your Dad and I have been talking. We might be able to send one of you. Auntie Nell has contacts in Dublin. But with digs and fees it'd be difficult. There's no question of both, I'm afraid," she sighed. "Your father's desperately upset over it, love, so the less said about it for the moment the better. I don't want him to feel guilty."

"I don't either, Ma," I said penitently.

She gave me a hug and left the room. Behind her the air was electric. I picked up a book and pretended to read. Anna got into bed and started to hum.

"You're a selfish little bitch, Anna Brown," I hissed.

"I am not."

"You are too."

"I am not."

"You are. You always have to have your own way."

"I do not."

"You do so." I threw a pillow at her.

"I do not." She gave a snigger and threw it back. It landed on the floor. I leaned out of the bed to get it and fell out.

She roared with laughter. "How could a thick like you go to college? You can't even have a decent pillow fight without falling out of bed."

I got back into bed, too angry to see the funny side of it. "I hate you, Anna Brown. I hate you. I hate you. I hate you."

"Ditto, ditto, ditto."

I didn't answer. I couldn't. I was still too angry.

"I'm sorry I was mean," she said after a few minutes.

"Forget it. I've decided not to go to college after all."

"Good. Then I won't go either."

The relief in her voice proved she never wanted to go in the first place. I hated her for that, but I decided my best tactic, for the moment, would be to pretend I'd changed my mind.

CHAPTER 6

St. Mary's prided themselves on using Fifth Year to expand our education. Mother Fintan was helping us put on "The Scarlet Pimpernel" as our Christmas play. It was a romantic story about the hero who pretends to be a fop, while risking his life to rescue people from the dreaded guillotine. She asked us to pick out the parts we wanted, and learn ten minutes of script by heart. I desperately wanted to play the lead role. I knew I'd have to lose weight, so I starved myself for days before the audition. Every chance I got, I studied the script. The evening before, I was able to recite the whole ten minutes to Anna, without once referring to the notes.

"You're bound to get it," she said when I'd finished.

"Thanks sis," I replied, delighted at the unexpected praise.

"Sure who else is tall enough?" I swallowed hard.

Naturally, she had selected the part of the wife for herself. Because of her looks, most of the class expected her to get it. She showed me how her hair could be made into ringlets after the fashion of the French court. "It'll be gas, you being the Pimpernel with me as your wife, won't it?" she giggled and jumped out of bed to practise her pirouette in front of the mirror. "Get up and see if we can do the polka."

We pranced about the room. Boom boom boom, boom boom boom.

"Girls, girls," Ma called up to us. "If ye don't get back into bed, there'll be no Scarlet Pimpernels in this house." We jumped back into bed at once.

The next day we had our chance to show what we could do on a real stage. Anna went first. I have to admit she was great, all feminine and gentle, not a bit like she was in reality. There was only one other girl who wanted to play that part, and she wasn't half as pretty as Anna.

Two of the others wanted to play Pimpernel as well as me. They were called up first. I listened to their performances with my heart in my mouth. Neither of them knew their lines very well. Mother Fintan had to prompt them several times. Then at last it was my turn. Up I got, and turned round to the audience. Mother Fintan gave me the signal to start. I looked down at the back of the hall the way she'd told us, took a deep breath and opened my mouth. Nothing came out.

"Right Maggie, off you go." She nodded again to me. I took another breath. Again nothing happened. "Come on now. Don't be nervous. I'll give you the first line... *'We have to rescue them, Charles. They'll be for the guillotine if we don't get them out of France tonight...'*"

"*'Out of France tonight,'*" I took up the cue, "*so comrades, we'll up anchor on the next tide and make Calais at... at dawn."* I stopped. It sounded flat, not a bit like the way I'd rehearsed. I repeated the line and then at last it happened. The words started to flow, just as I'd practiced. I continued and went on without stumbling to the end. *"And do remember, gentlemen, not a word to anyone. Many lives depend on your silence. Go quickly. We meet again at midnight."* I bowed with a great flourish. Everybody clapped.

"Very good Maggie," Mother Fintan beamed at me. "Don't worry about the stagefright. It happens to the best of us." I nodded, too breathless to speak. "Thank you, girls. I'll have the selection done by Friday."

Three sleepless nights followed. I tried to convince myself the others were hopeless, the part was mine.

There was no sign of Mother Fintan on Friday morning. We'd been fooling around in class for a good ten minutes before she arrived. Silence fell instantly. She walked unsmiling to the top of the class and sat down at her desk.

"Now girls I'm going to read out the cast but remember we all have parts to play both on and offstage, important jobs like prompting, looking after props, lights, costumes amongst other things. Please let me get to the end before asking any questions, and try to remember girls, it's all about teamwork. Each and every one of you will play a part on that team." She took a deep breath. "Scarlet Pimpernel Rosaleen Burke, his wife Anna Brown..."

"Who the hell's Rosaleen Burke?" I choked at Anna.

"Tall dark one in Sixth Year," Anna replied, her face rosy with success.

"But it's the bloody Fifth Years who are putting on the bloody play..."

Mother Fintan coughed, and looked across at me, "Monsieur Fauberge Maggie Brown."

"Who's Monsieur Fauberge when he's at home?" I gave Anna another dig.

"Innkeeper," Anna smirked, "congratulations."

Mother Fintan continued calling out the rest of the parts, followed by the stagehands. Somehow she'd managed to include the whole class. I should have given her some credit for that, but I wasn't in the mood for giving her anything. I was far too busy turning the pages trying to find Monsieur bloody Fauberge. I found him on page 42. Found his three lines, or to be more exact, his one line, repeated twice. A crazy man, all he had to do was to bang the table at the inn and shout, "Sacres Aristos" twice on page 42 and once on page 44.

A moment's silence followed Mother Fintan's litany. Then pandemonium broke out. Everybody started talking together. She held up her hand for silence.

"I know some of you are disappointed. Let me explain. First of all the main part of the Pimpernel—some of you may be wondering why I chose Rosaleen Burke." She looked at me and the other two who'd auditioned for the part. "To be perfectly honest, I didn't think that those who auditioned were up to it. We only have three weeks to get ready. The success of the production revolves around this part. I couldn't take a chance. I've chosen Rosaleen because she's already played this part in her last school."

"Where's she from anyway?" I asked, sulkily.

"Her family moved over from England last year."

"You mean she's not even Irish?"

"Maggie Brown, I'm ashamed to hear you talk like that."

"But it's not fair. It's supposed to be our class that's putting it on."

"I've explained why I gave it to her Maggie. We'll get on with the lesson now. Anyone who's still unhappy can come to me afterwards."

I couldn't wait for class to be over. She smiled at me when I approached her desk. "You'll enjoy your part, Maggie. It's small but dramatic. You'll be able to do a lot with it."

"Not as much as I'd have done with the Pimpernel."

"At least you have a part. Spare a thought for those who won't even get on stage."

"But I'll only be on for about five minutes."

"I know, but it's a critical part in the drama. Read it again. You'll see." She turned to another girl. "Yes Maria?"

I picked up my books and stormed out. *Sacres Aristos!* Two bloody words! I'd never hear the end of it from Anna. To avoid her I ran all the way home. I burst into the kitchen and thumped the table. "*Sacres Aristos!*" A cup of flour spattered over the baking tray.

Ma looked up from the oven. "Watch your language Maggie."

"It's the play, the one we're putting on for Christmas."

"Oh sorry, I forgot love. Did you get the part?"

"No. How come Anna always gets what she wants, Ma? It's not fair." I thumped the table again. "*Sacres Aristos*. It's not bloody fair."

Anna burst in through the door. "I got the part, Ma. I'll be wearing all those lovely dresses." She pirouetted around, knocking against the table. "I'll be able to put my hair up in ringlets and…" She spotted me behind the door. "Oh I wondered where you'd got to."

"I'm sure you did."

"Sorry about the part, Mags. But, as Mother Fintan says, it's all about teamwork," she grinned. I moved over, fist clenched but she quickly stepped behind Ma. "At least you got a part. You could be pushing furniture around backstage."

"Yeah, yeah" I muttered crossly.

"Will you be able to learn all the lines?" she sniggered and ran out of the kitchen slamming the door in my face before I could catch her. She leaned on it from the other side chanting "*Sacres Aristos, Sacres Aristos.*"

"You'll be sorry when I get you, little bitch," I roared, trying to push it open.

Ma sighed, and rubbed a floury hand over her forehead. "Go and tell your father all about it, there's a good girl. I have to get another dozen scones for the ICA into the oven. Anna! Let Maggie out, and go to your room until I call you for tea." There was a muffled sound at the far side. "Anna, did you hear me?"

"Yes, Ma."

Ma went to the door. I moved towards it too, but she put a hand out to stop me.

"Into the sitting room with you, Maggie. Anna! Upstairs to your room, this minute. You're wearing me out, the two of you. Ye wouldn't behave like this in front of the nuns."

Anna was half way up the stairs by the time I got out. I went into the sitting room and threw myself into a chair. Dad had his head buried in the newspaper. He looked up warily.

"Alright, Mags?"

"No, Dad. I'm not. Nothing's bloody right."

"Oh dear. Oh dear. That's too bad." He turned another page, shook out the newspaper and pretended to concentrate on some article. "I'm sure your mother will sort it out for you," he said, keeping his head safely buried in the paper.

But Ma couldn't sort it out, not this time.

When the rehearsals started, Anna became impossible to live with. She was acting all the time, on stage and off. Every opportunity she was muttering her lines, usually within earshot. When she'd forget a line she'd bang the nearest bit of furniture and scream *Sacres Aristos*. Rehearsals took place every second night. I didn't want to admit it, but Rosaleen Burke was good. From the beginning, she knew all her lines, and where to come on and off stage. She needed very little direction.

I was most uncomfortable playing Monsieur Fauberge. The part called for anger and emotion like Mother Fintan had said. At home I could thump the kitchen table and put real feeling into the two words, especially if I thought of Anna. But onstage it was another story. With so little to say, I felt stupid and moved awkwardly as a result.

I wished the school had never decided to put on the play. Each night I lay in bed praying that something would happen. '*Please God, put the play off. Better still, cancel it altogether. I'm going to make a mess of it. Everybody will laugh at me. Dear God, please. I'll work hard. I'll say the Rosary every night for a week, a month even...*" Every night the promises got more reckless. Some nights I dreamt it had been cancelled and everything was alright. Then I'd wake up to the awful reality.

Anna became insufferable. The more anxious I became, the more confident she got. She'd be muttering the lines at the table just loud enough for me to hear. No matter how hard I'd kick her she'd carry on. She was now saying *Sacres Aristos* every time anything went wrong at home, even the smallest thing.

On the Saturday before the play was due to go on, she was goading me all day. Finally I managed to trap her outside the bathroom door. I pinched her arm so hard that I drew blood. She screamed and ran downstairs to the kitchen.

"Ma, look what Lumpy has done." She held out her arm.

I was delighted to see the two red spots of blood. The surrounding flesh was already turning dark blue. I thought I'd pay for it, but even Ma had had enough of her airs and graces. "Don't make such a fuss Anna. A bit of makeup will cover that." She was busy making Madeira cake for yet another Bring and Buy Sale. "Leave me alone now. There's a good girl."

"No wonder Lumpy didn't get the part. She's so stupid she can't even say her two lines."

"Who're you calling stupid?" I said, moving threateningly towards her.
"Ma, get her off me."

Ma looked up wearily. "Maggie, behave yourself for goodness' sake."

"But I hate her, Ma. I hate her. I hate her. I hate her."

"Forget it." Ma sighed. "It'll be all over in a week or so. Then things can get back to normal."

"What's she going to be like next week?" I wailed.

"It's only one more week, love. What's a little week?"

I don't know how Anna got through that weekend without being killed in her bed.

On Monday morning Mother Fintan walked into the class, white as a sheet. She sat down at the desk and looked around the room.

"I'm afraid I've some bad news, girls." She waited for silence. "The play is off."

I held my breath, unable to believe what I'd heard. Then everyone tried to talk together. "Off? How can it be off?"

"We have to cancel, I'm afraid. The Scarlet Pimpernel's gone to England to do nursing."

"She can't," Anna shouted. "She'll have to wait 'til it's over."

"Sorry, Anna. Her mother and herself went over on the boat this morning. They had to enrol in the hospital today or she'd have lost the place." Talking broke out again. She rapped on the desk for silence. "Now I know it's a shock. I only heard it myself last night when her mother rang. Apparently she was trying to reach me since Satur…"

"She can't do that," Anna interrupted again. "Too many people are depending on her." The babble broke out again.

I sat in silence and prayed and prayed like I'd never prayed before. *'Thank you, God. Thank you, Dear God and His Holy Mother. I promise I'll never say a cross word to anyone again ever, even to that little bitch of a sister.'*

"I'm sorry, girls." Mother Fintan was trying to get the class to settle down. "I know you've all put a great deal of work into the rehearsals. But try to think of it as a learning experience. The next time we put on a play you'll be well prepared."

"We won't be able to put one on next year. We'll be doing exams," Anna grumbled. "I… we were all looking forward to Friday night. Weren't we girls?" She looked around. The others nodded in agreement. Her gaze landed on me. "Those of us who had decent parts anyway."

"It was a team effort, Anna," I said solemnly. "Isn't that right, Mother Fintan? It didn't matter what parts we had."

"Well said, Maggie. Thank you for reminding us all about that." Mother Fintan beamed at me. "It's the taking part that matters, and you've all done that for the last few weeks. Each and every one of you. I'm going to tell Mother Maria how good you were." Anna glowered back at her. "I know you were looking forward to going onstage, Anna, but it just can't be helped. A child's future was at stake, and that's far far more important than our little drama, isn't it?" Anna shook her head crossly. "Isn't it, dear?" Mother Fintan smiled encouragingly at her. Anna glowered back. "Good. Now if we could get on with the lesson. Please open your Macbeths at Act Two, Scene One."

I felt as if a great weight had been lifted from my shoulders. My prayers had been answered. There was nothing to dread any more. Life was wonderful again. Anna didn't talk to me for weeks of course. As if it was my fault the play had been cancelled. Perhaps it was. I *had* said an awful lot of prayers and made a great deal of promises.

CHAPTER 7

By Sixth year there were only five of us doing Physics and Chemistry. I was still hoping somehow to get to college. One evening, when we had the house to ourselves, Dad told me he might be able to manage it after all, provided it was only me. I was delighted. I didn't want to risk Anna spoiling things again, so this time I didn't say anything to her.

It was bitterly cold. It snowed for three days in succession. Kilmanogue looked like a Christmas card. For Anna and me it was our first-ever white Christmas. Auntie Nell bought herself a new car. Up to then, she'd been driving around in Uncle Pat's old Hillman.

"It'll make the trips to the wholesalers much quicker," she said, as we stood around admiring the shiny Morris Minor.

"You're so brave, Nell," Ma told her. "I'd be terrified."

"Women are just as good drivers as men." Nell laughed at Dad. "Isn't that right, John?"

"I can't keep up with you women." Dad made a sad face. "Ye'll be wanting to run the Government next. Then it'll be women priests, I suppose. Where will it all end? That's what I want to know. Where will it all end?"

"Why shouldn't we be priests?" I demanded.

"Or Prime Ministers for that matter?" Nell grinned.

"Or Chefs?" added Anna.

Dad turned back towards the house. "I'd better get out of here. I can see I'm outnumbered."

"To tell you the truth, Rose, I am a bit nervous." Auntie Nell turned to Ma. "I'm not used to this car. Some of the instruments are different from Pat's."

"Here's someone who'll keep you safe." Ma held out a tiny medal on a ribbon.

"Ah St Christopher. Thanks Rose." She kissed Ma. "With him to look after me, I'll be fine." She hung it round the little mirror over the dashboard, and as she closed the door brushed a mark off the shiny doorframe. "I was wondering if John would come out with me? I could do with some practice before I take it to Dublin."

"Of course Nell. He'd be delighted. Think what it'll do for his ego."

"Your John hasn't any ego."

"It's a miracle he hasn't then," Ma replied, walking up the path towards the house, "in a houseful of women."

Dad was delighted to be asked. They went for the lesson the following

Sunday after lunch. Anna and I wanted to pile into the back, but Dad said it would be too distracting for Auntie Nell so we went up to our room and did some study instead. We had mock exams as soon as we returned after the holidays, so we had lots of revision to do. Ma sat in the sitting room. She was knitting gloves for Dad's Christmas present.

A few hours later, Anna and I were checking each other's trial balance when we heard a knock on the door. Even though it was only five, it was dark already. We heard Ma answer it, and went back to our trial balance. A few minutes later we heard the front door open again.

"See who that is," I said to Anna who was nearest the window.

"See for yourself, Lumpy. I'm busy."

I got up and gave her a thump as I went over to the window. There were two cars outside our gate, neither of them Auntie Nell's. I strained my ears to hear what was being said below.

Anna lifted her head from the trial balance. "Sit down Mags and shut up. That's the third time I've gone over the same set of figures."

"I think there's something wrong." There was silence below, and yet I knew nobody had left the house. "I'm going down to see what's happening."

"Go on then and leave me in peace," she said crossly.

Three women were standing in the hall. Mrs Tobin was the only one I recognised.

"Where's Ma?"

"It's okay, love. I'm here." Ma emerged from the sitting room, face white as a sheet.

"What's wrong?"

She held out her arms to me. "They.... Auntie Nell and Dad had an accident." One of the women put her hand on her shoulder.

"Are they alright?" My mother closed her eyes as if too weary to answer me. I caught her hand. "Ma! Answer me. Are they hurt?"

She shook her head and held me. "I'm sorry, love. Nell's alright but... but your dad ... your dad's gone."

"Gone where?" I stared wildly at her, "to hospital?" She shook her head. Her eyes closed again. Mrs. Tobin took my hand.

"Maggie love, your father's dead, I'm sorry. That's what your mother's trying to tell you."

"He can't be." I pulled my hand away. "Ma, tell her she's wrong."

"Where's Anna?" My mother asked in a dull voice.

"Up in the bedroom studying."

"I'll go and tell her for you, Rose, will I?" Mrs. Tobin looked at her.

Ma shook her head and took my hand. "Come on, Maggie. For your father's sake." She led me upstairs. I held back. I felt if I delayed it might somehow make things different.

Anna was still bending over the trial balance, calling the figures to herself as if her life depended on them. When she saw us, the blood drained from her face. Ma held out her arms. "Anna you're going to have to be very brave. There's been an accident. He's dead, love. I'm so sorry. Your poor father's dead."

Anna ran to her and buried her head in her chest. Her body was shaking. Ma put her arms around her. "There there now. It'll be alright." She looked at me over Anna's shoulder. I moved over and put my arms around them. We stayed like that, the three of us, hanging onto each other for several minutes. Ma wasn't crying, neither was I, only Anna. I was numb inside. Dad couldn't be dead. That would mean he was never coming back. I felt a scream build up at the back of my throat. Ma hugged us. "There's only the three of us now, girls. We're going to help each other. That means no more rows between you two. If we're going to get through this, we'll have to ..."

There was a gentle tap on the door. "Sorry, Rose." It was Mrs Tobin. "Sorry to disturb you. Fr Doyle has arrived. He wants a word."

Ma's face tensed up. "Tell him I'll be down in a minute."

Mrs. Tobin turned to go. "I'll give him a cup of tea."

"Thanks."

"Don't go, Ma." Anna was sobbing her heart out. I stood there trying to comprehend what was happening. What was the priest doing here? Only a few hours ago Dad had been joking with Auntie Nell about women drivers.

"There has to be some mistake," I said, "It's not Dad. It must be someone else."

My mother's face twisted. "Jesus Mary and Joseph, if only it was." The cry came from deep within her. "Will ye be alright up here on your own for a few minutes?" We nodded. "Good girls. I'd better talk to Fr. Doyle." She left the room.

Anna looked at me and then out the window. I sat down on the bed. I couldn't think of anything to say.

"What's going to happen now?" Anna broke the silence.

"How d'you mean?" I stared vacantly at her.

"How are we going to live, stupid?"

I looked at her horrified. "Dad's dead and you're worried about money?"

She looked at me defiantly. "Well Ma hasn't any job."

I looked angrily at her. "Why did it have to be him? What did he do to deserve this? That's what you should be asking, not *what's going to happen now?*" I mimicked, deliberately exaggerating the whine in her voice.

She reached out and struck me with her fist. "Stop making fun of me."

I staggered back, the breath knocked out of me. "Little miss goody two shoes, always pretending to be nice when underneath you're…you're…horrible, mean, petty and horrible." I thumped her hard on the back, harder than I'd intended. She reeled under the blow and started to cough, a dry rasping cough like the one she'd had the previous winter. I ran downstairs scared. Anna staggered after me holding onto her throat. Bad and all as she was, she wasn't going to let me give my version of what had happened.

Ma was showing Fr Doyle out the front door. "We'll see you tomorrow evening, Mrs Brown. And again, anything you want, just let me know."

"Thanks Father." She closed the door and turned crossly to me. "I'm ashamed of you two. I'm sure he could hear ye through the ceiling."

"Maggie's … cough cough… after killing me," Anna rasped.

"It's her own fault," I retorted, "I wish it had been her that died, not Dad." My mother closed her eyes and moved away from me as if she couldn't take any more.

"I'll see to them, Rose," Mrs. Tobin said. "Go back into the sitting room and finish your tea."

At the calm voice Ma nodded and left us. Mrs Tobin closed the door behind her. "Shame on you girls for upsetting your mother at a time like this."

"Twas her fault," Anna said sulkily.

"Twas not. You started it."

"I did not."

"You did so. Mrs Tobin she said something terrible about Dad."

Anna blushed. "I didn't mean it."

Mrs Tobin smiled. "People often say terrible things when they're upset."

"She thumped me," Anna retorted. "She knows I have a weak chest."

Mrs Tobin looked at me.

"Twas only a little thump. Anyway she hit me first."

Mrs Tobin's eyebrows rose. "God, ye're worse than the boys." I doubted Jack and Tom fought half as much as we did, but I said nothing. "You two will have to try to get on better with each other from now on. Think of your poor mother." She looked from one to the other. "Ye can't be going on like this. Ye're all she has left now."

Suddenly, I didn't feel annoyed any more. *All she has left now.* It sounded so final. A sense of weariness washed over me. Ma was right. Everything had changed. We'd have to grow up. We had no father to look after us now. Nothing would ever be the same again.

The funeral took place two days later. Auntie Nell wasn't well enough to attend. Relatives came from all over the country. Anna and I never left Ma's side. The three of us walked up the church behind the coffin. We knelt on either side of her in the front row. I kept staring at it, wondering whether Dad could feel anything. Though I knew he wasn't really in there. His soul was somewhere up in the sky looking down on us.

After Mass, we followed the coffin down the aisle while everybody looked on. It was a bit like being on stage. I saw the Tobins. I caught Tom's eye. He looked so sad I smiled at him to cheer him up. He smiled back and looked away.

A short time later, we stood by the grave staring down into the deep hole. Fr Doyle blessed the coffin with holy water before it was lowered. *"Dust to dust. Ashes to ashes."* His voice droned on. *"We shouldn't grieve for John. Instead we must look to the resurrection on the last day when we will meet him again in our heavenly home."* Everybody was crying, but I knew that Daddy wasn't really in the coffin.

"Don't worry Ma. He's not down there," I whispered, trying to cheer her up. But she just gave my hand a little squeeze and said nothing. We watched as the clay was shovelled into the hole. Just then a bird swooped down over where we were standing. "See?" I pointed. "That's probably him watching over us."

"Yes, love." She squeezed both my hand and Anna's. "Your Dad will always be up there watching over his girls. Remember that whenever ye're sad, won't ye?"

Someone arranged the flowers on top of the clay. The smell was sweet, almost sickly.

Later everybody came back to our house, but this time Anna and I didn't have to make the sandwiches. Ma's ICA friends made them. I never saw so many plates in the kitchen. Ma was worried we wouldn't remember who owned them all. But Mrs Tobin collected them the next day and brought them to the meeting the following week so people could claim them.

CHAPTER 8

Auntie Nell came home from hospital on crutches the following week. We made up a bed for her in the sitting room. The house started to come alive again for the first time since the accident. Anna and I had been given a week off school. Neither of us felt ready to go back yet. The trial balance we'd been working on that night remained unbalanced.

"What time is Mr Joyce coming, Rose?" Auntie Nell asked Ma on Friday morning. Mr. Joyce was the local insurance man.

"Around three, I think."

"Are you sure you want me here?"

Ma nodded emphatically. "I'm no good with money. I left all that sort of thing to John."

"But I'd be intruding."

"You won't. Please Nell. I need you there."

"Do you want us too?" Anna asked.

"No. You girls go for a walk. Ye've been cooped up in the house too long."

Walks weren't the same now without Dad, but we went anyway. We walked along the beach, each lost in our own thoughts. I knew Anna was missing him too, but I wasn't ready to talk about it. When we got back, Mr. Joyce had left. Ma and Auntie Nell were sitting together on the sofa. Ma's eyes were red.

"… will be alright you'll see," Auntie Nell was saying.

"Are you okay?" Anna asked.

"I… er.. yes love, we'll be fine," Ma replied. "We might have to make some changes but we'll be fine. We'll be fine," she repeated, nodding to herself.

"I knew Dad wouldn't let us down," I said happily.

"Though you mightn't be able to do all the things you'd planned." Ma was looking directly at me. My heart sank.

"What sort of things?" Anna asked curiously.

"You might have to leave school," Ma continued hesitantly. "But Nell will get you jobs. Won't you Nell?"

"Leave now?" Anna stared, open-mouthed, "before we've even done the Leaving?"

"Lots of girls leave early," Auntie Nell said quickly. "Your mother only has a small lump sum. It won't last very long."

I could feel my safe world begin to crumble. "But Dad promised... He said only a few months ago that..."

"It's not his fault, Maggie." Ma interrupted with tears in her eyes. "Tell them, Nell. Make them understand. I don't want them blaming him."

"What your mother is trying to say is that he did make the right plans but..."

"Good. So we don't have to leave school then?"

"It's just he died too soon. That's the trouble. 'Twasn't his fault. You see he died before ... before he had paid enough money into the policy."

"But if he was paying money in, why can't we take it out now?" I asked.

Auntie Nell sighed. "The problem is..."

"The problem is, as I've said," Ma whispered, "that he died too soon, girls. That was the only mistake your poor father made. He died too soon."

"Why have insurance, then?" I asked crossly. "I thought people paid in so that when somebody dies, their families can get money out."

Ma looked at Auntie Nell. "That's what I said too. What was his answer?"

"There was some small print in the policy about having to pay in so many years at the beginning before there was any entitlement..." Auntie Nell stopped abruptly. "Oh God, if I hadn't insisted on his giving me a lesson, none of this would have happened. It's all my fault. John wouldn't have died, ye wouldn't be in this mess only for me." She broke down. Ma put an arm around her shoulders and waved at us to leave.

Anna and I wandered out again, this time up the town. Already it seemed our lives were beginning to change. Neither of us was trained for any job. And we'd need jobs, if there was no money coming in. We walked along automatically looking into the shop windows as we passed. But where could we get jobs in Kilmanogue? We passed Flavin's shop. Usually we'd be plastered up against the window looking at the latest fashions. Today we gave them only a passing glance and moved on. Suddenly I stopped. "That's what we'll do," I said, pointing at the two windows ablaze with Spring colours.

Anna shook her head. "You're mad, Lumpy, always was and always will be, forever and ever, amen."

"No I'm not."

"What's Flavin's got to do with anything?" Her lip curled derisively. "They haven't any vacancies, stupid!"

"No, but we could buy the shop."

If I was waiting for her to recognise my genius, I'd be waiting. She turned on her heel and walked off, muttering. "Mad as a bloody hatter. Always was and always..."

I grabbed her arm and pulled her back again.

"If we owned it we could work there, couldn't we? Ma said something about having a lump sum. It's worth a try, isn't it?"

Suddenly it dawned on her what a genius I really was. We ran all the way home.

"You're supposed to open the door, girls, not break it down," Auntie Nell protested mildly from the sitting room as we burst in.

"Ma?" Anna shouted.

Ma walked in carrying the carving knife. "What's all the commotion about?"

"You can use the money to buy Mrs Flavin's shop. Then we could all work there together," Anna said, the words tumbling out in her excitement.

Ma looked at Auntie Nell. "Has she ever said anything to you about selling?" Nell shook her head. "I thought not. Thanks, Anna. It was a clever idea. We probably wouldn't have enough money anyway. Okay everybody, tea will be ready in five minutes."

"Hold on a minute, Rose."

"Nell, you know how small the settlement is."

"Perhaps you're right. It wouldn't be enough." Auntie Nell's shoulders slumped again. "Sorry Anna."

"It was my idea, in case anyone's interested." Depressed, I flung myself into the sofa and picked up a newspaper.

"Rose, Rose!" Nell shouted suddenly. "Come back here a minute."

"I can't. I'm wetting the tea."

Auntie Nell couldn't wait. She grabbed her crutches and hobbled out to the kitchen. Anna and I followed on her heels. "What if you and I bought the shop between us?" Ma looked at her, the steaming kettle suspended in her hand. "I'd forgotten about the money Pat left me. We could use that along with your money."

"Oh" Ma's face brightened for a moment then fell. "Mrs Flavin loves that place. She'd never sell."

"She's not getting any younger. She might listen to an offer."

Ma poured the water into the teapot. "Would there be enough for us to live on?"

"We'd have to go into all that," Auntie Nell said eagerly. "At the moment she can afford to pay both me and the assistant Mary, apart from herself. On top of that, I get commission, so I know roughly what she makes. Oh Rose, think about it. It would give us all such independence. And you'd be making John's money work for you."

Ma nodded. "That's what Dr Tobin told me last week. Whatever money I get, I must make it work for me. I didn't really understand what he meant."

Her face was going pink with excitement. "Aren't ye great girls now to be able to think up such a clever scheme?" Anna beamed back at her.

"It was my idea actu…" But I let it go. It didn't matter whose idea it was if it was going to work.

"We must do this properly." Auntie Nell started to pace up and down the kitchen. "The first thing we do is have a look at the sales figures. Mrs. Flavin won't mind. Then we'll have to get the business valued by an independent party."

"But then we wouldn't get a bargain."

"Maggie!" Auntie Nell looked at me shocked and went on with her pacing. "We'll have to see what loan we can get from the bank, although we might be able to manage on an overdraft. That's cheaper."

"I don't think I'll be able to keep up with you," Ma said with a frown.

"'Course you will, Rose. Won't it be wonderful all of us working together in our own business? Won't it girls?"

Anna smiled, but I bit my lip. This wasn't exactly what I had in mind, but nothing was going to upset the excitement. Long after Anna and I had been packed off to bed, I could hear them talking downstairs. Auntie Nell it seemed was about to replace Dad as Ma's partner.

In the weeks that followed, that's exactly what happened. After a number of meetings with the bank manager and Mrs. Flavin, they finally hammered out a deal. The trick, as Auntie Nell said, was not to appear desperate. They had to revert to plan B in the end. One must always have a Plan B, according to Nell. I couldn't help noticing how much she'd changed since Uncle Pat died. For years she'd hardly ever had to think for herself. Now she was all plans and schemes. Plan B allowed Mrs. Flavin a share in the profits for two years, but after that we had an option to purchase the balance of the shop. For us of course having an income meant we could continue in school and sit the Leaving Cert before going into the shop. I didn't really want to work in the shop at all, but with family finances so tight I was obviously going to have to put up with it. It wouldn't be easy working with Anna though.

It was late in bed one night that I remembered something Mr Reid had said in class, that we should always think in terms of a career rather than just a job. Apart from Science, I'd always liked bookkeeping, so what about doing Accountancy? That way I could earn a living by day and study by night. It wouldn't be easy, but at least I'd have a career at the end of it, not just a job. The more I thought about it, the more I liked it. Yes, Accountancy would be my Plan B.

The next morning I looked up the phone directory. There seemed to be only one accounting firm in Wexford. When Ma and Nell were in with Mrs Flavin, I went to the public phone box on Main Street and rang them.

"I'd like to discuss apprenticeships please," I said in my most confident voice.

"We don't take apprentices." My heart sank.

"Can you tell me the name of a firm that does?"

I held my breath. There was a pause. A man's voice came on. "Hello?"

"I'm enquiring about apprenticeships."

"Is it for yourself?"

"Yes." There was a pause.

"We don't usually get requests from girls."

"Why?"

"Because of the long training period I suppose and…er…they tend to get married and have a family."

"That's okay because I won't. Have you a vacancy at the moment?"

"No, but… Sorry. Who am I talking to?"

I saw Anna coming towards me. "I'll have to ring you back." I put down the phone quickly. There was plenty of time still before the holidays. This wasn't going to be easy, but I was determined not to be put off.

Ma and Auntie Nell decided to make no changes in the way the shop was run for the moment. By the end of the month Mary, the assistant, who had always been lazy, had been given two warnings, both of which she'd ignored. During the second month, Nell walked into the storeroom and found her sitting, feet up, smoking a cigarette and reading Ireland's Own. She was still angry when she told us about it later.

"The brazen hussy didn't even bat an eyelid when I walked in. Do you realise how dangerous it is to smoke in here? I said, and grabbed the cigarette out of her mouth." Nell shook her head. "Bold as brass, she got up brushed her skirt down and walked out of the store room. I reminded her that she'd already been warned twice and this was the last warning. *Keep your auld job,* she said, *I wouldn't work for ye if it was the last job in Kilmanogue.*"

Ma smiled at Auntie Nell's imitation of Mary's accent. "Does that mean she's gone?"

Auntie Nell nodded. "We'll give her two weeks' pay. I'll send it off tomorrow. The exams are in a few weeks. After that we'll have the girls."

"I could start on Monday," Anna offered quickly.

"Oh no you can't," Ma said at once.

Anna pouted. "But how will you manage?"

"We couldn't bring you in straightaway, anyway," Nell said. "She'd say we got rid of her to make a job for someone in the family. It's better if she tells everyone she walked out. We'll say she left of her own free will."

Over the next few weeks they did manage on their own. A few people asked them about Mary. They just said she'd left of her own free will. Mary herself walked into the shop one day. Ma was on her own. Nell was gone to the wholesalers. Mary said she'd come to apologise.

"Apologise?" Nell's face was a picture when Ma told her that evening. "For what, her laziness?"

"For giving us so much trouble. She also wanted to thank us for telling everyone that she'd left of her own free will."

Nell smiled in relief.

"So she's not looking for her job back?"

"No. She's going to Dublin to look after an elderly uncle."

"Great." Nell sighed with relief. "Now we can fill the vacancy any way we like."

"So that means I can leave schoo… "

Ma cut in before Anna could finish the sentence. "Not 'til you've finished the Leaving, Miss. We'll be more than happy to have you then." She leaned over and pushed the fringe of blonde curls away from Anna's forehead. "We'll have a lovely time working together. You'll be a great ad. The customers will think that they'll look as good as you if they buy our dresses. We'll make a fortune."

Anna looked across the table at me with a sneer. "What about Lumpy? She'd put them off buying anything ouch!" My foot caught her shin under the table.

"When are you two ever going to grow up?" Ma said crossly. "If ye can't behave like adults, leave the table."

But we didn't leave. We stayed quiet instead, and the meal continued in silence. Lumpy indeed. I'd lose weight if it killed me. Starting as I meant to go on, I only had one slice of Ma's Madeira cake.

CHAPTER 9

The following week the exams began. The day they were over, Anna started in the shop. I told Ma I wanted a week to myself before starting. She agreed at once.

"I'm sorry we can't afford to send you to college, love. I know you'd set your heart on it."

"Doesn't matter Ma. I'll find something else."

That Monday, I put Plan B into action. I dressed up as smartly as I could and took the bus into Wexford. I stood outside the accountancy office for ten minutes before I plucked up enough courage to go in. The door squeaked open as I entered. A young girl looked up from her typewriter.

"Yes?" she said in a bored tone.

"I'm here to enquire about apprenticeships, please."

"Do you have an appointment with Mr. Forrest?" I nodded firmly. "Terrible man. He never told me. What time was it for?"

I looked at a clock on the wall over her head. "Eleven. I'm a bit early."

"Name, please?"

"Brown… Magg…er… Margaret Brown." My nerve was going but it was too late to pull out now.

"From where?"

"Kilmanogue."

"I'll see if he's available."

She disappeared through a small door on her left. I could hear muffled voices. After a few minutes the door opened again. She held it open for me.

"You're chancing your arm, aren't you?" she whispered in my ear as I passed her. I bit my lip and kept going. An elderly man stood up from behind a small desk and held out his hand.

"Don't worry, Miss Brown. Anyone can make a mistake. Close the door behind you, Maria."

It clicked loudly. I stood there quaking. He gestured to a chair opposite his desk. "What can I do for you?"

Now that I'd got this far, my tongue decided not to work. Gone were all the nice sentences I'd practiced in bed. It was the Scarlet Pimpernel all over again.

Mr. Forrest smiled at me. "You didn't really have an appointment, did you?" I shook my head. "Full marks for initiative. You were enquiring about doing Accountancy?" I nodded, wondering when my voice would return. "We don't actually offer apprenticeships here. We're too small." He looked at me curiously. "Are you sure you want to do it? It's a bit unusual for a girl."

"I know, but after Science I liked book-keeping best. Also, I'd like to be involved with business and..." My voice had returned with a vengeance. "You see, I'm looking for a career, not just a job. I know it will be hard work, and I know it will take ages, but I won't be getting married, having babies or anything like that, so I'd be able to concentrate on the study. I'll work really hard too. You won't be sorry."

He smiled. "Slow down. Start at the beginning Miss Brown. Tell me about yourself. Are you still at school?" I nodded then shook my head. He laughed. "Which is it?"

"I've just finished my Leaving Cert."

I started to tell him about St. Mary's and the subjects we'd done. He was a good listener. I found myself telling him about my father, and how we'd bought the shop with the insurance money, and how I could work there but I didn't want to.

He pressed a bell on his desk. The door opened. "Two teas, please, Maria. Sugar?" I nodded. The door closed again. "I'm not sure if I can do anything to help you, Margaret. As I said we're just a small firm here." My heart sank.

"Ah tea." He smiled as the door opened and Maria walked in with a tray. She put the tray down onto the desk and handed a cup of tea to him. She left the other one sitting on the tray. "Thanks, Maria. We'll manage," he said pointedly. She left with a sniff. I could understand how bad she must feel having to make tea for the likes of me. I sipped it. It tasted horrible. She must have put something in mine because he drank his and looked as if he enjoyed it. My tongue was taking a much-needed break.

When he'd finished his tea, he put down his cup and stood up.

"I'll make some enquiries Margaret. That's the best I can do, I'm afraid. I'm sorry we haven't anything here for you."

I left. So much for Plan B.

And I had no Plan C!

CHAPTER 10

The following Monday I started work in the shop. From the outset, it was clear that Anna and I wouldn't get on well in such small confines. We kept getting in each other's way. By the end of every day we were picking at each other for every little thing. Auntie Nell did her best by giving us separate jobs to do but by Friday I was beginning to wonder whether I'd be better off working in one of the cafés at the beach.

I was serving Mrs. Murphy when the phone rang. Mrs Murphy was one of our best customers but she was hard to please.

"It's for you, Lumpy." Anna brushed past me behind the counter. "I'll see to Mrs Murphy."

Grateful for any distraction, I went to the storeroom and picked up the phone.

"Hello?…who?.. Of course I remember you Mr Forrest." Anna was watching me suspiciously over Mrs Murphy's shoulder. She scowled as I pushed the door closed with my foot. "A vacancy but I thought you said you didn't do apprenticeships? …… Oh you mean as a typist. What happened Maria?"

He told me she'd given him a week's notice and had gone to Dublin to work for her Aunt. "I know it's not exactly what you're looking for, Miss Brown, but we are an accountancy practice and I'd give you all the encouragement you need with your studies. I'd even pay for typing classes during the summer," he added, clearly desperate for help.

At that moment Anna burst in through the door. "Come off that bloody phone, Lumpy. Who the hell d'you think you are?"

That settled any doubts I had. "Thank you for ringing, Mr Forrest. I'd love to come and see you." Anna was watching me like a hawk. I put on my most grown-up voice. "What time would suit best?" I didn't blame him for sounding surprised. "Monday at ten? Perfect, Mr. Forrest. See you then. Thank you for calling. Goodbye."

I put down the phone and stalked out past an open-mouthed Anna. My head was so high I nearly knocked down Mrs. Murphy who was just coming out of the fitting room. I smiled brightly at her. "I bet that suit was lovely on you, Mrs. Murphy. It's just your colour, isn't it?"

She nodded, surprised at my unexpected enthusiasm. I took the suit from her and was about to wrap it when Anna realised what was happening. "I was looking after Mrs. Murphy." She pushed me to one side and smiled ingratiatingly across the counter. Mrs. Murphy put out a restraining hand on her.

"On second thoughts, dear, I'm not sure it's exactly what I want. Is your Aunt around?"

"No" Anna scowled. "She's at the wholesalers."

I gave Mrs Murphy an understanding smile. "You'd like her to see it on you, Mrs Murphy, is that it? We could put it aside for you until Monday if you like?"

Few of the regulars ever bought a suit without checking it first with Auntie Nell anyway. She was known throughout Kilmanogue for her good dress sense.

Anna's face was purple with annoyance as Mrs. Murphy nodded gratefully at me. "You're a good girl, Maggie, a credit to your mother and your poor father, Lord have mercy on him."

I simpered, and put the suit carefully back on its hanger. "I'll just hang it in the storeroom and you can tell Auntie... er...Mrs. Maher on Monday where it is."

"Won't you be here yourself, Maggie?"

"No. I have a business meeting in Wexford, but Anna will happy to look after you." I smiled sweetly at Anna. "Won't you dear?"

Anna had to clear the scowl off her face, because Mrs. Murphy was looking directly at her. By the time Mrs. Murphy had left, I was already serving someone else, so Anna had no chance to get her own back.

I was hoping against hope she'd have forgotten about the phone call, but she challenged me at tea in front of the others. "Hey Lumpy, who's Mr. Forrest?" Fortunately Nell and Ma were in the middle of a discussion about whether or not they should buy the new trouser suits that were just coming into fashion.

"Nobody you need worry about. Pass me that fairy cake."

"No way. You've had your two."

I was glad my device had worked. I turned to Ma. "You should get some Ma. Everyone will be wearing them soon."

"Do you think so love?" she answered doubtfully. "It's your generation that'll be buying them, so perhaps you're right."

Nell nodded. "She is. They're wearing them in London already, so it's only a matter of time."

"That settles it then," Ma said. "Next time you're up in the wholesalers get two of every size. That'll start us off. Maybe you should take Maggie with you. She's nice and tall. She'd look well in one."

Anna let a snort out of her. "She'd look awful. They'd show up her fat thighs... ouch!" My shoe had found its mark again.

"Okay, little Miss Fashion Plate. You go if you like. I don't mind." I shrugged and bit into the cake she'd forgotten.

"That's settled then. Anna will go up with you on Tuesday." Ma smiled over at me. "We'll manage fine on our own, won't we Maggie?"

I said nothing and started to gather up the plates.

On Monday morning I was taking no chances. I arrived ten minutes early for the appointment with Mr. Forrest. The outside office was empty. The phone was off the hook, so I knocked on his door and went in. I found him kneeling on the floor gathering up the contents of a file that had obviously fallen off his desk.

"She rang me last night," he said, breathing heavily. "She's not even going to work out her notice."

"You know I haven't done any typing?" I said quickly. This man had been let down enough for one day.

"Yes, but I'd be happy to pay for night classes if you'll start straight away. I know you're just over the exams and all." He looked at me anxiously. "Please say yes!"

He obviously needed help, and it would get me away from Anna if nothing else.

"Okay. I'll take it."

"That's wonderful. Can you start tomorrow?"

"No I'll have to break it to my family first."

He heaved himself up from the chair and held out his hand. "Welcome aboard, Margaret."

"Call me Maggie."

As I waited for the bus home, I wondered which plan this was. It certainly wasn't A, neither was it B, but then Dad used to say, '*Man makes plans and God laughs*'.

When I walked into the shop, Nell and Anna were admiring Mrs. Murphy as she twirled round in the new suit. I grinned. "I knew it was right for you."

"You've good taste Maggie." Mrs. Murphy turned to Nell. "She was a great help to me on Friday. You're lucky to have her."

Nell smiled. Anna scowled.

"Have you seen the new Italian scarves that have just come in? They'd look great with that." I reached up to a shelf pulled one down and draped it over Mrs. Murphy's shoulder. "I think that's how they wear them. I've seen pictures in the magazines."

Mrs. Murphy stood back and admired herself in the mirror. Anna disappeared into the storeroom. Mrs. Murphy looked again at the price tag, still doubtful.

"Let's knock something off," I whispered to Nell. "She'll advertise them all over town." She nodded, so I went over to Mrs. Murphy. "We'll give you the scarf half price because you're taking the suit."

"Thanks Maggie. I'll take them both so." She did one last twirl before going back into the fitting room.

"Well done love." Nell smiled.

"There's something I have to tell you," I said nervously.

"Wait 'til Mrs. Murphy's gone. We'll have a cuppa." She looked at her watch. "Glory be to God, where does the time go?"

Anna emerged from the storeroom with her coat on. "If that one can gad around Wexford half the morning, so can I." With that she flounced out.

Auntie Nell packed up Mrs Murphy's purchases. I escorted her to the door.

"That will be on her at Mass on Sunday," I said, turning the "CLOSED" sign outwards as I locked the door. Auntie Nell looked at me curiously.

"Well, what's your big news?"

"I've got a job."

"But you've already got a job."

"This is a proper job, in Wexford, in that accountancy place on the quay."

"But I thought you were going to work here?"

"Anna and I wouldn't work well together. Mr. Forrest's secretary left him in the lurch. He's promised to pay for typing lessons."

"What's all this about typing lessons?" Ma had come downstairs without either of us hearing her.

"I'm just telling Auntie Nell about my new job."

"You have a job, Maggie, here with us."

"Yes, but it's not really what I want."

"And why in the name of God would you want to work for strangers when you can work with your own family?" I looked at her. Was it possible she didn't know how much Anna and I got on each other's nerves?

"She just wants to spread her wings, Rose," Nell interjected, "only natural isn't it?"

"Working with her family is natural," Ma said crisply. "Why would you go all the way to Wexford and work with strangers, when you could stay here in Kilmanogue where you're well-known?"

"I... I want to do accountancy."

Ma looked at me, a hurt expression on her face. I stared back defiantly. Nell shot me a warning glance.

"Put on the kettle Maggie."

I told them about Mr. Forrest over tea. I knew by Ma's expression she felt

I was letting her down. "Anna and I are in each other's way here. Aren't we, Auntie Nell?"

Nell nodded. "It might do them good to be a apart from each other. They'll...er... develop better."

"You mean they won't fight as much?" Ma said dryly.

"It's a great opportunity Ma," I pleaded. "You know how hard it is to get jobs, and you said yourself there's barely enough work here for three. Mr. Forrest is an accountant. Working for him will help my studies. I know it will."

"It makes sense, Rose," Nell added. "Kilmanogue is small. There's a limit to the number of customers. Another wage coming in will help."

Ma broke into a smile. "You two are ganging up on me. Okay I give in. The best of luck with your new job, love." She kissed me. "Your Dad would be proud of you."

She stood up. "Come on ladies. We'd better open up or we'll all be looking for jobs in Wexford." I ran to unlock the door.

Anna brushed roughly past me. "Enjoyed your lunch with the auld ones?"

"Yes, thanks." I smiled and waited for the bombshell.

"She's what?... I don't believe it." Anna turned on me, her face red as a turkey cock. "Who'd give her a job? She can't do anything."

"It's in Wexford with an accountant," I heard Nell explain as she opened some blouses that had just arrived. "Where do you think we should hang these, Anna?"

"If she thinks I'm going to be left here doing all the donkey work, she has another thing coming," Anna roared.

"Go out and get a job yourself then," I said calmly.

"Well indeed if you can, anyone can."

"Off you go. Nobody's stopping you."

"Stop fighting you two. Here, Maggie." Nell handed me a box of blouses. "Hang those up on the hangers like a good girl, and be sure to shake them out well. If any of them need ironing, give them a run over, will you?"

I nodded, and took the box. I was only too happy to keep my distance from Anna.

"Things are bound to improve when you're on your own," I said to her later, as I helped her stack jumpers behind the counter. "Come on, Anna Banana. We're still pals, aren't we?"

"How could we be pals? You're such a pig."

"A pig, as in oink oink?"

In spite of herself she laughed. "How did you manage it anyway?"

"Manage what?"

"The job, of course, you silly cow."

"I thought you said I was a pig?"
"Go on. Tell me."
"I went to ask about apprenticeships but he hadn't any."
"Are you really starting tomorrow?"
"Yes. Will you miss me?"
"Like a hole in the head." She laughed, and threw a sweater at me.
I caught it and folded it before giving it back to her.
"You'll be far better off without me here. You'll have the customers eating out of your hands." I was glad to see her good humour had returned.

Over the summer, slowly but surely, my typing improved, thanks to the classes. In October, I enrolled in the Technical school for Part One of the Accountancy program. Looking at the syllabus, I realised it would be a long haul, but I was determined to go ahead.

On Tuesdays and Thursdays I stayed behind in the office, had a sandwich and went to the Tech for lectures. I wouldn't get home to Kilmanogue until nearly eleven. Ma would take one look at my white face and put a bowl of hot soup and a plate of brown bread in front of me. It was about all I was capable of, before falling into bed.

CHAPTER 11

The autumn flew by. I sat my first exam the day before Christmas Eve. It was over by lunchtime. I went home and threw my books on the bed. The rest of the family were up in the shop, so I had the place to myself. I was just finishing a sandwich when a knock came to the door. I opened it to a tall dark stranger.

"Is this Tivoli Terrace?" he asked. I nodded. We didn't often get strangers in the middle of winter, especially handsome ones with English accents. "I'm looking for Elizabeth O'Shaughnessy. She lives in Number One, I believe?"

"Number One is next door, but there's nobody of that name I'm afraid."

"She'd be in her late forties, maybe fifties? Please. It's very important."

"Our next-door neighbour's Nell Maher. The O'Sheas used to live in Number three but they've gone to Dublin." He was writing each name down as I said it, then crossing them out again. "The Murphys live in Number four. Where's this woman from?"

"Cork originally, I think."

I thought for a few minutes, then had an idea. "Is Nell a form of Elizabeth?"

"I don't know."

"Auntie Nell's from Cork. What's it in connection with?"

"It's personal. I've knocked, but there's no answer."

"She'll be up in the shop. I'm on my way up now, so I can show you if you like?"

"I'll give you a lift." He nodded towards his car. We didn't get too many sports cars in Kilmanogue.

"Two minutes," I said, running in to get my coat. I sidestepped into the bathroom and put on some lipstick. I ran a brush through my hair, sorry I hadn't washed it the night before but there was nothing I could do about that now. We drove up the town and parked outside the shop.

"Is this hers?" he asked, running his eye over it before getting out.

"My mother and herself are partners."

"Women partners?"

"Why not?"

"Surprised, that's all."

"That equality has hit Kilmanogue?" I laughed and jumped out. "Come on. I'll introduce you. I'm Maggie Brown, by the way." I held out my hand.

"Jonathan Good. Pleased to meet you Maggie Brown."

"Me too."

Ma was at the counter. She was calling out from a list of prices to Anna who was marking dress labels. They both looked up when we came in. It wasn't often a man appeared in a dress shop. Anna flicked her hair over her shoulders and smiled up from under her lashes. "Can I help you?"

"This is Jonathan Good, Ma," I said. "He called to the house below."

Ma smiled at him. "Welcome to Kilmanogue."

"Thanks. I'm looking for Elizabeth O'Shaughnessy. Is she here?"

Ma frowned. "No sorry I don't think… "

"What about Auntie Nell?"

"Oh of course. O'Shaughnessy was Nell's maiden name. She's upstairs in the storeroom. Would you like me to get her?"

Jonathan shook his head firmly. "I'd prefer to see her alone."

"Is she expecting you?"

"No. Tell her Jonathan wants to see her."

"I'll go, Ma," I said and headed towards the stairs.

"Can I get you a cup of tea?" I heard Anna ask, as I ran upstairs. Good old Anna. She wasn't wasting any time.

I found Auntie Nell on her knees going through a large cardboard box.

"How did the exam go?" she asked. She was pulling some interlock knickers out of the box. "I didn't know we had any of these left. We'd better put them on sale and get rid of them." She held them up laughing. "Would you look at the size of those gussets?"

"Never mind the gussets. D'you know anyone called Jonathan?"

Her face went as white as a sheet. "What did you say?" she gasped.

"Jonathan. Jonathan Good?"

She sank back on her hunkers. "Where did you hear that name?"

"He's below waiting to see you."

"Dear God." She swayed and would have fallen only I knelt down beside her.

"What's the matter Auntie Nell? Who is he?"

"After all this time." She leaned against me. "Jonathan here in Kilmanogue, I can't believe it."

"I'll send him away if you'd prefer."

"No, no." She got up, and brushed herself off. "Of course I'll see him. I've waited all my life for this moment."

She walked down the stairs slowly, holding on to the banisters as if she were afraid of falling. Halfway down she stopped and turned. "On second thoughts, Maggie, ask him to come up, will you love?"

"Are you sure you're okay?"

She nodded. "Yes but better if I see him on my own."

Jonathan looked up as I came into the shop. When he saw nobody behind me his face fell. "Will she not see me?"

"Of course she will. It's the door at the top of the stairs."

He took the stairs two at a time.

"Who is he?" Ma asked.

"I don't know, but she got an awful fright when I said the name."

"He's a bit of alright." Anna's eyes were shining.

"Hands off. I saw him first."

"All's fair in love and war." Anna smirked, reaching for her hairbrush. "Did you see the way he was looking at me?" She ran the brush through her hair. I groaned as the blonde curls sprang up and then settled back into a shiny curtain. No man in his right mind would fancy me with her around. Depressed, I watched her put on some lipstick and stand back to admire herself in the mirror.

It was almost an hour later when Auntie Nell and Jonathan came downstairs. Her face was flushed. She was smiling up at Jonathan, her hand on his arm, as they walked in. "This is my s…son Jonathan," she announced proudly.

Ma's mouth dropped open "but… but …"

"Jonathan this is Rose Brown, the best friend anyone could ask for."

"Pleased to meet you, Mrs. Brown." Jonathan held out his hand to Ma.

"And these are her daughters, Anna and Maggie."

Jonathan turned to me and shook my hand. "Thanks for bringing me here, Maggie." He then turned to Anna, took her hand and held it. "A beautiful name for a beautiful girl. Hello Anna."

She blushed prettily. "Pleased to meet you Jonathan."

Nell put her arm around his shoulder.

"I was lucky. I married a wonderful man called Patrick Maher. I could never marry your father, unfortunately. Some day perhaps I'll tell you about him, but not today."

Ma found her voice at last. "There must be so much you have to say to each other. Why don't you take Jonathan home? We'll manage here."

"Thanks Rose." Nell squeezed her hand. "Come on Jonathan."

"Imagine Nell keeping a secret like that all this time?" Ma exclaimed, after they'd left. "She probably never told Pat. In those days girls, it was a shameful thing to have a child out of wedlock."

"Mary Murray from the cove had to run off to Dublin last week."

"Is she pregnant?" Ma's eyes widened. I nodded. "Good God, and her with such nice parents."

"What about Auntie Nell? I'm sure her parents were nice too."

"Don't be cheeky, Maggie."

"But Ma it could happen to anyone."

"If I thought for one minute that either of my girls would behave in such a manner, I'd... I'd... I'd die of shame."

"It wouldn't be your fault, Ma. Anyway it's not going to happen to me. It's Anna you should be worrying about. She's the one with all the boys after her."

"Do you want to send me to an early grave?" She looked helplessly at Anna. "Anna you wouldn't do anything like that, would you?"

Anna shook her head. "Of course not Ma and Lumpy would have to find a man first so..." I gave her a puck. She lashed back at once.

"Girls, girls, will ye stop for goodness sake." Ma looked around the empty shop. "Come on. We'll close early." We put the lights off, turned the CLOSED sign around and left. Things were far too exciting at home to be hanging around in the shop.

Minutes after we got home, Nell came in the back door. Ma hugged her. "That's great news. You must be so happy."

"I never thought I'd see this day."

"Is he staying?"

"Just for the night. He's going back tomorrow."

"There must be so much to talk about. Don't waste a minute of it with us. You can tell us all about it when he's gone."

Nell looked gratefully at her. "Are you sure?"

"Don't come up in the morning either. We'll manage." Nell gave her another quick hug and left.

It was funny having tea without her. Anna and I bombarded Ma with questions. She told us that women who found themselves pregnant usually had to go to England.

"So they wouldn't bring shame on their precious families, I suppose?"

Ma looked at me crossly. "They hadn't much choice Maggie. Times were different."

"What about Mary Murray?"

"Never mind all that." Anna interrupted. "I wonder who Jonathan's father was? He must have been a right smasher."

"Someone she could never hope to marry, probably," Ma replied, "someone from another class, or someone well-known in the area whose parents wouldn't have approved."

Anna had a faraway look in her eye. "It's so romantic, his turning up out of the blue like this."

"I bet it was someone who was cheating on his wife."

Ma looked at me, shocked. "Maggie. You'll have to stop reading those English magazines."

"Maybe he was foreign," Anna sighed, still in her romantic haze. "Italian or French?"

"Get away. He was probably a tinker."

"Enough of that sort of talk, girls. Clear the table. We don't want to miss the Archers."

Long lost sons may come and go, but missing the Archers, that would never do!

When they were over, Ma took out a bottle of whiskey from the cabinet and handed it to me. "Bring that in to Nell like a good girl. I'm sure she hasn't a drop in the house."

"No, let me." Anna grabbed at the bottle.

"She asked me first." I hugged it to my chest.

"You're only a kid. I'll take it."

"What's the big deal about being eighteen, for God's sake?" I said crossly, hanging onto the bottle. My eighteenth was still almost a year away.

Ma raised her eyes to Heaven. "Lord, give me strength! Both of you go then, but don't stay long. They need their privacy."

She didn't have to ask twice. We ran next door.

"Ma said you might want this for Jonathan." I handed the bottle to Auntie Nell.

"Thanks girls." We hesitated on the doorstep. "Do ye want to come in?" We nodded eagerly. "Okay, but don't stay too long," she whispered. "Jonathan and I have a lot of catching up to do."

Jonathan was lying on the sofa, a tea tray beside him. I could have sworn I saw a bored look on his face, but as soon as we entered the room he jumped up. "Nice to see you again, girls. Are we some sort of cousins?"

Anna giggled, and flashed her blue eyes up at him. "No relation at all."

"But you call my mother Auntie Nell?"

His mother smiled fondly at him. "They've called me that ever since they were born, and they used to call Pat Uncle too. We couldn't have any children of our own you see. So Rose and John shared their family with us. They've been wonderful neighbours, especially since Pat died. I don't know what I'd have done without them." She turned to us. "Can I get you girls some lemonade?"

Anna piped up. "Could I have whiskey please, Auntie Nell?"

"Did your mother say you could?"

Anna nodded. "Because of the special occasion."

Nell looked dubiously at her then at me. "What about you Maggie?"

"Yes please," I said quickly.

"In that case go in and get your mother. She should be here too."

"She said she wanted to go to bed early." Anna shot a warning glance at me. "Didn't she Mags?"

"Yes. She was tired."

Nell poured two small whiskies for us, and a big one for Jonathan. We all stood around and clinked glasses.

"Cheers."

"Good health."

"To my new family."

"To my son Jonathan."

One sip and I wanted to spit it out. I couldn't of course, so I let it slip down my throat. It tasted a bit like a cough bottle. The second sip wasn't as bad so I took another, then another. A warm glow started to spread around my chest. It seemed to get easier the more I took. Anna's glass was empty first.

"Allow me." Jonathan jumped up and refilled our glasses. He filled his own as well, almost up to the brim.

Anna seemed to be better at drinking than I was. Her second glass was empty in a few minutes. Her face was puce, so I thought we'd better leave. I drained my glass and stood up. I had to grab hold of the table to steady myself.

"That wash lovely Auntie Nell, but Ma shaid we musht let you get on with your cha.. cha.. chat." I put my glass down on the table with a bang and held out my hand to Jonathan. "'Twash lovely meeting you, Jonathan. Shee you again shoon, I hope?"

He took my hand and bowed low over it. "Yes indeed, Maggie. If I'm invited." He looked across at Nell who nodded warmly.

"This is your home now, love."

"I'll take you up on that," he said. "Nice to have met you Maggie, and of course, the lovely Anna too." He took her hand and held it. "I'm glad we're not really cousins."

Anna's face went even pinker. "Sho am I." I looked at her. Her face seemed to swim.

"Why are you talking funny?"

"No funnier than you, Maggshy."

Auntie Nell looked at us anxiously. "Sit down for a few minutes, girls. I can't send ye home to your mother like that."

"Like what?" Anna looked at her. "We're fine. Aren't we Maggshie?"

"Courshe we are."

I put my arms around her shoulders, and the two of us waltzed out of the house.

"Hey, look at thoshe funny starsh. I wash shupposed to be going up there. There musht be other life up there, lotsh and lotsh of it." I leaned back to admire the sky and fell onto the hedge.

"Rubbisshh," Anna said, pushing her way unsteadily through a gap. "Why won't thish hedge shtop moving?"

Nell came up behind us, pulled me up from the ground, took each of us by the arm and propelled us firmly through the gap.

"You agree. Don't you Auntie Nell?"

"Agree with what?"

"That theresh life up there. Shee?"

"Your mother's going to kill me. That's all I know." She dragged us to the door and rang the bell. She was gone before Ma opened it.

"Glory be to God, come in before ye fall down." She pulled us in and closed the door.

"We had a toasht." Anna beamed up at her.

"I can see that. What was Nell thinking of?"

"We only had two." I slumped onto the sofa.

Later that night, Anna threw up all over the bathroom. Her face was green when she came back to the bedroom. I was scared. "I'd better call Ma."

"No. She'll kill me." She rolled around in the bed holding her tummy. "Go back to sleep. I'll just lie here and die."

She was lying upside down, head hanging over the end of the bed, when I woke up.

"What time isht?" she asked, raising her head for a second before it flopped down again.

"Time to get up. Wonder when Jonathan will be leaving?"

"Who cares? It's his fault I feel like this. Oh God, Mags, why do people like whiskey?"

"'Makes them feel good, I suppose." I was up, dressing as fast as I could.

"Where're you going?" she moaned, holding her head.

"Work. Think he'll come over here to live?"

"I'm never ever going to touch that stuff again."

"I suppose it depends on who he has in London. See you later." I waved at her but she didn't stir. She was still lying upside down on the bed.

"How are you?" Ma asked when I got downstairs.

"Fine. Anna's not too well though." I reached for a slice of toast.

"We'll be seeing a lot more of that young man," Ma said, pouring out my tea. "Imagine Nell having a past? Isn't it funny the way we think we know people and we don't know them at all?"

"I have to go, Ma. Sorry. You can fill me in tonight on the big romance." She gave me a withering look. "Ah go on, Ma. You'd like to know too."

She shook her head. "Only if she wants to tell us. She's kept this a secret for so long now, she mightn't." A faraway look came into her eye.

"A few skeletons in your own cupboard too, eh?" I grinned at her. "Come on, Ma. Spill the beans."

"You'll miss that bus, if you don't get a move on."

I looked at the clock. It was gone eight thirty. "Jesus, I will. Bye."

"Watch your language, Maggie."

"Sorry, Ma." I grabbed my bag and ran out the door.

Sitting on the bus gazing out the window I saw that faraway look again. After what had happened with Nell, I was beginning to realise that our parents had been separate people, once upon a time. They'd led separate lives, lives we knew nothing about.

Mr Forrest was in before me. I went into his office and took the bundle of post from his desk.

"Sorry for being late."

"Everything alright at home, Maggie?"

"Yes. We had great excitement yesterday. Another addition to the family, or rather to Auntie Nell's family, but I can see you're busy so I'll leave..."

"Not at all, my dear. An old bachelor like me misses out on that sort of thing. Put the kettle on and tell me what happened."

I badly needed the liquid myself. I was beginning to feel the effects of the whiskey. Over tea I described the events of the day before. I left out the bit about the drinking.

"Sounds like the prodigal son," he laughed. "What's he like?"

"Tall dark and handsome. He's called Jonathan Good, and he's from England. Other than that we don't know anything about him. I'll probably find out more tonight."

"Well, Maggie, we'd better start earning some bread and butter. I'm off to Dublin for a meeting around noon. After that you can close early if you like and do some Christmas shopping."

"Thank you, Mr. Forrest."

My mind was only half on the work anyway. Jonathan's dark eyes kept floating in front of the typewriter. Several times I was tempted to phone and say goodbye but the calls kept coming in. Michael Moloney, a friend of Mr. Forrest's, rang several times. He worked in Flynn and Forsyth, a big Accountancy practice in Dublin.

After Mr. Forrest left for the meeting, I picked up the phone. Auntie Nell answered.

"Am I too late to say goodbye to Jonathan?"

"No, love. He's here. I'll put him on." I heard the phone being handed over, then Jonathan's voice.

"Maggie? Is that you?"

"Yes." Now that I had him on the line I became tongue-tied.

"Working hard?"

"Sort of." There was a long pause. Then I said the first thing that came into my head. "You sound different today."

"Different better or different worse?"

"Better. Deeper. Richer." I stopped embarrassed.

He gave a deep chuckle. "You sound different too, closer somehow."

There was a long pause. "I just rang to wish you a safe journey."

He sighed. "Is that all?"

My heart did a little somersault. "And to say… I hope we meet again soon."

"We will Maggie. We will." I heard Auntie Nell say something to him. "Sorry. Got to go. Goodbye Maggie. See you again soon. That's a promise."

The phone went dead. For a long time I gazed out the window. His words repeated inside my head, wrapping themselves around my heart. "*See you again soon. That's a promise. See you again soon. That's a promise.*" I couldn't wait to go home and hear all about him. Jonathan, Jonathan. Even saying his name gave me goose-bumps.

"Has he gone?" I asked, the minute I got in the door. They were all in the sitting room. Auntie Nell nodded sadly.

"You know right well he has." Anna uncurled herself from the sofa. "What did you ring him for anyway?" I blushed, and said nothing. "Hey, everyone. Lumpy fancies Jonathan."

I gave her what I hoped was a superior smile and sat down on the sofa. She moved closer and gave my arm a sneaky pinch. I yanked at her hair and pushed her away from me. A long blonde curl caught in my sleeve. Anna shrieked with pain.

"Ma. Quick. Lumpy's gone mad again! Get the doctor."

"Girls, girls, for goodness sake. Have ye no shame in front of your Auntie Nell? Come on. Sit up to the table and have your tea."

I suddenly noticed shadows under her eyes. "Are you alright, Ma?" I asked.

"Just a bit tired, love. Didn't sleep much after all the excitement. You must be worn out Nell, are you?" Nell nodded, but her shining eyes told another story.

"I still can't believe it. Jonathan turning up like that was the best Christmas present I could ever have. It's like a dream come true."

"Tell us about him, Auntie Nell," I asked, trying desperately to sound casual.

"Oh yes, do tell Lumpy all about him," Anna sneered.

"Don't be so rude, Anna," Ma said sharply.

But Nell smiled. "What do you want to know, girls?"

"Where does he work? What does he do? What age is he?" I asked quickly as I reached for a slice of bread. What I really wanted to know was whether he had a girl friend.

"Where's his father?" Anna piped up, an innocent look on her face. I kicked her under the table. She yelped.

"I'm sorry, Nell." Ma turned to Nell. "I don't know what's gotten into them today."

Nell's face had gone from red to white and back again. Anna and I started to eat, pushing the plates around, offering bread, butter, milk, sugar, anything we could think of to each other. Nell didn't speak. She gazed at her plate and refused all offers of food. Ma glared at us then turned to Nell and put a hand on her arm. "It must have been a terrible shock; his arriving like that out of the blue?"

"Funnily enough, it wasn't." She paused. "It's as if… as if I've been waiting for this day all my life. The only pity is that poor Pat isn't here." A wistful look came into her face. "Jonathan would have been the son he always wanted, the son I could never tell him about."

"That must have been hard," Ma said sympathetically.

"If you knew how often…" Nell looked out the window. There was a long silence. "But there were other people to consider." She spoke the words quietly to herself. She went off into another dream. It was as if she'd forgotten we were there. Even Anna had enough sensitivity not to disturb the silence.

After a while, Ma stood up and started to stack the plates.

"Come on, lads. Help me clear the table."

Nell shook herself. "Let me."

"No, love. Sit down. You must be exhausted."

I jumped up. "I'll do the washing. You do the drying. Okay?" I said to Anna. I was keen to get the wash-up over quickly. I wanted to go back and find out more about Jonathan.

"Who do you think the father is, Ma?" Anna asked outside in the kitchen.

"She'll tell us when she's ready. Don't you dare ask her again. D'you hear?" Ma said crossly, as she put away the remains of the Madeira cake. Anna nodded.

"Did she say what Jonathan does for a living?" I asked.

"Yes. He works in some sort of business place in London."

"Which one?"

"All those places sound the same to me, love. The name went in one ear and out the other. Some sort of management consultancy, I think."

We finished up and went back into the sitting room, but as soon as the Archers were over, Nell stood up. "I think I'll have an early night."

"Good idea." Ma smiled at her.

"He said he might ring me when he gets back."

"I'm sure he will."

"You should give him our number as well, Auntie Nell," I said quickly, "so he can get you when you're in here."

"I've already done that." Anna smirked. "But it'll be me he'll ring, Lumpy, not you."

"All I wanted was for him to be able to contact Auntie Nell. It doesn't matter to me." I shrugged airily, and walked with Nell out to the front door.

"Don't worry, Maggie. I've given him both numbers. Do you like him?"

"I think he's gorgeous."

"He's tall too, so he'd suit you, wouldn't he?"

I laughed. "Perfectly. I'm mad about him. Hope you don't mind?"

"Of course not, love." She smiled proudly and left.

I hardly closed an eye that night. I couldn't wait to speak to him again. He'd surely ring on Christmas Day. Jonathan, Jonathan. His name echoed in my brain over and over again. Compared to him, the Tobin boys seemed like children. He did ring the next day. Unfortunately, he only spoke to Nell. She told us he wished us all a happy Christmas and was sorry he couldn't be with us. Not half as sorry as I was.

CHAPTER 12

Mr. Forrest didn't come in until ten o'clock the first morning after the holidays.

"Happy New Year, Maggie. Make us a cuppa. Bring yours in too. We need to talk."

I wondered what was so important but I did what he asked.

"At last, it's official," he said as I gave him his cup. "We've been taken over."

"Taken over? By whom?"

"Flynn and Forsyth." I recognised the name at once. It was Mr Moloney's firm. "They'll probably want to close this office."

"Oh" All my dreams for a wonderful career evaporated. Long years stretched out ahead of me working behind the counter with Anna.

"But they're prepared to take you on in their Dublin office. You can continue your studies up there."

"Flynn and Forsyth? But why? I don't understand."

"It's a great opportunity, Maggie. You'll get all the accounting experience you need. They're a long-established firm." He smiled sheepishly. "They have other girls doing accountancy too, so you won't be on your own. Cheer up. It's the start of your career." He got up from his chair and walked over to the window and looked out. "It's the end of mine, of course. But I'm not complaining. They made me a generous offer. I'll keep on a few private clients."

"But they don't know me from Adam, Mr. Forrest. Why don't they just fire me?"

He turned and smiled. "I made it a condition of the takeover that they give you an apprenticeship."

I gasped. The full realisation of what I was being offered began to dawn on me. I jumped up and hugged him.

His face reddened with pleasure.

"Leaving home is a big step for you, Maggie. I know that. But they're a great firm. I wouldn't have forced the issue if I thought it wasn't right for you."

We did very little work for the rest of the day. Every so often I'd think of another question about the merger. He'd known about it for a month, but had been sworn to secrecy. I couldn't wait to tell the family.

Ma was about to pour the tea when I walked in. "Maggie, did you hear the latest? Jonathan's coming to Ireland."

"To Dublin or here?"

I held my breath.

"He's not sure yet." Auntie Nell beamed. The happiness shone like stars from her eyes. "He'll stay here while he looks around for a job."

I was thrilled. Whether he ended up in Dublin or Kilmanogue, he'd still be nearer than London.

"Sit down love. You must be starving." Ma pushed the salad towards me.

"I have some news too," I said nervously.

"Stop the lights everybody," Anna sniggered and went on eating.

"We've been taken over by a Dublin firm."

"In other words you've been fired. I knew that job wouldn't last."

"On the contrary." I looked at Ma. "The new firm has offered me an apprenticeship in their head office. So I'll be moving to Dublin."

Anna gasped. "Why would they do that?"

"Mr. Forrest made it a condition of the takeover."

"He must think an awful lot of you, love." Ma came around the table and kissed me. "I hate your leaving, but I suppose it's for the best in the long run. We'll have to find you good digs. Nobody eats properly up in Dublin."

Auntie Nell hugged me too. "I'll ask Mrs. O'Mahony to give you a room."

"Thanks Auntie Nell. I'd love that to start off with, but I'll probably go into a flat as soon as I can afford it." I'd been thinking about it on the way home in the bus. There was no point in exchanging one home for another. This was the chance I'd been waiting for, the chance to stand on my own two feet.

"Is that wise, love?" Ma's face creased with anxiety.

"Don't worry, Ma. I'll be going to classes at night so I'll need to be near the College."

"Sounds like you have it all planned." There was a sad note in her voice. "The first of my girls to leave the nest."

"Sure I'll be home every weekend," I laughed. "Ye'll be fed up seeing me." Ma gave a sad little smile. Seeing it Auntie Nell hugged her. Anna said nothing.

It was only later, lying in bed that night, I realised that my adult life was about to begin. It seemed as if everything that had happened up to now was only a preparation. A coincidence Jonathan's life was changing at the same time. I felt the hand of fate pulling us together, and fell into a deep sleep with that thought wrapped warmly around my heart.

CHAPTER 13

Mrs. O'Mahony was a plump kindly woman. Living in her house in South Circular Road in Dublin was like living in Cork. She'd stand at the bottom of the stairs and shout up in her strong Cork lilt. "Tea's on the table, Maggie." Not only could the people next door hear her, but the people in the top deck of the buses could too. There was a bus stop just outside the door, which was handy for the Flynn and Forsyth office. I'd never seen so much traffic. It made Kilmanogue seem like a ghost town.

Miss Ryan was the office manager. She was about forty, dressed mostly in navy and looked just like Sister Dympna without the veil. On my first day, she introduced me to the two other apprentices, Eileen and Maria. Eileen was from Wicklow, Maria from Waterford. "Eileen's doing Part One like yourself, but Marie has moved on to Part Two. This is Margaret Brown, girls. She's from Kilmanogue."

"Where's that when it's at home?" Eileen asked with a giggle.

"It's only a few miles from Wexford," I answered hotly. "Have you never heard of it?"

"No. Is it a nice place?"

"Gorgeous," I replied enthusiastically, "lovely beach, great swimming, tennis and lots and lots of…"

"Yes, yes! You can talk about that later." Miss Ryan interrupted. "Maria will be looking after you until you get used to our little ways."

"Welcome to F & F, Margaret." Maria shook my hand.

"F & F, Maria?" Miss Ryan's eyebrows shot up.

"Sorry, Miss Ryan. Flynn and Forsyth."

"That's better. Off you go then, girls. Save the chat for the coffee break."

Miss Ryan had a tiny office of her own. I was put at a desk opposite Eileen. Maria sat near us. We were in a long dark room in the basement. The rest of the office was taken up with rows and rows of numbered metal presses packed full with files. The windows were tiny, high up and covered in heavy net curtains that looked as if they hadn't been cleaned for years. My heart sank as I remembered the bright friendly office I'd left behind in Wexford.

"Where does everybody else work?" I whispered as we sat down.

"The real accountants are upstairs." Eileen pointed at the ceiling. "Only us plebs down here. Apart from Miss Ryan of course. She's next door."

For coffee break, Maria had brought in a sponge cake made by her aunt, with whom she lived in Rathmines.

"Where are you staying?" Eileen asked, as I bit into the cake.

"Digs in South Circular Road," I answered between mouthfuls.
"Whereabouts?"
"126. Why?"
"I'm in 28, and I'm looking for someone to share with me. My flatmate's gone back home. I can't really afford to keep it on my own. Would you be interested?"
"Is it big?"
"Big?" She laughed. "It's a bed-sitter, silly."
"What's a bed-sitter?"
"One room, two tiny beds and an even tinier kitchenette." I didn't know what a kitchenette was either, but didn't want to look like a complete fool so I didn't ask.
"It's near the Olympic, very handy for dances," she continued. "The landlord has halved the rent for two weeks so I can find someone."
"Can I think about it?" I didn't want to commit myself so quickly.
"Of course. Now let's see what I'll start you off on…the invoices I think."
During the afternoon Michael Moloney walked into our office. He came straight over to my desk "Welcome to Dublin, Maggie."
"Thanks, Mr. Moloney." I stood up and shook hands with him. "And thanks for giving me this opportunity."
"John wouldn't sign until you were part of the deal."
"I hope I won't let him down," I said, suddenly conscious of the girls' eyes on me.
"I'm sure you won't. How are the ladies?" He turned to Maria and Eileen.
"Fine thanks, Mr. Moloney."
"Maggie, if there's anything you want to know, don't hesitate to ask. I promised John I'd look after you." With that he left the office.
Eileen's eyes were out on stalks. "Wow! You're well in there. How d'you know him?"
"He's a friend of my former boss. Used to visit the office in Wexford."
"He's the Senior Partner here."
I nodded and went back to my invoices. The afternoon flew by.
Later that night, as I lay in bed in South Circular Road, listening to the buses screeching to a halt outside the door, I decided to take up Eileen's offer. It'd be great to be able to come and go as I pleased, not having to report back all the time like at home. I wondered if Jonathan had arrived yet. I decided I'd ring next day and find out.

But I forgot all about Jonathan, because the next day was Wednesday. Maria and Eileen were going dancing and asked me to go with them. The Royal Showband were playing at the Olympic.

"I can't," I wailed. "I've nothing to wear."

"Of course, you have. Better warn your landlady you'll be late."

"How late?"

"Three or four," Eileen said airily.

"Or five." Maria giggled.

"She'll never let me stay out that late." Ma wouldn't be too impressed either.

"That's a joke, dopey. The dance is over at two. You'll be home by half past."

Mrs O'Mahony wasn't too surprised when I asked her if I could stay out late. "Make sure someone walks you home. I don't want to be reading about you in the papers tomorrow."

I was to meet the girls outside the dance hall. I found it easily. The entrance was lit up. Rock and Roll music was thumping out onto the pavement. A long queue had already formed. The two girls waved at me from half way down the queue.

Maria pulled my coat open and looked at my red shirtwaister. "You'll do."

After Jonathan most of the boys seemed rather young. "Are they all students?" I asked.

"Course they are, silly." Eileen laughed. "It's the Waddies." I looked at her blankly. "Surely to God even in Kilmanogue ye've heard of the Yerrawaddies, the engineering students?"

"Oh, the Waddies!" I said, as if I'd recognised it at last.

"Quick, move up or we'll lose our place." Maria pushed the two of us along. The ticket office had just opened and the queue was starting to move.

A broad-shouldered man stood at the door. Occasionally his arm would come down in front of someone. He'd say something and then wave them through. Everyone was talking and laughing but when they came near him they'd stop.

"Who's that?" I asked curiously.

"That's our Paddy. A Guard by day, a bouncer by night." Eileen gave Maria a dig in the ribs. "A right eejit, isn't he Maria?"

"Don't mind her." Maria blushed.

Paddy beamed as we came to the top of the queue. "Good evening, girls. And who's this fine thing ye brought with ye tonight?"

Naturally I warmed to him immediately.

"This is Maggie from Kilmanogue."

"Sure I know it well."

"Pleased to meet you, Paddy." I held out my hand. It was immediately swallowed up in his.

"I spent my childhood on the beach there, Maggie. Is it still as beautiful as ever?"

Somebody called from behind us. "Paddy, stop chatting up the girls and let us in."

"Who said that?" Paddy looked back. Nobody answered. He waved us through. "Right, ladies, enjoy the dance. See you later, pet," he whispered to Maria.

Inside, the atmosphere was electric. The Hucklebuck had just started. Everybody was going crazy trying to imitate Brendan Bowyer, who was leaping around on the stage. A coloured ball, rotating from the ceiling, splashed blobs of light all over the walls and ceiling. I'd never seen so many people in one place.

After checking our coats in, we stood on the balcony looking down at the heaving mass of dancers below. The Hucklebuck had just finished. Brendan Bowyer was mopping his face with a towel.

"Come on. Let's go down in time for the next set." Eileen pushed us downstairs ahead of her as the band struck up again. She looked around searching for someone. "Where's he gone?" she asked loudly.

"Don't know," Maria replied, equally loudly.

"Who's she looking for?" I whispered.

"No-one," Maria giggled, "that's just her way of seeing and being seen."

It worked. A boy appeared from nowhere and took her arm. "Are you dancing?" Eileen nodded and they moved out onto the middle of the floor.

"One down, two to go." Maria smiled up at me. "You're lucky you're so tall."

I think she meant it as a compliment, but I hated being tall, especially at a dance. In Kilmanogue it had always been a problem. I looked around the hall now, and was sorry to see that the boys in Dublin weren't much taller.

Paddy came over and took Maria by the hand. "See you later," she smiled, as he wrapped his arms around her. They moved off to the strains of *Strangers on the Shore*.

Someone tugged at my arm. "Dance?"

"Yes please, I mean thanks," I mumbled feeling a right eejit.

"Come here often?" he asked, looking up at me.

"First time. You're not from Wexford are you?"

His eyes narrowed. "Are you making fun of my accent?"

"Of course not. I just thought I recognised it."

"Good. Come on so." He pulled me closer.

I got a whiff of stale beer and moved back. "I'm from there as well," I said in an effort to keep him talking.

"What's wrong with you. Can't you dance?" He pulled me close again, pinning my arms under his. I pulled away again. "You're a bit tall for a woman, but sure give us an ould squeeze anyway." He pulled me towards him again, more roughly than before. The smell was stronger now. I was beginning to feel sick.

"Please give me some room?" I pleaded.

He answered by pulling me closer. I stood on his foot and pressed down with my heel. He yelped. "Hey that hurt. What's wrong with you? Are you frigid?" I turned on my heel and left him standing. "You should have stayed in Wexford with the rest of the Yellabellies," he roared after me.

I pushed my way through the dancers and out to the side of the room. Terrified he'd follow, I headed for the Ladies. I could feel my face burning. People were staring at me. What a start to my dancing career.

I hung around in the Ladies for ten minutes. By the time I emerged I couldn't see him anywhere. I decided I'd go upstairs to sit down. From there I looked down at the heaving mass to see if I could find the girls. Eventually I spotted Eileen at the edge of the floor near the entrance, so I ran down to join her.

"Hi. Did you see what happened?" She pointed over to the entrance where a crowd had gathered. There were lots of raised voices. "Paddy's in the thick of it as usual. He's trying to sort out some drunk."

Maria arrived. "Come on, you two, it's Ladies' Choice."

They rushed away, but I stood there, near the door, wishing the night was over. I looked up at the balcony and wondered whether I'd find a seat up there. While I was trying to decide whether to go up or not the band struck up a Rock and Roll number. Somebody whisked me away to dance. In the rush I hardly saw his face but at least he seemed more interested in dancing than talking. The music was great so I followed his lead and let myself go. I was sorry when the set was over and he walked away. Suddenly they were announcing the last dance. Everybody seemed to be rushing out on the floor. I started to make my way towards the cloakroom but someone grabbed my arm. "Dance?" I nodded and turned back towards the centre again.

"What's your name?" I roared at him over the noise.

"What?" He cupped his hand over his ear.

"My name is Maggie. What's yours?" I roared again. But he just shook his head and nodded at the band and grinned. He put his arms around me and whisked me off. I sighed. Obviously there'd be no exchange of life experiences here either. In a few minutes we were standing to the National Anthem.

When it was over, my partner nodded and disappeared into the crowd. Everybody seemed to be rushing around. I heard my name being called.

The two girls were standing at the edge of the ballroom near the door. They were shouting something but I couldn't hear. They had their coats on. Eileen was holding up my coat and pointing to it. I pushed my way over. She thrust the coat into my hands.

"Come on. Maria's gone on out for the bikes."

Maria was waiting for us in the alleyway. They walked me home first. I let myself into O'Mahony's and crept quietly up to my room. Wearily, I climbed in between the cool sheets and wondered how I'd be able to function at work on the few hours' sleep that were left.

The banging on the door next morning came as a rude awakening. I dragged myself out of the bed and headed for the bathroom. Two black eyes stared out of a white face. I shook my head to try to wake up from a dream. I'd been swimming up and down a huge pool filled with water. Every time I'd tried to get out, Paddy the bouncer had prodded me back with a stick. I kept begging him to let me get out, but he wouldn't. I splashed cold water onto my face and held the cool face cloth against my eyes.

"Get a move on Maggie," Mrs. O'Mahony yelled up the stairs, "you'll miss the bus."

The two others were just as tired. Every so often one of us would yawn and the yawn would spread through the office like a disease. We made coffee every hour to keep us awake.

That evening I had the house to myself. Mrs. O'Mahony had left my meal ready on a plate in the fridge. Afterwards, I stretched out wearily on the sofa beside the fire and began to wonder whether I'd ever fit in in Dublin. I started dozing but the harsh ringing of the phone woke me up. It was a friend of Mrs. O'Mahony's from Cork. I took a message and put down the phone. Suddenly a wave of homesickness swept over me. I picked it up again and dialled our number.

"Hi, Anna."

"Oh, it's you," she said with a bored sigh.

"Any news?" I asked eagerly.

"No"

"How's everybody?"

"Fine"

"How's Auntie Nell?"

"Fine"

"Ma?"

"Fine" Another sigh.

"Is she there?"

"Yes." I waited. Nothing happened. "Call her. Come on. This is costing me money."

"Don't you want to hear about Jonathan?"

"What about him?"

"We're going out."

"Y'are not."

"We are so."

"But I thought… he said…" I trailed off miserably.

"You don't think for a minute he fancies you, Lumpy?"

"Shut up. Put Ma on."

"He'd have to be deaf dumb blind and…"

"Put her on, you bitch."

"and stupid."

"PUT HER ON THIS MIMUTE YOU LITTLE BITCH OR I'LL KILL YOU."

"Temper, temper!"

I heard the phone being banged down on the table. I pictured the hallway with the evening sun streaming in through the fanlight. I heard Ma's footsteps and the sound of the phone being picked up. "Hello, love."

"Hello, Ma."

"Are you eating properly?"

"Yes, Ma. Mrs. O'Mahony's a great cook. How's everyone?"

"We're all fine, love. Your Auntie Nell's working hard. She's thinking of giving Jonathan an interest in the business."

"I thought he was looking for consultancy work?"

"It's not so easy to find the right thing over here apparently."

"How is he?"

"Grand"

"Will you tell him I was asking for him? And Ma?"

"Yes, love"

"Make sure he has Mrs. O'Mahony's phone number."

"I will, love. This call must be costing you a fortune."

"I know, but I wanted to talk to you."

"I knew it. There's something wrong." Her voice rose. "Mags, tell me. What is it? I'm your mother remember. No matter what it is you can …"

"There's nothing to tell Ma, honestly." I laughed. "I was just a bit homesick. That's all."

"Are you sure? You're not sick, are you? Have you a cold? It's those damp beds, isn't it?"

"Of course not. I'm fine Ma. Stop worrying. Give my love to Auntie Nell."

"I will, and to Anna, I presume?"

"No, not her."

"You two aren't at it again, I hope?"

"No. Look, I'd better go, Ma. Don't forget to tell Jonathan I was asking for him."

"No, love. I won't."

"Bye, Ma."

"Bye, love. Take care of yourself. Eat well. Keep warm."

I put down the phone. Her words echoed softly in my head as I climbed the stairs to my room. *Eat well. Keep warm.* The words of mothering at long distance. Exactly the words I needed to hear.

CHAPTER 14

The following week I joined Eileen in the bed-sitter. For the first time I felt truly grownup and free. Together we played at being housewives. I made copious shopping lists while Eileen allocated the various cleaning jobs. I loved the freedom but not the housekeeping. After a few weeks I got bored doing the chores but Eileen didn't. In fact she relished them. A natural housewife, she was the first to notice when the carpet needed hoovering, the sheets changing or the bin emptying. Our bedsitter was big. But then it had to be to take two beds, a wardrobe and a sofa and of course the kitchenette.

Kitchenette was Mr. Kelly's name for it. Mr. Kelly was our landlord. The kitchenette was really only a corner of the room cut off by two presses. There was a tiny fridge, on top of which sat a two-plate electric cooker. One of the plates hadn't worked since Eileen had taken the flat. He'd promised to get it fixed when she came in but that was two years previously. Every time she saw him she reminded him. The snag was that we didn't see him very often. The rent system required little or no communication. Each Friday we'd put our money under the carpet inside our door. When we came home it would have disappeared. The odd time we'd forget and leave it a day late, it would be gone like magic when we'd return that day. It was as if he had some remote control mechanism which could home in on the money.

I was there several weeks before I actually met him. It was a Friday morning. I'd woken with a cold and told Eileen to tell them in the office I was staying in bed. Around noon the door opened. I saw an arm reach around the door under the carpet. I opened my mouth to scream, but only a hoarse squeak came out.

"Oh, you're there, sorry." A short flabby man squinted across the room through thick glasses perched halfway down his face. Wispy hair stood up from a pink scalp. He smiled and walked towards me. The smile showed two front teeth going in opposite directions. "Skiving off work, are we?"

I pulled up the bedclothes nervously around me. "No. I'm thick." A violent sneeze proved my point.

He stepped back. "Eileen, isn't it? Hot whiskey is what you need darlin'."

"I'm not Eileen, I'm Maggie."

"Pity she's gone. Nice girl." He turned absentmindedly and made for the door. "Well, must go. No rest for the wicked, eh?" He winked. "So much to do. So little time."

"Eileen's still here, Mr. Kelly. I'm sharing with her now. Didn't she tell you?"

He scratched his bald patch. "Don't think so, darlin'. Probably left a note with the rent. I don't read them much. Usually just complaints, things that need fixing, you know the way it is." He winked again. "I'm not saying she's any trouble or anything," he said correcting himself quickly, "none of you girls are."

"Now that you're here, Mr. Kelly, could you have a look at the cooker?"

His sigh sounded as if it came from the bottom of a very deep well. "What's wrong with it?"

"One of the plates isn't working."

"Ye must have done something to it."

"We didn't, Mr. Kelly. Eileen says it hasn't worked since she came here two years ago."

"Good." He beamed. "In that case, ye're obviously well able to cope without it."

He moved swiftly towards the door, his trousers flapping around his bum as he walked, like a child in a loose nappy. He could certainly move fast. Before I had time to find a suitable reply, the door had closed behind him. That was the first and last time I ever saw Mr. Kelly in the flesh.

"So you've met Pampers at last," Eileen said that evening when I told her. "You're honoured. Like Christ, he appears only to the chosen few."

"I don't think he's going to fix the cooker for us." I was lying on the sofa. Given my condition, I was expecting to be waited on.

"We'll manage," she said, carrying the groceries towards the kitchenette. "Is the cold any better?"

"Don't think so." I gave an experimental cough.

"You won't be up to dancing tomorrow night then?"

"Of course I will," I said quickly. "Why d'you call him Pampers?"

"Baggy trousers." She disappeared into the kitchenette. "Oh for God's sake Maggie," she roared, "this place is a kip."

"I'm sick, remember?"

"Sick or not, you're bloody hopeless."

She came out, grabbed a brush from behind the door and disappeared into the kitchenette again. I thought I'd better show willing, so I got up off the sofa to see what she was talking about. Within seconds she had the bin emptied and the floor spotless while I stood by, making suitable noises of gratitude.

"What's for tea?" I asked when I felt her humour had returned.

"Pig's feet and cabbage," she snapped so I went back to my place on the sofa.

Later, after a tea of beans on toast, she was still ranting on about the housekeeping. I wasn't listening. I was too busy looking out the window at the Garda station across the road. "Isn't that new recruit gorgeous?"

"Forget the bloody Guards and pay attention."

"Don't be so boring, Eileen. You sound like Sister Dympna." Being told that always stopped her nagging. "We're lucky to be so near them, aren't we?"

"Pampers will throw us out of here if the rats come back."

"Rats?" I screamed. "You never told me we had rats."

"Good. Got your attention at last." She smirked. "We haven't, not yet anyway. But they've been officially notified about you. They're packing up in Number Seven and are on their way up." I giggled. Number Seven was at the end of the block. Two old men lived there. There were lots of rumours about where they'd come from, but nobody knew for sure. The house looked like a refuse dump for every bit of old furniture in the city. The men used candles. Apparently didn't believe in electricity. We always ran past their house at night. During the day you couldn't see anything because of the old newspapers stuck up against the windows.

"I hope you're coming in tomorrow," Eileen grumbled. "Bossy Boots made me do your work as well as my own."

"How was she?"

"In great form. Why wouldn't she be? She's off on holidays next week. She was all sympathetic about you by the way. Couldn't wait to tell Moloney."

"Where's she going?"

"Sorrento."

"Where?"

"Didn't they teach you anything in Kilmanogue?" I shook my head. "It's in Italy."

"It'd be nice and warm there." I stared out at the rain and shivered. "Pampers was right. It'll take a few hot whiskies to shift this cold."

"That's not a bad idea."

"We haven't any left. I used the last of it today."

"Not the whiskey, stupid. The holiday."

"Holiday? And what would we use for money?"

"The Fund, of course. What else?"

"Fund?"

"Jesus, Mary and Joseph! How could I forget the most important part of your training?" She slapped her forehead. "In F&F we have this club, you see. We all put in so much every month. Each month someone draws the money out. That way you can go on holidays, even if you haven't saved up beforehand."

"Sounds too good to be true."

"We'll join you up tomorrow. I'll go into the travel agents next week. I've always wanted to go to Italy, haven't you?"

"Yes." It was easier to agree with her.

"Italy!" she chortled, dancing around the room, "land of sun, sand, sea and ice-cream."

With Eileen there was no hanging around. By Monday, I was an official member of the F&F holiday club. By Tuesday, the floor of the bed-sitter was covered with a multitude of brochures. By Wednesday we had put down a deposit on two weeks in Cattolica, the two weeks immediately after our next exams.

We crammed like devils after that. Despite Eileen's best effort, the bed-sitter turned into a tip. The news was out. It was official. We were now dirtier than Number Seven. The rats must surely be packing their bags. We had Accounting books everywhere, over every bit of furniture, including the beds and the floor. At night we'd push them to one side, and haul our exhausted bodies into bed.

"I don't think I could take another week of this," I moaned the night before the exam. "G'night."

"Buona notte, signorina," Eileen mumbled, and promptly fell asleep.

I was too tired to even try to imagine what Italy was like. Italy, with all those lovely dark-eyed men she kept raving about, and the sun and the sea, not to mention the ice-cream.

Forty-eight hours later, the torture was over. Eileen and I brought a bottle of whiskey home to celebrate. We sat on the floor in the middle of the paper mountain and got well and truly plastered, so plastered we fell asleep, instead of going dancing like we'd planned.

On our last day at work, we were going over our final list of things to pack, when Bossy Boots came in. Fortunately, she was still in a good mood after her own holiday, so she didn't take the head off us for making out packing lists instead of posting invoices.

"Allow me to give you the benefit of my vast experience, girls," she said grandly. "Travel light. There are only four essentials. Passport, Money, Tickets and Keys." She counted them off on her fingers. "Everything else is optional. Passport, Money, Tickets and Keys, that's it and that's all." She sailed out of the office with a breezy "Buon viaggio, Signorine" over her shoulder.

"Wow. That holiday did her a power of good, didn't it?" Eileen grinned over at me. "What's wrong with you?" I tried to swallow, but made a choking noise instead. "I hope you haven't caught anything. Time enough to get sick when you're back at work."

"Pa.. p.. pa..Passport." Finally I managed to get the word out.

"What's wrong with it?" Eileen demanded. I stared down at my feet. "Maggie, look at me." Her voice had gone tight. I looked up miserably. "You do have a passport?" I shook my head. She laughed harshly. "You're having me on." My head dropped. I gave a little whimper. "Whew. You had me going there for a moment." Relieved, she went back to her list again. "Now let's go over this once more. Don't mind Bossy Boots and her list. Perfume, mascara, make-up, bikinis. Come on! Show an interest, signorina. This is multo importante."

I had to sit down, because suddenly my legs didn't seem able to support me.

She looked up. "I don't want to hear this." She slammed her fist at the desk. The phone jumped. The files scattered. "You're not going to tell me you haven't got one?" I nodded dumbly, then shook my head. "Jesus, Mary, and Joseph what sort of … ."

Bossy Boots chose that moment to walk back into the office.

"Now come on, girls. Be fair."

"This bloody eejit has no passport." Eileen wasn't one to spare a person's feelings. "We're flying out on Saturday morning, and this thick, this … this… hasn't got a passport."

Bossy Boots' eyes opened wide. "Leave it to me." She turned on her heel and rushed out.

I sat there, head down, pulling an invoice into tiny little strips.

"I'll never forgive you for this Maggie Brown, never ever. Of all the incompetent, retarded, stupid, bloody geeks…" She ran out of words. I nodded in agreement. I was all that and more. Even the most stupid hick from the wilds of the bog knew you had to have a passport to go to Italy.

"The … the exams put it out of my head. I'm s..sorry."

She stared coldly back at me. I hung my head again. The invoice was now in a neatly shredded bundle. I patted the bundle for the umpteenth time. The phone rang. I jumped. The tiny shreds of paper scattered across my desk.

"If this is work, you handle it, okay?" Eileen barked at me.

"Of course," I answered meekly.

She listened intently and nodded her head a few times. "Yes, yes, I'll tell her… right. Thanks, Miss Ryan. You're a star." She put down the phone and made the Sign of the Cross. "Come on thicko. We've work to do. No, no, I don't mean that rubbish," she said, as I turned to the rest of the invoices. "Real work. Grab your coat. Come on."

I followed her out. We jumped on the bikes. I was feeling far too humble to ask where we were going.

Three hours later, I had the precious booklet stored safely in my bag. It was only a temporary one, of course, but it would get me out of the country. Who cared if I never got back? Bossy Boots had saved the day. She'd gone to Mr Moloney. He knew somebody, who knew somebody, who knew somebody who worked in the Passport Office. It was *multo buona fortuna*, she said. I think she meant we were lucky.

And we were. No work. No study. No exams. No rain. For two magic weeks we revelled in the excesses of hot sun and warm seas, crowned with all the admiration and devotion the hot-blooded Italians could lavish on us. Every night we stoutly defended our virginity against the lusty ravages of the passion-frenzied ice-cream sellers, with their long arms and short legs. I became the target of the owner of a restaurant on the cliff overlooking the bay. His name was Paulo Mandato. Paulo of the liquid eyes and passionate glances. I'd never seen eyelashes so long, so shiny. Each night I'd repel his advances, explain that everybody in Ireland was a virgin; that we never did *it* before marriage. Undeterred each morning he'd be back looking for more. One night he even produced a packet of you-know-whats. Serious measures were obviously called for, so I told him I was engaged. That he could understand. Jonathan was my lucky betrothed. I had to save my virginity for him, I said wistfully. It was such a heart-warming story I almost believed it myself.

If the nights were wonderful, the days were more so. The sun rose each morning and stayed out until the same time each evening. The sea shone like silver, almost blinding us with the glare. The sand was white and soft under our feet, the water warm and delicious. And then there were the markets. Eileen and I had begged, borrowed and stolen money for the holiday. So every afternoon we plundered the stalls with all the commitment and dedication Bossy Boots was trying to instil into us for F&F. We'd never seen mini-skirts so mini. Some of them leather, soft, not like the leather at home. We bought as many as we could. Eileen was almost raped by the stallholder when she fitted hers on. The shoes were great too. More of that lovely soft leather. Eileen bought a pair of stilettos, with heels so high I told her she'd have to report them to Air Traffic Control. I spotted this wine-coloured pair with the cutest little heels I'd ever seen. They were madly expensive, but I had to have them. Even my feet looked elegant in them.

Eileen and I thought we'd died and gone to Heaven. We stayed in the Albergo Roma, and danced under the stars every night. We knew we'd be paying for the rest of the year into the holiday club, but we didn't care. The ardent devotion of our Latin lovers was a pleasant change from the not-so-ardent attention we were used to at home. Surviving the constant assault on our virginity was hard work though. Long knickers and a strong bra was the secret. Eileen's mother had warned her what to expect. Not very multo romantica, but they worked. The real secret of our survival, though, was in staying together.

One night, things got out of hand. Paulo had had to work so I was with Giorgio, an ice-cream seller, my relief lover for the night. Eileen was with Luigi, Luigi of the garlic breath. Within minutes of arriving onto the beach, the two of them disappeared, leaving me on my own with Giorgio and his transistor radio. Before I knew what was happening, his zip was open, his willy gleaming up at me in the moonlight.

"You want make bambino, Margarita?"

"No, Giorgio. Thank you very much for asking, but no." I backed away but he kept advancing. He didn't look like a man who was in the mood for stories of Irish virgins and fiancés, so I turned to run and promptly fell over the radio. The music stopped. Giorgio picked up the radio and shook it. The music started again. Now that he knew his precious radio wasn't broken, he turned his attention back to the task in hand.

"Come, Margarita. Now we make luff." But I was off again, running as fast as my legs could carry me up the road and back to the safety of our hotel.

"How'd you get on with Giorgio?" Eileen asked, when I burst in the door.

"The bollocks tried to rape me."

"Oh, Mags. You're such a liar."

"I am not. He even showed me his willy."

Her mouth dropped opened. "What was it like?"

"Black pudding." Her eyebrows raised in disbelief. "Well to be fair, more like white pudding."

"Was it long short fat thin? Was there any hair on it?"

"I can't believe we're having this conversation," I said crossly.

"Come on, Mags," she giggled. "Travel is supposed to broaden the mind."

"If I hadn't managed to get away from him, God knows what would have happened."

"Was it like the puddings in Smelly's?" Smelly's was the corner shop near the flat in South Circular Road. Weird smells emanated from the back of the shop, hence the nickname. "Or was it more like the puddings you bring up from Kilmanogue?"

Purely in the interests of further education, I tried to be as specific as possible, but I couldn't resist embroidering what had happened. In a few minutes we were rolling around the beds with tears streaming down our faces.

We defended our honour even more strenuously after that. We stuck together like glue. Even the night Paulo drove us up behind the town to watch the sunset. We stood there mesmerised, all four of us, Luigi, Eileen, Paulo and I, as the orange ball slipped down beneath the horizon. Before our eyes, the sky turned into a black canopy of stars, the water a sheet of silver. Luigi said he wanted to come to Ireland. His plan was to marry Eileen and sell ice-cream on the beach in Bray. He had a cousin there apparently. We did our best to explain about the Irish climate, but he was in love. He didn't want to hear.

On the last day, in a fit of culture, we went to Pisa. "What did the Dubliner say when he saw the leaning tower of Pisa?" Eileen asked, as I marvelled at the angle of the building that had withstood the test of time.

"I don't know, what?"

"*Hey looka. It's crooka*"

"You've no soul, Ilena. Who told you that one?"

"Bossy Boots," came the unexpected reply.

Paulo drove us to the airport. He kissed me on both cheeks. "I'll never forget you, Margarita."

"Me neither Paulo, but you know the way it is." I smiled wistfully. He nodded and squeezed more blood out of my hand.

Luigi's eyes were brimming with tears. In the interests of Irish/Italian relations, I took hold of him. "Please don't cry, Luigi. You're too nice for the likes of Ilena." The tears spilled over. Not wanting my new skirt to get wet, I pushed him away as gently as I could. "Ilena will never forget you, sure you won't Ilena?" I frowned across at Eileen. Her eyes were shining with amusement. I pushed her quickly towards the check-in desk. They waved madly at us from the balcony as the plane took off.

Four hours later, we landed in Dublin. We spent the next day unpacking. I hung up the new miniskirts lovingly in the wardrobe. I found some shoe-cream under the sink, and gave the red shoes a good clean. They'd look great on the dance floor. For me, the holiday had been well worth it for them alone.

CHAPTER 15

It was back to reality on Monday. We staggered into the office half-asleep. Everybody wanted to know how we'd got on. We told them how utterly desirable the Italians had found us. Paulo's car had become a Mercedes overnight, his restaurant a chain of nightclubs. Luigi was now the proud owner of an ice-cream factory. Bossy Boots wasn't too convinced, however. She said we'd missed out on everything cultural. She wasn't a bit impressed with our ten-minute visit to Pisa, and was annoyed when we repeated her joke about the leaning tower.

Soon the excitement died down, and we had no excuse to put off work any longer. As I struggled to find my way through the first ledger, I looked out at the drizzle and thought longingly of the beach and the warm sea we'd left behind.

We were paying into the Holiday Fund for the rest of the year. Each month I gave my subscription and waved someone else off, but I couldn't complain. I had a good job and a career in the making. I could do what I want, wear what I like, go where I please, dance every night of the week if I took a notion. In Italy I'd begun to realise that we'd been dressing like younger versions of our mothers, with our tweed skirts, woolly twin-sets and sensible stockings. Now, for the first time, in Ireland, fashions were changing. Hemlines were shooting up. Soon I might even be able to wear the skirts I'd bought in Cattolica.

I hadn't really thought much about being Irish up to then, but now I was beginning to realise that it was something to be proud of. John F Kennedy was proclaiming his Irishness all over America, and if the President of the most powerful nation in the world was proud to be Irish, it was high time we were too. Eileen and I started to read newspapers that summer, not just to see what was on in the cinemas, but to see what other countries were up to. People were saying that Ireland was coming of age. She was ready to cast off the spectre of the Famine, the shadow and gloom of the post-war years, and walk out onto the world stage. For the first time being Irish was a good thing, not something to apologise for. It was a nice feeling.

Shortly after we came back, the news broke that President Kennedy was coming on a visit. The office was agog with details of his itinerary. He'd be visiting his old homestead outside New Ross. Auntie Nell was going to drive Ma over from Kilmanogue. They had to be up at dawn to be sure of getting a good view. There was standing room only on the quay. Anna told me she'd never seen Ma so excited. We reckoned it was because he was a Catholic.

Eileen and I would gladly have gone down too, but we hadn't any holidays left. Instead, we had to make do with waiting for him outside the Passport Office in Stephen's Green. We bought American flags. Everyone was in great form. We sang songs while we waited. Then, at long last, the waiting was over. He stood up in the open car, looking like a super-star in his white tuxedo. In our whole lives we'd never seen anyone so glamorous. Eileen and I waved our flags like crazy women, and nearly fainted when he turned and waved back at us.

In Limerick, he congratulated our first Lady Mayor on her speech. The women all over the country cheered. In Dublin, he delivered an address to a joint assembly of the Senate and the Dail. He said that Ireland was one of the youngest Nations in the world, but she had the oldest civilisation, that we should be proud of our past, and look forward to the future. He got a standing ovation.

The visit was over in a few days, but we talked about it for weeks. In that short time, he'd captured the hearts of everybody. After his visit, we followed the American news with special pride. He was the President of America, but far more important than that, he was Irish and Catholic, one of our own.

Then the unimaginable happened. The Russians sent the first woman into space. I wondered what she was like. I'd dreamed of going there myself of course, but that was before Dad had been killed. Becoming an accountant was my dream now, a dream founded in reality and hard work but I didn't mind because Dublin was the happiest city in the world that summer. I was revelling in the newfound freedom of life in a bed-sitter. For the first time in my life, I had money in my pocket. I could buy clothes without Ma's approval. Eileen and I vied with each other. As our skirts got shorter, our hair got longer. Fresh from our Italian holiday, the two of us basked in wolf-whistles as we walked down Grafton Street in our newest shortest minis.

Anna was the only blot on my horizon. She kept teasing me about my age, just because she was eighteen and I had to wait until the end of the year. "What's that child doing tonight?" she'd say, when I'd go home for the weekend, or "What's that child up to now?" She made fun of the exams too. "That child will never be an accountant. She hasn't got the maturity." The more she went on, the more it got to me. I couldn't wait for my birthday.

Our exams over at last, Eileen and I made up for time lost in study. Decked out in our Italian gear, we went dancing every night. As summer turned to autumn, the flimsy Italian shoes began to look the worse for the wear.

One frosty night in November, just outside the dancehall, disaster finally struck. One of the heels came off in a grating. Dicky Rock's *From a candy store…* was wafting out onto the night air as I stopped to examine the damage.

"Feck it, anyway!" I said, showing the broken heel to Eileen. "I'll have to go back."

"You can't. We haven't time."

She was right. I wrenched the heel off the other shoe and tossed the two heels into a litterbin with a flourish. The shoes looked a bit funny without them, but they'd have to do. Someone tapped me on the shoulder as we entered the hall. I whirled around and looked up at a face I hadn't seen for months.

"Jonathan, what are you doing here?"

"Is this the Italian Jonathan?" Eileen's eyes danced, as she looked him up and down. I could have cheerfully throttled her.

"What do you mean?" Jonathan asked looking from one to the other.

"Nothing." Eileen laughed. "Enjoy yourselves." With that she was gone, weaving her way through the crowds.

"Come on. We can talk later." Jonathan took my hand and pulled me onto the dance floor where a new set was starting. He was a good dancer. As we spun round the floor, I forgot all about the missing heels. When the set was finished we stood chatting about Kilmanogue. The next was a Rock and Roll number.

It wasn't until the end of the night we saw Eileen again. She reminded me that she was staying with Carmel again that night.

"Oh fine," I replied quickly, hoping he wouldn't get the wrong impression. "See you in the office tomorrow."

"I know when I'm not wanted," she said with an airy wave and moved off into the crowd.

Jonathan put his arm around me. "Won't you be lonely on your own?"

"Not at all. There are lots of other flats in the house."

"I could keep you company if you like?"

"We're reared by the nuns over here, Jonathan, remember?"

He laughed. "You can't blame a guy for trying."

It was after three by the time we got back to the bed-sitter. I saw him looking at the two beds, but steered him firmly towards the sofa. I made tea, and for the next couple of hours he brought me up-to-date with the news from Kilmanogue; how they'd acquired the small premises next door and hoped to develop it into a Men's section. I noticed he was discussing the business as if it was his own.

"Has Auntie Nell made you a partner?" I asked curiously.

"Why wouldn't she?" He sounded slightly defensive.

"No reason. The Men's Section is a great idea."

"We're going to break in an entrance between the shops. This will encourage the women to buy something for the hubby after they've treated themselves." He yawned and stretched. "Are you really going to throw me out? What if I promise to behave myself?"

"I'm not so sure you would," I laughed and stood up.

"You don't really want me to go, do you?"

"Yes, I do," I said, pushing him towards the door.

"But you'll be lonely on your own."

"No I won't."

"Are you sure?"

"Yes" I said, trying to sound firm but friendly, like the nuns had told us.

At the door, he kissed me. I felt a funny tingling sensation as his fingers caressed the skin on the back of my neck in a slow circular motion

"Are you sure you're sure?"

"Yes"

"Really?"

"Yes positive," I said and pushed him out.

He sighed. "Bloody nuns. They've a lot to answer for."

I giggled, and closed the door behind him. It was almost four, but I was far too excited to sleep. He'd asked me to the pictures the following night. The problem now was what I should wear.

I was still trying to decide, when I heard the milk bottles being dropped on the doorstep. Who needs sleep, I thought, jumping up and pulling on some clothes. I ran out into the frosty morning, grabbed Eileen's bike and hared off down the street. Twice I nearly skidded on the wet road, as I took a curve too quickly. P*lease God, don't let the bin-men have been yet*. At the dancehall, I jumped off the bike and rooted feverishly in the bin. The nuns were right. *Ask and ye shall receive*. Gleaming redly up through the empty mineral bottles and twisted cigarette packs were my precious Italian heels. Now all I had to do was to call into the shoemaker. They'd be perfect with the new mini. Out of the bin with them and into the basket of the bike. Jonathan need never know where they'd spent the night.

I caught Mr Fallon just as he was opening up. He promised a full resurrection. All well with my world, I cycled off happily to work.

As it happened, Eileen was staying with Carmel again that night. When Jonathan arrived I handed him the Evening Press. "Just finishing the makeup," I said, trying desperately to sound casual. "You can decide which film we'll go to."

I was so excited I had difficulty getting the lipstick on straight. I could feel his blue eyes watching me through the mirror.

"What's the point in putting that on?" he demanded. "It's only going to come off again."

"Read the film guide and do what you're told."

"Okay, okay. Let's have some music so," he said turning on the radio.

We were both leaning over the film page a few minutes later, when a shaky voice cut into the music. *'We interrupt this program to bring you a news flash. Reports are just coming in that President Kennedy has been shot.'* The print swam in front of my eyes. *'The presidential cavalcade was on its way from the airport. The shots appear to have been fired from a book depository in downtown Dallas.'*

"There must be some mistake." I looked wildly at Jonathan.

"Don't worry. He'll pull through."

"Please God," I wailed, "don't let him die." That wonderful man, who just a few months ago had put Dublin on the world map, our cool clean hero who had stood in the open car at Stephen's Green, and waved specially at Eileen and me.

We sat in silence on the side of the bed, waiting for another news flash. I was almost afraid to breathe in case we missed it. After a few minutes it came. The President had been taken to Dallas Memorial Hospital where he was being operated on.

"I told you he'd be all right," Jonathan said. "They'll have the best doctors in the world working on him."

And so we waited. And waited. Then came another bulletin. It was over. John F. Kennedy, the youngest ever President of the United States, had been assassinated. Our wonderful safe world had become dark and dangerous. It was 1963, the 22nd of November, and nothing would ever be the same again.

Jonathan and I didn't go to the pictures that night. Instead, we lit the fire and sat listening to the bulletins as the same words were repeated over and over again. Between bouts of sobbing, I told him all about the famous visit to Dublin, how Eileen and I had waited for hours for the cavalcade, how we were so sure he'd waved at us specially we'd nearly died of excitement.

Around eleven, he and I went out for some fresh air. Ordinary life was suspended. Everywhere we looked, small groups of people were huddled together, talking in hushed tones. We walked along the canal in silence. The Rathmines clock struck midnight. "History has been written today," Jonathan said.

I shivered. "Let's go back."

"You're freezing. Must be the shock." He put his arm around me. "I'll stay. This is no time to be on your own."

"I'll be alright," I said shakily.

"After all that's happened? Don't be silly. I insist."

"Are you sure you don't mind?"

"Of course not. I'm glad I'm here."

"Me too."

When we got back, the fire had gone out. I started to shiver again.

"Anything to drink?" Jonathan asked, looking around the room.

"There's some whiskey in the wardrobe," I told him. "I'll put on the kettle."

We sipped the hot drinks, but still I couldn't stop shivering. I sat hugging the glass. He looked at me. "You'd be warmer in bed."

"Hope you'll be all right in Eileen's." It seemed awfully small for his tall frame.

"If you're sure that's what you want? I could always get in with ... "

"No, Jonathan. You can't."

"I'm sorry. I forgot about the nuns."

I got undressed in the bathroom. By the time I got back he was in the bed, his bare feet sticking out at the end. He was trying to pull the bedclothes up around him but every time he pulled them up, his legs were stripped.

"I'm sorry we haven't more blankets," I said guiltily.

"If we were together, we could double what we have."

"Sorry." I got into my own bed. "Night, night, sleep tight." I turned off the light and tried to settle down.

A few minutes later he called across the room "Are you okay?"

"Fine thanks. How are you?"

"Freezing."

I jumped up. "I'll make us more hot toddies. That'll do the trick."

"This isn't very hot," he complained, when he tasted it.

"That's because I put in so much whiskey," I giggled.

Five minutes later he jumped out of his bed, and padded over in bare feet. "I'll make proper ones. Finish that up." I drained the glass obediently.

This time, he sat on the side of my bed while we drank. I was beginning to feel quite woozy. The last thing I needed was more whiskey, but I drank it down to please him.

"What we need now is a little cuddle," he said, as I slipped under the covers. Too sleepy to argue, my eyes were already closing as I felt him slip in beside me.

"God Almighty, do the nuns design the beds too?"

I giggled, and moved over to give him some room. I was pinned up against the wall at this stage, but I didn't mind. At least the shivering had stopped. Somehow we managed to settle down. I could feel his breath on my neck. For the first time that night I began to feel warm.

"Cosy?" he mumbled into my ear.

"Snug as a bug ... rug," I said, starting to drift off.

"A goodnight kiss," he whispered, and turned me round to face him.

It was a little one to start with. Then he kissed me again. This one was deeper, closer, more urgent. Somewhere in the back of my brain an alarm bell went off. I knew I should tell him to stop. Maybe if you're drunk it's not a sin, I thought drowsily, as his hands stroked my neck. The warmth was flowing out from his fingers and moving down my back. His legs twined themselves around mine. I opened my mouth to say something. His tongue sent a shockwave through me. He started to move over on top of me. His legs were pushing against mine now, coaxing them apart. I tried to push him away, but he was too heavy. I could barely breathe under the weight of him. Suddenly, his hand reached down and the nightdress wasn't between us anymore. Something was pushing into me, hurting me. Frightened, I shouted at him to stop, but he was breathing hard and moving to some sort of rhythm of his own. In a last desperate attempt I pushed against him. I felt a sharp stab of pain. He fell back against the pillow.

I lay there shocked. I couldn't believe what had just happened.

"Better get back to my own bed, I suppose," he muttered. Then he was up and padding across the floor to Eileen's bed.

Seconds later he was asleep.

A few weeks later I went home to Kilmanogue. They were throwing a party to celebrate my eighteenth birthday, my coming of age. At least Anna wouldn't be able to tease me anymore.

That same night she and Jonathan announced their engagement. Hugs and congratulations all round. Everyone was delighted, for them on their engagement, for me on my coming of age. I hugged them all too and smiled, though my head was spinning, not only because of the surprise announcement, but also because no matter how often I checked and rechecked the dates, the answer was still the same. My period was two weeks late.

PART TWO

PUTTING AWAY CHILDISH THINGS

CHAPTER 1

"There is no *us*." Jonathan stared ahead grimly, hands clenched around the steering wheel. "I'm sorry, Maggie. What happened was a mistake."

"*You're sorry? Is that it? You're sorry?*"

He nodded. I opened my mouth and closed it again. He was sorry. I was sorry. We were all bloody sorry. Some mistake, I thought, staring out the window.

He was giving me a lift to the station. It was the first chance I'd had during the holidays to talk to him. But what was the point?

He put his hand on my knee and squeezed it. "I was only trying to comfort you after the news about Kennedy."

I brushed his hand away. "Well, you can comfort Anna from now on. Leave me alone."

He nodded eagerly, like a kid who was expecting a whole Rosary as penance and who only got a Hail Mary. "Thanks, Maggie. You're a brick."

I shot a stony look at him. "Wonder what she'd say if she knew?"

"You won't tell her, will you?"

"God help her, placing her trust in someone like you for the rest of her life."

"Promise you won't say anything?"

"Of course I won't," I snapped, "for her sake and Ma's though, not yours."

"Thanks." He gave a sigh of relief.

Nothing else was said. I couldn't tell him my real fear, that I could be carrying a permanent reminder of that awful night, the night we were all so bloody sorry about.

"You needn't wait," I said curtly, when we arrived at the station. He looked relieved.

As I watched him drive off, I couldn't help wondering what I'd ever seen in him. I looked around for an empty carriage. As I sat down I prodded my tummy. I couldn't be, could I? Not after only the once. The train started with a jolt. For what must have been the hundredth time, I counted up the days and dates, still hoping I'd made a mistake. But the answer was the same. I looked out at the fields whizzing by, and tried to empty my mind. I was just beginning to drift off into a doze when the train pulled up at a station. Two young girls got in giggling, as they hauled heavy cases behind them. Full of their mother's Christmas baking no doubt. I smiled at them, and closed my eyes again. They were chatting about the presents they'd got. I felt years older than them. My eye drifted to an ad up over their heads.

It was one of those ads you see all the time. See, but don't see. *Think you might be pregnant? Have a test and be sure. Discretion guaranteed.* My eyes snapped open. It gave a Dublin number. I looked sideways at the girls, but they weren't paying any attention. I read it again slowly. Counting days and dates was all very well. This was the only way I could be sure. And it did say, *Discretion guaranteed*.

By the time the train pulled into Amiens Street every word of the ad was burnt into my brain. I could recite it backwards as well as forwards. I called from a phone booth in the station. No answer. I'd call again in the morning on my way to work. Eileen had left me a note to say she was taking another few days off. She wouldn't be back until the New Year. By then my fate would be sealed. *Please God, let it be negative. Don't make me pregnant. I'll go to Mass every day. I'll say the rosary...I'll...*

I lay awake the whole night. Around five I got up and made tea. I looked at the pile of food I'd brought back. Ma didn't realise how small our kitchenette was. By seven I was up. I rang the number on the way to work, but again there was no answer.

There were very few back in the office, so I was busy. The work took my mind off the problem for several minutes at a time. There was no answer at lunchtime either. That could mean nobody would be there until the New Year, and that was four days away. Four days. Oh God! I took some accountancy books home with me. Studying might help me stop worrying, and if I stopped worrying, my period might come. That's what they tell you in magazines anyway.

By New Year's Day I was a wreck. I'd tried the number each morning and evening. Still no answer. Still no sign of my period either. The first chance I got that morning, I dialled the number and nearly dropped the phone when a chirpy female voice answered. I was so surprised to get an answer I didn't hear what she said.

"Is that the.. er… clinic?" I gulped.

"Yes. Can I help you?"

"I think .. er.. sorry, I'd like to make an appointment."

"A pregnancy test I suppose." I thought I heard a yawn quickly stifled.

"Uh-huh" I replied, trying to sound like I'd had dozens of tests before.

"When do you think you might have conceived?" A personal question of the highest order. All the chirpiness back in the voice.

"Oh.. er.. about five weeks ago or thereabouts," I said, knowing not only the day but the exact hour of conception, committed forever to history along with Kennedy's assassination.

"We'd better have you in straightaway in that case. What about nine o'clock tomorrow morning?"

"Tomorrow?" I gulped.

"Yes, is that a problem?" Chirpy was beginning to lose some of her chirpiness.

"Oh... okay."

"And don't forget your fasting sample."

"My what?"

"Urine sample, first thing when you get up." Chirpiness all gone now, a hint of impatience even.

"Oh... right."

"And the name?"

She had me there. There was some graffiti on the back of the phone booth. *Margaret Byrne loves Charlie Dickhead*. It seemed appropriate. "Byrne, Margaret Byrne," I said into the phone. Someone had drawn a big hairy willy beside the names. Giorgio's was the only one I'd ever seen. Odd, I hadn't seen Jonathan's.

"Hello, hello? Are you still there?" Definite impatience now.

"Sorry. Yes?"

"See you tomorrow at nine, Miss Byrne. It is Miss, I presume?" The faintest suspicion of a chuckle.

"Yes, it is," I snapped and put the phone down. I'd had enough chirpiness for the moment.

It was a long day. Thoughts going round and round in my head. Fortunately Eileen arrived back that night.

"Ah go on, Mags. Pull the other one," she laughed when I told her.

"For God's sake Eileen, stop cleaning that bloody table and tell me what to do."

She looked up at me. "You're serious?" I nodded miserably. "But how the hell.. who... when... I mean where was I when all this happened?" I started to cry. "I'm sorry, Mags." She put her arms around me. "Sit down and tell me the whole story."

Between sobs, I told her what had happened the night Kennedy was killed. Also about Christmas and the engagement, and the appointment I had in the clinic.

"How long will the test take?" she asked.

"Don't know."

"How soon will they be able to tell you?"

"Don't know."

"It probably takes about a week." She counted on her fingers. "Right, the baby will be seven weeks, but you can't be having a baby. You're far too young..." She got up went into the kitchenette for the whiskey. "Damn, is that all we've left? I was hoping we could wash it out of you."

That reminded me of a sermon from a school retreat. The priest had spoken in hushed tones about bad girls who got into trouble and tried to wash out the babies by drinking a bottle of gin while taking a bath. We'd all giggled about it afterwards, confident in the knowledge that it could never happen to us. Well here was I, and it was happening to me. My stomach heaved. I ran out to the bathroom and slammed the door behind me.

"Are you alright?" Eileen called a few minutes later. "Say something, Mags, anything, just to let me know you're alive." I opened the door and walked stiffly back into our bed-sitter. "Would you like a cuppa?" Her voice was low, as if she was talking to an invalid. I lay down on my bed and closed my eyes.

"Yes please, and a slice of Ma's Christmas cake."

She put on the kettle and sat down beside me. "Was it your first time?" I looked at her offended. "You didn't do anything with Giorgio or Paulo?"

"Of course not. We were all virgins then, remember?"

"Good," she nodded and got up to make the tea. "It's probably just a scare then. This time tomorrow it'll be all over. Where'd you put the cake?"

I pointed at the wardrobe. "Blue tin, near the shoes."

Where else? She pulled the door open, automatically reaching up to stop the sweaters falling out. She found the tin. "Are you sure this won't make you sick again? Though of course on the other hand it might dislodge…"

"Would it?" I looked at her hopefully.

"No. Perhaps not."

She cut four slices. We sat on the bed and started to eat. I hadn't realised how hungry I was.

"You do know that in some houses Christmas cakes can last for months?" Eileen said, as I cut two more slices. "Your mother's a great cook."

"Aren't they all?" I answered, with my mouth full.

"Ha! I must bring you some of my mother's offerings."

It was a relief to be able to tell someone all the same. That night, for the first time in weeks, I slept soundly. When I woke, I could hear the traffic building up outside as people started to return to work after the long holiday. Eileen was already awake.

"I don't know how you managed to sleep," she grumbled. "I didn't close an eye."

"Makes a nice change," I said jumping out of bed. "What am I going to put it into?"

"Put what into?" she yawned.

"The sample, dopey. Do we have a bottle?"

She sat up, wide awake now. "Only the whiskey bottle, and that's too big. Hey! What about this?" She held up the Holy Water bottle Ma had made us bring to Italy.

I gave her one of my Sister Dympna looks.

"Eileen Farrell, that's hardly appropriate."

I was dying to go to the loo. We searched around frantically for a few minutes. Finally, in desperation, I grabbed the Holy Water bottle from her.

"What will I do with the Holy Water? I can't just throw it down the sink. Here quick. Bless yourself." I sprinkled it over the two of us. We made the Sign of the Cross several times. "Please God, let the test be negative. Please God, let me be negative. Please God, let me be negative. Negative, negative, negative."

"Lay off," Eileen protested. "You have me drenched."

I rushed into the bathroom, and emerged five minutes later with the bottle full of warm yellow liquid. I held it up triumphantly. "I spilt most of it, but there should be enough here."

She pushed past me. "Quick. Out of the way. I'm bursting now."

I wrapped the bottle in a page from an old ledger, and put it into my handbag. The plan was that Eileen would tell them in the office that I'd been sick all night but I hoped to be in later.

CHAPTER 2

The wintry morning sun shone brightly on the window boxes of Northbrook Road as I walked up the tree-lined avenue. The odd numbers were on one side, the evens on the other. The sun disappeared behind a cloud just as I reached 57. Bad omen that, I thought, climbing the steps to the front door. I rang the bell. The sound echoed through the house. After a few minutes a young girl in a dressing gown opened the door.

"Yes?"

"Is this the… er …Clinic?"

"Downstairs." She stepped back into the hall.

"Sorry."

"No problem. Happens all the time. Good luck with the test," she said cheerfully and banged the door shut. So much for discretion. I walked back down the steps. The basement door was almost hidden from view at the side of the steps. I knocked on the door. Nothing happened so I knocked again.

"Come in. It's open," a voice called from inside.

I entered a tiny hallway and walked through into a larger room. A young girl sat on a chair near the window. A middle-aged woman looked up from a desk and smiled at me.

"Miss Byrne?" I nodded. "You've brought the sample?" I nodded again and took it out from my bag. The bottle was still warm. Embarrassed, I handed it to her.

"Will that be enough?" I whispered, desperately conscious of the other pair of eyes watching. The lady held the bottle up to the light for the whole world to admire.

"Plenty. It will take about ten minutes. Can you wait?"

I nodded. She indicated a chair beside the other girl and disappeared into an inner room.

The silence hung in the air. We examined each other surreptitiously. She didn't look like the sort of girl who would get into trouble, but then, maybe I didn't either.

"Nice day," I mumbled eventually, desperate to break the awful silence. She nodded and said nothing. "Bit cold still though, isn't it?" I added. She nodded again. Defeated, I stared out the window then turned back to have another go. "Wasn't December dreadful?" Again she nodded and said nothing but I wasn't finished yet. "The long-range forecast says we're going to have an early spring. Did you know that?" I asked in a tone that left her no option but to answer.

"No" she mumbled at last.

"It'd be great if we did, wouldn't it?" I pleaded. She nodded. "Not before time, sure it's not?" I insisted.

"No" she sighed.

Silence fell again. I looked sideways at her. She was doing the same thing. Our eyes met. She blushed and smiled. "What a way to start the New Year off, eh?" Her smile got sort of twisted in the middle. "I'm a bundle of nerves."

I smiled back gratefully. "Me too. Haven't slept for weeks."

"It's been two months with me. Kept hoping 'twas a mistake. Every morning I'd wake up expecting my period, and then nothing." She sighed heavily. "How far gone are you?"

"Six weeks…er…about six weeks… I think." I didn't want to let the side down.

She gazed out the window. "The sun's out again."

"A good omen, eh?" I gave a nervous giggle.

She looked at her watch. "Not much longer now."

The hands on mine seemed to have stopped, even the second hand. My whole life was in suspended animation, waiting for the sentence to be handed down. Would I walk out of here a free woman?

After what seemed an age, the older lady entered the room. We both looked up. She smiled at the other girl. "You're fine, dear. You're not pregnant." My friend sat there stunned. "I'm sure your period will come in a few days now you're no longer worried. That'll be five pounds please."

I never saw anyone part with five pounds so willingly. She looked as if she wanted to empty her whole purse out on the counter.

"Won't be much longer now, Miss Byrne." The lady disappeared into the back room again.

My new friend put her arm on my shoulder. "I'm sure you'll be alright too. Would you like me to wait with you?"

"No, no. You go on. I'm glad your news was good."

"Thanks. I can't wait to tell my boyfriend," she grinned. "I feel I've been let out of prison." She picked up her bag. "Bye now and good luck to you."

Now that she'd gone, the room began to close in on me. I looked at my watch to see if it had started working yet. At least she had a steady boyfriend. What had I? Eileen was the only human being in the world who knew where I was at that moment. *Please God, let me not be pregnant. I'll go to Mass every morning for a month. I'll go to confession more often. I'll be nice to*

Anna, even to Jonathan if I have to. Please God, give me back my period. I'll never complain about the leaking again, ever. I'll even do an act of...'

"Miss Byrne." I opened my eyes. This time she wasn't smiling. "I'm sorry, my dear. Your test was positive. You'd better get in touch with your GP."

"GP?" I stared at her wildly.

She sat down beside me and took my hand. "How old are you?"

"Seven... er... eighteen."

"Does the father know?"

"My father's dead."

"I mean the baby's father."

"Who?"

"Wait there. I'll get you a cup of tea."

I looked at my watch. It seemed to be working now. It was a quarter to ten. I jumped up. "I can't."

"But you've had a shock. At least wait for..."

"No, I really must go. I'll be fine, honestly."

"Is there anyone you can talk to?"

"My friend Eileen. Don't worry. I'll be alright."

"You'll need to see a doctor, and you should tell your mother as soon as possible." I looked at her incredulously. "You must, dear," she carried on smoothly. "Motherhood's a big step. It'll change your whole life." I edged towards the door. I didn't need to hear this. "Aren't you forgetting something, Miss Byrne?"

"Of course, I'm sorry." I rooted in my bag for my purse. "Five pounds, isn't it?" I handed her the note.

"Thanks. Let me make another appointment so we can talk about the next stage." She pulled a book towards her. "What about next week? Monday, same time or would you prefer after work? We're open late on Wednesdays?" I nodded. Anything to get out of that room. "Right. Wednesday 6.30. By then you'll be used to the idea. Here, I'll give you our card." She wrote the time and date on a small yellow card and handed it to me. "Remember what I said about your mother, won't you, dear? You're far too young to be going through this alo..."

I ran out the door, down the path and leaned against the railings to give my heart a chance to slow down. I looked around amazed. The sun was still shining. The grass was still green. The traffic was still moving. Everything looked so normal. I started to walk fast along the footpath. Very fast. Fast enough to blot out any thought. I heard a screech of brakes.

"Where's the fire, Missus?" A bus driver roared. I ignored him and hurried on. I couldn't be pregnant, not after just once. It must be a mistake. I was only a few weeks late. What's a few weeks? Suddenly, I realised what had happened. A great surge of relief ran through me. That other girl was two months overdue. She had a steady boyfriend. She'd been doing it all the time. I whirled around. That was it. They'd mixed up our two samples. She'd got my results. I'd got hers. I started to run. I pushed open the door of number 57. The older lady was on the phone. She looked up surprised. I paced the floor until she hung up.

"I didn't expect you back so soon." She smiled. "Do you want to make an earlier appointment?"

"No, no. It's not that," I said, excitedly. "You see I know what's happened but it's alright. Anyone can make a mistake." She looked at me blankly. "You mixed up the last two samples. That other girl, the one who was before me? She and her boyfriend were at it all the time, whereas I was only … I only…" My voice trailed off. I didn't like the way she was looking at me. There was too much sympathy in her gaze.

"I'm sorry, dear. We're very careful. We have to be."

"But you tested the two of us together."

"No, we didn't. That girl had already handed in her sample when you arrived. Don't you remember?"

"Are you sure?"

"I'm sorry, dear. Truly I am."

At her words, the last remnants of hope drained away. The room started to spin. She caught me and sat me down on the chair.

"This time you're not leaving 'til you've had a cup of tea." I was in no position to argue. She disappeared into the back room. The tea was ready in five minutes. The two Marietta biscuits tasted delicious. No wonder. I'd had no breakfast. She sat with me, watching every mouthful I took. "Good. The colour's coming back in your face."

"I'm glad."

"Is there anything you need to ask, or do you want to wait 'til Wednesday?"

I put the cup down and looked at her. "Are you really sure there couldn't be a mistake? Surely sometimes you mix up…"

"I'm sorry. I wish the results were different, but you're going to have to face up to it, I'm afraid." She took my hand as I stood up. "I'm here every morning if you want to talk. We'll see you next week. You might like to bring your boyfriend in with you." She saw my face. "Or perhaps your girlfriend?"

I nodded bleakly. "I have to go now. I'm late for work."

"Tell them you had a virus or a tummy bug. From now on, you won't always be able to tell people where you're going. There'll be tests, examinations, visits to the doctor, things like that." She smiled at my worried expression. "Don't worry Miss Byrne." I blushed, as I remembered I hadn't given her my real name. "There's nothing to be afraid of. Having a baby is the most natural thing in the world. Goodbye, my dear. See you Wednesday."

"Yes" I mumbled, and left the clinic for the second time.

CHAPTER 3

I felt a bit like that girl in the Wizard of Oz, as if I'd gone through a door and emerged into a world where the rules were different. Even the language was different. So, it was *The most natural thing in the world* was it? It sure didn't seem like that. I tried to remember how many months it was before pregnancy started to show, but my mind was blank. Either the pregnant women of Kilmanogue had been very discrete, or I'd had more important things on my mind, like tennis and swimming. This had to be some sort of a dream. Surely I'd wake up in a minute and have to get up for work. This wasn't Margaret Brown from Kilmanogue walking down Northbrook Road on the second day of the New Year, pregnant. *Pregnant. Going to have a baby.* I repeated the unfamiliar words, trying to get used to them. *Going to have a baby* sounded less lethal. *Going to have a baby. The most natural thing in the world.*

"*So Miss Brown, is it true you're going to have a baby? The viewers are all dying to know.*" The imaginary reporter from the BBC stuck the microphone in front of me. I nodded glumly. "*And how does it feel?*" The intrepid reporter asked.

"Feels like a load of codswallop. You can tell them that from me, it's all bloody codswallop, the biggest mistake that ever happened on this planet."

"*I don't think that's what they expect to hear Miss Brown. To win the prize you must answer the question. How does it feel to be pregnant?*"

"Let them find out for themselves, the lazy gits." I stepped off the footpath to cross the road and bumped straight into a woman dragging a little boy along by the hand. The kid took one look at me, opened his mouth and started to scream. His mother glared at me.

"Don't mind her, Jameser. She's harmless, just a wee bit mad. Now, stop that bawlin' or I'll give you something to cry for." They gave me a wide berth and rushed off. She wasn't talking about me, was she? *The most natural thing in the world* eh? In my Aunt Fanny! I crossed the road and started to walk fast, trying to keep up with my thoughts. E*xpecting a baby, awaiting the happy event*. There seemed to be quite a few ways to describe it, but *happy event* was pushing it a bit. Not too happy for Maggie Brown, who had neither husband nor boyfriend. A nightmare, more like. Oh good, a nightmare. In a few minutes now the alarm would go off and I'd wake up. Something loomed out of the corner of my eye. Brakes screamed, as a bus swerved and shuddered to a halt inches from my face.

"For Christ's sake watch where you're going Miss," the driver roared from his cab, face white as a sheet. He looked back at his passengers. "Anyone hurt in there?" The passengers were all staring out their windows at me, disappointed no doubt that I wasn't stretched on the ground. I was a bit disappointed myself. It might be one way of solving the problem. I saw an elderly man pull himself up from the floor of the bus and stagger back to his seat. His voice carried through the open window. "I'm okay, son, but that young wan should be locked up." He was looking at me. Someone gave him a hat, which he put back on his head.

The driver jumped out of his cab and ran over to where I stood rooted to the ground. "What the hell d'you think you're doing?" I backed away. "Are you trying to kill yourself? I've a good mind to call the Guards."

"I'm sorry." I could feel the tears starting. "I'm s..sorry. I didn't m…mean to…"

"So well you might be. Look Miss," his tone softened, "do you want to get on the bus? I'll bring you into town. Is that where you're going?"

"I d..don't," I blubbered, "don't want to go anywhere. I just want to … to die."

"Sit down. I'll call an ambulance."

"No, I'll be alright." I mopped my eyes and blew my nose. "I just want to be on my own."

"You're not fit to be on your own."

"I am so. I'm f…fine."

"I can't delay much longer." He looked back at his bus "Oh my God!" I followed his gaze. All I could see was a row of white faces looking out. The faces sitting down had been joined by another set, presumably the passengers from the other side of the bus who'd crossed over to watch the entertainment. Up on the top deck it was the same. Every window had a face. Some had two. Windows were opening as the passengers entered into the spirit.

"Now, now, Charlie, take your mitts off that nice young girl."

"Put her down, Chas. You don't know where she's bin."

This was greeted by a burst of raucous laughter.

Charlie dropped his arm from me like lightning. "I'll have to get this lot out of here before there's a riot. Will you be okay?"

I nodded eagerly. "Don't worry. I won't do anything stupid." I'd have said anything to get away. What if there was someone from Kilmanogue on that bus, or someone from the office?

He ran back and climbed into his cab. Hands waved at me, as the bus pulled out into the traffic. "He's not a bad auld sod, love. You could do worse."

"Bye, bye Miss. Be good."

"And if you can't be good, be careful."

"And if you can't be careful, you know what to do."
"Hey Miss, hope you didn't give him your number?"
"And if you did, I hope it wasn't the right ……"

The voices faded as the bus moved off. People on the pavement were looking at me as if I was mad. I started to run. I turned down one side street, then another. My heel caught in a grating. I stumbled and would have pitched headlong only somebody caught me.

"Well, if it isn't the one and only Maggie Brown?" I looked blankly into a pair of green eyes. "Don't tell me you don't recognise me?"

"I don't." I pushed him away, crossly. I was in no mood for games.

"Okay, I'll give you a clue." He started to sing. *"Bring flowers of the rarest. Bring blossoms the fairest from gardens and woodlands and boll …"*

I gaped at him. "Tommy? Tommy O'Connor?"

"The very one," he grinned. "I'm mortally offended you didn't remember me, because I certainly remember you." He was taller, more filled out, but had the same cheeky grin. "How long has it been? Seven, eight years?" I nodded. Kilmanogue seemed like another world. "Come on. Let's go for a cup of coffee and a chat."

"Sorry. I have to get to work." I blew my nose, hoping he'd put the red eyes down to a cold. I was in no mood for reminiscences.

"Come on, little Maggie. I won't take no for an answer. You look like you could do with a break."

He put his arm around me. We started to walk. At least this way I wouldn't bump into any more buses. Nobody had ever called me little Maggie before. It felt kind of comforting. We headed for a coffee shop, and sat down at a table in the corner. I watched him order tea and scones. A far cry from the young ragamuffin who'd taught me words for the hymns. Unconsciously, I started to hum. *"Bring flowers of the fairest…"*

He grinned. "Remember Sister Dympna?"

I nodded. "Life was so simple in those days."

"Of course it was. We were young." He gazed out the window. "Everything was simple then."

Without warning, the tears came. This time I had no control over them. Silent, wordless tears. He stared at me, horrified. "What's wrong, Maggie? I'm sorry if I upset you. I didn't mean to." He put his hand under my chin and lifted my head. "What is it? Maybe I can help." I shook my head as the tears rolled down my face. "Oh, come on. Surely it's not that bad?"

"I'm … I'm p… pregnant."

I don't know which of us was the more shocked.

"You poor little mite." There was that *little* word again. "You obviously don't want to be. What does your boyfriend think?"

"I d.. don't have a boyfriend."

He smiled gently. "Maggie, my love, I remember those endless processions too, but this is hardly an immaculate conception."

"He…er… doesn't know. I've just had this test you see and…" I stopped abruptly as the tea and scones were brought to the table.

"Will you be mother, dear?" the waitress asked brightly as she put the teapot down in front of me. I looked up at her shocked. Tommy's face contorted. I didn't know whether to laugh or cry. I chose the former. "Honestly. Young people nowadays." She stalked off, tut tutting all the way into the kitchen.

"I'd better leave her a big tip to make up to her," Tommy said, lifting the teapot. "In the circumstances I'd better be mother eh?"

We ate in silence. Either he didn't know what to say, or he felt I needed more time. I watched him out of the corner of my eye, noticed the clean-cut jaw, the cropped hairline. He'd certainly changed from the scruffy tearaway. Once he caught me looking, but he just smiled and continued eating. There were tiny gold flecks in his eyes I'd never noticed before.

"I don't know what you must think of me," I said at last.

"None of us is perfect, Maggie." He reached over and touched my face. "Sorry. Butter on your chin." I felt my face redden. "Do you want to talk about it?"

I shook my head. "No. What about you? What's been happening with you since…"

"Since we were run out of Kilmanogue, you mean?"

"I can't believe you've grown up so much. Is it really you?"

"Oh it's me alright, Tommy O'Connor, the terror of Kilmanogue, the best hymn-singer in town."

"My mother used to skin me alive for playing with you."

"Is Anna up in Dublin too?" He lifted the teapot to refill my cup.

"No. She's working in Kilmanogue. She's… she's er … engaged to be married."

"You don't sound too enthusiastic. Don't you approve?"

I looked out the window. "It's a bit… complicated."

"He's not the one who… ?"

I looked at him; appalled he could be so perceptive. To my horror I found myself nodding. I averted my eyes. I couldn't bear to see the condemnation in his.

"It's not what you think. They only got engaged at Christmas. I didn't know about him and Anna, you see. He was up here the night Kennedy was assassinated. We had a date. I was upset, and..and.. and that's how it happened." For some reason I was desperate to make him understand. "We'd had a lot to drink. I was shocked by the news but I never intended for anything to happen... he got carried away I suppose. I couldn't stop him... anyway now I'm p..."

He pushed a handkerchief across the table. "Here take this. He doesn't sound too much a gentleman. Being pregnant's not the end of the world, you know." He smiled gently.

"That's easy for you to say."

"I watched my mother often enough." His face darkened. He gazed out the window. "I don't suppose any of us were planned, but we were all wanted in the end." He reached across the table and gripped my two hands. "Don't harm the baby, Maggie. If we lose respect for human life we've lost everything."

My head shot up. "How could you even think that?"

"You weren't going to get rid of it?" His eyes looked deep into mine searching for an answer.

"Of course not."

He heaved a sigh of relief, and dropped my hands. "You'd regret it the rest of your life. There's far too much killing in the world."

"But it's the end of my career. I'll lose my job. I've nowhere to go. I can't go home with Jonathan there. Anyway it would break Ma's heart. Oh God, Tommy, what am I going to do?"

"Don't worry. We'll work something out." He thought for a minute. "My mother might be able to help."

"How?"

"We moved to London after we left Kilmanogue. It was a new start for us. I ran away and joined the army. I lied about my age. They couldn't find any papers, so I got away with it. As soon as I could, I transferred to the Air Force and learnt to fly. I took to it like a duck to water." His face lit up. "Oh Maggie, if you knew how clean the world seems from up there. You're looking at a fully commissioned officer of Her Majesty's Royal Air Force." He smiled and gave me a cheeky salute.

"Now that's the Tommy O'Connor I know and love."

"Don't distract me, Miss Brown. Let me concentrate on your problem."

"I'd much prefer hear about the flying."

"Later. Let me think. There's only Mary at home now, and she's getting married shortly, so there'll be plenty of room."

"Plenty of room for what?"

"For you, of course. You could stay with Mam for the last few months."

I gaped at him. "Me stay with your mother in London?"

"Why not? She's better than any doctor with all her experience. She'd be happy to help. I know she would. She was very fond of your father."

I gaped again. "I didn't even know they know each other."

"Right." He sat back with a satisfied air. "London it is then."

"Hold your horses for a minute." He looked so hurt that I put out my hand. "It's not that I'm not grateful, Tommy. But I have to think it all out, when I'm going to show and all that sort of thing. And then there are the exams. Did I tell you I was doing Accountancy?" He shook his head. "My next exam's in March. That's another reason why I don't want to lose this job."

"Accountancy? Good for you. Don't worry about showing. You're tall so you probably won't for about four months, maybe even five. So let's see. When did you... oh yes, Kennedy's assassination wasn't it?" I nodded. I could feel the colour spreading hotly across my face. "That means that you'll be alright until..." He counted the months off on his fingers. "December, January, February, March. Being pregnant won't interfere with your next exam and if you took six months' leave you could come back in September when it's all over."

I started to giggle. "Do they teach you this stuff in the army?"

"Air Force," he corrected. "No. I'm from a big family, remember."

"I'll still have to give up my job though, won't I?"

"Not necessarily. Where do you work?"

"Flynn and Forsyth."

"If they had a branch in London they might transfer you. In London, women are kept on after having babies. We're a bit behind in Ireland but it will change, you'll see. At least ask them for leave. Tell them you want a career break."

He made it all sound so reasonable.

"Just as well I bumped into you. I was about to jump off the nearest bridge."

He laughed. "Be careful who you tell, Maggie, won't you?"

"Eileen my flatmate's the only one I've told."

"Which doctor are you going to use?"

"Don't know."

"Tell your boss you want to move to London for personal reasons. Do you know anyone high up who might be able to arrange it for you?"

I thought of Mr. Moloney. "There is one man. He's a friend of the man who got me the job in the first place."

"I hope he's a decent bloke." I smiled at his concerned expression. "What are you smiling at?"

"They say a problem shared is a problem halved. I feel as if mine is halved already."

A serious look came over his face. "You mustn't depend on me, Maggie. I'm not around very often."

Panic swept over me. I grabbed his arm. "Oh God, how long are you staying?"

"I fly off again next week."

My world collapsed around me in an instant. "You can't go away on me. I can't possibly manage on my own."

He burst out laughing. "Don't be so dramatic. You've managed fine for the last seven years."

"How am I going to get through the preg…?"

"You'll be fine. If you stay with Mam, I'll be able to see you from time to time."

"But there'll be all sorts of decisions to make."

"Yes, and you'll make them very well on your own. Now, isn't it time you got back to work?"

I looked at my watch. "Jesus, Mary and Joseph, Eileen will think I've been taken to hospital." I grabbed a paper napkin. "Here's the number of the flat and the office. Call me tonight. Okay?" I folded the napkin and put it into his breast pocket.

"Okay, boss," he saluted with a grin. "I'll walk you to the office."

"No. I'll have to dash. Thanks for…" I gave him a quick peck on the cheek and ran out of the cafe.

Bossy Boots was most sympathetic when I mumbled something about a tummy bug. She even thanked me for coming in. Eileen bundled me into the Ladies' before I could get my files open. She was shocked when I told her the test was positive. For some reason, I didn't tell her about Tommy. By working through lunch, I managed to sneak a look at some personnel files. F&F did give career breaks in certain cases, usually to pursue special study programs. Mr. Moloney was on holidays for another week, so I'd have to wait until he came back to find out more.

There was no phone call from Tommy that night. I lay in bed panicking. Suppose he disappeared again for another seven years? Blackness crowded in on me. I tried to push the thought away. Tommy would ring. Of course he would. He had to. Without him I was lost.

The next day crawled by. Every time I heard the phone I jumped. That night, while Eileen and I were washing up, the phone rang. I tore downstairs to the hall and picked it up. Someone was humming at the other end of the line. "*Bring flowers of…*"

"Thank God."

"No, it's me."

Giggling, I pulled up the chair to sit down for a chat. The receiver flew out of my hand as I hit the floor. I'd forgotten about the broken leg, yet another item on Mr. Kelly's list of things to be fixed. Every time we said anything about it, he'd put the broken leg back under the seat and stand the chair carefully up against the wall with a "sure isn't it grand the way it is?" before doing another of his disappearing acts.

"Hello, Hello, Maggie? Are you there?" I could hear Tommy's voice as I rescued the receiver.

"Yes. Sorry. 'Twas only the chair."

"Chair?"

"Never mind. I'm glad you called."

"You're not still planning to throw yourself off the nearest bridge, I hope?"

"No."

"Have you thought about what I suggested about staying with Mam?"

"Yes, but are you sure she won't mind?"

"She's happy to have you, but you should go over and see her first, get to know her."

"It's a terrible imposition."

"Not at all. I'll fix up a weekend. Have to go. Ring you in a few days. Bye."

The phone was down before I could reply.

The following week he rang again. We agreed I'd go over to see his mother the next long weekend. That same week I made an appointment to see Mr. Moloney.

"How can I help you, Maggie?" he asked, after I'd sat down. I was a bundle of nerves.

"It's about career breaks, Mr Moloney."

His eyebrows shot up. "I thought you were settling down nicely. What about your exams?"

"My next one's in March. It's after that I was thinking of. I need to get away for about six months." I could feel my face reddening. "To London. It's.. er.. personal."

He shifted uneasily. "Is it important?" I nodded. "It's a pity to drop your studies. You've been doing so well."

"I intend to continue studying in London," I said quickly, "so I'll be able to sit the autumn exam when I get back."

"How will you manage without a salary?"

"I'll look for temporary work."

"Why do you want to go?"

"I'd rather not say," I mumbled.

"It'd be a shame to give up your career."

"I've no intention of giving it up, Mr. Moloney. I want to come back to F & F. I love it here."

"I'm glad to hear it," he smiled. "Okay, I'll see what I can do. We don't want to lose our newest recruit. I'll be in touch in a day or two."

It was another week before I heard from him again. By then I was a nervous wreck. Every possible scenario had been played out in my mind in the meantime, none of them good. He was standing at a wall planner as I walked into his office. He motioned me towards a chair.

"You wanted to leave in April, didn't you?"

I nodded. He smiled broadly and looked down at a company memorandum in his hand. "Something has just come up. As it happens it would suit us fine to send you over to our London office around that time."

My heart sank. "Sorry, you must have misunderstood. I need the time off, Mr. Moloney. I'm not going to be able to work."

"Maggie, forgive me if I'm overstepping the mark, but are you pregnant?" I nodded miserably. "That's alright then. You can work in the London office right up to a couple of weeks before the birth, and return a month or so after." I looked at him in disbelief. "They're a bit more advanced over there about maternity leave. This means you'll continue to be paid and I'm sure you'd prefer that?"

I nodded speechlessly while he continued.

"They're getting a computer. Everybody has to be trained. Even the Smart Alecs in London don't know their way around them yet." He started to pace the floor. "It's actually a great opportunity for you, Maggie. It'll suit your own…er… personal situation, and you'll be able to bring your knowledge back to us. It'll be good for your career in the long run too. Well, what do you say?" He stopped pacing and held out his hand. "Is it a deal?"

"I suppose so." We shook hands.

He went back to his desk. I got up to leave. I was beginning to feel like a puppet dancing on a string that could break at any minute. I needed to get home to Kilmanogue and think everything out for myself, but first, there was this visit to Tommy's mother.

Tommy rang me a few days later. "What about the weekend after next?"

"That would be fine."

"What's that, Mam?" I heard muffled talk as he went off the line for a few minutes. He came back on the line laughing. "She wants to know if you're eating properly. What'll I tell her?"

"Tell her I am and I look forward to seeing her."

There was another pause, then he was back on the line. "Sorry, Maggie. She insists on having a word with you herself."

"Hello, Maggie?"

"Hello, Mrs. O'Connor."

"Remember, you're eating for two now, love, so no skipped meals and drink plenty of milk."

"Yes, Mrs. O'Connor."

"Good girl and I look forward to seeing you too."

Then Tommy was back. "I have to go, Maggie. Take care of yourself. Bye."

A few days later I was engulfed in her arms in the foyer of her apartment block in Richmond.

"You couldn't be more welcome. Come in quickly, you poor thing. Are you frozen? When did you eat last?" Her last sentence would have been my mother's first. Apart from that, she was Ma, albeit a plumper, noisier version, and I loved her straightaway. She picked up my bag and pulled me into the lift. "How's the little one? When is he due? I'm dying to hear everything. Are you exhausted? Was it a bad trip? Were you seasick?" I decided that most of her questions didn't require answering, so I just kept smiling and nodding with the occasional shake of the head. "I hope you've been taking care of yourself like you promised. None of you young people eat properly nowadays. But don't worry. From now on I'm going to look after you."

The barrage continued all the way up in the lift. I felt I was drowning under a tidal wave, a wave I was far too tired to resist. "Everything's ready. You sit down and rest yourself, or do you want to go to the bathroom? It must have been a long journey all on your own. Now let me look at you properly." She paused for the first time and studied me. Then she shook her head. "You did have a poor crossing, didn't you? The forecast said gales over the Irish Sea. Was it awful?" I nodded. "Were you seasick?" I nodded again. "It's not fair, is it?" she said angrily. "Some people never have problems. I only have to look at a boat myself and I get sick. Tommy's different. Just as well with all his flying, I suppose. I worry about him all the time, but I'm sure you do too. He can't be safe in those strange countries, sure he can't?"

It was definitely time to get a word in now. "But we're not... he and I aren't.. we're only..."

"Get that wet coat off quickly, lovey, before you catch your death." I stood like a child while she unbuttoned my coat. "Slip out of the shoes too. They're soaked. Sit down over here near the fire." It took less energy to do what I was told. She put a pair of men's socks and slippers in front of me. "They're Tommy's. I've had them warming. When I saw the rain earlier I knew you'd be wet. None of you young people wear sensible shoes." I slipped my feet into the slippers. They were far too big for me, but for the first time since I'd got on the boat I started to feel warm. "The food will be ready in a minute. You just relax."

She turned on the television and left. Some sort of competition was on. I looked at it with interest. Eileen and I didn't have a television in the flat in Dublin. Through the open door, I could see her darting about the little kitchen. Within seconds, she was out with a steaming glass wrapped in a napkin. I reeled at the strong smell of whiskey. "This will heat you up on the inside. Go on, lovey. It won't do the baby any harm, not this once anyway." Who was I to argue? I took a sip, leaned back against the cushions and looked around the cosy room.

If the last few minutes were any indication, I'd found a home from home, complete with a mother to mind me. After the whiskey, came a plate of Irish stew followed by hot apple tart and cream. While I ate, she talked. Every so often she stopped and ate something but never for long. Then she showed me to the bedroom. I fell into bed and passed out.

The next day we took the tube into Oxford Street. Three hours later we emerged from Marks and Spencer's. We'd been to C&A's, and BHS as well. I'd never seen such a selection of clothes. The mini-skirts were even shorter here than at home. I spent my last few pounds on one for Eileen. I'd given them up myself for the moment.

"Where to next?" she asked, as we stood on the path outside Marks.

"Could we call it a day, Mrs O? If I go up one more escalator I'll take off."

She laughed. "Mrs. O. I like it."

"Sorry. Mrs. O'Connor seems a bit of a mouthful. Do you mind?"

"I don't mind what you call me, lovey, as long as you don't call me early in the morning. Come on so. We'll beat the rush hour."

The rest of the weekend went by in a twinkling. She stood fussing over me in the lobby as we waited for the taxi. "Are you sure you have enough sandwiches?"

"I'm fine honestly. I don't know how to thank you."

"Eat properly and look after yourself, that'll be thanks enough for me." The taxi drew up outside. The driver honked. "Give my regards to your mother. Oopps!" She put her hand to her mouth. "Sorry, I forgot."

CHAPTER 4

The next two months went by in a haze of morning sickness, work, lectures and study. I wore oversized blouses and loose sweaters to hide my disappearing waistline. Nobody could see that I had to leave some of my skirt buttons open. I pretended to be disgusted at the weight I was putting on. I blamed the studying. Eileen backed this up by telling people how much I was eating at home.

I went down every few weeks to Kilmanogue. I dressed particularly carefully on those weekends. Luckily they were working too hard to notice anything. The man who owned the shop next door had died and the property was on the market. Auntie Nell and Ma had a chat with the bank manager. They took out another loan and bought it. Jonathan was "away on business" most of the time. I was glad. He might have noticed the extra weight and put two and two together. To conceal the morning sickness, I started to go home early on the Saturday morning train rather than on Friday night. I'd pretend I had a party to go to and put the nausea on Sunday morning down to the results of something I'd eaten at the party. Usually, in the rush of getting ready for Mass, nobody noticed.

One day the phone rang in the flat just as I was coming in after shopping. I heard the familiar notes of *"Bring flowers of the fairest"*. In the excitement I dropped the bags onto the chair, which collapsed immediately. The shopping scattered all over the floor.

"I hope that was the chair and not you?" Tommy chuckled.

I hadn't realised how much I'd missed the sound of his voice. "It's a bad line. I can barely hear you."

"What did you do to Mam?"

"Where have you been?" I roared back accusingly. "Haven't heard from you in ages."

"Is that all the gratitude I get for ringing you from a distant land?" The line got stronger then faded again.

"What's wrong with your mother? The last time I rang her she was in great form."

"What did you do, put her under a spell?"

I laughed. "She's great Tommy. You're lucky to have her."

"Isn't she lucky to have me?" he retorted. "Will you be okay with her?"

"Of course. She's terrific."

"How are you keeping? Not sick or anything?" The line went faint again.

"I'm sick, fat," I roared "and looking more like an elephant every week."

"Ah sure that's only natural. When are the exams?"
"Week after next. I start in London a week later."
"Have to go. The line is terrible. Take care of yourself, and Maggie?"
"Yes?" I roared.
"I'm glad you have Mam to mind you. Bye."
The line went dead. I slammed down the receiver. Talking to him was more frustrating than not hearing from him at all. I hadn't a clue where he'd been ringing from, or when I'd hear from him again. I propped the chair up into its usual position, picked up the parcels from the floor, and climbed the stairs wearily. A few more weeks and I'd be in London at the start of my big adventure. At least there I wouldn't have to pretend.

The study paid off. The exams passed over with none of the usual regrets. Then suddenly it was my last week in the Dublin office. Everywhere I went, people I hardly knew came up to me to wish me well with the new computer system. I was beginning to wonder whether I'd done the right thing agreeing to take on the project. I'd be the only Irish person in F & F trained on the computer. What if I didn't make the grade? What if after the six months I still didn't understand the bloody thing? A fine end to my career.

That evening, they had a party in the office for me. Mr. Moloney made a speech and handed me a package. They all clapped and waited as I unwrapped it. It was a leather brief case. I looked up at all the faces.

"If you think you're getting a speech out of me…" They laughed and waited, obviously expecting more, so I struggled on. "Thanks for this lovely present and for the party and for all your good wishes. I only hope I can live up to your expectations about this new computer thingy." A titter went round the room. "I'll try not to let you all down. Thanks again." They clapped, probably with relief that it was so short.

"Well done, Maggie." Mr. Moloney shook my hand. "Remember if you need me, you've only got to call. Day or night. You have my phone number?"

"Thanks," I gulped. He turned away to speak to someone.

Eileen jumped up behind me and pulled the briefcase out of my hand. "Wow, pure leather, great for the old sambos."

"I feel awful about this, Eileen. If they only knew."

She shot me a warning glance as one of the junior accountants came up to me. "If they only knew what? Good luck Maggie. Don't forget to come back."

"I was just saying I'd feel a bit of a sham walking around with one of those yokes, Jimmy. Get us a cuppa, Eileen. I'm parched."

"What did your last one die of?" she laughed, and poured me a cup of tea. "That fruit cake looks nice."

Bossy Boots came over. "Not long now, Maggie. How do you feel?"

"Terrified," I said, detecting a twinge of envy in her voice. "Have you ever worked in London, Miss Ryan?"

She shook her head wistfully. "No, unfortunately. You should make the most of it. It's a wonderful opportunity." I looked at her curiously. There was a lot we didn't know about Bossy Boots. "Good luck, Maggie." She shook my hand warmly. "Don't forget to send us the odd card, sure you won't?"

"Of course not," I answered. She moved off. "I think I'm going to miss her." I whispered to Eileen.

"Bossy Boots? Are you sick?"

"I'm sure she was young once."

"Not her," Eileen said, reaching for another slice of cake.

Nobody wanted to be late leaving the office for the long weekend. By five o'clock the place was empty, except for Eileen and me.

"Wonder what I'll be feeling the next time I climb these steps?" I said, holding the skirt-band out to give me some relief, "somewhat lighter, I hope."

I was off to Kilmanogue for the weekend, but I planned to return on Sunday to get ready for my flight on Monday. I was dreading saying goodbye to Ma. Fortunately they were all up to their eyes at home with the Easter Sale. They roped me in on Saturday morning to mark down what was left of the winter stock. That kept me in the storeroom, away from prying eyes. It also meant fewer questions about the next six months. The first thing I planned to do was to buy some maternity dresses. I'd had my fill of ripped waistbands and safety pins. The doctor at the Clinic had warned me that over the next few weeks even my biggest skirts and trousers wouldn't fit me. He'd given me a note to take to a doctor who had a clinic near Mrs O's flat. I felt like a backward child being passed from one teacher to the next.

On Sunday, as I tucked into the roast beef, I could feel my mother's eyes watching me.

"Maggie, have you put on more weight?"

I nodded without a blush. "It's all the study, Ma. I told you." I prodded another roast potato with my fork. "I'll go on a diet in London."

"Watch yourself, won't you love? Where in the name of God is she going to get a fresh egg over there, Nell?"

"She won't," Auntie Nell replied morosely.

"Could you bring a few with you if I packed them carefully?"

"No, Ma, I could not." I laughed. "Anyway, they have food in London. Millions of people live there, I believe."

"She'll survive, Ma." Anna looked at me scornfully. "She's so fat she can live off her own body."

"That's a terrible thing to say to your sister," Ma said, "you'll miss her when she's gone."

"Like a hole in the head," Anna retorted, but there was a slight weariness in her voice. I couldn't help wondering whether everything was alright between her and Jonathan. I felt a sudden pang at leaving her. What if she needed me while I was away? I'd be in no condition to come home.

"Don't be rude Anna." Ma looked crossly at her.

"Why are you all fussing about Lumpy?" Anna replied sulkily. "What about me? Of course I'm only the old slob who stays at home. None of your fancy computers and transfers to London for me, oh no!" She slammed down her knife and fork, and pushed her plate away.

"It's ice-cream and apple tart for dessert, girls," Nell announced brightly. "I'll go and get it. Will you help me, Maggie?" I nodded eagerly. I was beginning to feel a bit like a visitor in my own home, and I didn't like it. I gathered up the plates and followed Nell out to the kitchen.

"What's wrong with Anna?" I asked as soon as the door closed behind us. "Are things all right between Jonathan and herself?"

"Don't talk to me about that fellow," Nell said crossly, taking the tart out of the oven. "Get the ice-cream, will you love?"

"What's he done now?"

"It's nothing. It'll pass. I know he's my son," she sighed, "but I don't know what's going on in his mind half the time." She moved around our kitchen with the ease that comes of long practice. "We'll take it in on the tray and serve inside." She stopped for a moment and looked at me. "Sometimes I feel as if I don't know him at all, Maggie. Imagine a mother admitting that? Kettle on? Good. We don't want you to miss your train. Come on." She handed me the loaded tray. "I have the plates."

Nothing more was said on the subject.

I had to leave immediately after lunch, so the goodbyes were short and sweet. It wasn't until the final moment that the full realisation dawned. As far as they were concerned, I'd be home for the Whit weekend. But of course that wasn't going to happen. I'd have to fake some emergency at work. The deception was starting. Already I hated it.

They all came to the station to see me off, even Anna.

"Take care of yourself," I said, giving her a quick hug.

"Yeah yeah" she answered, wearing her bored expression.

"Mind you watch the traffic, Maggie," Auntie Nell said, hugging me breathless. Ever since the accident she was nervous about traffic. "I'll tell Jonathan you were sorry to miss him."

"Thanks. Bye Auntie Nell." I hugged her warmly. Hopefully she'd have him sorted out by the time I saw her again.

Ma held her arms out to me.

"We're not going to be sad, love. Just promise me you'll mind yourself." She looked into my eyes. "Eat properly, keep warm and ring as often as you can."

"I will, Ma, I will." I hugged her and closed my eyes tightly. In that moment I wished with all my heart to be a little girl again, to be able to tell her everything, knowing she'd be able to fix it. If only I was. If only she could. If only we could put the clock back. If only, if only.

"Don't sleep in any damp beds, sure you won't? Tell the landlady I said she was to look after you. She's a mother too. She'll know how much I'll be worrying." I nodded. The only information I'd given her about my landlady was that her name was Connors, and that the firm had made the arrangements.

As the train moved off, I leaned out the window and waved at them. I didn't stop until the three figures were tiny dots. The next time they'd see me I'd be a mother. Me, a mother! The word sent shivers up my spine. I was the one who'd never wanted to have children, so how come I was five months' pregnant and on my way to London? What about all my great plans for going to the moon? I sat back. My eyes closed with weariness. Within seconds I was asleep, and I didn't wake until the train pulled into Dublin.

By noon the following day, I was all packed and waiting for the taxi. I'd left a funny note for Eileen. At least I'd tried to make it funny. As I wrote I was looking around the tiny bed-sitter wondering when I'd see it again. Eileen was hoping to find someone to share it for the six months. In the drama of the moment I'd also left a note for Mr. Kelly, begging him to fix the chair in the hall at least, even if he never fixed the cooker or the curtains. By the time the notes were written, I felt so lonely I seriously considered cancelling London and telling everyone the truth. Fortunately the taxi arrived.

By eight o'clock that evening, I was in the lobby of the Richmond apartment being smothered by Mrs O'Connor. "Welcome, welcome, welcome," she panted. "The lift was busy so I ran downstairs. Let me look at you." She stood back and appraised my bump with the eye of an expert. "Carrying high, I see. Has he moved yet? Is the morning sickness gone?" The lift arrived and we piled in, but the barrage continued. "Where will you be working? Did they give you a map? I have a big one of Tommy's if you need it. Did they tell you what trains to take? We must study the timetables. How's your family? Did you tell your mother yet?"

She eventually stopped for breath. We sat on her couch sipping several cups of tea, and I brought her up to date with all the news. She wasn't pleased to hear I still hadn't told Ma. To distract her, I pulled out the piece of paper showing the address and the exact whereabouts of the office.

"I don't have to check in until Tuesday."

"What sort of gombeens are they?" She jumped up and went to a press. "Tommy left a proper map here somewhere." She found it and within minutes we were pouring over it trying to pinpoint my new office. "You're lucky," she said when she found it. "According to this, you'll only have to change once on the underground."

"But they said it was very close."

"It is, by London standards. You'll be there in less than an hour, and don't worry; I think it's only a matter of crossing from one platform to another. We'll do a practice run tomorrow."

We did. I couldn't believe how crowded the Underground was. "This is nothing," she warned. "Wait till you see it at rush hour!"

The office itself was a large granite building on a Square. We crossed the busy intersection, and walked into the tree-lined park in front of the building. The noise of the traffic quietened as soon as we entered. There were lots of benches around the place and flowerbeds. We could hear birds singing in the trees over our heads. "This will be a nice place to relax in," she remarked with approval. "Let's go see what the cafes are like. It's important you eat properly."

We entered the one nearest the office. The waitress handed us a menu. She wore heavy white make-up. It looked like a mask. She was chewing gum.

"What do you recommend, love?" Mrs. O asked, looking up at her.

The chewing stopped for a moment. "You wa?"

"What do you recommend?" Mrs O asked again, enunciating each word carefully.

The pencilled eyebrows twitched. There was a long sigh. "Up to you, ain't it?" The chewing recommenced.

"What's *Dish of the Day?*"

"For two?" The Mask started to write on her pad.

"Not so fast, dear. First tell us what it is?" The Mask raised her eyes to heaven and stood there, pencil poised over the pad, sighing but saying nothing. I could see that Mrs. O was getting cross. "If you know what it is, dear, kindly share the information with us. If you don't, run inside and ask, like a good girl."

The Mask didn't look like someone who was used to being called either dear or a good girl. She tapped her pencil impatiently against her pad. "Same everyday."

"Well, don't keep us in suspense?" Mrs O smiled up at her. "Go on, dear. I promise we won't tell anyone."

The eyebrows twitched again. " 'otpot."

"God Almighty, you don't waste words, do you? I suppose there's no point in my asking you to describe it?" The pencil was tapping against the pad. Mrs. O knew she was beaten. "Go on, then. Hotpot for two, and a pot of tea, and make sure it is hot."

Smirking, the Mask turned on her heels and disappeared in through a swing door at the side. "'otpot for the two Oirish dames, and make sure it's 'ot Paddy," we heard her roar, just before the door closed fully.

The other tables were beginning to fill up, young business types, judging by the dark suits. I wondered whether any of them worked in my building.

"They dress well over here," I said anxiously, "I'll be a holy show."

"We're going to remedy that this afternoon."

The Mask arrived and slapped two plates down in front of us. "Careful. They're 'ot."

"So the cook's Irish then?" Mrs. O looked up at her. The eyebrows twitched, but she said nothing.

The food was surprisingly good.

"That was very nice, thank you, dear," Mrs. O said as she paid the bill. "You can keep the change in return for all the chat." The eyebrows twitched once more as she closed the till and disappeared into the kitchen.

"'Ere Paddy, the Oirish liked your 'otpot," we heard her shout before the door swung closed.

"God blast her anyway," Mrs. O laughed as we emerged into the afternoon sun, "she bested me."

"There's not many who would, I'd say." I took her arm. "Now, come on, let's 'it these shops while we're still full of Paddy's 'otpot."

On our way home on the tube she turned to me suddenly. "Have you heard from Tommy recently?" I shook my head.

"No, but then I didn't expect to."

"But I thought you and he…?"

"No. We're just good friends," I said, glad of the opportunity to put her right. "He's been a life-saver about this baby business. But we're not. I mean we're not …he doesn't see me as a girlfriend or anything."

"Rubbish. He thinks the world of you, Maggie. Surely you know that?"

"No, he doesn't." But I couldn't help feeling pleased.

"And I'm delighted he's found such a nice girl," she prattled on as if I hadn't said anything. "I worry about him, Maggie. So far away from home. Out in those foreign countries, eating God knows what. I'm glad he has you. It means a lot to a mother. But you'll learn. It's all ahead of you." She gave my tummy a little pat

It's all ahead of you. She was right. It was time I started thinking about after the baby was born. Every time I started my mind went blank. It was as if I couldn't accept that there would actually be a baby at the end of the nine months. Now that the bump was getting bigger, I knew I'd have to face up to it, sooner or later. Adoption seemed the obvious solution, some nice couple who could give him a good home. But first, I had to cope with the new office. I lay in bed that night, twisting and turning, my brain refusing to settle down. Would they accept me? What if I wasn't any use? I'd probably be hopeless with the computer. They'd bundle me back to Dublin.

It must have been well after three o'clock when I finally fell asleep. I was walking down a ramp in Paris showing off the latest space-wear for women when a bell rang. I pirouetted gracefully at the end of the ramp. Flash lights of the world press exploded in my face.

"Rise and shine, Maggie." Mrs. O was opening the curtains. The early morning sunlight streamed into the room. "You don't want to be late on your first day. I'll get your breakfast."

"No, no, go back to bed. I'm awake." I struggled into a sitting position, trying to shake off the glamour of the catwalk and sank back exhausted against the pillow.

But she wasn't falling for that one. She pulled me up again into a sitting position and pulled my legs out onto the floor.

"You're as bad as Tommy. There you are. Can I leave you now?"

I nodded and yawned.

Half an hour later I entered the tube station. It was like heading for a match in Croke Park. Everyone going the same way. Everyone in a hurry. There was standing room only on the train. I checked the map on the wall of the carriage and counted the number of stops to my change. The first stop was the one I expected. So far, so good. This tube business was child's play. I stood there, briefcase in hand, trying desperately to look like I'd done the trip dozens of times before. The other commuters stared ahead into the middle distance, eyes slightly glazed, bodies swaying with the motion of the train. Nobody was taking the slightest notice of me. I jumped off at the connecting station. Some people were heading for the exit steps but I was careful to join the others who were transferring to the Central Line. A train was just coming in. Again I allowed myself to be swept up in the crowd who ran to make the doors before they closed. Standing room only.

As before, I checked the name of the first station we stopped at. This time it wasn't the one I expected. I looked at the map again. Jesus, I was going the wrong way! I dropped my briefcase and took the note of instructions Mrs. O had given me out of my pocket. I read it and checked the map again. Yes I was definitely going the wrong way.

"Something wrong?" A young girl beside me smiled. I told her where I was heading for. "No problem," she said calmly. "I'm going there too. There's another change stop further on. Follow me when I get off." I followed her up one flight of stairs, and down another to a platform. In less than two minutes a train arrived, jam-packed. "Just push your way on. Nobody minds," she shouted over her shoulder. I did what she said, and stood beside her, hanging onto a handle as the train took off again.

"Thanks a million. I don't know what I'd have done without you."

"You're new in London?"

I nodded. "First day. I've never seen such crowds."

"You'll get used to them. Be ready to move when I do or you'll get left behind." I watched her like a hawk. At last we arrived at the Square. "Right, come on!" We pushed and elbowed our way through the crowds and out onto the platform. "The exit is up those stairs. I'm late so I have to rush. Good luck." With that she was off up the stairs ahead of me.

"Thanks again," I called after her.

I walked up the stairs more slowly, and out into the sunlight. I was relieved to see the Square. My tummy gave a nervous twitch as I recognised the F & F building. The steps up to the entrance seemed higher and more unwelcoming than yesterday. *'Into the valley of death rode the six hundred.'* I knew if I wavered for a minute I'd lose my nerve. Inside the door, a man in uniform tipped his cap as people passed.

"Morning, Sean."

"Morning, Miss Fairchild."

"Morning Sean. Nice day."

"Yes Sir, it is."

He looked at me curiously. "Can I help you Miss?"

"I'm Maggie, Maggie Brown from Kil... from Dublin." I felt my face redden.

"You're welcome to London, Miss Brown." He saluted smartly and held out his hand.

"Please call me Maggie." I shook his hand nervously.

"A pleasure I'm sure Miss..er.. Maggie. What part of the country do you come from?"

"Dublin," I replied.

"Did I not detect a touch of the South?"

"I was told to ask for Mr. Fothergill's secretary," I said quickly.

"That'll be Miss Peters. I'll call her." He picked up the nearby telephone.

I looked around. My eyes followed the arch over the doorway as it ran up into a wide dome. It was as big as a church. I had to bend backwards to follow the line of the roof.

"She'll be down in a moment," he smiled and indicated a long bench inside the door.

"With a name like Sean, you must be Irish too." I looked at him, admiring his army-like bearing.

"Nearly. Ex-Irish Guards, Miss." He clicked his heels smartly. "My parents were."

"They must have taken you back there on holidays?"

"No unfortunately. They died when I was a toddler. I was reared in an orphanage."

"Oh God! I'm sorry." Not five minutes in the place and already I'd managed to put my two feet into it. "Please forgive me."

"That's alright Miss."

The lift door opened. A young girl emerged and walked over smiling. "You're welcome, Margaret. You've met Sean I see." I nodded. "Come on. Mr. Fothergill's expecting you."

"Call me Maggie."

"Okay, Maggie. I'm Edwina by the way. Welcome to London."

"Thanks." I followed her into the lift.

"Good luck Maggie," Sean called, just as the doors shut. Something about the way he said it reminded me of Dad. Unconsciously, I straightened my shoulders. As the lift ascended smoothly I could have sworn I heard him whisper *Good luck Mags*.

The lift door opened onto a large room lined with desks. Edwina led me through the maze. I'd never seen an office with so many people. All girls, most of them young, although I noticed one or two older ones at the far end. These, no doubt, were the London equivalent of Bossy Boots. I wished fervently I was back in Dublin with Bossy Boots and the rest of the gang instead of standing here petrified. I'd have willingly given back the brief case.

"That's mine," Edwina pointed to a desk close to where we were standing, "the one with the plants."

She opened a door at the back of the room.

A short balding man, with gold-rimmed glasses at the end of his nose, got up and held out his hand. He was in shirtsleeves. A jacket hung crookedly across the back of the chair. "Miss Brown, I presume?" He laughed self-consciously. "Golly, that sounds a bit like *Doctor Livingstone I presume,* doesn't it? Come in and sit down. Thanks, Edwina." I looked around for a chair as she left. "Oopps! Sorry about that. Here. Take mine." He plonked himself on the side of his desk while I went round rather nervously and sat on his chair. I tried to avoid sitting on his jacket. A file lay open on the desk. The top page was marked 'Computer Project.' There were loose pages scattered all over the file. I recognised one of them as my CV.

"So, Miss Brown. You found us alright?"

"Yes, Mr Fothergill."

"Any bother with the tube?"

"No, Mr Fothergill," I lied. "It's very efficient. We could do with one in Dublin."

"Yes, I'm sure you could. Well now Miss..er.. "

"Please, Mr Fothergill, call me Maggie." *Call me Maggie* was beginning to sound like the name of a show.

"You know why we need you here?" I nodded uneasily. "We need help with our new computer system. We're on the brink of new technology that's going to change the face of the accounting business forever." He got up and started to pace the floor, arms waving to emphasise what he was saying. "Few people realise it, Mary, but the changes are going to be more comprehensive than any of us can imagine. Do you know that the machines we're getting in here are already becoming obsolete in the States? A few years from now they'll be manufacturing computers smaller and ten times more powerful than the ones we're buying for this project. Imagine that!" He slapped the file with the back of his hand.

"Why don't we wait and buy the next ones then?"

He beamed at me. "I can see why they picked you for the job, Mary."

I smiled modestly. "It's Maggie actually Mr. Fothergill. It doesn't seem very sensible to buy something that might be out-of-date so soon."

"I know. I know, and I agree with you entirely, but we have to start somewhere." He waved expansively at the office. "We can't sit around forever with these old-fashioned ledgers. We have to get our people trained. That will give us some sort of a head start on the competition. We have to keep ahead of the competition these days, isn't that right, Mary?"

"It's Maggie."

"Yes, yes, of course. Well, that's it for the moment. I'll introduce you to the rest of the team in the afternoon." He sat back onto the desk. "Settle in for the morning. Get the feel of the place. I've asked Edwina to copy this file so you can bring yourself up-to-date with the project. I have to go to a meeting, I'm afraid. Budgets, budgets, and more budgets. You know how it is?"

I smiled conspiratorially. "Of course Mr. Fothergill."

"You seem rather experienced for such a young girl?"

Fortunately for me the phone rang. The wire was tangled so he had to almost lie down on top of the desk to reach the mouthpiece. "Fothergill... hello?" he bellowed. His shirt was missing a button. I could see the hair on his chest through the gap. "Yes, yes, of course. On my way. Where did you say it was?.. Oh fine. Where?.. Yes don't worry. I'll find it. Bye."

He slapped the phone down and stood up to go. It missed the receiver and landed on the desk. I picked it up and started to untangle the wire.

At the door, he turned. "You'd better use my office for today, Mary. The team is going to be in another wing of the building." He looked at me anxiously. "You don't mind?"

"Of course not," I said, busy unwinding the phone.

"Edwina" he called out the door.

"Yes, Mr. Fothergill?" Edwina appeared instantly.

"Where's this place they call the Annex?"

"Up on third."

"Whereabouts?"

"At the end of the corridor. Go out of the lift, turn left and keep going. You were there before."

"Was I?"

She laughed. "You didn't like it, remember? The Architect was annoyed. You told them they'd made a mess of it?"

"Oh yes." He smiled. "The place they spent a fortune on?"

"I think they're waiting for you," she said gently.

He looked at her, puzzled. "Why do they call it the Annex?"

"The catering staff nicknamed it. It sort of stuck."

"I see. Right I'm off. Bye ...Mar... Miss...er.."

"Maggie," I offered humbly for the umpteenth time.

"Right then, I'll see you in the afternoon. Edwina will look after you."

Edwina picked up a file and ran after him. "You'll need this for the meeting."

"What would I do without you," he chuckled and ran off.

She grinned at me. "Well, what do you think of my boss?"

"I like him. He seems to be a tiny bit absent-minded."

Edwina giggled. "He is. In fact, we call him Fusty Gully when he's not in earshot, but don't underestimate him. He's one of the brightest accountants in London. He's years ahead of his time with these computers. Nobody else knows what he's talking about half the time." She looked at me proudly. "He's our representative on the feasibility study that's being done in the States. We're all mad about him. He's a widower by the way. That's why he always looks a bit un-ironed. Oh! There's my phone." I marvelled that she could distinguish her phone in the general bedlam.

I sat down and started to go through the file. They had set aside a huge budget to bring in the new system. I looked at the proposed timetable. After installation of the new machines it would take months of trials, followed by two further months of training before the old system would be let go. They had a number of names listed beside each month. I saw my name at the bottom of each list. It was still there in August, but with a question mark beside it. The same for September. Just as well, because I should be gone back by then. I turned another page, and read the advantages they hoped the new system would bring to the company. This was followed by pages and pages about the possible risks to the security and accuracy of the client accounts, and how they could be overcome. I was deeply engrossed when the door opened and Edwina popped her head in.

"Lunch time," she called cheerfully.

"Already?"

"I go with two pals. We'll take you to the place we usually go to."

One of the pals was Rosie. The other was Jill, a small dark girl who looked as if she might be pregnant. We left the building and walked along the side of the Square into a cafe. There was one table empty at the window.

"Quick, grab that one." Edwina pushed us towards it. I looked around. It was the same place Mrs. O and I had been the previous day.

"The usual, ladies?" It was the Mask herself, still made up like a ghost, and still chewing gum. "I see the Irish contingent has arrived. Don't let them take over, sure you won't? How's it going, Irish?" She winked at me.

"So far, so good." I grinned back. "I'll have whatever they're having."

"Fine. Four 'otpots it is then."

"See? Queuing already." Edwina nodded at the door, where already a small queue was starting to form.

The lunch arrived in a couple of minutes.

"Paddy must be in good form," I said to the Mask later, as she cleared our empty plates. "That was delicious."

"Glad you liked it. Pudding, ladies?"

The girls nodded. "Yes, Molly."

"You too, Irish?"

"Yes, please."

"Tea for everyone?" Everybody nodded. Molly hurried off.

"Is she Irish too?" I asked the girls.

"Her mother was, I think," Rosie said.

Molly arrived back a few minutes later with dishes of steaming rhubarb tart, the ice-cream melting over it. Paddy had surpassed himself again.

"I'm going to put on weight if I'm not careful," I said, scraping up the last piece of tart onto my fork.

"Don't forget you're eating for two," Jill whispered, "like me. Is it your first?"

I gulped and nodded. The other two were looking out the window at someone Susie had recognised. "How did you know?"

She shrugged, and went on with her pudding. I sighed. How many others would know too? Still, in a few weeks I'd be so big everybody would know, so I'd better get used to it. "When are you due?" I asked her.

"End of August." She looked quizzically at my bulge. "I'd say you're around the same?"

I nodded. It was a relief to be able to speak openly about it.

"We'll be out together in that case." Jill turned to the other girls.

"That's not fair," Edwina protested. "You're supposed to be my relief."

"Can't help that," Jill smiled. "We don't plan these things do we, Maggie?"

"No. We certainly don't."

In the afternoon I was introduced to another member of the computer team, an accountant called Michael. Michael was so tall he had to stoop entering the office.

Mr. Fothergill looked like a dwarf beside him. "This is Mary, your assistant."

Michael dropped the files he was carrying, and held out his hand. "Hi Mary. Pleased to meet you."

"You too." I smiled up at him. "I'm Maggie, by the way."

"Come on, team. Let's get to our proper office," Mr. Fothergill said, bristling with sudden energy.

"Fine," Michael replied, and picked up his files again.

"You and Michael will be working together," Mr. Fothergill explained, as the three of us walked down the corridor into a big office at the end. "You should be okay in here, but anything you need, ask Edwina."

After a quick run-through of the timetable he left us to it. It was a long afternoon. Michael explained, in some detail, what we'd be doing over the next couple of months. He was the person who had done the detailed designs for the new system. He'd only just returned from the States. For the next few months the old and the new systems would be run in tandem. Most of the data had been copied onto the new system, but the accounts had to be gone through, balances checked, details itemised and double-checked, using control totals from the old system to make sure the new one was accurate. The firm couldn't take chances with their client accounts. The old system would not be let go until they were absolutely sure that the new system was reliable.

By the end of the afternoon I was almost cross-eyed from squinting at the tiny computer print. Around five-thirty Edwina popped her head in.

"Come on, Michael. Have a heart. It's her first day."

"Sorry, Maggie. I'm inclined to forget about the time." Michael looked up. "You go on. I'll finish this."

"Thanks." I stood up before he could change his mind. "See you in the morning?"

"Bye." He was back, engrossed in the figures before I closed the door.

Edwina travelled on the first leg of my journey home. I got off the train changed platforms and managed to make the right connection. It was a relief to get off finally at the Richmond station and walk down the quiet tree-lined road to the apartment block.

Mrs. O fussed over me the minute I walked in the door. We ate shepherd's pie, sitting on the sofa in front of the television. I realised, again, how lucky I was to have someone like her to come home to in a city the size of London. A tiny silver-framed photograph on the windowsill caught my eye, a bride and groom, taken in the thirties judging by the style of clothes. The man was tall dark and handsome, with a swirling moustache. The woman was beautiful, with a head of dark curly hair and bright eyes that seemed to be laughing straight into the camera.

"Is that you?" I asked, as Mrs. O walked back into the room with two dishes of apple-tart. She nodded. "You were beautiful."

"No, I wasn't," she smiled as she sat down. "Come on, have this, while it's hot."

"Yes, you were."

"Well maybe I was, that day."

"We have a wedding photo just like that at home," I said as I put my fork into the apple tart.

She smiled. "Your Dad was a perfect gentleman. What a shame he died so young. You must miss him dreadfully."

"I do. We all do."

"He was always very good to me."

"Was he?" I looked up surprised.

"It's better not to dwell on the past too much. More tart?"

"No thanks," I protested. "I'll be fat as a fool if I go on like this. I've already had lunch and here I am eating again."

"You're eating for two, remember."

"That's what Jill said." I laughed. "We had Paddy's hotpot again, and by the way, Molly's the name of that waitress. Her mother's Irish."

"Did she talk?"

"Oh yes, lots."

"Tell me about the people you're working with."

Over tea, I told her everything that had happened in the office. She was particularly interested in Sean the porter.

"Orphanages were quite common then. Nowadays, lots of couples want to adopt so children get a good home." She looked at me. "Is that what you'll be doing?"

"It's the best thing for the baby, I suppose," I sighed, "or is it?"

"It's not easy bringing up children, even with a father around." She sipped her tea. "Must be terrible without one."

I nodded, thinking of a young girl I'd noticed recently pushing a pram along South Circular Road. She had a flat in a house two down from ours. She was painfully thin, rarely smiled, and usually had black circles under her eyes.

Mrs O looked at her watch. "Do you mind if we watch the quiz? I want to see how the man from last week gets on. He's made it into the final."

My eyelids were starting to droop anyway. "I'll go on to bed Mrs. O, if you don't mind."

"Good girl. Get as much rest as you can. The water's on if you want a bath." She waved me away without taking her eyes off the screen. "I'll run in later and say goodnight."

I had a long hot soak in the bath and climbed into bed. I must have been asleep before my head touched the pillow, because I never heard her come into my room.

CHAPTER 5

The next day I managed the tube without incident. In the office, I checked pages and pages of printouts, comparing the computer balances against those on the ledgers. I went to lunch with the girls again and continued the checking in the afternoon.

The work continued like that over the following weeks. At first, I just did what I was told without really knowing where it fitted into the overall system. Michael reported my findings to Fusty Gully. Gradually, however, I began to differentiate between the various printouts and was soon able to write my own reports. This left Michael free to go ahead with the more complex parts of the system.

I continued going to lunch with the girls. Michael didn't bother with lunch. He preferred to go for a run. We worked late most nights. More often than not I'd leave him behind me when I went home. He was young and single, but didn't seem to bother going out much. He was totally engrossed in his work.

Mrs O insisted on feeding me every evening, so I ate lightly at lunchtime. Eating for two was all very well, but I was getting as big as an elephant. I felt the first fluttery movement in my tummy one night getting out of the bath. It frightened the life out of me. After that, I got used to the occasional flutter. They made me realise I was carrying a real live person in my tummy, someone who would soon have a separate existence from me. I began worrying about how I'd feel when it came to giving him or her away.

As instructed by the clinic in Dublin, I checked in with the local doctor. He was quite elderly. His clinic was full the night I went to him. His examination was over in a few minutes.

"You're fine. Come back in a month," he declared, looking at his watch. "Pay my secretary on your way out. Tell her to send in the next patient." I walked back to the Towers hoping I'd never need to call him out in the middle of the night.

Every weekend I rang home. I was beginning to feel desperately guilty. Here was I, facing what was probably the most important event in my life, and poor Ma didn't know a thing about it. She kept asking when I'd be home. So far I'd managed to find excuses, but she wasn't the sort of person you could put off forever. She was making big plans for the Whit weekend. I still hadn't a clue how I was going to get out of it.

One day Tommy rang. Mrs. O told me about the call when I arrived in from work.

"He was ringing from Cyprus. He wouldn't tell me what he was doing, never does."

"A bit of a mystery, your Tommy, isn't he?"

She nodded. She was only too happy to talk about her favourite child. "He was always a bit of a mystery, if you ask me. Always looking for something different. Reaching for the impossible. Even as a child. Never content with ordinary things like the others. I think he resented…" She stopped.

"Resented what?" I prompted gently.

"Being born on the wrong side of the tracks, I suppose," she replied. A sad expression flitted across her face. "We were you know, as far as Kilmanogue was concerned. His father didn't help, always getting into scrapes with the drinking. Your father was great though."

"Was he?"

"Oh yes. He helped us get set up over here, gave me the courage to make a fresh start. I hated it at the time, but he was right. I'm grand here, aren't I?" She looked around the cosy apartment with a contented smile on her face.

"Yes it's lovely, a real home from home," I added, mystified that there was so much I didn't know about my own father.

That night in bed I thought again about what she'd said about Tommy, always searching for something, reaching for the impossible, never content with what he had, a bit like me in some ways, I thought. He'd probably never settle down, either. I tried to shift my bump into a more comfortable position and finally drifted off to sleep. I dreamt about guns and battles and Tommy in the middle of them all, screaming at his troops to follow him over the hill into certain death.

As the summer went on, I realised that London was a far stickier place to work in than Dublin. Even though I'd open every window in the office, I couldn't seem to get enough air. I don't think Michael even noticed, he was so caught up in the work. Despite all our hard work and late nights, the new system started to fall behind schedule. Mr. Fothergill called us both to a meeting with the Finance Director, Chris Jones. He was the one who had to answer to the Board for the money spent on the project. People were usually summoned to the firm's headquarters in Knightsbridge, but on this occasion he came to our office.

After the most perfunctory of introductions, Michael went through the problems, detailing the weaknesses we'd found so far, and why we needed to do more testing of the new system. He said he couldn't recommend that it go ahead until we had. Mr. Jones frowned, and looked at Fusty Gully.

"Any suggestions Jim?"

Fusty nodded, and put up a chart on the board with a detailed plan. He explained that as a final check we'd select two weeks in the next month and do a parallel run on both systems for every transaction of those two weeks. We'd take on the opening balances, run all the transactions and then check the closing balances on the new system against those of the old system. It would mean working through both weekends. He had selected the two weeks around Whit. He looked guiltily at me as he made the proposal, but I nodded eagerly.

"That's fine, Mr Fothergill. I don't mind working through the weekends."

"Are you sure, Maggie?" Michael said. "Are you fit enough?"

I nodded and smiled. "Fit as a flea."

But Fusty still looked worried. "It'll mean really long hours. And we'll have to deliver once we're committed. Are you both sure you can handle it?"

Michael nodded and looked anxiously at me.

"Of course," I replied. "I'll be only too glad to prove the system works."

"I must say, Jim, I'm impressed by your team's commitment." Mr. Jones smiled. "That's settled then. Keep me informed."

After he left, Fusty breathed a sigh of relief.

"Whew, that was a close one. He came in assuming the worst. You two succeeded in turning the thing around."

Michael turned to me. "Are you really sure, Maggie? Your family must be expecting to see you at Whit."

"They won't mind," I said quickly. I felt guilty about betraying Ma, but what could I do? It was the perfect excuse not to go home.

"You've saved our bacon."

"Michael's right," Fusty smiled. "Thanks, Maggie. We're very grateful."

I felt a bit mean taking all the credit. Especially when the system gave me such a good alibi. A month later I'd have to find another reason not to go home. A month after that, the baby would be born, I'd be thin again, and I could go home whenever I liked.

I broke the news to Ma on the phone on the Saturday night. She was desperately disappointed.

"How long is this testing going to take?"

"Difficult to say, Ma. Depends on what sort of problems we find."

"At least you're needed, that's something I suppose," she admitted grudgingly. "Don't let them take you for granted though, sure you won't love."

"No, Ma. I won't."

"How are the digs going? Are you eating properly?"

"Yes." I rubbed my bulge. "In fact I'm still putting on weight."

"Ah well, your father always said that sitting at a desk never made anybody thin." Thank God she couldn't see me. I was a long way from thin.

"I'd better go Ma. I'll ring next weekend, usual time."

"Okay love. Take care of yourself. Goodbye. God bless."

Putting down the phone I wondered, not for the first time, whether I should, after all, have told her about the pregnancy and stayed home, instead of running off to London. An immediate vision of me heavily pregnant working beside Anna in the shop, the various neighbours coming in every day asking after my health and Ma head down in the corner, too ashamed to talk to them, cured me in an instant.

"The kettle's on," Mrs. O called out from the sitting room.

She took one look at my expression as I walked in, and put her arm around me. "It's hard telling lies, isn't it?"

I looked at her amazed. "How did you know?"

She smiled. "I'm a mother too, remember?"

"If you were mine, would you want to know?"

"Of course I would."

"But she'd be so ashamed."

"She's your mother, Maggie."

"You don't know Kilmanogue."

Mrs. O took one look at me and burst out laughing. I realised what a stupid remark I'd made and joined in the laughter. But my tummy started to ache so I stopped. It had been doing that a lot lately. The only remedy was to lie down and rest.

CHAPTER 6

If I thought I'd been working long hours up to then I was sadly mistaken. With the first week of the parallel run, the real work started. It was followed by the first of the working weekends. While everybody else was out enjoying the long weekend, Michael and I were in the office pouring over computer printouts. As a concession we allowed ourselves a late start of ten o'clock, but we worked until six each evening for the three days. Fortunately, the tube trains were blissfully empty and the journeys in and out trouble-free.

I hadn't bargained however for feeling so washed-out on Tuesday morning. The others came in all bright and bushy-tailed after their long weekend. I envied them their energy. My heart sank as I sat down and started into yet another printout, which had been churned out by the computer overnight. By the time I'd checked it and made my report, another had arrived. And so it went on through the week.

As I faced another weekend of work, I was exhausted and desperate for fresh air. I'd intended going for an odd walk after dinner during the two weeks but kept falling asleep on the sofa. The ache in my tummy was becoming more regular now. Fortunately, it never lasted too long.

The following week when I went for my check-up, the Clinic was full as usual. I fell asleep waiting to be called.

"You haven't been looking after yourself, young lady, have you?" the doctor said, wagging his finger at me. I was too tired to get into a long discussion so I didn't deny it. "Hop up there on the couch for me like a good girl." *Hop* wasn't the word I'd have used. I didn't particularly feel like a good girl either, but I heaved myself up and lay down as comfortably as my bulk allowed. He poked and prodded and asked the usual questions. I nodded and grunted on cue. All I could think of was getting home and into bed. He made some notes on my chart.

"You'll have to do better than that if you want to deliver a healthy baby," he said crossly. "Now jump up on the scales for me." *Jump* was another word I wouldn't have used. I slid awkwardly off the couch. Holding onto the windowsill for balance I stepped on the scales. He manipulated the weights and peered over his glasses. He frowned and peered again, pushing his glasses up further. "How far gone did you say you were?"

"You mean when did I…?" He nodded impatiently. "Twenty-second of November," I replied stifling a yawn.

His eyes opened wide. "You know the exact date?"

"Doesn't everybody?"

He laughed. "No, they certainly don't. Now let's see... twenty second of November..." He looked again at my chart and back at the weight and made some more notes. "Each pregnancy is different, but I want to see you every week from now on. You'll have to take things easier. Get to bed early. I know you young ones." He smiled, as he put down my chart. "Out on the town every night, in spite of your condition." I shook my head, but he was already picking up the next chart. "Tell Mrs. Richards to come in, like a good girl."

I gave Mrs. Richards her instructions and left, only too glad to be done with the poking and prodding for another while.

Neither Mrs. O nor I heard the alarm the next morning. It was almost ten by the time I got in. Michael looked up anxiously as I burst in the door.

"Maggie, are you alright? Can I get you a glass of water? You look like you could do with it."

"Sorry. Slept it out." I threw off my jacket and sat down. "The tube was like an oven."

"You look awful. Are you sure you're alright?"

"I'm fine," I said, picking up the printout from the top of the pile, where I'd dropped it the previous evening. "I'm nearly finished this one. Couldn't quite manage it last night." We got on with the work.

Even though I'd opened all the windows and the door, by lunchtime I was gasping for air. I couldn't face the girls or the café; so instead, I spent the hour on a bench in the park. During recent lunches there'd been nothing but baby talk. Listening to Jill, I'd stopped being afraid of the actual birth itself, but I was counting the days until it would be over. By contrast, Jill was really enjoying her pregnancy. She kept assuring me that the first was the hardest. I kept telling her that my first would be my last. "Everybody says that," she laughed. "Believe me that will all disappear when you hold the baby in your arms."

And that would be another problem, I thought. Should I hold him in my arms? Would it not make it harder when I had to give him up? By now, I was sure I was carrying a boy, a footballer, to judge by the way I'd been kicked over the last few weeks, though the kicking seemed to have subsided lately. Perhaps he was taking a rest before his grand entrance?

After lunch I waded through more printouts. Fusty joined us for an update. He wanted to know how Michael planned to make up the few days we were behind.

"We need more resources," Michael replied firmly. "Maggie can only do so much. We need someone to help her."

Fusty looked at me. "How do you feel about that?"

I shook my head. "By the time I'd train them, I'd have it done myself. What if I stayed on later during the week?"

Michael frowned. "We don't want to wear you out."

"I'll be fine," I replied confidently. The last thing I wanted was to have to train someone new.

"Good girl." Fusty beamed at me. Michael still looked uneasy but said nothing.

We worked until nine o'clock all that week, in a desperate attempt to catch up. On Saturday evening I looked so awful, Michael forbade me to come in on Sunday. He made me promise to spend the day in bed instead. There was a note from the doctor when I got in. I'd forgotten to keep my appointment. So what, I thought, I can't be in two places at once.

Sunday was bliss. Mrs. O brought me my meals in bed. I stayed awake long enough to eat them and then fell asleep again. That evening I got into my dressing gown and watched television for a couple of hours. I was back in bed by ten.

The alarm clock shattered my brain the next morning. I got up as quickly as my bulk allowed. Back to the grindstone. I'd had my day's rest. What more could a body want? I waddled my way to the Tube Station and took the escalator up to the platform. I stood in the middle of the Monday commuters trying to catch my breath. I remember the sound of the train as it trundled through the tunnel towards us. I remember it stopping. I distinctly remember heading for the nearest door with the other commuters. Then everything faded.

CHAPTER 7

I woke up, squinting into bright lights. Faces loomed in and out of my vision. I heard my name. I tried to sit up, but a hand pushed me back. "It's okay, Miss Brown. Don't worry. Everything's alright." I must have believed them because everything faded again.

The next time I woke, Mrs. O was sitting beside my bed. "Welcome back, Maggie."

"Sorry," I said, struggling to sit up, "I must have forgotten to set the alarm again."

She put her hand on my shoulder. "Don't move, lovey. You're in hospital."

My mouth dropped open. I was about to contradict her when a glimpse of the tube station flashed into my brain so I closed my mouth.

"Hello, young lady."

Mrs. O moved back to allow two men in white coats move closer.

The older one prodded me with a stethoscope. "What day is it, Maggie?"

"Monday, of course," I replied crossly, "and I have to get to work. I'm late already so if you don't mind... ."

"Wrong on both counts. It's Wednesday, and you're not going anywhere."

"Wednesday?" I gasped. "What happened to Monday and Tuesday?"

"You slept through them." The younger doctor smiled.

I flopped back against the pillow. If I'd slept through them how come I still felt desperately tired. My whole body ached, in fact. But there was something else. I couldn't figure out what it was. I put my hand down to my tummy and screamed. I screamed and screamed and went on screaming. There was a sharp jab in my arm. Then everything faded again.

When I woke Mrs. O was asleep on a chair beside my bed.

"Mrs O, Mrs O," I shouted. "Where is he? Where's my baby?"

She woke at once, and came over to me. "Shh, Maggie. Shh. Shh love. It's all over. You're fine."

"What have they done with him? Why isn't he here?"

"They had to take him, lovey." She wiped my forehead with a cold cloth. "It was for the best."

"But I wasn't due for six weeks."

"You couldn't carry him any longer, pet. You were too tired."

It took me a few minutes to digest what she was saying. I should have been delighted it was all over, but instead I felt cheated. "It's a boy?" She nodded. "I said it would be, didn't I?" She nodded again and turned away. I pulled at her sleeve. "I know I shouldn't ask when I'm giving him away, but what's he look like?"

"Don't think about him, love. Just concentrate on getting stronger yourself."

"Six weeks early. Will he be alright?"

"No more questions, Maggie. You must rest. You've been through a terrible ordeal. I'll go and get a cup of tea for us." She got up and left the room.

I lay back, eyes closed. At last it was all over. I was a mother. I had given birth. I had a son. I'd expected to feel different, triumphant or something but instead all I felt was empty.

She came back with the tea, and the older doctor in tow.

"Are you going to stay awake for us this time, young lady?" He smiled down at me. I nodded and struggled up to a sitting position to drink the tea. "No sudden movements for a while, eh? Allow me." He put one arm behind my back and held me, while he doubled the pillow behind me. "Better?"

"Thanks." I lay back gratefully. "How is he? How's the baby?"

He sat down on the side of the bed and held my hand. "Not as good as we'd like, I'm afraid. But leave him to us. You need to rest."

"When can I see him?"

He looked across at Mrs. O.

"Maggie, remember what we agreed?" she said. "It will be easier if you don't."

"I just want to make sure he's okay."

"Better not." Mrs. O patted my shoulder.

"I agree," the doctor said firmly, "you're too weak."

"But he's my responsibility. I just want to make sure…"

"And you're mine, young lady," he interrupted. "Your system has taken quite a beating. You've had the equivalent of a major operation."

"But all I want is to…"

"Maggie, listen to the doctor for goodness sake."

"But…"

The doctor's bleeper went off. "Sorry. I'm due in theatre." He smiled down at me. "I'll be back tomorrow. In the meantime try to get some rest. Okay?"

"I'll see she does, Doctor," Mrs. O said. "Drink this tea, love. I had enough trouble trying to get it for you. It's amazing how few kettles there are in a big place like this." She settled herself down on the chair again. She looked worn out, poor thing.

"I'm sorry, Mrs. O. You must have a thousand things to do at home."

"Home will look after itself."

I struggled to sit up. "The office! Did anyone tell them?"

"Of course they did," she said pushing me down. "You created quite a fuss in the Underground. Luckily one of the passengers was a nurse and knew what to do."

"All I remember is the train coming in and trying to get onto it."

"You passed out in the doorway and blocked the entrance. The train was held up. The ambulance was late because of the rush hour."

"Ambulance?" I gasped.

"Of course. How do you think they got you to the hospital? Your friend from the office happened to come along. They found my phone number in your handbag. They sent these by the way." She pointed at a vase of flowers in the window. "This is the card that came with them." She handed me a card. '*To Maggie, with all our love from Mr Fothergill, Michael and the girls.*'

"That's nice," I said. "When can I see my baby?"

"Maggie, I think you should stick to what we agreed." Mrs. O held my hand. "What's the point in torturing yourself? Concentrate on getting better and going back to work."

Again I tried to sit up. "Oh God, the system will be miles behind. I promised not to let them down. I'll have to ring myself and explain."

"No, Maggie. Lie down. I'll ring them for you."

"Okay but be sure to tell them I'll be in in a day or so."

"I will."

"And tell them how sorry I am for letting them down. There's nobody else trained in. Michael will be going mad trying to do it all himself."

"Maggie," she said crossly, "lie back there and try to sleep like a good girl."

"I'm hardly a little girl any more now I'm a mother," I muttered but settled back against the pillows to please her. "They will let me see him tomorrow, won't they?"

"Let him go, darlin', let him go." Her words repeated inside my head as I started to drift off. *Let him go. Let him go.*

I didn't wake again until much later. Through the window I could see that the moon was out. Dark clouds were scudding across the night sky.

"I'm sorry to disturb you, Miss Brown. Just checking." I recognised the face. It was the younger of the doctors from earlier. He was holding a stethoscope to my chest.

"What time is it?" I smiled sleepily up at him.

"Almost nine. The night shift is about to come on. How do you feel?"

"Empty. But not so tired as I was before."

"I'm sorry about… ." He stopped. I saw alarm flash across his eyes.

"Your vital signs are good anyway." He picked up my chart and started making notes.

"What do you mean sorry, sorry about what?" He didn't answer me. "Is there something wrong with the baby? There is, isn't there?"

"I'll go get Dr. Mulvey."

"No." I caught his sleeve. "You tell me."

"We delivered him by Caesarean Section but he was very small. He won't... he's unlikely to..."

My stomach lurched. "Unlikely to what?"

"He's in an incubator. We're doing all we can but..."

"He's not going to make it?" I whispered. "My baby's going to die."

"I'll get someone to come and talk to you." With that, he scurried out of the room.

My baby was going to die. I closed my eyes to blot out the pain. I'd brought him into the world too soon. Anyway what had he to live for when I was going to give him away? None of this was his fault. Oh God why did you let it happen? What was it all for, if he was going to die anyway?

"IT'S NOT FAIR," I screamed at the top of my voice, "IT'S NOT BLOODY FAIR."

The door opened. A young nurse looked in frightened.

My anger faded as quickly as it had risen. "Don't worry." I smiled weakly at her. "I'm not going to do anything."

"There's a message from a Mrs. O?" She looked at me questioningly.

"My landlady."

"She was here all morning but you were asleep. She can't make it back tonight, she said. She'll be in first thing tomorrow."

"Thanks, nurse." I lay back against the pillow.

"If there's anything you want, ring the bell okay?"

I nodded. She shut the door behind her, and the emptiness closed in around me again. Poor Mrs. O hadn't been able to tell me herself. Being a mother she knew what it would mean. That's what I was now too, a mother, but for how long? Oh God, I'd made a mess of everything. Tentatively, I felt my tummy. There was a thick wad of bandage but it felt sore even through the thickness. Sore and empty. The emptiness overwhelmed me, made me feel physically sick. But I hadn't planned to see him, much less keep him, so why did I feel like it was the end of the world? And it was. I hadn't the energy to wipe the tears away so I let them go. I cried like I hadn't done even when Dad was killed. I'm not sure what I was crying for. For my baby? For the waste? For myself? I don't know, but it was as if a well of sadness had sprung up inside me, a well that had been blocked all my life until that moment. My son had unblocked it, the son they wouldn't even let me see. The sadness was pouring out of me and I was lost in the flood.

It was sheer exhaustion made me stop finally. I lay there drained. Then I thought I heard something. I listened. There it was again, faint humming from the corridor outside. I recognised it straightaway, '*bring flowers of the fairest, bring blossoms the rarest...*' A light tap and the door opened. Tommy stood there in full military uniform, looking larger than life and a trifle silly with a big bunch of flowers in his arms. At the sight of his familiar face I burst into fresh tears.

"There you are again, crying the minute you see me," he snorted, "doesn't do much for a man's ego."

"Oh Tommy." I held out my arms to him. He laid the flowers down on the bed and held me. I buried my head in his neck.

"I know, love. I know." His voice was muffled. " I'm here now. Sh…ssh…"

I held onto him, like a drowning man to a life raft. He made soft comforting noises like one would to a child. I felt some of the emptiness drain away. Finally, I loosened my grip on him.

"Can I move? Oh thank God for small mercies." He smiled into my eyes. "My poor little Mags. You've been through the wars, haven't you?"

"Why did it have to happen, Tommy?"

"Ma would say it's God's will. Here use this." He handed me a handkerchief.

"Thanks. I must look a sight."

"Allow me." He took the handkerchief back and gently wiped around my eyes. "I've never seen you so tired."

I lay back and looked at him properly for the first time. "Where did you spring from anyway?"

"From the base."

"Where's that?"

"Cyprus."

"You came all that way just to see me?"

"Of course."

I looked at him. Our eyes held for a moment and then he looked away. "Any chance of getting a cup of tea around here?" he said, reaching for the bell over my bed. The nurse ran in. She stopped abruptly when she saw Tommy. "Sorry for disturbing you, nurse." He smiled down at her. "I know you're busy."

I watched her melt under the warmth of his smile. "It's no bother honestly. What can I do for you?"

"I've come straight from the airport. I was wondering if…"

"A cup of tea? No problem. Do you take sugar and milk?"

"Yes to both, I'm afraid." He beamed like a Cheshire cat. "Thanks a million. You're very kind."

"Not at all. You're welcome. Back in a minute."

"Tommy O'Connor," I snorted as the door closed behind her, "you're shameless."

"It's the uniform," he smirked, "not to mention my natural charm which you don't appreciate of course." He pulled a chair close to the bed and sat down.

"I do so."

"You do not."

"I do."

There was an awkward silence for a few minutes. Then we both spoke together.

"Are you fed up?"

"I'm delighted to see you."

We laughed nervously, and promptly did the same thing again.

"Sorry"

"You first."

He slapped his forehead. "God Almighty, what's wrong with us?"

"It's the jetlag."

"Must be the anaesthetic."

We'd done it again. We were still giggling when the nurse returned with a tray. She had a pot of tea two cups and a packet of chocolate biscuits. I noticed she'd put on fresh lipstick. She looked up at Tommy for approval as she put the tray down on a trolley and moved it over to the bed. "I thought you'd be hungry, so I robbed some of Matron's biscuits."

"Thanks, nurse. You're a lifesaver."

"You're very welcome. Will you be staying long Sergeant er... er...?"

"O'Connor, Flight Lieutenant Tommy O'Connor at your service." He gave a little salute. "Not very long, I'm afraid."

"That's a pity. Enjoy the tea. Call if you need anything, won't you?" She flashed her long eyelashes at him and left.

"Will I do mother?" He smiled and picked up the teapot. "Remember?"

"Feels like a hundred years ago." I sighed, recalling the day of the pregnancy test. This was the nearest to being a mother I'd ever be. A few short days, hours even, if the doctors were right.

Over tea, I filled him in on what little I'd been told. He listened in silence, various expressions flitting across his face. I repeated what the doctor had said about the baby's chances of survival.

"Perhaps it's for the best, Mags."

"Best for whom exactly?" I looked at him crossly. Suddenly I couldn't bear the calm expression on his face. "Tommy, answer me. What did you mean it's for the best?"

"I'm sorry, Mags." He put down his cup. "I'm only a man. It's difficult to know what to say."

There was silence for a few minutes. I heard him stifle a yawn. Moments later I saw him sneak a look at his watch.

"I can't believe it. You've had enough now, I suppose," I shouted angrily. "Well go on. Get out of here. Nobody's keeping you. You've done your duty. Go back to wherever you came from."

"Be reasonable Maggie." He stood up and stretched. "I haven't slept in forty-eight hours. When Ma told me what had happened I just upped and left, didn't even wait for permission."

"I don't know why you bothered."

"I thought you needed me."

"Well I don't," I snapped turning my back to him. "I don't need you. I don't need anyone." I heard a sharp intake of breath behind me. Good. Serve him right. How dare he think I need him? How could a man possibly know what I was feeling? "Men have it so easy," I ranted to the wall. "It's not fair. Little boys, the lot of them. Never have to grow up. All they can do is play at being soldiers."

I heard him sigh.

"Right, I'll be off so," he said.

I said nothing.

"I'm really sorry Mags. I have to get some rest. I'm dead on my feet." I remained silent. I heard him sigh again, heard his chair move as he got up. "Goodbye, love. Take care of yourself."

"No, Tommy wait." I turned, but the door had closed behind him. The room was empty again. I wanted to jump up and run after him but moving was out of the question. I was too soar and anyway he'd be down the corridor by now.

I couldn't believe what had just happened. He'd travelled halfway across the world to see me and all I'd done was throw insults at him. I lay there going over everything that had been said. Me and my big mouth. I started tossing and turning. Every time I moved, it was agony. Twice I rang for the nurse and begged her for more painkillers. Finally, I dozed off into a fretful sleep, full of shapes and shadows.

From the moment I woke next morning, I couldn't wait to see him and beg his forgiveness. I knew he'd understand. I tried to do something with my hair. I even put on some makeup. Mrs O was first to arrive.

"Where's himself?" I asked, hugging her. "I hope he's not buying more flowers. There's no room in here."

She shook her head. "Sorry, lovey. He's gone. He said to say goodbye for him."

"But he can't be." I looked at her appalled. "There's so much I have to say to him. I was terrible to him last night."

"I'm sure he understands, love. He hadn't permission to come so he had to get back straight away."

"But I was really awful to him."

"Don't worry. He knows what you've been through. He said to give you this." She handed me an envelope. "He said to read it when you're alone." She sat down on the side of the bed and took my hand. "Try not to feel too sad about the baby love. It might be all for the best."

"The poor little mite doesn't have a chance according to the doctors. How could that be all for the best?"

"God's ways aren't our ways, Maggie."

"So it would seem."

"You must learn to accept it and move on."

"And you still think I shouldn't see him?"

"I do," she said firmly. "Trust me on this, love. You've so much to live for, your job, your career. Your father would have been proud of you."

The tears threatened, but I wiped them away. I couldn't risk breaking down again.

After she'd left, I read Tommy's note. *Dear Maggie, I took a terrible chance leaving Cyprus the way I did. I have to get back at once or I'll be court-marshalled. But I'm glad I came. I had to see for myself how you were. What you said last night was right. I can't possibly understand what you're going through. What I do know is that you're strong. Life goes on. In time you'll come through this. Being so far away, I know I'm not much use to you but my mother loves you. She'll always be there for you.* "What about you, Tommy?" A hidden voice asked inside me. "Will you always be there for me?" He'd finished *'Take care of yourself, Maggie, love, Tommy'*.

I read it again. No commitment, no promises, but what did I expect? All I knew was that now he was gone I felt horribly alone again. He was right about life going on though. In a few weeks I'd be back in Dublin and could go home to Kilmanogue. There'd be no more secrets from Ma. The time for crying was over too. There'd been enough tears in the last couple of weeks to last a lifetime.

CHAPTER 8

I stopped asking to see my baby after that. The doctors, the nurses, everybody, seemed to think it was best if I didn't, so who was I to argue? Over the next few days my wound began to close up. As the pain lessened, I needed fewer painkillers. Soon I was able to take a short walk in the grounds during the afternoon, and slept better as a result.

A week later I was discharged. The first thing I did when I got to Mrs O's flat was to ring home. Anna answered.

"Hi Sis" I said brightly. I felt as if a lifetime had passed since we'd last spoken.

"Oh, it's you," she said in the bored voice she reserved for me.

"Yes, the bad penny. How's everyone?"

"The same as we were when you last rang."

"Nothing's changed then."

"Why would it?"

"Don't know. Is Ma there?"

I heard her sigh, and the phone was dropped. It was awful how much we seemed to have grown apart. She had Jonathan, of course, and I had… nothing now, I suppose, now that the baby was … .

"At last. How are you Mags? Are you alright?" The tenderness in Ma's voice flew down the line and broke through my control. "It's been so long. Has anything happened?"

"No, Ma." I coughed, fighting the impulse to break into tears. "Must be a bad line."

"Sounds like you've picked up another cold. It must be all that overtime you've been doing. When are we going to see you? It's ages since you've been home."

"The project is nearly over. I'm going to ask for the weekend off."

"Good. I've missed my little girl," she laughed, "although I suppose you're still big as a house, are you?"

I had to think for a minute what she meant. "No, Ma. You'll be glad to hear I've started a diet."

"Don't overdo it now, sure you won't? I'd prefer have you fat and healthy than thin and sick."

"I've lost a stone already. How's Auntie Nell?"

"She's grand. We're all dying to see you. When you didn't ring we were worried. I wanted to contact your landlady, but Nell said I shouldn't interfere."

"I'm glad you did… " I stopped horrified at my mistake. "I'm glad you have her to advise you. With the cold, my voice was gone. I didn't want you to worry," I carried on glibly, appalled at how easily the lies flowed.

"You should have gone to the doctor and got something."

"I did, Ma." I looked at the range of pills on the hall table and thanked God once again that phones were carriers of sound not vision. "And don't worry. My landlady looked after me very well."

"God bless her for that. Now don't you be standing out in the cold any longer." Ma hadn't yet got her head around the concept of central heating. "Go and get a hot cup of tea inside you. Let us know when to expect you… and, Maggie?"

"Yes, Ma?"

"Be sure to thank her for all her kindness. On second thoughts I'll have a word with her myself. Put her on."

I had to think quickly. "Sorry, Ma. She's in the bath. Next time okay?"

"Okay, but be sure to thank her, love, won't you? Bye now. Sleep well."

I put down the phone and wondered how many other daughters were away from home suffering through one of life's dramas, unknown to their nearest and dearest. But, for me at least, the deception was nearly over. I went into the sitting room and brought Mrs. O up-to-date with the news from home. I didn't tell her that Ma wanted to speak to her. Mrs. O was incapable of deception. I couldn't risk it. Not now I'd come so far.

In the tube station next morning I started to panic as the train pulled up at the platform. It took all my nerve to get on. Luckily I found a seat, and by the time I had to change trains, the strength had returned to my legs.

We had a meeting first thing. Fusty Gully and Michael brought me up-to-date on the system. They'd now revised the schedule, but they still needed me to help them for what was left of the six months. There'd be no more weekend work they assured me. The system had passed all its checks, had received final approval from Head Office, so we could start training the bookkeepers without any more delay.

I was looking forward to my weekend at home. My figure was almost back to what it had been, so my clothes were falling off me. During one of my lunch hours, I took a tube to Oxford Street. Marks and Spencers' sale was on, and I had three weeks' wages to spend. I bought a suit for myself, silk scarves for Ma and Auntie Nell, perfume for Anna, and a new sandwich toaster for Mrs. O.

That Friday I went straight from the office to the airport and caught the early flight. By taking a taxi from Dublin Airport to Amiens Street station, I managed to catch the afternoon train to Wexford. They weren't expecting me that early, so I took a taxi from there to Kilmanogue. I dropped all the luggage in home, and walked up town to the shop. Never having been away so long before from Kilmanogue, I savoured every step.

Auntie Nell was on the phone when I walked in. She dropped it when she saw me "ROSE, IT'S MAGGIE!" she roared down the length of the shop. Ma was serving a customer. She ran up leaving the customer looking after her.

"It's great to see you, love," she said, hugging me breathless. "We weren't expecting you for hours yet."

"I wanted to surprise you. Oh, Ma, I've missed you so much."

"Not half as much as I've missed you, love." She started to cry. That started me off too. Then Auntie Nell started. Ma laughed as she mopped her eyes with a handkerchief. "Look at us. Anyone would think you'd been away for years."

"It feels like that to me Ma. Where's Anna?"

"Next door. Go in and tell her to close up early. We've so much catching up to do. Oh Mrs. Byrne, I'm sorry. I'm coming." She almost danced back to the customer she'd left standing.

I was nervous about meeting Jonathan, but curious to see how the extension had worked out. It was a much smaller version of the main shop, and had menswear only. Fortunately, he was nowhere to be seen. Anna was sorting sweaters. She had her back to the door so she didn't notice me come in.

"Hi, Sis."

She looked up. "Oh, it's you," she said, and returned to the sweaters.

"No hug for your baby sister?" I went up to her.

She blushed, and allowed me to give her a quick hug before pulling away. "They've done nothing only talk about you all week," she grumbled. "I'm here all the time and nobody appreciates me."

"Just call me the prodigal son. How've you been? Where's Jonathan?"

"Away on business. Won't be back 'til Monday night."

"That's good." The words were out before I could stop them. Fortunately, she didn't notice. At least this way I could really enjoy the weekend. What would he say if he knew what had happened in the last few weeks?

"What's wrong?" Anna asked suddenly.

"Nothing. Why?"

"You looked funny there for a minute." She eyed me up and down. "New suit?"

"D'you like it?" I gave a little twirl.

"It's alright. Doesn't make you look as lumpy as usual."

I grinned back at her. "Coming from you, that's a compliment. I've been on a diet."

A customer walked in from the other shop.

"Some of us have work to do." Anna turned to the customer. "Yes Mrs. Cantwell. Can I help you?"

"Is it yourself, Maggie?" Mrs Cantwell smiled at me. "You're looking great. Your mother told me you were working in London, is that right?"

"Yes. I'm just home for the weekend, but I'll be back for good, soon."

"You must be delighted to have her back, Anna." Anna scowled and said nothing. "You two used to be inseparable when ye were young."

"Can I get you something, Mrs. Cantwell?" Anna asked, sharply.

"Yes dear, you can. I'm looking for a shirt for Sean to wear with his navy suit."

"What size?"

"Seventeen and a half."

"White, blue or cream?"

"White, please." Anna turned to a row of boxes behind the counter. "What sort of work are you doing in London, Maggie?" Mrs. Cantwell asked.

"Computer work," I answered, ignoring the loud sigh from Anna.

"I thought your mother told me you were doing accountancy?"

"I am but computers will do a lot of that work in the future. They're new at the moment."

"Sounds exciting, doesn't it, Anna?"

"Riveting," Anna said, holding up a white shirt. "Will this one do?"

"It'll do grand. Sure that fellow would go on wearing the old ones 'til they fell off him. Men have no clothes sense, girls, sure they haven't?"

"Not much," I grinned.

"That'll be five pounds, please," Anna said curtly.

"Glory be to God! In that case, he'd better look after it. He won't get another one 'til Christmas. Bye, girls. Nice to see you looking so well, Maggie."

She was hardly gone out the door when Anna mimicked her. "*Nice to see you looking so well, Maggie.* That old bag sees me every week and never remarks on how I look. What are you hanging around here for anyway?"

"Ma says to close up early."

"Just because you're here?" Anna looked incredulously at me.

"Yes. Awful isn't it?" I laughed. "Come on, Sis. We've a lot of catching up to do. Tell me all about this extension."

"Won't be half as exciting as your bloody computers," she muttered with a scowl.

"Ah, come on, Anna Banana. They're not going to hit this place for a while, so you don't have to worry. It's a good excuse to close early anyway, isn't it?"

She relented. We came out and locked the door behind us. Nell and Mother were turning the key in the other door. Ma put her arm around the two of us.

"Just like old times. My two girls together again. Aren't I the lucky woman, Nell?"

"Indeed you are, Rose. I'm lucky too, having you as my surrogate family."

"Nothing surrogate about Nell, is there, girls?" Ma laughed as we got into the car. "What do you think of her new car, Maggie?"

"Lovely. What make is it?"

"Tell them, Nell. Some foreign job with a funny name. She insisted on buying it though there was nothing wrong with the Morris Minor."

"It's a Volvo, Swedish, safest car on the market." Nell smiled, as she started the engine. "I know it's a bit of an extravagance but I wanted a solid car." There was an uneasy silence. She still had a hang-up about safety. It wouldn't bring Dad back, of course. Nothing would.

The kettle was put on straight away. I told them all about London, the shops and the Underground, also about Michael, Mr. Fothergill, and the girls in the office.

"How's Mrs. Connors? Is she keeping well?" Ma asked.

"Who? Oh she's fine. Sends her best."

"Why would she do that?" Anna asked curiously.

"Because I told her about you all, of course," I said quickly. "I was lucky to have such a nice landlady. London would have been awful on my own."

"When do we get to meet her? Nell and I were thinking one of us should go over, visit some of the shops in Oxford Street, get some ideas."

The last thing I needed was Ma over in London. "What's for dinner?"

She jumped up. "Dear God, with all the talking, I forgot to put the potatoes in the oven."

"I'll scrub," I said, following her out to the kitchen.

"Better put an apron on, love. I don't want you spoiling that suit."

"D'you like it?" I gave a twirl before I pulled on the apron.

"Yes. It's lovely. You look different." She stood back and examined me. "You've certainly lost weight, but it's more than that. I can't put my finger on it."

"The same boring old me, I'm afraid. Less of me, that's all." I opened the bag of potatoes. "Two for Anna and me, one each for you and Nell, and one for the pot. Okay?"

But she wasn't letting go so easily. "Has something happened in London?"

"No."

But I'd answered too quickly.

"Something did happen, Maggie. What was it?"

"Nothing, Ma. Honestly."

"Did you meet someone?"

I felt I'd better give her something to distract her. "Okay, if you must know, I did."

"I knew it." She smiled, delighted with herself. "Well?"

"Well what?"

"Tell me about him."

"There's nothing to tell, really."

"He's not… he's not…" She stopped.

"Not what, Ma?"

"He's not English is he? I couldn't stand it if you went to live in England. I know that sounds selfish but I can't help it. I'm your mother."

"No, Ma. He's not. He's Irish, actually. Tommy is his name."

"He works in the office, I suppose? You'd better do another few." She looked doubtfully at the potatoes. "They're small."

"No, Ma. He works abroad. He's in the Air Force."

Her face went pale. "He's not…he's not a Protestant!"

"No, Ma." I laughed.

"Thank God for that." She made a fast Sign of the Cross.

"Anyway, he's away most of the time so you needn't worry. I'll leave the marrying to Anna. I prefer my independence."

"We all need someone to love, Maggie."

"Not me," I said, scrubbing the potatoes with a vengeance.

She put her hand under my chin and turned my face up to her, so she could see my eyes. "Are you telling me everything?"

"Of course I am," I said, returning her look. "Cross my heart and hope to die." I held up my wet hands and gave her a hug. "I'm just glad to be home, that's all."

Neither of us said anything more. For the first time since it had happened, I was glad I'd got over the pregnancy early. I don't think either Ma or myself would have lasted the full nine months. Perhaps Tommy and Mrs O were right after all. Perhaps what had happened was for the best, for me, if not for my baby.

Later, lying in my own bed for the first time in months, I thought about him again. Mrs O had promised to take care of everything. She said it would be too painful for me. I'd taken the coward's way out and agreed. God knows I'd had enough pain, both physical and mental. The doctor had said the wound was *healing beautifully.* Beautiful was not the word I'd have used. It looked positively hideous.

It was because of Mrs. O I'd made such a quick recovery of course. Without her, I don't know what I'd have done. And it was all thanks to the chance meeting with Tommy after the pregnancy test. I'd never have had the nerve to go off to London on my own. I'd probably have stayed here and brought shame on the family.

As it was, everything would soon be back to normal. Mrs O could concentrate on her own family now. I knew how much she missed Tommy. I wondered how he'd got on since he returned to Cyprus. *God keep him safe,* was my last thought before I drifted off.

I woke to birdsong. I'd forgotten the sound existed. I'd been dreaming of Tommy again. I glanced at my watch. Six o'clock. What time would that be in Cyprus? I smiled. He'd looked so handsome in his uniform. No wonder he could twist the nurse around his little finger. I shot up in the bed, suddenly, as a horrible thought struck me. He probably had a girlfriend, a real girlfriend, not just a pal like me. I got up and went to the bathroom. I stared at my reflection in the mirror. What business was it of mine, anyway? After what I'd been through, who'd give me a second glance? I was a mess, thanks to Jonathan. Physically and emotionally he'd spoiled me for anyone else. I shivered in the early morning chill. All the plans for standing on my own feet, for taking charge of my life again, suddenly seemed pointless.

No one else was even awake yet. It was a long time since I'd gone for an early morning walk. I got dressed, slipped out of the house quietly, and headed down to the beach. *Best time for mushrooms,* Dad used to call it, *while the dew is still on the grass.* I wondered how he'd have reacted to my pregnancy. The sand was soft under my feet. The tide was on the turn, just starting to slip back down the beach, the time when as kids we'd rebuild the sand castles and replace what the waves had swept away. How long ago that all seemed now? So much had happened. Dad gone. Uncle Pat too. Anna and I hardly speaking. Jonathan here in Kilmanogue, part of the family. I kicked angrily at a stone and winced with pain. It scuffed along the wet sand and stopped a few feet away. I wasn't healed yet, no matter what the doctors said.

I stood for a while and looked out over the water. There wasn't a cloud in the sky and only the slightest hint of a breeze. It was going to be a fine day, a day when there'd be lots of buses, full of day-trippers. Or had that changed too? It probably had. Nothing stayed the same. Not even in Kilmanogue

I walked along the beach towards the sand dunes. They seemed slightly shrunken now, bruised by the elements over the years. Like myself, I thought, searching for the hollow that Tommy and I used to like. It was still there, more overgrown than I remembered. My heart was thumping with the unaccustomed exercise. The walk had brought back the old ache in my tummy. I lay down on the grass and closed my eyes. After a few minutes, the pain eased. I opened my eyes and stared up at the sky. I'd wanted to be the first woman in space. What had gone wrong? I searched the blue depths for an answer. The odd wisp of cloud looked like pieces of cotton wool waiting to be picked up. I reached up as far as I could to catch them, like we used to as kids, but then my arm got too heavy. I'd wanted to be the second Marie Curie too, and find a cure for every disease. Dreams, dreams and more dreams, so many dreams, and all of them gone like the wisps of cloud.

The sun felt warm on my face. It was going to be a hot day. I felt the warmth wash over me. Some of the tension began to lift. As the inner turmoil melted away, my heartbeat slowed down. I lay there, flat on my back, perfectly still, and listened to the sound of the waves breaking and receding down the beach. They had a gentle rhythm of their own. My breath slowed down to that rhythm, nature's rhythm, calming, healing. The tide came in, turned and went out, the same simple pattern repeating every few hours, every day, every month, every season, forever. Why couldn't life be that simple? But maybe it was. We were born. We lived. We died. 'Though some of us don't even get that much. My baby hadn't. I was wrong not to have insisted on seeing him, because now, when I desperately wanted to remember him, I couldn't. The awful emptiness swept over me again, the emptiness I thought I'd left behind in the hospital. Only with it, this time came helplessness as well. It was over, finished. I put up my hand and felt the tears on my face, cool silent tears, tears I had no control over. They didn't seem as painful as the earlier ones. Perhaps these would heal rather than hurt.

I woke with a start, a dog nuzzling my face. Someone whistled, and he ran off. I looked at my watch. It was after ten. They'd be wondering where I was. I got up slowly, walked up the beach and back into my life.

The rest of the weekend was a flurry of talking, eating, and more talking. Ma raised the subject of meeting Mrs. Connors again. "You'll have to ask her over on a visit, Maggie. I want to thank her for looking after you so well."

"She's more a city person, Ma. Anyway, she has her own family."
"How many?"
"I'm not sure." Lies, lies, and more lies.
"Connors. That's Irish, isn't it?" Auntie Nell asked.

"A few generations back, I think," I answered glibly. "What time can you bring me to the station? My plane leaves at seven thirty."

"Good God, I'd forgotten you were flying." Ma put her hand to her mouth. "You'll have to catch the early train, won't you?" I nodded. "That means we'll go to ten Mass and have lunch early." She nodded, satisfied. Ma was happiest when she had the Sunday timetable organised. "What would you girls like to do this evening?"

"D'you want to go out for a drink?" Anna asked, in an unexpected spurt of friendliness.

"Great idea." Ma beamed at her. "You two must have loads to talk about."

I agreed at once. It'd be good to talk to her, break through the barrier that had risen between us since Jonathan's arrival.

It wasn't until we were well into our second G&Ts that Anna even mentioned his name. Apparently, he was still away most of the time. Ma concentrated on the day-to-day running of the shop, while Anna looked after the men's section. Apart from giving the occasional hand in the shop, Jonathan did all the travelling and purchasing.

"Who keeps the accounts?" I asked curiously.

"Auntie Nell."

"Sounds like it's working out okay," I said, sipping my drink. Anna nodded. "Are you and he still…?"

"Of course." She waved her engagement ring around, letting it catch the lights. "We'll be getting married after my birthday. I'll be a respectable married woman then. Are you jealous?"

"Hardly. I don't intend ever getting married."

She looked at me, shocked. "'Course you will. Everyone does."

"I prefer my independence."

She banged her glass down on the table. "That's so typical of you. Why do you have to be different from everyone else?"

"But why should I give up my freedom if I don't want to?"

"Freedom? Don't be stupid." She picked up her glass and drained it. "Your round."

"I'm not being stupid. Why can't women stay single if they want to?"

"Because they can't."

"Why not?"

"Because people would think them odd."

"People don't think men odd when they don't get married."

"That's just because they haven't met the right girl, and in any case…" She caught my amused expression. "You think you're smart, don't you?"

"Maybe not so smart," I said, getting up. "Sorry, Anna Banana. Another G&T?"

"Yes, please. Anyway what about babies?" I turned away quickly so she wouldn't see my expression. "You can't have babies without getting married, can you?" she said triumphantly.

"I suppose not," I replied, with a sigh of defeat.

"See? You're not so smart after all."

I went up to the bar. We'd need more fuel if we were to continue this stimulating conversation.

When we got home, the hall light was on.

"Enjoyed yourselves, girls?" Ma called down from the bedroom.

"Yes, Ma. Go back to sleep," we shouted up in a chorus.

"How could I sleep when my little girls are out on the town? Ye won't forget to put the bolt on the door, sure ye won't?"

"No, Ma, we won't," we chorused again, giggling as we banged the door shut behind us. I tripped over the mat and fell against the wall. I wasn't used to three G&Ts, and certainly not to the Irish measures.

"What was that?" Ma called.

"Nothing Ma. It's only Lumpy being awkward as usual," Anna said, as she hauled me to my feet.

"Is the bolt on?"

"Yes, Ma."

"That's good. G'night girls."

"G'night, Ma."

Giggling, we tiptoed back to put the bolt on the door.

I slept heavily, assisted no doubt by the unaccustomed alcohol. The next morning passed in a flash. Before I knew it, lunch was over and I was getting into Nell's car. There were more goodbyes, but these were happy ones. In a few short weeks I'd be home for good.

Mrs. O was bursting with news when I walked in that night. Tommy had taken up a new contract. He'd be away for a year. "I suppose I'll have to get used to it," she moaned. "He says it's what he wants."

This latest move of Tommy's settled my resolve. I'd gained valuable work experience in London. I'd continue my studies. I'd work hard and pass all the exams. As an accountant, I'd always be able to stand on my own two feet. I'd never have to rely on anyone else.

The girls took me somewhere posh for lunch on the last day. I was glad. I felt if anyone put a plate of hotpot in front of me again I'd become pregnant again by association. Afterwards, I cleared out my desk, and said a tearful goodbye to Michael and Fusty Gully. They thanked me again for my help though, given my rather abrupt departure for the labour ward, I wondered privately whether I'd been more a hindrance than a help.

Saying goodbye to Mrs O wasn't easy. I knew she'd miss having me around, especially now that Tommy was going away again.

"I'll never be able to thank you enough for what you've done, Mrs. O," I said as I hugged her. "I don't know what would have happened if…"

"Your father would have wanted me to look out for you." She looked into my eyes. "Don't ever be afraid, love. He'll always be there for you. You know that, don't you?" I nodded unable to speak. The doorbell rang. "That'll be the taxi."

We hugged one last time. I picked up my two bags and got into the lift.

"Take care of yourself, Mrs O."

"God keep you safe, Maggie," she called as the doors closed.

CHAPTER 9

Eileen opened a fresh bottle of whiskey to celebrate my return. I'd forgotten how generous her portions were. "Don't worry, Mags," she giggled, "you won't be long getting back into training."

Not much had changed in the office either, as I discovered the following morning. The same old jokes were being bandied around, the same old personal rivalries. For the first hour or so, I felt I'd returned from another planet. Some of the trainees called down to the basement to see how I was. Bossy Boots asked me what diet I'd been on. I told her it was all the travelling by Tube, having to climb up so many stairs to change platforms.

"Must be more than that," she said, eyeing my waistline.

"Probably all the salads I used to eat for lunch," I offered, hoping to God she'd never hear about Paddy's 'otpots. "Which ledger do you want me to start on?" Anything to distract her. But I needn't have worried. By eleven o'clock I was relegated to the category of a nine days' wonder.

Later that week, Mr. Moloney sent for me. Rather nervously I went up to his office. "Welcome back, Maggie," he said as he shook my hand. "You did us proud by all accounts."

"Thanks."

"They couldn't have brought in the system without you, according to Fothergill." He looked at me quizzically over his glasses.

"Not at all. They're exaggerating."

"You worked yourself into hospital according to what I heard." He frowned. "I was really sorry to hear about the... about your loss."

"Thanks." I looked down at my hands. He shifted uncomfortably in his chair. "That's all in the past now. You wanted to see me?"

"Yes. Firstly, to say thank you for working so hard on our behalf. We'll be giving you a bonus next month."

"That's great. Thanks a million," I said, getting up to go.

"Secondly, I want to let you in on a little secret." I sat down again. He started to pace the floor. He reminded me of Mr. Fothergill, as he outlined his plans to extend the computer system into the Irish branches of F&F.

"There'll be lots of resistance over here. People are used to doing things the old way. They might find it hard to change. What do you think?" He stopped pacing and looked at me.

"The London staff certainly did at first," I replied, "but once they got used to the printouts they realised it was just another way of doing the same thing. Some of them even admitted that the computer would make their lives easier but then... "

"Fothergill was right." He slapped the table. "You'll be perfect. Sorry. Go on with what you were saying."

"Perhaps you should talk to them first, explain the system, put their fears at rest? Maybe even let them try it out? That way, they'd see for themselves."

"D'you think you could do it for us?"

I gulped. "Me?"

"Yes, you."

"But how?"

"You've been through it over there, so you know what to expect."

"Well I could show them through the printouts, I suppose, and maybe explain the controls?"

"I was hoping you'd say that." He leaned back against his chair. "We want you to become Systems Trainer for a year, Maggie. We'll pass your ledgers on to one of the others and free you up so you can concentrate on the training."

"Systems Trainer but..."

"It will mean automatic promotion. We'll expect you to continue with your studies, of course."

I didn't know what to say. It wouldn't be easy. People like Bossy Boots might take some convincing but at least I knew what could go wrong, and Mr Moloney had been the one who let me go to London in the first place, so I couldn't very well turn him down.

"Okay. I'll give it a go."

"Good girl." He held out his hand. "I appreciate it, especially after what you've been through."

"I've put all that behind me now, Mr. Moloney."

"I'm glad. Better not say anything downstairs yet. I'll make the announcement next week. Your promotion will be effective immediately."

"Thanks," I said, and left the office.

Later that night I told Eileen. She wasn't as excited as I expected her to be. "You don't know some of them like I do, Mags. They could make life very difficult for you."

"Why would they?"

"Some of the older ones will be afraid."

"Sure computers are only glorified totting machines. The new system will either work or it won't. What's the problem?"

"You really don't see it, do you?" She looked at me. "This machine could do them out of a job. People like Bossy Boots will be terrified."

"Bossy Boots terrified?" I laughed incredulously. "Why?"

"Because, stupid, she's done the books the same way for the last twenty years. She's used to pen and paper. She's always been able to check every entry in the ledger. How can you expect her to trust her life's work to a bloody machine?"

In bed later, I thought again about what she'd said. To me computers were just a quicker way of doing the same job, but if I was going to be able to convince other people, I'd have to try to see things from their point of view. The excitement of the promotion was beginning to pall.

My visit home the following weekend was spoiled too because Jonathan was there. Large as life and twice as invasive

"Wow what have you done to yourself?" he asked, eyeing me up and down.

"Nothing."

But he wasn't put off so easily. He was everywhere, smiling and winking at me, when he thought nobody was looking. Several times I was tempted to wipe the smirk off his face and tell him what had really happened over the last six months. But for Anna's sake I had to keep my mouth shut. Instead I tried to keep out of his way as much as possible.

At tea, I told them about my promotion. Nell and Ma were delighted. Anna just shrugged and looked bored. Jonathan came up behind me and planted a kiss on both cheeks. I swallowed hard, and pulled away as fast as I could. He disappeared up the town only to reappear ten minutes later with a bottle of sparkling wine and flowers. He apologised that he couldn't find any real champagne in Kilmanogue. His extravagant behaviour did nothing for Anna's mood. For the rest of the weekend, every chance she got, she held his hand or put her arm around his shoulders, making it clear to me that he was her property. My heart ached for her when I saw him brush her away. He was bound to hurt her sooner or later, and nothing I could say or do would stop that happening.

On Monday, everybody in the office was told about the plans for the new system and my part in those plans. The training would start the following month. I'd be working in a spare office on the second floor. It was the first time I'd ever worked in an office on my own. I was looking forward to it, and dreading it at the same time. I knew I'd miss Eileen and Maria, but I needed the space for the printouts. Visions of the untidy office in London floated into my head. What if I'd taken on too much?

Most people's reactions weren't too bad. Even Bossy Boots. "I've seen new systems come and go all my working life. Not worth getting into a tizzy over." She smiled serenely. "Some of them work. Some of them don't. Just like people." A real philosopher, our Bossy Boots.

    Between work and my lectures at the Tech I hadn't the time or the energy to brood about my lost baby. I fell into bed each night exhausted. Every other weekend I went home for some fresh air and Ma's cooking. Anna must have said something, because miraculously, Jonathan stopped harassing me. Their big day was approaching. Everybody kept saying what a lovely couple they'd make. He was away several nights each week and would come home with some new business contacts. I seemed to be the only one who had any reservations about him.

CHAPTER 10

As the months went by, Anna became a bundle of jitters. The only subject worthy of discussion in our house was *THE WEDDING*. If anybody had the temerity to talk about anything else, she'd cut them off. Everything was gone over again and again – the cake, the flowers, the hymns, the prayers, the dresses, not to mention the most painful of all, the guest list. Jonathan had nobody coming from his side. His foster mother was a widow and had no children of her own. He said she wouldn't be up to the journey. There were so many from our side that it didn't seem to matter.

I was to be bridesmaid. As the only sister it was not a subject for debate. The dresses were being made locally under Auntie Nell's watchful eye. Anna would look beautiful in white. The material chosen for mine was salmon pink. I almost threw up when I saw it. The design was the same as hers, all frills and flounces, a veritable bundle of femininity. It would look ghastly on me. I knew it. The dressmaker knew it. Ma knew it. Auntie Nell knew it. Anna herself knew it too. But nobody said anything.

I pleaded with Ma and Nell to intervene on my behalf, but they ganged up on me. I tried every argument short of blackmail, but was overruled. We had weekly fittings. Anna's went well. Mine were nightmares. First of all, the sleeves were too short so they were lengthened. Then they were too long, so they had to be shortened again. This time the dressmaker cut too much off and couldn't get any more material, so she changed them to three-quarter-length. Every Sunday night, I returned to Dublin in a filthier mood. Kilmanogue was no longer a place of refuge. Every room was strewn with bridal magazines. Even the bathroom had a little pile beside the toilet seat. Swatches of rejected material lay everywhere. Anna caught me looking through them longingly one evening and a row broke out. I told her in no uncertain terms how much I'd have appreciated being consulted about my dress.

"It's not your dress," she snapped.

"How d'you make that out?" I retorted, "I'm the dope who has to traipse down the aisle in that ... that pink thing."

"It's not pink. It's salmon."

"IT'S PINK."

"IT'S SALMON."

"IT'S BLOODY PINK. ANY FOOL CAN SEE THAT."

"IT'S BLOODY SA... it's salmon," she corrected herself quickly. "You've no style, Lumpy. That's always been the trouble with you. You're nothing but a tomboy. I'm wasting my time trying to make you look nice. No wonder you don't have a boyfriend."

I flounced out of the house slamming the door behind me, and marched down to the beach to cool off. The fact she was right only served to turn the knife deeper. It was ages since I'd heard from Tommy. This bloody circus might have been more bearable if I had him with me, but God knows when I'd hear from him again.

The walk did the trick. After all, it wasn't me who was putting my head in a noose. Nobody would be looking at me. It was her day. I couldn't really blame her for getting so uptight with all the problems she had to deal with.

And there were problems. The church, for instance. Following the recent discovery of rising damp, the main church was under repair. It should have been completed several weeks before the wedding, but while the workmen were stripping off the outer plaster, they had discovered major problems in the brickwork underneath. As a result, they were now running several weeks behind schedule. As the big day drew closer, it became clear that the work would never be finished in time for the wedding. Everybody in the house was worrying about it, but nobody was brave enough to say anything.

One weekend I was home, having what I hoped was to be the final fitting of the pink monstrosity. As we drove past, I was shocked to see the scaffolding still up around the church. "Have you seen the state of the Church, Anna?"

"What about it?"

"Doesn't look like they're going to be finished in time."

"Of course they will," she snapped. "They know I'm getting married on the fifteenth."

"Perhaps you should…"

"Mind your own business."

"But shouldn't you at least…"

"It's you that's awful, not the dress."

"You could always go out to Kilcashel," I suggested, determined not to get riled. Kilcashel was the small neighbouring townland. There hadn't been a wedding in Kilcashel since the turn of the century. The few inhabitants were all in their eighties. She went back to the magazine, but I knew I'd started her thinking.

We got through that fitting without fisticuffs. Both dresses were finished. I hated mine, of course. Hers was perfect on her, and she knew it. She looked like a delicate crinoline doll. The smug look stayed on her face all the way home.

Later I overheard her and Ma talking in the kitchen about the state of the church.

"Maybe you should have a word with Fr Ryan, love?"

"He promised it would be ready Ma," she wailed. "It's not fair. I wanted everything to be perfect."

After a couple of phone calls next day, it became clear that the wedding of the century would have to take place in Kilcashel after all. So the four of us drove out to have a look. The tiny church sat in the middle of an old graveyard, its walls covered with lichen and wild roses.

"Oh Anna, this is much nicer than Kilmanogue," Ma enthused.

Nell immediately joined in. "Yes, it's so romantic. Come and smell these roses." She was picking her way through the old gravestones when she tripped. "On second thoughts don't. The ground's not good over here."

Anna and I were first into the church itself. As she sniffed the stale air, her lower lip trembled. I put my arm around her, but she pushed me away.

"Don't worry, love." Ma came up behind her. "Fr Ryan swore to me he'd have it cleaned and full of flowers for your big day."

"We might as well not get married if we have to use this dump." Anna stamped her foot in temper. "Who's going to see us out here?" She ran out of the church crying. As far as I was concerned the fewer people who came to look at the wedding the better, but I couldn't help feeling sorry for her.

The following weekend, Jonathan and the friend who was going to be best man were to meet for a rehearsal. The boys were supposed to pick Anna and me up at four, but they didn't turn up until half past. Anna was in a huff. She and I got into the back seat of the car. Jonathan made hasty introductions. "Tom, Anna." Anna barely nodded at him before turning to look out the window.

"I'm Maggie, the sister." I smiled and held out my hand.

"Pleased to meet you, Maggie. Oopps! hang on to your hat," he added as Jonathan put his foot on the accelerator. The car shot off down the country road. Anna's mood was so pervasive that nobody dared speak.

Fr Ryan was pacing up and down outside the church. He looked at his watch pointedly, and almost ran under the car when we pulled up. Anna's face was like thunder as she followed him inside. I followed. Jonathan and Tom brought up the rear. Fr Ryan ran through the procedure with the minimum of reverence, due no doubt to the icy atmosphere between the about-to-be-wedlocked couple.

"Glad it's them, not us, aren't you?" Tom winked at me, as Fr Ryan whisked them into the side office to show them where they'd have to sign the Register.

Judging by the expressions on their faces as they emerged, the atmosphere hadn't lightened. After a few final words about the sanctity of marriage and the commitment they were about to enter into, Fr Ryan shepherded us all out of the church. "I'll have to run, if you don't mind. I'm late." He looked over his glasses at Jonathan. "Don't keep the bride waiting on the big day, young man, will you?"

Jonathan smiled sheepishly. "Sorry about that."

"It's me you should be apologising to," Anna snapped and strode off to the car.

Jonathan sighed and rolled his eyes to heaven. "Am I mad or what?" he muttered to Tom under his breath. "I feel like a lamb being led to the slaughter. Sorry, sister-in-law." He suddenly realised I was listening. "That was a joke."

"I certainly hope so," I replied coldly.

"We'll be one big happy family, won't we?" He put his arm around me. I pushed it away and hurried after Anna.

The evening before the great day arrived. Tea was over. Only twelve hours to go. Everything was in hand. The Archers were just finishing when the phone rang. It was Tom. He was still in England. He'd been delayed on some urgent business and couldn't make the wedding. Jonathan slammed down the phone. Anna screamed. Auntie Nell bit her lip nervously. Ma ran out to the kitchen and put on the kettle. We all racked our brains for a substitute while we drank several cups of unwanted tea. Obviously at this late stage it would have to be someone from the family, someone who wouldn't need instruction, and above all, someone who wouldn't get drunk and let us down. Not easy. Every time a name was suggested, it was shot down by either Anna or Ma. Then I remembered our cousin Matt. There was an uneasy silence.

"At least he'll do what he's told, and he won't get drunk until I let him," I said, anxious to further his candidacy.

Everybody looked at Anna. She sat there with a frozen jaw, staring into space.

"What do you think, love?" Ma asked hopefully.

Anna's lip started to tremble. "He's such an eejit. Surely there's someone else?" One by one, we all shook our heads. "It's not f..fair. This was supposed to be the best day of my life."

Ma put her arms around her. "And it will, love. Everything will be fine, you'll see. Here, let me put a hot drop in that." She filled Anna's cup of tea up to the brim.

"Wasn't he Best Man last year for one of Uncle Eamon's?" I looked at Ma. "Remember you spotted his photo in the paper?"

"That's right." Ma beamed. "That means he'll know what to do. Go ring him straight away Maggie. He always had a soft spot for you. I'm sure he'll oblige."

I looked at Anna. She was staring out the window. I took that for a yes, and went out to the hall. It took ten minutes of pleading before Matt agreed. It was the promise of a bottle of best malt that clinched it. When I got back, Anna was gone to bed. Ma was delighted Matt had agreed. I didn't tell her about the bribe.

When I went upstairs, I found Anna sitting in front of the dressing table mirror bawling her eyes out.

"What did the eejit say?" she asked crossly, "not that I care at this stage."

"Don't be crying, Sis. He'll be grand." She burst into fresh tears. "He will. He promised to do exactly what I tell him and he knows how to propose a toast and all that." But she continued crying. "Stop it, Anna, you'll make yourself sick." I handed her a tissue. "Is there something else on your mind?" She shook her head vehemently, too vehemently. "What is it? Come on, Sis. Tell me." She stopped crying and lifted her head. I looked at the sore red eyes, the blotchy face and wondered how she'd play the part of a happy bride in a few hours.

"I'm... I'm pregnant." The words hung in the air between us. "I'm pregnant. That's why I'm crying, you dummy. I don't give a twopenny damn who's Best Man. Auntie Nell can do it as far as I'm concerned."

"Jonathan?"

"Of course."

"Typical." So that's why he'd stopped harassing me.

"What d'you mean, typical?"

I shook my head. "Nothing."

"You're just jealous 'cos I got him."

She was obviously on the mend, so I shrugged. "Do you really want to spend the rest of your life with that man?"

"Of course."

For one awful moment I wondered whether I should tell her what had happened between him and me. Fortunately, the moment passed. "And you do love him?"

"Of course I do." She gave me one of her withering how-could-you-be-so-stupid looks. "The girls here are dead jealous." She looked into the mirror and groaned. "Oh God. I've ruined my face with all this weepin' and wawlin'."

I looked at her tummy. "How far gone are you?"

"Six weeks."

"Have you told him?"

"Of course not. Don't be stupid." She opened a jar of face cream, scooped some onto her fingers and slapped it on her face.

"You're that sure of him?"

"What d'you mean?" She stopped in the middle of her creaming, and looked at me.

"Nothing" I said quickly. She started to smile. "What are you smiling at?"

"That's another thing I'll beat you at." She gave a triumphant little laugh.

"What?" I asked, glad to see how quickly she was recovering.

"Having a baby, of course," she chortled. "There'll be a big fuss. Everybody will think it's a honeymoon baby."

I stood there, watching her fingers work the cream into her skin with well-practised movements.

"Where are you going?" she shouted, as I turned on my heel and left the room.

"Out," I called over my shoulder, and ran downstairs.

Please God look after her, I prayed as I walked, half-ran, along the road towards the beach. It would have been so easy to wipe that smile off her face, to tell her some home truths about the bastard she was about to marry. But there was no way I could tell her the truth about him because now everything had changed. There was a baby to consider. Another baby.

CHAPTER 11

The first thing I saw, when I opened my eyes the next morning, was the big pink cloud hanging from the back of the bedroom door. I groaned and turned away.

Ma walked in.

"Come on, girls. Wakey wakey!"

Anna leaped out of bed and ran to the window.

"Hurrah, it's sunny. Come on Lazybones. Up you get." I groaned in response. "Proper makeup now. Use that eye-shadow I gave you." I pulled the pillow over my ears but she dragged it off me. "Come on, Lumpy. Up. In a few hours your baby sister is going to be a married woman. Can you believe it?"

I opened my eyes and turned around to look at her. Gone was the tragedy queen of the night before. Her eyes were shining like stars.

"It's so beautiful. I almost can't bear to put it on," she said, plucking at the folds of her dress, which Ma had laid carefully across the end of her bed.

Maybe I was worrying about nothing. I jumped out of bed and started to get ready. Maybe by some miracle, he'd make a good husband and father.

I helped her into her dress before stepping into my own. She looked beautiful. I could hardly bear to look at my own reflection in the mirror. Revolting. Desperately, I clutched the flowers close to my stomach, and tried to conceal some of the material, which hung down in massive folds from the waist.

Anna was the perfect bride. Her eyes were still shining, her cheeks glowing, as we stood an hour later in the tiny porch waiting for the organist to strike up the Wedding March.

"Are you sure you still want to go through with it, Miss Brown?" I whispered to her in a threatening voice. "This is your last chance. In a few minutes it'll be too late." The colour drained from her face. "Only joking, Sis." I corrected myself hastily. "Isn't it amazing how such a short ceremony can change your whole life?" The colour flooded back into her face. "You're so lucky. I really envy you," I added for good measure. That clinched it.

"You'll find someone too, Lumpy. Don't worry." I shook my head and said nothing. "But you're a mess most of the time. You'll have to make more of an effort, wear decent clothes and makeup. Men like women who make an effort, you know. And you'll have to stop wearing trousers so much."

She was really getting into her stride now. "Especially if you want to find someone classy like Jonathan. Follow my example and you won't go far wrong."

The tentative notes of the organ saved her from a punch in the face. She shut up at once, gathered her skirt and shook the folds out so that they lay all around her like a cloud, just like the dressmaker had instructed. Then she straightened up and put out her arm to Uncle John, who was looking like someone about to walk to the gallows. He'd been mopping his brow with a big white handkerchief. Now he stuffed the handkerchief into his pocket and took her arm.

"Right then. Let's go. Nice and slowly now," I said starting to count. "one and two and ... slowly does it." The three of us moved cautiously up the aisle, as if unsure what we'd meet at the top. All heads turned around to watch. I felt my face go crimson. I knew they were all laughing at me, but this was Anna's day. I had to do it for her.

"one and two and..." I could hear Uncle John obediently counting in time with me under his breath, while Anna floated forward smiling and nodding regally from side to side, like a queen to her courtiers.

Jonathan stood waiting at the altar. As we approached, he smiled at Anna, and across her shoulder at me, nodding his approval at my dress. I scowled back, wondering what he'd say when he found out there was a baby on the way. Fr Ryan beamed around the tiny church, as Anna stepped forward and took her place beside her groom. At a gesture from him, they both knelt down.

Matt and I had special pews behind them. Matt moved over and knelt down. I went to kneel down too but found my knee wouldn't bend. Something was caught. I couldn't see through the mountains of pink. Ma's eyes were boring into me so I pulled to free whatever was caught. There was a ripping noise. Anna's ears twitched. I tugged again, more cautiously this time. There was another rip. I tried to kneel down but couldn't.

"Kneel down, please, Maggie," Fr Ryan whispered. I tried again but couldn't.

Anna turned around, her eyes glittering. "Kneel down, you bitch, and stop looking for notice," she hissed. Jonathan gaped back over his shoulder. Her face assumed a bride-like smile as she turned back to him.

I gave one last desperate tug at the fabric. There was a loud rip, but I didn't care because at last I was able to kneel down. Fr Ryan heaved a sigh of relief, and started the prayers. I tried surreptitiously to figure out the extent of the damage. One of the frills in front had somehow swung around to the side and seemed to have caught on the decorative buckle of my shoe. In my frantic efforts to free the material, I had detached it from the dress and with it the buckle from my shoe. I was sure nobody would miss either, so I kicked the buckle under the kneeler, and grabbed the piece of fabric up off the ground. I looked around for somewhere to hide it. The handiest place was Matt's pocket.

The initial prayers over, Fr. Ryan signalled the bride and groom to come forward. Matt and I stood on either side. The important part of the ceremony was about to start.

"We are gathered together to join this man and this woman in the Holy Sacrament of Marriage... "

I looked at the back of both heads and hoped they were doing the right thing. My mind drifted. What was Tommy doing right now? Not thinking of me, anyway. That's for sure. Suddenly everything had gone very quiet. Fr Ryan was looking at Matt. Jonathan and Anna were too. They all seemed to be waiting for him to do something. Matt himself was away with the fairies as usual.

"The rings," Fr. Ryan whispered urgently. "Who has the rings?"

I gave Matt a poke.

"Sorry," he muttered, scarlet-faced. He put his hands into his pocket and pulled out the lump of pink fabric. Fr Ryan's eyes widened. Anna gasped. I heard a loud moan from Ma in the pew behind us. There was a rasping noise as Matt started to hyperventilate. I grabbed the fabric from his lifeless fingers and plunged my other hand into his pocket. There were sighs of relief all around as I laid two gold rings on the cushion.

"Well done, Maggie." Fr. Ryan beamed his approval. I tried to ignore the waves of icy contempt coming from Anna. Matt's breathing began to slow down as Fr Ryan got on with the ceremony. Soon, all attention was on the couple again. I stuffed the fabric back into Matt's pocket.

"Do you, Jonathan, take Anna for your lawfully-wedded wife?"

"I do," Jonathan replied hoarsely.

"Do you Anna, take Jonathan for your lawfully-wedded husband?"

I held my breath and waited.

"I do." Anna's reply was barely audible.

"I now pronounce you man and wife. You may kiss the bride."

Jonathan leaned over and kissed his new bride. The congregation started to clap. The smiling couple turned around in acknowledgement. As she turned back to the altar, Anna scowled at Matt and me.

"I had to put it somewhere," I whispered.

She sniffed. "You're determined to ruin my day. You're jealous 'cause you'll never have anyone like Jonathan." She turned back to the altar with a swirl of her veil.

"You're welcome to him," I muttered.

Jonathan was staring straight ahead of him, though I knew he could hear every word. Fr Ryan had gone up to the tabernacle to get the Hosts so he was out of earshot.

Ma wasn't.

"Behave yourselves, girls, for goodness sake," she whispered crossly. "Remember where you are."

Fr Ryan came back and started to give out Communion. The bride and groom first, then Matt and me. As he moved down into the body of the church, I closed my eyes and started to pray. There was a sharp dig in my ribs. It was Matt. His eyes were bulging, his two palms locked tight together.

"What'll I do?" he whimpered, opening his palms to show two Hosts.

I marvelled how this man managed to get up in the morning, much less hold a job down.

"Put them in your mouth, of course," I said, closing my eyes.

"I can't," he wailed, "I'd choke."

"Do what you're told and shut up."

He put one in his mouth. The whole church must have heard the gulping noise he made as it went down.

"What about the other one?" he whispered.

"Oh for God's sake," I said crossly, picking up the remaining Host from his hand and popping it into my mouth. "Now, shut up and say your prayers."

"That's a Mortal Sin," Anna hissed, her eyes flashing back over Jonathan's bowed head.

"So I'll go to Hell." I rolled my eyes at her.

"You will too."

"It'd be more fun there anyway."

"It would not."

"It would so."

"STOP IT, GIRLS." Ma's voice had a slightly hysterical note. "Stop it at once."

Anna turned back to the altar and bent her head in exaggerated prayerful mode.

"You look like Sister Dympna in that veil," I whispered.

"More sexy, I hope," she sniggered, flicking the veil back over her shoulder, the way the nuns used to.

"I always thought Dumpy was sexy."

"Dumpy, sexy?" Anna snorted. Her shoulders started to shake with the laughter.

"Stop giggling you two," Jonathan said, crossly. "This is a solemn occasion."

At that we collapsed. Jonathan looked at his new wife with an injured expression.

"I'm sorry," Anna said, biting her lip in an effort to control herself. "Really, I am." She bent her head forward but soon her shoulders started to quiver again. After a minute she leaned back. "Why was Matt worried about the second Host?" she whispered.

"He thought if he swallowed it, he'd choke."

"I never heard of anyone getting two before, did you?"

"It could only happen to him."

"GIRLS, PLEASE," Ma called out in desperation.

But the more we tried to sober up, the worse we got. Jonathan was glaring at Anna. Matt was glaring at me. Ma was glaring at both of us. She was crimson with embarrassment. "Control yourselves, girls. You're letting the whole family down."

Fr Ryan finished giving out Communion and walked back to the altar. As he passed by, he shot a withering glance at each of us. The hysteria continued for another few minutes, and then stopped as quickly as it had begun. I took a crumpled hanky out of Matt's pocket and blew my nose. I chanced a quick look over the hanky at Anna. Jonathan was whispering something, his mouth close to her ear. All her attention was on what he was saying. He reached out and took her hand. They were smiling into each other's eyes, oblivious to everyone else. Ma was beaming. All well in Paradise again. A family scandal had been averted. I looked at my watch and wondered how long before I could take off the dress.

The reception was in Moore's Hotel. Thirty bottles of wine had been ordered. The waiters had been given strict instructions to serve it slowly and make it last. Knowing only too well the consequences of a free bar, Ma and Anna had spent many tortuous hours on the seating arrangements. With no relations from Jonathan's side to keep things polite, they were hoping that family feuds would be forgotten for the day.

As soon as I walked into the dining room and saw Uncle John sitting opposite Uncle Michael, I knew somebody had rearranged their carefully planned place-names. Those two had been bitter enemies since our grandmother's time. Some joker had obviously changed the settings. It was too late to do anything about it now, but from her vantage point at the top table, I could see Ma watching them as the meal progressed.

At the dessert stage, Uncle Michael got up to leave the room. I assumed he was going to the toilet, but when he returned with two bottles of wine, I knew he'd been to the bar. He started filling all the glasses at his table including Uncle John's. That wasn't a good omen. Ma was just getting up to go over to them when Matt tapped a glass for silence. The talking stopped, and everybody looked at him. He stood up nervously and called for a toast to the happy couple. We all rose to our feet and raised our glasses. The cameras flashed. '*Be happy, Anna Banana*' I whispered, holding up my glass to her.

Matt started to read out the telegrams. Each one was greeted with applause. As the nervousness left, he started to read them with great gusto. Everybody laughed and clapped at his efforts. They all seemed to be having a great time. Even Ma had started to relax.

It wasn't until the cutting of the cake that we got the first indication that something was wrong. Jonathan and Anna were leaning on the knife. The guests were clapping and egging them on. As the clapping died down, raised voices were heard. They came from Uncle John's table where Uncle Michael and himself were on their feet. Uncle Michael's face was bright red; Uncle John's almost purple. They were arguing about something. Uncle Michael was waving his arms to make a point. He must have forgotten he had a glass in his hand because wine was spilling all over the carpet with every gesture he made. A vexed-looking Uncle John was shaking his head in disagreement.

Ma got up and rushed over. The two men towered over her. Everybody watched and waited to see what she would do. She took the glass gently from Uncle Michael's hand and put it on the table. Then she laid a restraining hand on Uncle John and started to speak. Whatever she was saying seemed to be having some effect. At least they'd stopped shouting now. There was still a lot of shaking of heads, and then an occasional nod as one of them appeared to agree with her. Both heads were down as they listened attentively to what she was saying. Then suddenly they were nodding at each other and smiling. She gave Uncle Michael a hug. He smiled and held out his hand to Uncle John who frowned, shook his head and turned away. She nodded firmly, picked up his hand and held it out to Uncle Michael, who by now had stopped smiling. Now it was his turn to refuse the hand of friendship. Ma shook her head crossly and started talking again. Uncle Michael turned back to listen. He shook his head at her but she kept nodding and talking. Finally, he shrugged and held out a reluctant hand to Uncle John, who shrugged equally carelessly and took it. At this everybody clapped. The two men smiled and sat down. Ma kissed them both on the top of their heads and returned to her table. She sat down and picked up her glass of champagne. The war was over for another few years, and not a drop of blood had been spilt.

The dancing started. Everybody followed Anna and Jonathan onto the floor. Matt and I shuffled around to the music. Then Jonathan asked me to dance. The music slowed down and he pulled me close. I could smell the whiskey. I pushed him away, crossly.

"There was a time you wouldn't push me away," he said, his breath hot on my ear. For Anna's sake I didn't want to make a scene.

"You're married now, Jonathan."

"So what?" He pulled me closer, and looked deep in my eyes.

"What do you mean?"

"You and I will always have something special."

I pushed him back, roughly. "Don't you dare… don't you dare try to…"

Anna's voice cut in suddenly from behind. "I hope you're not making a pass at my husband, Lumpy?" Uncle John pulled her away in a swirling movement. Uncle John was the dancer in the family. He seemed to have forgotten the row with Uncle Michael and was out strutting his stuff. From the change of colour in Jonathan's face, I knew he was as relieved as I was that nobody had heard what we'd been saying. We broke up the minute the set was over.

Later, Anna went off to get changed. She came back in her going-away suit, and stood on the stairs in the hallway of the hotel, brandishing the bouquet. All the girls gathered round, waving at her to throw it in their direction. Impatient to be off myself, I was near the door, looking at my watch, when I saw the coloured blur out of the corner of my eye. I looked up just in time to catch it. Everybody clapped. "You're next, Maggie."

"No, thanks. Who wants this?" I said tossing it up in the air again.

There was a shocked silence for a second, then all the hands went up again to grab the bouquet. Ma frowned and turned to Aunt Mary who was beside her. "…always an awful tomboy you know. Used to play with those rough O'Connors." My Aunt smiled, and nodded. They both turned towards me, but I was already half way up the stairs to change. The last thing I needed was another lecture. I decided to ring Tommy's mother when I got back to the flat. I needed to talk to somebody who'd understand how mixed up I felt about Jonathan and his marriage to Anna. If anyone would she would.

CHAPTER 12

Ma was close to tears as she said goodbye to me on Sunday night at the station.

"I feel I've lost ye both now."

"It's only Dublin, Ma." I laughed. "It's not Beirut." I turned to Auntie Nell. "Take care of her, won't you?" Nell nodded.

"And who'll take care of you, Maggie?" Ma asked quietly.

"I'm quite capable of taking care of myself, thanks. We don't all need a man to look after us."

"What about that chap you met in London?" She didn't miss much.

"I haven't heard from him for ages."

"It would be nice if you had someone though, wouldn't it?"

"You should be glad I'm so independent Ma. "

Ma shook her head. "You and your independence."

"I've years of study ahead. I won't have time for anything else."

"Oh, Maggie. I don't know what we're going to do with you," she said, hugging me. "You'd better get in or you won't get a seat."

As soon as the train had pulled out of the station a sense of isolation swept over me. Perhaps everybody else was right. Maybe Anna was the smart one after all? Jonathan mightn't be the most honourable man in the world, but, at least now, she had someone to take care of her. Who had I, when all was said and done? Who could I turn to in my hour of need? Wearily, I lay back against the headrest and closed my eyes. Tommy's face loomed in front of me, those green eyes and little gold flecks. Where was he now? Probably off in the Middle East somewhere.

I didn't wake up until we were in Amiens Street Station. It was dark and pouring rain, when I finally jumped off the bus in South Circular Road. I had the umbrella up with one hand and my bag full of Ma's baking in the other. "Ooops sorry," I muttered, as I bumped into a dark figure leaning against the railings. I hurried past and put my key in the door. Then I heard it, *'Bring flowers of the fairest, bring blossoms the rarest...'*

"I don't believe it," I gasped and turned. "I was just thinking about you."

Tommy beamed. "Sounds hopeful. Have you a kiss for the returning hero?"

"Of course." I smiled, turning my cheek to him.

"Not so quick. Let me put these down so we can do it right." He was holding a big bunch of flowers. We went inside and he laid them on the hall table. "Now young lady, come here to me." Blushing, I moved closer. He put his hands on my chin and tilted my face towards him. When we were about an inch apart, he looked deep into my eyes. "Hello again, little Mags," he whispered.

"Hello yourself," I murmured. His lips were soft. I moved closer into his arms. His mouth moved against mine. My head spun as our bodies melted together. I felt as if I was drowning in him.

"I'm so glad you're here," I said, shakily.

"Oh God, Maggie, if you only knew…"

"Everything seemed so empty…"

"I had this sudden… Ma told me about the wedding. Are you okay?"

"I am now."

He pulled back, and looked around. "Chair's still broken, I see. Kind of reassuring in a way." He picked up my bag.

A note from Eileen was propped up on the mantelpiece. *"Welcome back, Mags. Hope the wedding of the century went off well. Dying to see the pink yoke. Back Wednesday."*

"Was it awful?" Tommy asked, dropping the bag on the floor.

"The wedding or the dress?"

"The wedding, of course."

"Never mind the bloody wedding," I said, putting my arms around his neck. "How come you're always there when I need you?" I smiled into his eyes. "I missed those little gold flecks."

He pushed me away from him. "Maggie, lay off. I'm only human."

"So I've noticed," I whispered, moving closer again.

"Maggie, stop. There's only so much I can take."

Then he was kissing me and holding me tight, so tight I could barely breath. My head swirled. I felt myself being picked up and carried to the bed. There was a feverish pulling-off of clothes, giggling as something caught. Then, at last, we were lying next to each other, all barriers gone. He was covering my body with kisses.

"Oh, Maggie, if you only knew how often I've dreamt about this."

"Shh" I put my fingers to his mouth. His lips caught them, sucking each of them in turn, slowly, wetly, until I couldn't bear it any longer. I pulled back. His arms went round me again, trapping me. His fingers travelled down my spine. Waves of heat passed through my body from wherever he touched. I was caught in a spell, unable to move, conscious only of his touch, waiting to see where his fingers would go next.

Afterwards, we lay side by side.

"Are you alright?" he whispered.

"I often wondered what it would be like with you," I smiled tenderly at him.

"And how was it?" He looked at me, anxiously.

"Unbelievably, magically, perfect."

"Me too. Dangerous, though. Makes a person vulnerable." He sighed. "You're very special to me, Mags. You know that?" I nodded happily. "Is this still sore?" He traced my scar with his finger. I flinched and turned away. "When I think of what that guy has put you through..." His face darkened with anger.

"Don't let's talk about him." I shuddered. "Tell me about your work. Where are you at the moment?"

"Out in the Gulf."

"What are those badges I saw on your uniform?"

"I got involved in a few hairy incidents, that's all."

I frowned. "You mean you could have been killed?"

"Naw. I'm too tough."

"Nobody's that tough."

"I was reared tough, had to be." He smiled suddenly. "Remember throwing mud at the cars, knowing Anna would sneak home and tell your mother?" He grinned at me. "Not to mention taking on the wrath of Sister Dympna." He started to sing. *Bring flowers of the rarest...* "

"Seems like a lifetime ago, doesn't it?"

"What's a few little wars compared to being thrown out of Kilmanogue?" he said, in a more sober tone.

"Your mother said something about that. What happened?"

He shook his head. "That part of my life is over. I don't want to go back over it."

"Just as long as you keep coming back to me..." I said, cuddling into him.

He sat up abruptly. "Listen, Mags. Maybe we shouldn't have done this. You deserve someone steady, someone who'll be there for you. I can't promise you anything like that."

"So what? We could be happy."

"I won't make promises I can't keep. I'd feel trapped. I know I would. I'm sorry Mags but that's the way I am."

"You're right," I said, lightly. "I'd probably feel the same way."

"That's my girl." He gave me a warm hug. "We're two of a kind, I guess."

"Made for each other," I mumbled into his shoulder.

He drifted back to sleep. For hours I lay quietly in his arms listening to his breathing. I felt far too alive to waste this time on sleep. I was overwhelmed by my feelings for this man, this childhood friend, who kept appearing in my hour of need. Of course I valued my independence too, but...

In spite of myself, I must have fallen asleep too, because suddenly, the light was streaming in through the frayed curtains, and the noise of the early morning buses was beginning to build up outside the window. I turned as quietly as I could. Tommy looked like a young boy lying there, chest rising and falling with each breath. I didn't want to break the magic by waking him, but couldn't resist leaning down and kissing him ever so gently on a corner of his mouth, barely brushing his lips. When he didn't stir, I felt safe to do it again. He stirred and reached out for me.

"What would a conquering hero like for breakfast?"

"What's on offer?" He smiled lazily, his half-closed eyes sending me warm signals.

"Wedding cake, Ma's brown bread, or some of Auntie Nell's apple tart."

"You know what I really want?"

"That's not on the menu."

"Why not?"

"We have to be sensible."

"Do we?"

"Yes."

"Why?" He smiled challengingly up into my eyes.

"Because someone's bound to get hurt."

The smile faded. "Oh right, in that case I'll have some of your mother's brown bread and a cup of tea." Disappointed, I started to get up. "And where d'you think you're going?" He pulled me back and kissed me. Our mouths opened to each other and then I was drowning in him again. He moved on top of me and I was lost. For the second time, his lovemaking took my breath away.

Afterwards I lay there, incapable of moving. A bus screeched to a halt outside the window. He stirred and looked at his watch.

"Blast it, I have to go."

"Typical man, going when he's got what he wants."

He pulled me roughly towards him, and held my face in his hands. "Don't joke about it, Maggie. You're the most precious thing in my life. If you don't know that by now, you never will. If I were ever to love anyone it would be you, but I'm not cut out for this sort of thing. Please try to understand. I never know where I am from one month to the next. You could never count on me. You deserve more. Now, up you get, me darlin'."

He gave me a playful slap on the bottom. "Put the kettle on. Man does not live by love alone."

Twenty minutes later he was gone and I had absolutely no idea when I'd hear from him again.

CHAPTER 13

A week later the photographs arrived. Eileen got out the gin. She laughed herself sick over the pink creation. I laughed with her, but my mind was elsewhere. To me the wedding seemed years away.

A few weeks after that, Anna told the world she was expecting a baby. A honeymoon baby, everybody said. Cards of Congratulations poured in.

"We're going to call him John if it's a boy after Dad, and Rose if it's a girl," Anna said, when I went home that weekend.

"That's nice," I replied, ignoring the twinge of jealousy. I hadn't even had time to put a name on my baby before he died.

I returned to Dublin earlier than usual. The coming exams gave me the perfect excuse.

For the next few months I buried myself in work and study. I cut down drastically on the visits home. Anna was blooming. The perfect mother-to-be. She wallowed in her pregnancy and all the fuss everybody made of her. How incredibly different her pregnancy was from mine.

The baby was born six weeks early, surprise, surprise. It was a boy. Ma rang to give me the good news.

"That's great Ma. Are they still going to call him John?"

"Yes, love. Your father would have been so proud of his girls. When are the results out?"

"Next week, I hope. I'll be home at the weekend."

"Surely you'll come down to see the baby?"

"He'll still be there at the weekend, Ma."

"But Anna's dying to see you. She misses you, Maggie. She'll never admit it, of course."

"Hasn't she Jonathan?"

"That's not the same thing, love, and you know it."

"Okay Ma, I give up." I laughed, "I'll get some time off and go down tomorrow."

"That's my girl. He's the spit of you when you were born, by the way."

"God help the poor child so. I have to go Ma. Bye." I put the phone down quickly. There was only so much I could take.

I was dreading the visit. I had to brace myself walking into the baby unit. My breath caught as the nurse held up the little wrinkled bundle. I leaned against the wall to steady myself. Had mine looked that tiny, that helpless?

Oh God, why hadn't they let me see him? At least there'd be something to remember, instead of this awful darkness. The nurse put him back into the cot. I read the tiny white card pinned over his head. *John Anthony Good, 7 pounds 2 ounces.* I reached out and touched the wispy fuzz on the top of the skull.

"Welcome to the world, John Anthony," I whispered.

I went up to the ward. Jonathan was standing looking out the window, a bored expression on his face. Anna was sitting up in the bed putting on lipstick. She barely smiled when I walked in.

"Congratulations, Sis." I leaned over to kiss her.

"Thanks," she said, and turned back to the mirror.

I looked over at Jonathan. "Congratulations to you too, Daddy." He shrugged and said nothing. "Ye're so lucky, the two of you."

"Lucky?" Anna said, poking at an imaginary spot on her face.

"To have such a perfect baby."

"What did you expect, a monster?" Anna retorted, "I only hope I get my figure back soon."

I turned, exasperated, to Jonathan. "What about you? Aren't you delighted with your son and heir?"

He shrugged again. "It wasn't my idea. And I'm not looking forward to a houseful of smelly nappies." He scowled across at Anna.

"Well you'll just have to get used to them," Anna snapped. "Won't he, Mags? I can't be expected to do everything."

Jonathan continued to stare out the window. I thought of the tiny miracle I'd just seen. It was a few minutes before I realised tears were running down my face. They were so wrapped up in the sulks that neither of them noticed. I felt if I stayed another minute, I'd say something I'd regret, so I wiped away the tears quickly and left. They couldn't possibly understand how I was feeling. How could they? Nobody could. I didn't go on to Kilmanogue as planned. Instead, I drove back to Dublin.

That night I rang Mrs O and told her about the new arrival. As usual, she hit the nail on the head. "It must have been hard for you, Maggie. It's not that long since you had your own."

"You never told me what happened after I left the hospital? Was it long before he... before he...?" I couldn't say the actual word.

There was a pause at the other end of the line. "Why don't you come over at the weekend and we can talk?"

"I will, but first tell me how long it was before..."

"Sorry lovey, didn't catch that. Must be a bad connection. I'll expect you on Friday then, usual time."

"Okay."

We talked for hours the night I arrived. After we'd covered the wedding and the new arrival, she plagued me with questions about the family. She listened carefully when I tried to describe my feelings about the new baby, and laughed when I told her how Anna and Jonathan were already quarrelling about who would change the nappies. It was after one o'clock when we finally got to bed. It was only then I remembered she hadn't told me about my own baby.

I asked her at breakfast next day. She was about to pour tea, but she quickly put the pot back on its stand. "You mustn't worry about him, lovey. It all happened for the best in the end."

"Then why do I still feel such a failure? You know I can't have any more?" She nodded sadly as I went on. "I didn't mind too much at the time, but now…"

She got up and put her arms around me. "Apart from that you're okay though, aren't you? Everything's healed?"

"I thought I was fine 'til I saw Anna's. When does it stop Mrs O? When does the pain go away?"

"Soon, love, soon. You're young. You have your whole life ahead of you."

I sighed and said nothing. What was there to say? I felt more like an old woman.

"Are you going into the shops today?" she asked, trying no doubt to change the subject.

"Only if you come with me."

"I don't think I'd be able for them." I looked up at her anxiously, but she just laughed. "I'm a wee bit tired, that's all. Anyway you'd cover more ground on your own."

Later that evening, she was frying steak and onions and I was standing at the door of the kitchen, a glass of wine in my hand. She looked up suddenly. "By the way, Maggie, did I tell you about Tommy's latest contract?" I had to hold the glass tightly to stop it shaking. "This one's for three years." She turned the steaks carefully. "It's a long time. There'll still be letters and the odd phone call, but I loved those visits of his. I'll miss him dreadfully. I'd never let on to him, of course. He has his own life and…" She looked up at me. "I'm being stupid, aren't I?"

"Of course not. You're his mother."

I busied myself laying the table. There'd be plenty of time to worry about Tommy later. I was too confused now. Three years! But he was a free agent.

We both were. And Mrs O was right. I was young. I had my life ahead of me, and my career. I could bury myself in work and exams. They were the only things I seemed to be good at. This way was safer too, less likely to hurt. Anyway, life would be very boring if everybody did the same thing. Yes, independence was the answer. I'd have my career and my independence. What more could anyone want?

PART THREE

INDEPENDENT – ANOTHER WORD FOR LONELY?

CHAPTER 1

The alarm buzzed. Just gone seven. I stretched lazily in the bed and looked around. Since my last promotion, F&F sent me to First Class hotels only. Just as well. There'd been far too much travelling lately. Perhaps as a New Year resolution I should let my staff do more of it. I wasn't getting any younger, after all. Thirty-seven next week. No wonder they'd stopped asking in Kilmanogue when I was going to give them *the big day*.

1982 had been a good year. I was head of my own department now. I had a company car, and my own expense account, not to mention my fancy title, New Projects Manager. What more could a girl ask for? Did I say girl? Richard's face drifted in front of me. Kind, dependable Richard. Shipwrecks in life, the two of us. He was not long out of a painful separation, and I was… I was what?

I pulled the bedclothes away and jumped out of bed. With Tommy always away in some God-awful country waging someone else's war for them, I needed someone like Richard. I walked into the bathroom and stepped into the marble shower. First Class hotels in London were a far cry from the old bed-sitter in South Circular Road. Had that chair in the hall ever been fixed, I wondered, or was it still propped up against the wall waiting to trap the unwary visitor? Buying the apartment in Rathmines had been one of my better decisions. It gave me a sense of permanence, life in my own control, as well as somewhere to relax and be myself.

I turned on the shower. No time to waste. I had another busy day ahead today. Apart from the F&F work I had to see two fashion houses who supplied the family shop in Kilmanogue. They were insisting our accounts hadn't been cleared, even though Auntie Nell distinctly remembered giving the cheques to Jonathan. He said he'd paid them during one of his trips, but then Jonathan was still a law unto himself. I held my face up to the water.

He and Anna seemed happy enough. Their two children were a constant source of wonder to me. John, almost fifteen now, a tall gentle boy, totally unlike his father. Emily, eight going on nine, blonde like her mother and bright as a button. Anna had enough to do minding them, without worrying about unpaid bills as well. No wonder she needed the odd tranquilliser to get through the day. She kept insisting they were just a temporary need. I hoped she was right.

Kilmanogue was still my special place, my retreat, a place to recuperate when work and travelling got me down. It was on one of those weekends that Auntie Nell told me about the shop accounts. She was sure Jonathan was right and the suppliers were wrong, but then she'd always been too trusting when it came to her son.

Thanks to her and Ma's efforts, the business had done well over the years. They had three London suppliers apparently, the two who were complaining and a third in the East End. We'd been making monthly payments to the East End company for two years now. The payments had been authorised by Jonathan. I thought I might as well look that company up too, while I was over here. I finished my shower and wrapped myself up in a bathrobe.

There was a knock on the door. "Room Service." A girl entered and carried a tray to the table at the window. "Enjoy your breakfast Madam," she said, slipping out of the room as neatly as she'd come in.

I lifted the lid off the plate and sniffed the crispy bacon. A cooked breakfast, one of the few joys of travelling. And I'd need it if I was to get through the day's schedule.

It was a long day. By six I was exhausted, but I still had to see to the family business. I was half an hour late for the first of the suppliers. Mrs. Little was the Accounts Manager.

"I'm so sorry," I said as we shook hands. "I hadn't allowed for the traffic."

"It's getting worse instead of better, I'm afraid." She smiled. "At last I get to meet one of the Brown sisters. You're the accountant, I believe?"

"Yes. Thanks for agreeing to see me," I replied, "I don't want to waste your time so I'll come straight to the point."

"Ah, yes, the unpaid account." She frowned. "If it was anybody other than your Aunt, we'd have gone to our legal people by now."

This startled me. "There must be some misunderstanding. We thought the account was settled." I opened my briefcase and drew out the notes I'd made. "My Aunt wrote the cheque and gave it to her son to bring over. Did he not give it to you?"

"No, he didn't." Her reply was crisp and definite.

"But he did come to see you?"

"Yes, and when I asked him for payment, he said the cheque would be in the post the following week. Apparently there'd been some breakdown in your system."

"Breakdown?" Auntie Nell had said nothing to me about a breakdown.

"Yes." Again her response was crisp. "I remember it distinctly, because when I asked him what sort of breakdown he was somewhat evasive. I told him we'd wait one more week for the money." She looked at me. It was obvious that she was waiting for me to hand over the cheque.

"I'm sorry about that, Mrs Little. You'll have your cheque next week."

"That's what Mr. Good said, but he didn't deliver on his promise."

"There's obviously been some misunderstanding. I'll need a couple of days to clear it up."

She relented and held out her hand. "Very well, Miss Brown. Better make it a money draft." I nodded. "And if it's not on my desk by Friday I'm putting the matter into the hands of our legal people. I'm responsible to my Board. I can't make any exceptions."

"Thank you, Mrs. Little. I do appreciate your patience."

"Just so long as we understand each other."

"Perhaps you could help me with another mystery?" I pulled the East End statement from my briefcase. "Do you know anything about this firm?"

"*Fashion Consulting Services*," she read. "Sorry. Never heard of them. *Box 111, The Mews, Shanley Industrial Estate.* Sounds like a drop address. Are you having trouble there too?"

"No, no. Nothing like that," I said quickly. "Sorry to have bothered you."

It was almost half-past six, but the second supplier was only a block away. The story there was the same. They had exacted a promise from Jonathan to send the cheque the following week. When it didn't arrive, they gave instructions to their legal people to start proceedings. It took a lot of persuading there too to convince them to wait for one more week before taking things further.

I hailed a taxi. "Shanley Industrial Estate, East End, please." The car edged out into the traffic. I sat back, wondering what further revelations were ahead of me. When we got there, I asked the driver to wait. The office was closed but I rang the bell anyway. No answer. I tried to look inside, but the windows were covered by security panels. The premises on either side were shuttered too, so I got back into the taxi.

The following afternoon I called again to the East End address. This time the shutters were open. I could hear the sound of horseracing. I pushed the door and walked into a dingy office. A big man was slumped in front of a television screen, a cigarette dangling from his mouth, his tummy hanging out over his trousers. "Yeah?" He threw the question over his shoulder without taking his gaze from the screen.

"I'm looking for Fashion Consulting Services, please?"

"Come on, damn you. Come on," he roared at the screen as the horses thundered towards the winning post.

"Fashion Consulting Services?" I shouted above the din.

"Ya wha?" His ear cocked for a moment, then his attention went back to the screen as the horses romped past the post. "Ah go home, you useless bum. God blast it anyway. Another fiver down the Swanee." He turned around. "That's the last time I'll listen to that boll... sorry miss. What can I do you for?" He smiled at his cleverness, revealing a gap in the front teeth. His tongue ran in and out of the gap, as he looked me up and down.

"I'm looking for Fashion Consulting Services."

His eyes wandered down to the racing pages. "Only problem now, is how to get the fiver back, idn't it?"

"Can you tell me where to find them?"

He stared back. I waited. He didn't flinch. Finally, I got the message and took a fiver out of my purse. "What was that name again?" he smirked, pocketing the note.

"Fashion Consulting Services," I answered between clenched teeth.

"Hmm Fashion Consulting Services...." He swivelled his chair, remained sitting and walked it along the floor towards a steel cabinet. He started to flick through some files in one of the drawers.

"'ere we are." He held up a tiny card triumphantly.

"Well, who are they?"

"I'm not supposed to give out information, Miss." He smiled archly at me.

"But I've just given you a fiver."

"Another one'll do it, Miss, seein' as how it's yourself." He waved the card in front of my nose.

"I don't have another fiver." I held out a ten-pound note. He put his hand on it, but I snapped it away from him. "Change?"

"Sorry. Don't have any."

"You have so. I've just given you a fiver."

"What fiver?" He smiled his toothless grin. I glared. He didn't budge. I glanced at my watch. I had less than an hour before check-in. Big mistake. "I'm not the one in a hurry, Miss."

He was a good judge of character. I handed him the tenner, and snapped the card crossly out of his hand. It read *Fashion Consulting Services, c/o M. Barrett, 23 Broadway Close, Richmond.*

"'ere. You can't keep that." He grabbed the card back again. "How would I know where to address their post? You'll just have to make a note of it." He held the card in front of me, near enough so I could read it, but just far enough away so I couldn't grab it back. I scribbled the name and address on the top of their statement and rushed out of the office. Whatever service he did or didn't provide, Mr. Barrett of Richmond would have to wait until I was back in London again.

By the time I got to the airport the other passengers had already boarded. The airhostess escorted me, crossly, to the waiting plane. Yet again, I'd been to London without taking the time to visit Mrs O. Next time, I promised myself, as the plane took off. Definitely, next time.

I rang home as soon as I got in and spoke to Auntie Nell. When she heard what had happened she promised to organise the money drafts at once.

"Thanks for talking to them, Maggie. Jonathan was so insistent, but he seems to have made some mistake. God knows where that money has gone. We'll just have to find some more." She sighed. "Every mother's an eejit when it comes to her son, I suppose. He works hard enough, but sometimes I think his mind is elsewhere. What do you think happened?"

"I don't know. I'm sure he'll be able to clear it up. Is he there at the moment?"

"No. He's gone to London. Do you want to talk to your mother?"

"Yes, please. What's he doing in London?"

"Some match or other."

I didn't know he was interested in football, but then there was a lot I didn't know about Jonathan, it seemed.

Ma came on the phone. "When are you coming down, love?"

"Soon, Ma. How are you?"

"Grand. You should come more often. Anna needs you."

"Hasn't she got Wonder Boy?"

"You're her sister, Maggie." Her voice had an edge in it.

"Okay, Ma. I'll be down next weekend."

"Good girl." She sounded relieved.

"Are you alright?"

"Of course."

"You're not worrying about this cheque business, I hope?"

"No, love. I leave the finances to Nell."

"I'm sure the money will turn up."

"What money?"

"Auntie Nell will bring you up-to-date, Ma. I'd better go."

"Okay, love. God bless. Take care."

"I will, Ma. You too."

"Oh, and Maggie"

"Yes, Ma."

"These nights are very cold. You are using the electric blanket I hope?"

"Yes, Ma." There was no point in telling her I only put it on when she came to visit.

"I don't trust that central heating. They say it only gives people colds."

"Yes, Ma. Well, I'd better go up and turn on the blanket."

"Are you making fun of your mother?"

"Who? Me?"

"I won't be around forever, you know."

"Sorry, Ma."

"It's alright. Goodbye love. Take care."

It was only after I put down the phone I remembered I hadn't told Nell about the Fashion Consultancy in the East End. It would do another time. She'd enough to worry about, having to find the money to settle the overdue accounts.

I ran a bath. Richard was taking me out to dinner tomorrow night. I yawned. That was more than enough excitement after the week I'd had. I'd have a lie-in in the morning, get up around eleven, stroll down to Rathmines, do some shopping, come back, tidy the flat, put on the glad rags. Who knows? I might even let Richard stay over. Sunday we could go out for lunch, and maybe go for a walk on Howth Head. I yawned again.

Like most weekends, it was gone in a flash. An idea had started to form in the back of my mind. The more I thought about it, the more I knew it was the right thing to do. On Sunday night I jotted down a few figures. Monday morning I was back at my desk dictating a report on the lack of progress in the latest computer project. Like many a project before, it was running behind schedule and over budget. I summarised the situation briefly for the Finance Director, and suggested a couple of remedies. First, they'd have to find someone to deputise for the Project Leader in his old job for a few months. Tim was a good man. The others looked to him for advice and leadership, but his hands were tied having to run back every other day to make sure his old job was covered. Secondly, instead of trying to implement the new system on all sites at once, they should implement it first on the three London sites. When it was up and running, they could use the city staff to train the regional staff. That way the city would test the system and have the bugs ironed out before the system went countrywide.

"Enjoyed London?" my secretary asked, as I handed her the tape.

"I wasn't there for enjoyment, as you well know."

Maura laughed. "That was a joke. You need your coffee. Give me your receipts and I'll do the expenses."

"Thanks. You're a star."

"Don't forget your ten o'clock."

"What have I in the afternoon?"

"Only the Monthly Section Heads at 2.30."

"Right. Can you get my bank manager on the line?"

I took the call in my office. "Good morning, Tom," I said, when I heard Tom Murphy's voice. "What sort of mood are you in this morning?"

"What sort of mood would you like me to be in?"

"A lending one. How are the interest rates at the moment?"

"Low, too low."

"You're not looking for sympathy, I hope." I heard him chuckle. "It's the unfortunate punter like me who has to make the money work."

"I often wondered why that is," he replied dryly. "Could it have something to do with the fact that *you* make profit out of *our* money?" I laughed. It was difficult to win an argument with him. "So now that we have the sparring out of the way, what can I do for you Ms Brown?"

"I have a proposition for you. Can we meet?"

"Hold on a minute." There was a slight pause before he came back on the line. "Four o'clock?"

"Great. See you then."

A moment later, Maura walked in with two mugs of coffee. We usually had coffee together unless I had a client with me. It gave us a chance to catch up on things. We went over the messages that had piled up while I was in London. The phone rang. It was a call from downstairs asking if I was going to the meeting. I jumped up grabbed the file and ran out.

Later that afternoon, Tom ushered me into his office with a flourish.

"Okay Ms Brown, how much and for how long?"

"Fifteen for ten."

He laughed. "Perhaps Madam could give me a few details?"

"Fifteen thousand for ten years. How much more detail do you need?"

"Remember I hold the purse, so you'd better tell me exactly what you have in mind?"

"I'm thinking of buying into the family business." I handed him a page of figures. It was a rough picture of the shop's assets and liabilities which I'd done out earlier. He listened quietly as I explained how they were strapped for cash at the moment, even though the business was doing well. "I'm not sure they have enough controls in place. Officially, I don't have the right to interfere," I explained. "but if I had a share in the business, I could keep a closer eye on things."

He nodded. "Tell me more about this Jonathan." Typical bank manager, he'd put his finger on the weak link straightaway.

"He's Auntie Nell's son and he's married to my sister Anna. He works hard enough, goes away a lot. He's the main salesman, so that makes sense, but sometimes I'm not sure…"

"Not sure about what?"

"About him, I suppose. It's all rather sensitive but if I had reason to look at the books on a regular basis, I might be able to spot problems before they start."

"Fifteen thousand would give you about twenty percent?" I nodded. "What collateral would you be putting up?"

"The apartment. I only have a small loan out against it as you know. Property in that area has appreciated more than most."

"You'll have to give me time to think about it. And I'd need to see the books." He frowned. "What's his background?"

"He was brought up in England. Has a business degree from some university in the North. Other than that I don't know too much." I wasn't happy with the way the conversation was going. "But surely all the bank has to worry about is whether I can make the payments?"

"I don't like to see any client of mine investing unwisely." He grinned at me. "On the other hand, given that it's a family business, I'd have to say, in principle, we probably will be able to give you the loan. But if we do, Maggie," he cautioned, "it will be strictly a personal loan in *your* name and secured by *your* apartment." I nodded. "Before I commit formally I'd like to make some more enquiries." I nodded again and pointed to a poster on the wall, advertising small business loans. '*JUST CALL IN AND ASK. WE'RE THE BANK THAT LIKES TO SAY YES.*'

He laughed. "Give me twenty-four hours."

"I suppose I'll have to be content with that." I stood up. "Thanks, Tom."

"Always glad to see you, Maggie." He stood up and we shook hands. It was nice to be able to stare a man in the eye. Unfortunately, Tom was happily married. "I'll ring you tomorrow afternoon. Thanks for coming to this bank."

"What other one is there?" I retorted with a smile and left.

It was a pity I had to wait until the next day, but I knew he'd give me the loan. Property prices were going up in Dublin and he knew my salary was well able to carry the extra payment, even if the investment didn't bring in any profit for a while.

I got a call two days later. The loan was mine, but strictly as a personal loan. We agreed the terms. He promised to have a formal contract drawn up ready to sign by the end of the week. I put down the phone and rang home. Ma answered.

"What's wrong, Maggie?"

I laughed. "Does there have to be something wrong for me to ring you?"

"You don't normally ring at this time. Are you checking up to see if we made those payments?"

"Did you?"

"Of course. It wasn't easy to find the money, though. Nell says we're very short of cash at the moment."

"That's what I'd like to talk to you about."

"Oh?"

"It'll wait 'til Friday. I'll try to get off early."

"Be down in time for dinner. I know you don't feed yourself properly up there in Dublin."

"I do, Ma. Honest. We all do. All one million of us."

"Don't be cheeky to your poor mother, Maggie. What would the nuns say?"

"How did we get onto the nuns, Ma? I'd better go do some work. See you Friday."

"In time for dinner, remember."

"Yes, Ma."

That weekend, I put my proposal to Nell and herself. We had it discussed and agreed before we told Anna and Jonathan. Jonathan looked at me, but said nothing. He could hardly object to more money coming into the business. He hadn't been able to offer a satisfactory explanation for the missing cheques. He still claimed that the bank had made a mistake. Our bank was in the throes of computerisation. The money had definitely left our accounts, but the cheques themselves had somehow got mislaid. In any case, by Monday, the Kilmanogue business would now have cash and I'd have my 20% holding.

Jonathan was quiet all through the weekend. I suspected the last thing he wanted was someone examining the books on a regular basis. I knew I was taking on additional work on top of the day job, but it felt right to be part of the family business.

The initial excitement drained away, however, when I returned to the empty flat on Sunday night. I'd have liked to have gone out and celebrated, but Richard was away. There was nothing on television. I was just beginning to think of an early night when the phone rang. I picked it up. '*Bring flowers of the fairest...*'

"That's beginning to sound a bit sad, old chum," I said, interrupting the medley.

"Time was when you almost jumped down the phone if you heard those notes."

"That wasn't today or yesterday."

"What's wrong, Mags?"

"Just feeling my age, I suppose."

"Another birthday coming up?"

"Been and gone, I'm afraid."

"Sorry. You should have said."

"Some birthdays are worse than others."

"You're as old as you feel, Mags."

"I feel old tonight. Tommy whatever happened to all those dreams we had as kids?" He didn't answer. "Are *you* happy with *your* life?"

"What sort of question is that?"

"Well?" There was silence again. "Not like you to be stuck for words, Mr. O'Connor?"

"It's a difficult one. I miss the flying, of course. But other than that.... Anyway, who's really happy?"

I sighed. "I thought I was, but lately I don't know."

"Go away outa that. You have it all sewn up."

"Who? Me?"

"Yes, you. You're the only person I know who knows exactly where they're going and what they want out of life."

"Oh, for God's sake, Tommy, how long have you known me?"

He chuckled. "How far back do you want me to go?"

"Okay, okay, forget it." I didn't want to get more depressed. "How's your mother? I was thinking about her the other day. I owe her a visit. It seems ages since... "

"That's why I'm ringing you, Mags. She's not too good, I'm afraid."

"Sorry to hear that. She was fine the last time I saw her."

"That was over a year ago." There was a slight criticism in his voice.

I was shocked. "It can't be that long surely?"

"There's something she wants to talk to you about, something important."

"A year? I don't believe it. Whenever I'm over I'm buried in meetings, but I keep meaning to..."

"She's had some tests done. The results weren't good."

"Oh God, Tommy. I'm sorry. I'll go see her straight away."

"I never thought the day would come when she wouldn't..." His voice broke.

"I'm sorry, love. Anything I can do?" A long silence.

"I'm okay," he said finally. "Has Jonathan been behaving himself?"

"As far as I know. Why do you ask?"

"I was talking to a friend of mine. Did you know he was in the army?"

"The British Army?"

"Yes. For about five years. He was discharged apparently."

"Discharged?" The alarm bells were ringing.

"But that was a long time ago. Maybe he's changed, although..." He stopped.

"Go on. What else did you hear?"

"There's probably nothing to it. I don't like spreading rumours."

"Knowing him, they're probably true."

"There was some woman he got into trouble."

"Another one?" I said sarcastically.

"I'm only telling you because Mick seems to think he's still involved with her."

I gasped. "You mean he's cheating on Anna?"

"It may be nothing," he continued. "I've asked him to check and come back to me. Perhaps I shouldn't have mentioned it. I'm a bit distracted with Mam being so sick and all…"

"Poor Tommy. I wish I was there with you but I'm in the middle of this big project at the moment."

"I know. Me too. This is the last thing I need right now."

"The story of our lives, eh?"

There was another long pause. "Look, Mags, I have to go."

"To fight someone else's war no doubt. Don't let me keep you."

"I'm sorry. Try to see Mam, won't you?"

"I will. Do you have to go away with her so sick?"

"You know the way it is."

"Sure. God knows I ought to by now." I slammed the phone down in a sudden fit of temper. I instantly regretted it but it was too late. He could have been ringing from anywhere. I picked up the phone at once and booked a flight to London for the following Friday. Poor Mrs O. I'd neglected her for too long. I was shocked that Jonathan could be seeing someone else. But not surprised. It would certainly explain some of his absences.

Tommy had sounded depressed. Lying in bed later, his words continued to echo in my brain. Perhaps all his gadding around the world was beginning to wear thin? He'd always been so sure of what he wanted. The world and freedom. Especially the freedom. He'd said it often enough over the last number of years. Even in those moments of closeness after making love. *Find someone who can be there for you, Mags. I'd feel trapped in one place.*

The trouble was that nobody could reach me the way he could. During those perfect moments there was nothing else in the whole world I wanted. But in the cold light of reality our relationship was impossible. We both knew it. I punched the pillows angrily, and for the tenth time that night tried to settle down. I should be satisfied with what we had. He had the knack of being there when I really needed him, starting with the day I'd walked out of the clinic, dazed with the results of the pregnancy test. Then the awful time in the hospital. I turned on the light and picked up a book. Relying on Tommy would be a recipe for disaster. The print blurred as a moment of self-pity washed over me. Blast him anyway. He really got to me and he'd never promised anything, not even in our most intimate moments.

I flung the book at the wall. Why couldn't I just hate him? He had a nerve walking in and out of my life, leaving me for his bloody wars. Why does he have to be running around the world all the time? Why couldn't we be a normal couple?

CHAPTER 2

"God bless us and save us, if it isn't herself." Mrs. O's face lit up when she saw me standing at the door. "You're a sight for sore eyes."

"It's wonderful to see you too, Mrs O. You look great," I said, allowing myself to be smothered in one of her bear hugs. In fact, I was shocked by her appearance. She'd turned into an old woman since I'd last seen her, her skull etched out underneath her skin. "Not too much of the old tummy left, I see?" I laughed.

"Come on in. You'll catch your death." She shivered, and shut the door quickly behind me. It was stifling in her apartment. "Everything's ready. I'll just put on the kettle," she said, pulling her cardigan around her.

"No, let me do that. You go sit down."

"Thanks, lovey." She sighed, and flopped down on a chair. "Oh God, it's such a bore being tired all the time." She was rubbing her chest, but stopped as soon as she saw me looking at her. "Thank God you're here. If you knew how often I've wished…"

"I'm sorry. I get so wrapped up in my work." I sat down beside her. "I can't believe I've left it so long."

"Not at all." She smiled up at me. "You have your own life. You shouldn't waste time on an auld one like me."

"I'd never even have known you were sick if Tommy hadn't told me."

"Ye're still great pals, aren't ye?" She looked into my eyes searching as only she could. I blushed. "No need for false modesty." She laughed. "There's nothing in this world that would give me more pleasure than you two getting together. Now, get the tea brewed like a good girl, so we can relax."

"You and your tea."

"Not many pleasures left at my age."

The tray was all ready. I made the tea and carried it to the table. She lifted a cover off a plate of cold meats and salad.

"You shouldn't have gone to such trouble," I said when I saw all the food.

"I've already eaten. Get that into you now like a good girl. You must be starving."

"But I had something on the plane."

"This is real food, not plastic."

She winced as she tried to lift the heavy teapot. I took it out of her hand in case she'd drop it. "I must be getting old when I can't lift the old teapot. It's wonderful to see you again, Maggie. There's so much I need to.... but eat first, then we'll talk."

To please her, I buttered a roll and started to eat. I examined her out of the corner of my eye. The hand had crept up to her chest again. I couldn't believe how much she'd changed. Her skin was grey, almost transparent. Her skirt-band was doubled over and held by a safety pin. She seemed to have several layers inside the heavy cardigan. Her hair was thinner than I remembered too. Only her eyes were the same. She seemed a bit edgy, as if something was worrying her.

"I know what you're thinking," she said, suddenly. I looked up, shocked. She smiled at me. "You're thinking when will this auld one come to the point?"

I laughed. "I am not."

"Finish all that meat like a good girl." She pointed at my plate. "Otherwise it'll go in the bin."

I looked, dismayed, at the plate. "But there's far too much here for me."

"Eat it. I got it specially for you."

I had another slice to please her, then sat back. "I'm sorry. I really can't manage another morsel."

"You did your best." She smiled. "Stick a hot drop in that for me." She pushed her cup towards me. I topped both cups up then sat back and waited.

"There's something I should have told you a long time ago." Two pink spots had appeared in her cheeks. I waited for her to continue. "It's about... about your... your son," she whispered. I had to lean forward to catch the last word.

"My son?" He was the last person I'd expected her to talk about. "What did you want to tell me about him?"

She reached over and caught my hand. "Oh God, it's so hard to know where to begin."

"You shouldn't be worrying, Mrs. O. I've put all that behind me, long ago."

"He's... he's...oh God and His Blessed Mother help me." Her face had gone deathly pale. She looked frightened.

"What is it? What is it you're trying to tell me?" I was getting nervous now.

She turned and looked at me. "Maggie, your son could still be alive."

Whatever she was suffering from had obviously made her delirious. I gripped her hand tightly.

"I'll look after you Mrs O. Don't worry. Everything's going to be alright."

She pulled her hand away. "You don't understand, Maggie. Your son might still be alive," she gasped.

"But…"

"Please. Hear me out." She waited until her breathing became normal before continuing. "He didn't die that time in the hospital. The doctors expected him to, but after ten days in the coma your son woke up."

"Why wasn't I told?" My tone was harsher than I'd intended.

"You'd already been discharged. You were still very weak, but at least you were on the mend." Her voice trailed off dismally. "They told me, of course, but they warned me not to say anything to you, that the shock would only set you back. They said he wouldn't live anyway; he was so weak that he'd go back into another coma and …… I'm sorry." Her voice trailed off again into a whisper.

"He did go into another coma." She started to tremble. "This one lasted almost a month. They kept him alive on tubes and things. It was awful, Maggie, the worst time of my life." She looked at me, willing me to understand. "I was frightened to tell you. You were still weak but you were coping quite well. You were back at work. They said it would only upset you needlessly. Then you returned to Ireland."

"But I was his mother. I had a right to know."

"You'd already signed the adoption papers. Telling you would have only brought more heartache. And he was such a sickly little thing; they said it was only a matter of time. Oh Maggie, as God is my judge, I thought I was doing the right thing." Her voice dropped to a whisper. "Was I wrong?" She gripped my hand. "Was I, Maggie?" Her nails dug into my skin. "Should I have brought you back from Ireland and let you see him before giving him up?"

"And why are you telling me now?" I asked shakily.

"My doctor says I should get my affairs in order." She smiled crookedly. "Funny phrase, isn't it?"

My heart took a dive. "Why? What's the matter?"

"I'm dying." She smiled. "No need to look so shocked, darlin'. We all have to go some time."

"Oh God, I'm sorry." I held her hand. "I'm so sorry."

"Please, Maggie. Tell me you forgive me."

"Of course I do," I said, quickly. "You only did what you thought was best." I got up and went to the window. "When did he… when did he die?"

She shrank back, frightened by the question. "I don't know. I'm sorry, love. All I know is that he was taken away eventually. You'd signed all the necessary papers so they were free to… " She stopped. Her face changed colour and she fell back against the sofa. I ran to her and tapped her cheek.

"Are you alright?" There was no response. I lifted her legs up onto the cushion and ran to get a blanket. I tucked it in around her. There was still no move out of her. Her breathing sounded funny. Beside the phone was the book for phone numbers I'd bought her during my pregnancy. I remembered filling it in for her at the time. I found the doctor's number and dialled praying he'd be there.

"This is an emergency. I'm ringing for Mrs O'Connor, Tower Apartments." The words jumbled over themselves in my panic. "She's passed out. Can you come quickly, please?"

"On my way," the voice answered crisply. "Keep her warm and don't attempt to move her." The phone rang off.

Her face was now waxy white. Her breathing was shallow and so quiet I had to lean close to hear it. Poor thing. The strain of telling me had almost killed her. *Please God let her be alright.* I suddenly thought of Tommy and picked up the phone book again. Under T, there was a name and number in Tommy's handwriting. *'Michael Power, to be called only in emergencies.'* It was a London number. I dialled again. A curt male voice answered.

"Securities."

"Could I speak to Michael Power, please?"

"Nobody here of that name."

"This is an emergency," I said, trying not to scream. "I have to reach Tommy O'Connor. It's about his mother."

"Give me your name and number and I'll see what I can do."

"Tell him to ring Maggie at his mother's. It's urgent."

The doorbell rang. I slammed down the phone and ran to open it. Within seconds the doctor was leaning over her with a stethoscope.

"I was afraid of this. We have to get her into hospital at once." He looked at me. "You are?"

"Maggie Brown. I'm staying with her for the weekend. Thanks for coming so fast."

"I knew something like this would happen. I told her she should be in hospital, but she's a very independent lady." He smiled. "She's told me about you. You're a friend of Tommy's, aren't you?" I nodded. "He should be here. Can you get in touch with him?"

"I've already called and left a message."

"Good. I dread to think what might have happened if she was on her own, but she's stubborn. Wonder what caused it?" He looked around the flat. "Was she doing anything strenuous at the time?"

I nodded. "She was telling me about something that happened a long time ago, something she felt guilty about."

He shook his head. "I warned her that any kind of stress would trigger an attack. I wasn't happy with her living on her own in her condition." He sighed. "I wish my patients would listen to me sometimes."

"Will she be alright?"

"I can't be sure. Her son should be here, just in case. She has other children too, hasn't she?" I nodded.

"Should I try to contact them?"

He frowned. "Perhaps wait until you hear from Tommy. The less fuss there is the better. But her condition is serious. The ambulance shouldn't be too long. St. Thomas's is on emergencies tonight so at least she'll recognise her surroundings if… when she comes to."

"Is there anything I can do?" I asked looking around the apartment.

"You could put some things together for her."

"Of course." I went into her bedroom and packed a couple of nightdresses. The doorbell rang. This time it was the ambulance. In a matter of minutes they had her strapped to the stretcher with an oxygen mask over her face. I held her hand all the way, but there wasn't even the faintest flicker of response. When we arrived at the hospital, she was transferred onto a trolley and whisked away. Somebody brought me to a reception area where I gave them her details. I wondered whether Tommy had received the message. By some lucky fluke I still had her phone book in my pocket, so I rang Mary, his sister. There was only an Ansaphone reply, but I left a brief message for her to ring the hospital. There was nothing I could do then but sit and wait.

After what seemed an age, a nurse came up to me.

"Maggie?" I nodded. "She insists on seeing you, but you mustn't stay long."

"How is she?" I asked, as we hurried along the corridor.

The nurse shook her head. "Not good, I'm afraid. Has her son been informed?"

"Yes. He's on his way."

"Let's hope he makes it in time." She lifted a curtain to let me through. "Don't mind all the tubes," she whispered, as I walked past her. "She's not in any pain."

Mrs O was lying on the narrow bed, the mask still over her face. Her eyelids flickered as I came in.

"Maggie is that you?" Her voice was weak.

I leant over her and kissed her forehead. "Yes love, it's me." I took her hand, careful to avoid the drip. Her skin felt like parchment. The nurse pushed a chair under me. I pulled it as close to the bed as I could and sat down.

"I'm sorry, Maggie." Her fingers were twitching. I held them tightly to steady them. Her voice was desperately weak.

"And what would you have to be sorry about?" I said forcing a smile.

"For not telling you sooner." She struggled to raise her head. "Did I do wrong, Maggie? Please tell me."

"Of course not."

Her eyes darted anxiously over my face. Her fingers gripped mine in a vicelike grip. "I only did what I thought was best, love."

"Don't talk, Mrs O. Save your strength."

"He was sent to the nuns at the orphanage. That's all I know. But the hospital will have details. He probably didn't live for long, but who knows? I'm sorry, Maggie. Will you forgive me?" Her eyes fixed me with such intensity I could barely breath. I nodded. "Say it."

"Of course I forgive you, Mrs O."

Relief spread over her face. She slumped back against the pillow. Her fingers slid out of mine. She gave a little sigh and her eyelids closed. They flicked open again almost at once. "Take care of Tommy. He needs you." She waved my words of protest away with a weary flick of her hand. "He'll never admit it, of course. He's stubborn, independent…"

"I know." I smiled.

She returned the smile, lay back and closed her eyes. I was glad of a moment to think. Was it possible my son could still be alive? If the doctors got it wrong once they might have been wrong a second time. There was a movement outside the curtain. The doctor came in, ran his eyes over the machines and picked up her hand. He felt her pulse and frowned as he looked at the various monitors. He held a stethoscope to her chest, and then straightened up and nodded for me to follow him out of the cubicle.

"Her heart is very weak and she has almost no pulse."

"How long, Doctor? Her son is on his way."

"It could be a matter of hours, or she could last a few days." He put his hand on my arm. "Don't worry. She's not in any pain. The morphine will see to that. We have all her vital signs monitored, so you never know."

A nurse ran over. "Doctor?" He followed her into another cubicle.

I sat down again. *Please God, let Tommy get here in time.* It had always been as if she'd only the one child. His letters and cards were scattered all around the apartment. Little or no sign of the others, not even from Mary, the one who lived in London. Having children certainly didn't guarantee anything. But what was it all for then? I wondered. This woman had raised a number of children in spite of enormous hardship, and here she was dying on her own. It wasn't fair. *Please please let Tommy be in time* I prayed again, feverishly. I felt the touch of a hand on my head and looked up. She was awake. She was smiling. All anxiety gone from her face.

"Don't be sad, love. He's waiting for me. I can see him."

"Who?"

"Your Dad." Her eyes closed again, but the smile remained. Her mind was obviously going. She thought I was one of her daughters. "Don't forget to look after Tommy." The words were surprisingly strong. One of the machines bleeped. I looked at it. There was a red light. It went on bleeping. The curtain was pulled back and two nurses ran in. The doctor rushed in behind them. I stood outside and listened as the bleeping sounds continued. Voices called out words and numbers. Then a pause, followed by the sound of various machines being switched off. Then silence. The doctor walked out slowly.

"I'm sorry." He put his hand on my arm. "It was quicker than we thought in the end."

"But you said…"

"It's always difficult to tell with older people. Sometimes, they've finished their work and they're happy to go. The nurses are fixing her up now. You'll be able to see her then. I have to go I'm afraid."

After a few minutes, the two nurses emerged and nodded to me. She looked so relaxed when I went in, for a moment I thought there'd been a mistake. Her colour was normal. All the tension was gone from her face. She looked like she was asleep.

I leant down and kissed her. "Goodbye, Mrs O," I whispered. "Thank you for telling me about my baby." It had probably cost her her life. I was sorry she'd slipped away too quickly for Tommy to say goodbye. Perhaps she'd decided it was less painful this way. *May her soul be taken as quickly into Heaven.* If anyone deserved their reward, she did. She'd spent her life looking after others. Oh God, if only I'd known about the baby, if only she'd told me years ago……

There was a commotion outside. The curtains parted and a tall red-faced woman entered. She fell across the bed sobbing. The nurse beckoned me out.

"Her daughter, Mary. Any news of the son?"

I shook my head. "I'll try the number again."

I pulled the notebook out of my pocket and went to the phone. This time I asked for Tommy by name.

"Sorry, we can only get a message to him," the crisp voice responded.

"I've already left one. Can you at least tell me whether he's received it?"

"Hold on a minute." The line went dead. I stood watching the activity going on around me. It was ironic that it was St. Thomas'. I tried to remember what the place had looked like eighteen years ago. Nothing seemed familiar, but then it was a long time ago. Suppose by some miracle he was still alive? Suppose he's out there being raised by another woman…

"O'Connor got the message." The harsh tone interrupted my thoughts. "He's on his way."

"Do you have any details of his flights?"

"No, Ma'am." The line went dead. I went back to the cubicle and found Mary drinking tea.

"Would you like a cuppa?" The nurse smiled at me.

"Please." I nodded gratefully and sat down. "Tommy's on his way."

"That's nice of him," Mary said curtly.

"He'll be devastated not to have got here in time."

She looked me up and down."How would you know?"

"I'm sorry. I'll go." I got up and touched her mother's face. "Goodbye, Mrs O," I whispered, "say hello to Dad for me." I could have sworn I saw a smile on her lips as I straightened up. "I'm sorry for your loss," I said, taking Mary's limp hand.

I don't remember the taxi ride back to the Towers. I do remember going up in the lift. Her presence was everywhere, in the kitchen, the sitting room, especially the bedroom. I threw myself down on her bed and started to cry. Deep down, I knew I wasn't so much crying for her as for myself.

I must have fallen asleep, because the next thing I remember was Tommy's arms around me. My eyes filled up again.

"Don't, Mags. You'll start me off too." He held me for a minute then straightened up. "How was it? Did she suffer much?"

"No. It was very gentle. Her last words were of you." I smiled. "She asked me to look after you."

At that, his face crumpled. I'd never seen a man cry until that moment. Once he started he couldn't stop, as if he was making up for years of sadness locked away, which he'd never allowed himself to acknowledge. All I could do was hold him. We lay side by side on his mother's bed. I pulled the cover up over us. His sobs finally subsided, and we fell asleep.

CHAPTER 3

The phone rang harshly. I looked at my watch. It was after nine. The sun was streaming in through the window. Tommy was stretched across the bed, one arm hanging over the side, the other flung across me. I lifted his arm gently, and slid out to answer it. He'd need all the rest he could get to cope with the funeral. I ran to the sitting room and picked up the phone. "Hello" I whispered.

"Who's that?" Mary's harsh tones were unmistakable.

"Maggie. What can I do for you?"

"Tommy ran out of the hospital last night and hasn't been seen since. Do you know where he is?"

I couldn't help being amused at her phrasing. "He's not a child, Mary. He's here."

"With *you*?"

"Of course."

"Put him on please."

"I don't want to disturb him," I said firmly, "can I help?"

"It's a family matter."

"In that case I'll ask him to ring you when he wakes up."

"You'll do no such thing. Get him to the phone. We have to make arrangements."

"I've already said he'll ring you when he wakes up."

I flinched, as she slammed down the phone. I was replacing the receiver when Tommy walked into the room. He looked around, dazed.

"What time is it?"

"Time for you to have a shower and a shave while I make breakfast." I gave him a cheerful peck on the cheek. "Your skin feels like a yard brush. You're to ring Mary."

"Oh God." He ran his fingers through his hair. "I guessed 'twas the Witch."

I laughed. "Why d'you call her that?"

"Because she's always brewing up trouble for someone."

"Shower first then food, okay?" I said, pushing him towards the bathroom.

"Okay, boss." He grinned and gave a mock salute.

There were rashers and eggs in the fridge. She must have bought them in honour of my visit.

"That smells nice." His arms slid around me as I stirred the bacon on the pan. He gave me a peck on the back of the neck.

"The rashers or me?" I turned around, glad to see the greyness had disappeared from his face.

"Both" came the quick reply. His lips lingered on my skin.

"Sit." I waved him away with the splice. "We don't have time for diversions."

"Okay, boss." He pulled out a chair.

"Up to Air Force standards?" I asked, watching the food disappear.

"There's something you should know." He looked up guiltily, a forkful of egg poised in front of his mouth.

"What's that?" I picked up the teapot to give him a refill.

"I'm not in the Air Force any more." He put the fork into his mouth.

"What are you talking about? Of course you are."

"I was thrown out that time. Any chance of more toast?"

"Never mind the toast. What time?"

"When you lost the baby, remember? When I came home?" He spoke softly, as if frightened of reminding me.

"But that was years ago." I put down the teapot with a bump.

"They declared me AWOL even though I returned straight away."

"But that was an emergency. They can't do that."

"Believe me, Mags, they can. They can do anything they want."

I looked at him, shocked. "Oh God, Tommy. I know how much you loved the flying."

He shrugged. "I still get to fly sometimes, though it's mostly combat duty nowadays. Ah to hell with them. It's their loss."

Combat duty. So he was a mercenary. That explained all these mysterious absences around the world, all those times I'd blamed him for being secretive. "I'm so sorry. You lost a promising career because of me. Do you miss it?"

He shrugged. "Water under the bridge. Anyway you lost much more," he said softly. I suddenly remembered I still hadn't told him what his mother had said.

"He... he lived, you know. My son didn't die in those first few days, like I'd been told. That's what your mother was so anxious to tell me." The pain came back into his face at the mention of her. "The doctors said I shouldn't be told, that it would only make me ill again. They felt there was no point if he was to die eventually."

"And Mam knew all along?"

I nodded. "He probably died shortly afterwards anyway, but..."

"But Mags if he survived the first few weeks who's to say he didn't make it in the end?" His eyes gleamed. "He could still be alive."

I was glad it was he who'd said the actual words. It gave them more credence.

"Your mother said he was given to nuns in some orphanage. I'd signed all the papers anyway, so even if he did survive, they could go ahead with the adoption." I trailed away miserably. "So I suppose nothing has changed really. I'm back where I started."

Tommy reached out and took my hand. "No, no you're not. Everything has changed. Make enquiries. Start at St Thomas's."

I tried to pull my hand away. "I don't want to get my hopes up and…"

"I'd never have taken you for a coward, Mags. I'll help you all I can. If he's dead, we'll visit his grave and lay him to rest. If he's alive, we'll find out where he is." He tilted my chin up. "You have to know one way or another, don't you?" I nodded. "Was Mam very upset when she was telling you?"

I looked at him guiltily. "It was the strain of telling me that k… killed her."

"Rubbish." He leaned over and kissed me gently on the forehead. "Nothing you would say or do could hurt her."

"You weren't there. She pleaded for forgiveness, begged me to tell her she'd done the right thing. Oh God, Tommy all these years she's been worrying about it. The doctor even said it was the strain…"

"It's over now, Mags. You were more of a daughter to her than her own. Speaking of whom, I'd better ring Mary."

"Of course." I pulled away from him. "I'll have a quick shower and come with you if you like? Although she did make it very clear I wasn't family."

"Don't mind her. You're far more likely to know what kind of funeral Mam would have liked." The pain was back in his face again. He shook his head. "God, I can't believe we're talking about her funeral."

"I know, love. I know." I kissed him and went into the bathroom.

By the time I came out, the washing up was done and the flat looked less like a bombsite. He grinned at me. "If they get you young enough, the training never leaves you."

"How did you get on with Mary?"

He looked at me uneasily. "Do you mind if I go see her on my own?"

"Of course not." I looked around. "Is there anything I can do here?"

"I'd like you to have something of Mam's, so have a look around. Better decide now before the Witch takes over."

"Would you like me to tell Father Ryan?"

"Good idea. Ask him to pick out some of her favourite readings." He glanced at his watch again. "I said I'd be there in half an hour. Thanks Mags, and thanks for last night. I'd never have made it without you."

"You were always there for me, weren't you?" I smiled, and pushed him out the door.

The flat felt empty again. After I'd contacted Mrs O's priest, I made myself a fresh pot of tea. As long as I'd known her, she'd used the same teapot. She often said that the tea didn't taste the same in the new ones. I could almost feel her warm touch on the handle. I smiled. Now at least I knew what I wanted to take as a memento. Even the Witch couldn't object to my having the teapot. It would be like having a part of Mrs. O in my apartment. I still couldn't believe she was dead, that her funeral was being arranged at that very moment. I rang the office to tell them what had happened. There was no point in telling my mother. It would only lead to questions.

I was glad I'd been there for Tommy. His mother's death had brought us even closer. Sometimes it was as if we were two parts of one whole. I'd never felt anything remotely like that with any other man, probably never would. I got up from the couch wearily, and went over to the window. The problem was, that the longer I was with him the harder it was to find someone else who'd measure up. Perhaps I'd be better off to avoid him and keep some semblance of control over my life.

Avoiding personal relationships was one thing, but being cut off from my own flesh and blood was something else. Tommy was right. If my son was alive, I'd have to find him. I had a good job now, and a nice apartment. I no longer cared whether people approved. I could look after him, try to make up for the past. With my son by my side, I'd never be lonely again. Oops! Where had that word come from? I was independent. I didn't need people so how could I be lonely? I looked out at the city stretched below me and remembered something Auntie Nell had once said, about independent being just another word for lonely.

The phone rang. It was Tommy. The funeral would take place two days later. She'd be buried in a little cemetery on the outskirts of Richmond, where his father had been buried several years ago.

In the days that followed, Mary took every opportunity to isolate me. Anxious not to be the cause of further rift between herself and Tommy, I went off to the hospital to make some enquiries. The girl in the records section dug out the old files from the basement, but all she could tell me in the end was the name of the orphanage to which he had been sent.

"But surely you know whether he's still alive?" I asked.

She shook her head. "Once they leave here, that's it, I'm afraid. Unless of course they return as patients."

The orphanage was called St Dominic's, with an address in the suburbs.

When I got out there, I was told by a passer-by that it had been closed down years ago.

"Do you know where they might have moved to?"

"No, but somebody in the Post Office might." She pointed across the road.

I thanked her, and went over. There were three assistants behind the counter, two young ones, and an elderly lady with glasses halfway down her nose. There were queues in front of all three. I joined the one in front of the old lady, even though it seemed to be moving more slowly than the others. There'd be no point in asking the younger ones. We shuffled forward until I finally came to the hatch.

"Glory be, imagine anyone remembering St. Dominic's?" She looked at me quizzically over her glasses. "Are you Irish by any chance?" I nodded. "I thought so, from your accent. And what part of the country would you be from?"

"Dublin."

Someone coughed behind me.

"Are you sure you're not from down South?" She looked hard at me. "I'm from Tipperary myself."

"Really? That's very interesting but… "

"Yes. Left there as a little girl many years ago." Her eyes took on a dreamy look.

"Excuse me." A crisp English voice cut in over my shoulder. "There are people waiting."

I turned, apologetically. "I'm terribly sorry, but…"

"Did you say something, Madam?" The Post Office lady's eyes had lost their dreaminess.

"Sorry. I just wondered if you could get on with the … er … business."

"You can either wait or join another queue, Madam. Your choice. It's a free country." The complainant closed her mouth at once. "Now where were we, dear? Oh yes, you were telling me where you were from?"

"Wexford originally."

She smiled triumphantly. "There, you see? I was right. My mother, God rest her, always used to say I had a good ear."

"You were telling me about St. Dominic's?" I prompted. The shuffling behind me was getting louder.

"Ah yes. And what business would you have with the nuns, dear?"

"I… I just want to know where they've gone to," I said, sidestepping the question.

"Most of them died. They were very old, you know. Even older than me." She smiled.

"All of them?" I was shocked. Was my search over before it had even begun?

"Well, perhaps one or two transferred to the Mother House."

"Where's that?"

A few people coughed impatiently.

"Quiet please back there." She rapped her pencil sharply against the railings. "Where was I, dear?"

"You were about to tell me where the Mother House is?" I said, glancing nervously over my shoulder.

"Ealing, I think."

"Thanks very much for your help. I... er...don't suppose you remember any of their names?" I looked at her in desperation.

"Indeed I do, m'dear. Sister Gertrude was teaching when I was there. She taught Latin. Nobody learns Latin nowadays." She sighed. "A great shame too. Maybe that's why people have lost the art of writing. Illiteracy rules supreme nowadays, doesn't it? Or should I say supremely?" she added with a girlish giggle.

Judging by the murmurs behind, the queue was ready to riot. She gazed over her glasses at them. Her voice rose sharply. "If there's another sound back there, I'll close this hatch." There was instant silence. She turned back to me. "Now what was I saying, dear? Oh, yes. Most young people are illiterate nowadays, don't you agree?" I mumbled something noncommittal. "Is there anything else I can help you with at all?"

I shook my head. "No, thank you. I'm very grateful."

"You're welcome, my dear. It's always a pleasure to meet someone from home. NEXT PLEASE." The queue shuffled quickly up to fill the gap I vacated.

I kept my eyes fixed on the floor as I moved quickly towards the exit.

"WHEN YOU SEE SISTER GERTRUDE TELL HER VERONICA MULDOON WAS ASKING FOR HER, WON'T YOU, DEAR?" Her voice boomed like a megaphone across the crowded Post Office. Several pairs of eyes glared at me as I slunk out the door.

CHAPTER 4

Next morning I stood by the graveside at Tommy's side. He maintained his control to the end. As we were leaving, he looked back.

"Too many here today. I'll come back tomorrow, say goodbye properly."

The next day we stood there looking down at the newly filled-in grave. I held his hand, wishing I could ease his pain. A bird squawked loudly as it swooped down close to us. "Your mother's at peace now. Maybe that's her soul breaking free." I pointed up, smiling, as I remembered the same thing had happened at Dad's grave. It seemed so long ago now. Another time, another place. We walked slowly out of the graveyard. This time, he didn't look back.

Later, I left him and Mary sorting their mother's things and hailed a taxi outside the apartment.

"The Dominicans in Ealing," I told the driver and sat in.

"Going back inside, eh?" Cockney eyes grinned into the mirror at me.

I smiled back. "D'you know the place?"

"Sure do. Fine buildin'. The banks are tryin' to buy it. Those nuns are sittin' on a bleedin' fortune."

I was glad to hear that the place still existed, but I was trying not to build up too much hope. After all, the nuns from St. Dominic's could be dead now. The records might have been destroyed in the move.

"'Ere y'are then, miss." Cheerful tones interrupted my thoughts. The driver pointed to a tall granite building. "'uge, idn't it?"

I nodded and reached for my bag.

I walked up the steps and rang the doorbell. I could hear it echoing. There was a long pause. Nothing happened, so I rang again. This time I heard footsteps. The door swung heavily open. A nun stood there, dwarfed in the massive archway.

"I'm looking for Sister Gertrude, please. She used to work in St. Dominic's?"

"I'm sorry. She's not allowed visitors." She looked at my crestfallen face. "Step inside out of the breeze, dear. Could someone else not help?" She drew me into a marble-tiled hallway and closed the door.

"Not unless they used to work in the orphanage?"

"Oh, I think they've all gone to the Lord at this stage. Let me see now." She frowned as she tried to remember. "Oh yes, there was another nun, a younger one who transferred with her, Sister Monica. I wonder what happened to her?"

A tall nun hurried by us. Her skirts made a swishing sound along the floor. "'Morning Concepta," she called out cheerily.

"'Morning Bonaventure," the tiny nun answered automatically. "Oh, wait. Bonaventure might know."

"Bonaventure might know what?" The other nun spun around.

"This young lady is enquiring about the sisters who worked in Railway Street. She'd like to speak to Sister Monica."

"You're too late, my dear." She smiled at me. "She died in the Congo last year."

"She wanted to see Sister Gertrude, but I've told her she's too sick. How is she this morning?"

"Quite lucid, actually. Is it very important?"

I nodded emphatically. "I'm flying home to Dublin tonight. I'd be very grateful if I could see her, even for a few minutes?"

"Dublin, I thought so." The tall nun smiled, and turned to the other. "I think we can make an exception for a fellow Irish woman, Concepta."

"Thanks." I breathed a sigh of relief.

"Come follow me, as the Good Lord said," she chuckled as she swept up the marble staircase. I followed her. At one stage I made the mistake of looking up to admire the domed roof and nearly lost my footing. I could see what the taxi driver had been talking about.

"Is it true the bank wants to buy it?"

"Yes, but they'll have to put their money where their mouth is." Sister Bonaventure turned back and smiled archly at me. "We're well aware of the value of the property."

We were at the top of the staircase now. She moved quickly along a wide corridor, which narrowed at the end. Then we entered a side wing, which was permeated by antiseptic smells. Several doors opened off the corridor. Sister Bonaventure stopped and tapped on one of them before pushing it open.

"It's me again, Gertrude. I've brought you a visitor from Ireland."

A frail figure lay in the bed. She smiled as we entered and tried to lift her head. Sister Bonaventure put a second pillow behind her back.

"Who have I?" Tiny bright eyes looked at me from a waxen face.

"My name is Maggie Brown," I said, taking the seat Sister Bonaventure pushed towards me. "I'm hoping you can help me."

"A good Irish name," she whispered. "What part do you come from?"

"Wexford."

"I know it well."

"I need your help, Sister. I'm looking for my son. He was in your orphanage years ago."

She looked at me. "And what was his name, my dear?"

"I'm sorry. All I can tell you is he was born in St. Thomas' in July 1964. Nobody expected him to live. Up to recently I thought he had died." I swallowed. "Everybody expected him to, you see, but…"

"And you don't have his name?"

"No. I'm sorry." I stood up. "I shouldn't have bothered you. But I had to try…"

"Wait." Thin fingers clutched at my arm. "I wonder could it be little Johnny?"

I gulped. "John was my father's name."

"We were told to call him that." Her eyes had a faraway look. "He was an awfully weak little thing when they brought him in. Nobody expected him to make it."

I sat down quickly. "And did he?" I held my breath.

"We looked after the poor little mite for days. We almost lost him at one stage…" She lay back exhausted. Her eyelids fluttered and closed.

Sister Bonaventure touched my arm. "Sorry, dear. She's very weak. She needs to rest."

"One minute more, please?" I begged. She nodded reluctantly.

"Sister Gertrude?" I called gently. Her eyes fluttered open. "Did he live?"

"Oh yes," she sighed heavily, "though perhaps better if he hadn't."

"What does he look like?"

"Long legs, blue eyes." She smiled. "I particularly remember the eyes."

"Who adopted him? Where is he now?"

She shook her head. The smile faded. "I'm sorry. We failed the poor boy. Nobody would take him, you see. He was such a difficult child. Got worse as he got older. Everyone who had anything to do with him despaired of him." The feverish fingers plucked at the bedspread. "He kept running away. He'd be found, brought back, and in a few days, he'd be gone again." She sank back onto the bed.

"But you must have some idea where he is?"

She shook her head. "At nine he ran away and was never found again. Johnny was our one failure. That's why I remember him. All the others we found homes for, but we failed him, poor child." She gave a weary sigh and closed her eyes. "We failed him."

Sister Bonaventure tapped me on the shoulder. "Please. You can see how weak she is."

I stood up dazed. We left the room and walked back down the corridor. Halfway down, I stopped dead in my tracks. "My son's alive," I said, looking up at her. "I've been given a second chance."

"God does that sometimes," she replied with a gentle smile.

"I'll give you my name and address. She might remember something later that would help me find him." I took a card from my bag and handed it to her. She lifted up one of her many layers of skirt and tucked the card away into one of the hidden pockets. I couldn't help smiling. The last time I'd seen that gesture was in St Mary's.

We walked downstairs. "Try not to get your hopes up too much," she said. "There are hundreds of young people living rough in London."

"But at least now I know he survived."

"Yes, thank God. It's a miracle she remembered him."

He'd broken their hearts. That's why she'd remembered him. After the thrill of discovering he was alive, I was depressed again. What did I really know? Long legs, blue eyes, half a name. Not much to go on.

At the door she sprinkled me with Holy Water from a font on the wall. "God works in strange ways, my dear. I hope you find peace."

"If she remembers anything else, you will get in touch?" I pleaded. "There's nowhere else I can turn."

"There's always Himself, my dear." She pointed upwards.

The door closed with a dull thud. The roar of the city assaulted my senses after the peace of the convent. Everybody seemed to be in such a hurry. I walked slowly along the pavement, trying to come to terms with what I'd learned.

Tommy and I clung to each other that night. We knew we mightn't meet again for a long time. Part of me was glad he was leaving. I needed time to think. Nothing was going to stop me finding out what had happened to my son. I'd hire a detective agency if necessary. I didn't care what it would cost.

Back in my apartment in Dublin next evening, I was unwrapping the teapot when the phone rang.

"Thank God." Ma sighed with relief when I picked it up. "You said you were only going for the weekend. What happened?"

"Something came up, Ma. Sorry."

"Doesn't matter now you're alright. How did you get on at the Richmond address?"

"Sorry, I didn't have time."

"You sound tired, love." Her mother's antennae were up in an instant. "When are you coming home?"

"For God's sake, Ma. I'm only in the door."

"You'll be down soon?"

"I will." I yawned. "I'll get someone to check up on that Richmond address."

"Thanks, love. Go to bed early. You need your sleep."

"Yes, Ma." I put the phone down.

There was a message on the Ansaphone. I pressed the playback button and heard Richard's careful tones. *"Still not home? Give me a ring when you get in and let me know you're alright."* I couldn't cope with him tonight. I'd ring him tomorrow in the office. That way neither of us would have time to talk. I dropped a quick note about the Richmond account to Tommy, care of Mary's address. Hopefully, he'd get the message.

As I lay in bed, trying to sleep, visions of Jonathan kept floating into my mind. My son must have Jonathan's blue eyes. What else did he inherit, I wondered, as I tossed and turned. With my son alive, I had something to look forward to, now, someone to plan for. It would make a change from just looking after myself. Tommy would always be a free spirit. It was high time I accepted that. If only he was different. I sighed. If only I hadn't given the baby away. If only I hadn't been so worried about bringing shame on the family. If only. If only. I punched the pillow savagely. Tomorrow I'd hire a detective agency. Too much time had been wasted already.

CHAPTER 5

In the weeks that followed, I put the matter into the hands of the best detective agency I could find in London. Work kept me busy. It was several weeks before I heard from Tommy again.

"I've news for you, Mags, but you're not going to like it," he warned.

"What is it?"

"Remember that Richmond person you asked me to check on?"

"Fashion Consulting Services?"

"Yes. Are you sitting down?"

I laughed. "Don't be so melodramatic."

"D'you know who lives there?"

"If I knew I wouldn't have asked you to find out, would I?"

"Jonathan's wife."

"Talk sense, Tommy. Anna's his wife."

"This Barrett woman is too, I'm afraid. Barrett was her single name. He was married to her long before he met Anna. They lived together in Richmond at that address."

"You're joking." I waited for him to laugh, but there was silence at the other end.

"Afraid not, Mags. When they split up, he came over to Ireland. The wife had a good job apparently, so she was able to look after herself. No divorce. In fact, she was just glad to see the back of him. But a couple of years ago the firm she was working for went bust. She hasn't been able to find a job since, so she claimed maintenance from our friend. Which explains the monthly cheques into the account from the shop."

"He's a bigamist!"

"Yes," replied Tommy, "and there's more."

"Oh God, how much more could there be?"

"He's a gambler. Has a real problem, I'm afraid. He owes money all over the city, according to my friend in MI5."

"MI5?" I laughed crazily. This was taking on all the dimensions of a farce.

"Yes," Tommy answered firmly. "In fact they'd be very interested in knowing his present whereabouts."

"You haven't told them," I gasped. "You can't, Tommy. You can't."

"Relax, of course I haven't," he said calmly. "I'm only telling you so we can decide what's the best thing to do. His file hasn't been active for years.

They think he's on the continent. That's why it took so long to find out about him."

"Oh God. This could wreck Anna's life. Kilmanogue's so small. They have the children to consider."

"Whatever we decide, we'll do it together, okay? Don't attempt to see him on your own."

"Don't be ridiculous, Tommy. This is Jonathan you're talking about, not some master criminal."

"I'm serious Mags. You don't know the company he keeps."

"Okay, okay. I'll be careful."

His tone softened. "I'm sorry to be the bearer of bad news."

"That's alright. How are you coping yourself?"

"Not great." He sighed. "Can't believe she's gone. I sometimes find myself dialling her number, then I remember."

"And she's probably thinking what an eejit she reared." I laughed. "But don't worry, love. She's a mother. A little thing like being dead's not going to stop her looking after her favourite son."

"I suppose not," he chuckled. "Speaking of sons, did you find anything out about yours?"

"No. The Agency rang last week, but they haven't found anything yet. Where are you, so we can discuss this Jonathan business?"

"London. I'll ring you tomorrow when you've had time to think. I have to go now. Bye, Mags." With that the line went dead. Still the same old Tommy, I thought, replacing the receiver.

I'd read about people living two lives. Usually in England, or some other country. But here in Ireland it seemed hard to believe. And in a small town like Kilmanogue, where everybody knew everybody, where you had to live for twenty years before you could shake off the title of blow-in, it was even harder. What would Auntie Nell say, and what about poor old Anna? If the truth came out, it would destroy them both. I thought about it all morning. Did they have to be told? What if I confronted him, did a deal with him? No more gambling, no more running up debts, no more payments to the Barrett woman in exchange for my silence. Bigamy and embezzlement were criminal offences. Jonathan liked the good life. He wouldn't want to go to jail. This way, Anna and the family could still hold their heads up in Kilmanogue.

The more I thought about it, the more sense it made, but when I put my plan to Tommy next day, he wasn't happy. He did everything he could to change my mind, but finally he gave in. "I'm coming over to Dublin for a few days anyway, so at least I'll be on hand."

I laughed. "Always there when I need you, aren't you, me auld pal?" There was an uneasy silence.

"Be careful, Mags. He's a nasty piece of work."

"I will," I promised, and put down the phone.

There was no point in putting it off, so I rang Jonathan that evening.

"To what do I owe the pleasure?" he asked, sarcastically.

"There's something we need to discuss."

"Sounds mysterious. When will you be down?"

"I'd prefer see you up here, if you don't mind. What I have to say is better kept between us."

"Oh. It's like that, is it?" he said with a snigger.

"What about tomorrow night, around seven? That'll give you time to return home."

"You mean I won't be staying?" he asked silkily.

"Don't be ridiculous. You know my address, I presume?"

"The famous apartment? Of course."

"See you here at seven, then."

"I'll bring a bottle."

"It's not a social visit," I snapped and slammed down the phone.

The next evening, I went over my speech carefully. I was nervous, but I knew the element of surprise would be to my advantage. He arrived on the dot, strolled into the apartment.

"So this is where the lady executive does her entertaining?" he smirked, looking around.

"Sit down," I said curtly. "Information has come into my hands…"

"Information?" His head shot up. At least I'd wiped the smirk off his face.

"About you and a certain woman in Richmond."

He gasped. "I don't know what you're talking about."

"Your wife, that's who I'm talking about, Jonathan, your real wife." He shifted uneasily in the chair. "Well? Anything to say?"

"You haven't a clue, have you?" He leaned back in the chair with a sneer.

"I know all I need to know."

"Rubbish. You're just bluffing."

"I know about the gambling debts too." He sat up straight. The blood drained from his face. "I'm sure the English police would be interested in your whereabouts."

"Police? Don't talk nonsense."

I knew I'd hit the mark, so I continued. "You've been sending her money, money you stole from our company."

He got up and came towards me. "You think you're clever, don't you?"

I stepped back. "I'm prepared to offer you a deal."

He stopped in his tracks. "What sort of deal?"

"I'll keep silent about your unsavoury past on certain conditions."

His eyes narrowed. "And why would you want to do that?"

"To protect my family, my sister and the children."

"I see," he sneered, "the small town syndrome, the shame and all that."

Waves of anger flooded over me. "It's your call," I said coldly. "Break off connections with that woman in Richmond, stop your gambling and thieving or else…."

He started towards me again, his fist clenched. "Or else what?"

I backed away.

"Or else, I'll go straight to the police and tell them what I know." I was up against the window ledge now. "You'll get prison for the bigamy alone, apart altogether from the gambling debts."

"What conditions?" His eyes were narrow slits.

"You'll give me back the cheque book. From now on all cheques will be signed by either my mother, Auntie Nell or me…"

"I thought you said you weren't going to tell them."

"I won't. I'll say that my new position of internal auditor means that I have to keep a closer eye on payments."

A bus passed by. He stared out the window. "And you won't tell Anna…?"

"No. Not if you behave yourself."

He stood thinking for a couple of minutes. I started to relax. The plan was working.

"If you think I'm going to let a little bitch like you dictate…" He moved so fast that all I saw was a glimpse of hatred in the blue eyes before his fist connected with my forehead. My head exploded with light and I keeled backwards into oblivion.

When I came to, I was slumped against the wall, my head supported by the windowsill. I put my hand up and felt something warm and sticky. I lay there for a few minutes, trying to find the energy to move. Then I picked myself up and went to the bathroom. As I bent over it, the basin turned red. Frightened, I dabbed at the wound with a face cloth. The phone rang. I staggered over. It was Tommy.

"How did it go?" he asked, eagerly.

"Not … not too well."

"What's wrong?" I didn't reply. "Mags, what is it? Talk to me."

"You were right. We should have seen him together."

"I'll kill that bastard," he shouted. "Don't move. I'm on my way."

I flinched, as the phone was banged down.

He was at the door in fifteen minutes. I was still holding the facecloth to my head. "I knew I shouldn't have let you tackle him alone." He rushed in. "If he's hurt you… I'll…I'll… "

"Calm down, Tommy. It's not as bad as it looks."

"Let me be the judge of that." He sat me down and removed the cloth. "You need an ice pack." He ran to the fridge and was back a few minutes later with a tea towel packed with ice cubes. "Lie down and hold that to your forehead."

"Yes boss." I winced as the cold pack touched my skin.

"It's Casualty for you."

"Don't fuss. He didn't hit me very hard. I must have fallen against something."

"Anything broken?" I shook my head, wincing at the pain the movement caused. "Did you get him to admit anything?"

"Oh yes. He's guilty alright, guilty as sin."

"Did he make any promises?"

"No. I'm sorry Tommy. I should have listened to you." He jumped up and ran to the door. "Where are you off to now?" I called after him.

"Lie down and don't move. I'll be back soon."

The door slammed behind him. There was nothing for it only to do what I was told.

A couple of hours later he was back. His face was white with tension. "It's sorted."

I'd never seen that expression on his face before. It frightened me.

"Tommy what have you done?"

"You don't need to know."

"How did you sort it?"

"I caught up with his car on the dual carriageway."

"The Wexford road?"

"Yep," he grinned. "I knew the bastard would run for home, try to give himself an alibi."

"It's a wonder he stopped for you."

He laughed harshly. "He didn't have a choice."

I looked at him, shocked. "What did you do, run him off the road?"

"More or less." He started to pace the floor. "He and I had a long talk."

"Sit down before you combust. I'll make tea."

"Forget your tea. I'll have whiskey. Don't move. I'll get it myself. How's the head?"

"Better," I replied, sinking back gratefully as he fixed the drinks. "Okay, cowboy," I smiled and accepted a glass of whiskey from him. "Tell me exactly what happened."

"Never mind. He has no option now but to cooperate." He drained the glass in one gulp and helped himself to another. "He won't be bothering you again, Mags. Take it from me."

I was having difficulty holding the glass steady but I managed to swallow something. The whiskey burnt its way down my throat. "All he has to do is wait 'til you go back, then he can come after me again."

"Don't worry," he said calmly. "He'll behave himself from now on. Oh, and by the way," he put his hand into his pocket, "he gave me this for you." He handed me a chequebook with the shop's name on it. As I took it, I started to shiver again. Tommy gripped me by the shoulders. "Maggie, look at me." I looked up obediently. "He won't touch you again. Believe me. He knows he's a dead man if he does. Finish that, and I'll give you a refill."

I raised the glass to my lips obediently, but I couldn't blot out the vision of those hate-filled eyes just before Jonathan had struck me. "Can you stay?"

"Try and stop me," he said with a smile.

But neither of us was in a funny mood. We didn't talk much that night. The shivering returned when I went to bed. Despite the warmth of Tommy's arms, I never closed an eye.

Long after he'd fallen asleep I lay awake, reliving what had happened, and worrying about what Jonathan would do when Tommy went away again. Beside me Tommy slept soundly. I shifted closer trying to draw on some of his strength. His breath felt warm and comforting against my skin, but every time I started to drift into sleep, I saw again the cold blue eyes and the raised fist.

Tommy had to leave early to catch his flight.

"You look awful," he said, frowning at me over the breakfast.

"Thanks a lot," I replied, disappointed the makeup hadn't done a better job of concealing the bruises.

"You're not to worry about Jonathan, Mags. The bastard's not worth it. He has a cushy number here in Ireland and he knows it. I made it quite clear what I'll do to him if he bothers you again."

"The only problem is that you won't be here, and he knows that."

"He also knows that if he steps out of line, I'll get him, and next time it'll be for keeps." He looked at his watch. "Damn, I have to go." He jumped up from the table and threw on his jacket. He looked around the room and grabbed a pen from beside the telephone. "Look, if there's an emergency, ring this number and ask for Mick, okay?"

"Thanks," I said dryly.

"Remember, I'm only a flight away."

"Only a flight away. That'll be a great help when he breaks down my door in the middle of the night." I looked at the hurt on his face and ran to him. "I'm sorry, love. I shouldn't be such a wimp."

"If anything happened to you, Mags, I'd never forgive myself." He looked into my eyes. "You're everything in the world to me. You know that."

"Yeah, yeah, go on. You'll miss your flight." I pushed him towards the door.

He was suddenly reluctant to go. "Will you be alright?"

"I'll be fine," I said, trying to sound confident. "The lack of sleep has me jittery, that's all. Go on. Get out of here."

He was still hesitating. "Mags, some day you and I have to settle this once and for all."

"Settle what?"

"Us."

"Us?"

"Yeah, us."

With that he turned and left. I closed the door behind him, turned the key in the lock and slid the bolt across. I looked across at the window. Two flights up. High time I got security locks there too.

All through the day, I felt as if I was working in a dream. In the afternoon I made a quick call to Kilmanogue, and broached the subject of cheque-writing procedures.

"Oh yes," Ma replied, "Jonathan told me about those." Ah so he'd got the message after all. "According to the new regulations apparently, there has to be a couple of signatures on each cheque."

"You know what auditors are like Ma," I said, introducing a bored tone into my voice. "I'll put a few details on paper and send them down."

"Will we not see you at the weekend?"

I caught sight of my bruises in the mirror. "No, sorry."

"Better things to do, I suppose?"

"Something like that. I'll be down next weekend instead."

"Okay, love."

When Tommy rang that night I told him about the phone call. He was jubilant. "I told you he'd behave himself from now on, Mags, didn't I? How's the forehead?"

"I look like I've done fifteen rounds in the ring."

"That will never happen again." His voice was cold.

"I told them in the office my boyfriend beats me up."

"It's not funny, Mags."

"I know." I sobered up instantly. "But I feel better since I talked to Ma. I'll have to go home next weekend. I just hope he won't..."

"He'll make himself scarce. Don't worry. He won't have the nerve to face you."

"I hope you're right," I said fervently.

By the following weekend, all that remained of the bruising was a yellow tinge, which was easily disguised by makeup. Despite Tommy's reassurances, my heart was thumping as I parked the car in front of the house. When I went in there was no sign of Jonathan.

"Away on business," Anna said, when I enquired after him. "Had to go to London for a couple of days. He's staying the weekend as well. There's some match on."

"What sort of business?" I asked.

"Don't know," she said, vaguely. "He looks after the sales side of things. Is that a new suit?"

"Never mind the suit. Who does he report to when he comes back from these trips?"

"Report?" She looked at me puzzled.

"Yes." I was beginning to realise how easy it was for him to lead a double life. "Who decides what trips are necessary?"

She shrugged. "Auntie Nell I suppose. D'you think that colour would suit me?"

"Of course it would." I sighed in exasperation. "Every colour suits you."

Later, at dinner, I put the same question to Auntie Nell. I didn't get very far with her either. "He's his own boss, dear. We give him a free hand. He makes a lot of contacts for us."

"What sort of contacts?"

"New suppliers for the most part. He brings back lots of brochures. Although..." she hesitated. "I'm not sure if we've actually ordered from any of them. They're usually a bit out of our league."

"Why do we keep sending him then?" I asked, looking across the table at Ma.

"He says we have to keep our eyes on new trends. London leads the fashion world, so I suppose it makes sense."

"We have done business with some of them." Auntie Nell turned to Ma. "What was the name of that consulting place who did work for us a few years ago?"

"Consulting Services," I said, without thinking.

"That's the one. How clever of you, Mags." Auntie Nell smiled. "Jonathan said they gave him lots of advice, advice we'd never get in Ireland. They were very expensive, so he arranged for us to pay them off a little at a time. A special arrangement, just for us apparently," she said, proudly.

"Do we have to talk about business at the table?" Anna interrupted crossly. "It's so boring."

"Are we still paying them, Auntie Nell?" I held my breath.

"No. He told me last week we're finished now," she answered. "Anyone for more sprouts?"

Young Emily was pushing her food around the plate with her fork. The fork was making a scratching noise. "Mind your manners, Emily." Anna slapped her daughter on the wrist. "Finish what's on your plate or you won't get any pudding."

Emily pulled a face at me. I winked back at her.

"Why all the questions, Maggie?" Ma looked at me, puzzled.

"As your internal auditor," I said helping myself to sprouts, "I'm supposed to ask questions."

"We're lucky to have such talented children. Aren't we Nell?"

Nell beamed and nodded. Anna scowled and grabbed the dish from my hand.

"Leave some of those for other people."

"I didn't know you liked sprouts, Anna." I grinned at her. "Here let me help you." I pushed what was left onto her plate.

"I'll get the pudding," Ma said, picking up her plate. "Nell, as it's your creation, will you help me dish it out?"

"Certainly." Nell jumped up and followed her out to the kitchen.

Emily grinned a toothless grin across the table at me. "Wait 'til you thee what we have for pudding, Auntie Maggie. Ith yummy."

"Who'th Auntie Maggie?" I made a horrible face at her.

She giggled. "What elth can I call you?"

"You can call me anything you like as long as you don't call me early in the morning." I lunged across the table and tickled her. She yelped. "Now tell me about thith yummy pudding." I caught one of her runaway blonde curls and flicked it back from her eyes. "Ith it really yummy, little Emmy? Did you help bake it?"

"Don't call her Emmy," Anna said crossly, "Emily is her name."

Emily looked at her mother, and then back at me. "Yeth, I licked the bowl." She nodded emphatically, causing her curls to fall back over her eyes again.

"Wath that very hard work?" I asked solemnly.

"Yeth, but I didn't mind."

"That'th 'coth you're a good girl, ithn't it?" I lunged at her again. She dissolved into a fit of giggles.

"Jonathan's not going to like it when he hears about all these questions," Anna said. My blood froze.

"You won't tell him, will you?" I looked at her. "Please Anna. It's very important."

"What's wrong?" She looked at me curiously. "You've gone a funny colour."

"Please, Anna. Don't tell him I was asking questions."

"Why? It's only because of this auditor business, isn't it?"

"Yes but he might be a bit sensitive," I said in desperation. "Men don't like women doing those kind of jobs."

"I suppose not." She nodded, apparently satisfied with my answer.

"Men and their egos, eh?" I grinned at her, but she gave me a funny look.

She was about to say something when Nell walked in, carrying a dish of baked Alaska. She laid it down on the table with a flourish.

"This isn't going to do much for my waistline," I said, winking at Emily.

"You're far too thin anyway," Ma declared, brandishing the carving knife. "Now who's for pudding?"

John shot both his hands up into the air. "Me, me."

"Me too," Emily chorused, raising both podgy arms up trying to reach as high as his.

"Me three and four," I said, holding both my arms up too.

"You look thilly," Emily giggled, her golden curls bobbing up and down in time with the giggles. "Doethn't thee, Mummy?"

Anna nodded and smiled. I was relieved. Jonathan seemed to have been forgotten for the moment.

Tommy rang late Sunday night to see how the weekend had gone. He was delighted when I told him about the payments being finished.

"Any word from the Agency about your son?" he asked.

"No. I rang them again on Friday. I think they're fed up hearing from me."

"Don't give up, Mags, not yet," There was some interference on the line. "Sorry, I'm between flights. Have to go."

"So what else is new?"

"Talk to you soon. Take care."

"You too." But the line was already dead. I banged down the receiver. One minute he was so close. Next minute he was on the other side of the bloody world.

I was in bed and almost asleep when the phone rang again. I picked it up;

pleased he'd rung me back. "Okay dopey, what did you forget?" Silence at the other end. "Tommy?" More silence. Then I heard the breathing and knew at once who it was. "Jonathan, is that you?"

"If you ever again ask questions about me I'll finish what I started. Is that clear?" His voice was deep, soft, intimate. It sounded like it was almost inside my head. "Answer me, bitch."

"How dare you ring and threaten me…"

"IS THAT CLEAR?"

"I'm calling Tommy. You can't just…"

"SHUT UP AND LISTEN. I'm just across the street. I can be over there and gone long before that stupid boyfriend of yours." I gasped in horror. I'd assumed he was ringing from Kilmanogue. "Now, do I have your attention?"

"Yes," I mumbled.

"Any more interfering I'll come visiting and next time I won't be so gentle. Even your precious boyfriend won't recognise you by the time I'm finished. Do you understand what I'm saying?"

"Yes." By now I was shaking so much I could barely hold the phone.

"All you have to do is butt out of my life and you won't get hurt. Keep interfering and you'll be sorry. Got that?"

"Yes, yes," I whispered hoarsely. The line went dead. I tried to put the receiver back but I was shaking so much it fell on the floor. My heart was thumping, my nightdress soaked with perspiration. God blast you, Tommy. Where are you now when I need you? I lay there for several minutes waiting for my pulse to return to normal. Then I got up took two sleeping pills and washed them down with a glass of whiskey.

But they didn't work. I kept the lights on for the rest of the night. I passed the time making lists of things I had to do. Get a burglar alarm fitted. More bolts on the windows. A mortise lock on the front door. Ask the Management Committee to put security cameras up outside. Every time my mind went back to the phone call, I forced myself back to the list. At about five, my eyes were burning with exhaustion. I decided to try and sleep for a few hours. I covered my head with the pillow and settled down. I was being chased along a road by Jonathan. He was driving a big truck. As he came up beside me he turned the wheel of the truck sharply into my car. I tried to pull away but the truck came in on top of me. I could feel the weight of it pushing me across the seat.

Something buzzed in my ear. The alarm clock. I opened tired eyes to the world, as reality came flooding back. I dragged myself out of bed and stumbled to the phone. I dialled the number Tommy had given me. An English voice answered.

"Emergency call for Tommy O'Connor," I said, trying to keep my voice from shaking.

"Message?"

"Tell him to ring Maggie as soon as possible."

"Right." The phone went dead. I staggered into the shower. Perhaps work would help.

It was almost noon when I heard from him. The connection was bad. "What's wrong, Mags?" His voice sounded far away.

"Jonathan rang."

"Did he hurt you?"

"No, but he said he'd come and get me if I asked any more questions at home."

"Ignore him. It's just bluster."

"That's easy for you to say," I retorted. "You're not the one lying in bed, waiting to be attacked."

"He's just trying to frighten you, Mags. He's a coward. I know the sort, all bark and no bollocks."

"It's not funny." My voice started to shake. "You weren't there. You didn't hear him."

"Stop panicking, Mags," he said, speaking slowly as to a child. "All you have to do is get extra bolts on the door. Lock up properly and take the phone off the hook when you go to bed. He can't hurt you if he can't get to you."

"No but... "

"Trust me."

"But..."

"Have I ever let you down?"

"No but..."

"Then do what I say and stop worrying. He has too much to lose and he knows it."

"I suppose you're right." I was too tired to argue any more.

"You know I am." The line started to break up. "... to go, Mags... worry."

"Fat lot of use you are thousands of miles away."

"I know... be going soo..."

The line went dead. I put the phone down. For the first time in my life, I didn't feel any better for having talked to him.

CHAPTER 6

In the weeks that followed I heard nothing further from either Jonathan or Tommy. I took all the security measures on my list, and avoided Kilmanogue like the plague. Instead, I asked Anna to come up for a few days to Dublin. On her first day up, I took the day off and brought her around the shops.

"We should do this more often," she said, as we relaxed over coffee and scones in Bewley's. She was lying back enjoying her cigarette, watching the crowds come in for their elevenses. I noticed shadows under her eyes.

"What's up, Sis?" I asked casually, "the kids getting you down?"

She lit a second cigarette from her first one. "No. Why?" She inhaled deeply and sat back again.

"You don't look well."

"You don't look too wonderful yourself! I see you're back on the fags."

I stubbed out my cigarette guiltily. I'd bought a packet after Jonathan's call. I'd bought another one when the first one was gone. I hadn't actually realised I was back on them until she said it.

"What's going on between you and Jonathan?"

I gaped at her. "What do you mean?"

"He said to be sure to pass on his regards."

"To me?" I gulped.

"If it were anyone else, I'd be jealous." Luckily her attention was drawn to someone at the next table. "Quick. See that dress, the blue one?"

I turned to look. "The one with the slit?"

"Yes. Nice isn't it?"

"They're in the sale at Brown Thomas's. We'll go there next, if you like?"

She shook her head. "At their prices? Jonathan would have a fit."

I couldn't help smiling at the irony of Jonathan worrying about his wife's extravagance.

"What so funny?" Anna snapped. "We can't all have big jobs."

"Nothing, Sis." I jumped up and linked her out of the restaurant. "I'm just glad we're spending time together. Makes a nice change."

"That's your fault. You're the busy one. I'm only the country bumpkin."

I laughed. "Well, come on bumpkin. Let's get those bargains before the jackeens snap them up."

As Anna rooted frantically through the racks of reduced clothes, I wondered what Jonathan could have possibly meant by sending me such a message. Perhaps it was another warning, reminding me to keep my nose out of his affairs. Ma had told me that the new cheque-signing system was going well. I could see from the books and bank statements that he hadn't taken any more money from the company. Perhaps he was content with the new regime. Was that the message?

We stayed on in town, had a meal in a small Italian restaurant off Wicklow Street. I had booked seats for a play in the Olympia. By the time we got back to the apartment we were both exhausted and fell into bed.

In the middle of the night, the phone rang. I'd forgotten to take it off the hook. I picked it up, sure it was Jonathan but it wasn't. It was Auntie Nell.

"You need to come home, Maggie. It's your mother."

"Oh God." I poked at Anna to wake up.

"She's in hospital. I'm sorry it's so late, but I've been trying to get you all evening. She collapsed in the shop this afternoon. The doctor insisted on taking her in."

"What did he say was wrong with her?" I held the phone out so that Anna could listen to her reply.

"It's her heart, I'm afraid. She's had chest pains for the last few months. I tried to get her to see about them, but she kept putting it off. You know the way she is."

"Is she bad?"

"I think you and Anna should come home."

My heart sank. Anna's eyes started to fill. "We'll leave right away. Is she in the Regional?"

"Yes. Drive carefully Maggie, won't you?"

"Don't worry. There'll be no traffic on the road this late. We'll be there in a couple of hours."

Anna was pulling at my sleeve. "Where's Jonathan? Ask her where's Jonathan?"

Auntie Nell heard her. "Tell her not to worry. He's at home with the kids."

For once, he was in the right place at the right time.

We dressed quickly. I made us some coffee. It was almost three as we headed out onto the dual carriageway. I tried not to think of anything as I drove. I could hear Anna breaking into a quiet sob from time to time, but my eyes stayed dry. Heart attacks were for old people. Ma wasn't old.

The minute we walked into the Intensive Care Unit I knew how wrong I could be. I barely recognised her in the bed. She had a mask over the lower part of her face. She gave a weak smile when she saw us.

"I'll kill Nell for getting ye out of bed," she whispered. "What are you crying for, Anna?"

Anna kissed her. "Are you going to be alright?"

"Of course, love." Ma turned to me. "How are you Maggie? Long time since you've been down."

"Sorry, Ma." I bent down and kissed her. "You know how it is."

"Anna, go and get tea for the two of ye, will you, love?"

"Why can't Maggie go?"

Ma gave a tired sigh so Anna left at once to do what she asked.

"Look after her won't you, Maggie?" Ma's words shocked me. "I know the two of you don't always get along, but she needs you, especially if I…"

"You're not going to…"

"You were always the strong one."

"You'll be alright, Ma. Nothing's going to happ…"

"Stop interrupting. There isn't much time. I worry about Jonathan sometimes." I looked up surprised, but didn't say anything. "He's not the perfect husband." She smiled sadly. "But then there's probably no such thing."

"Except for Dad, of course."

"Your poor father wasn't perfect either, but I loved him, so I forgave him." She gave a deep fluttery sigh. "I know he never really stopped loving me."

I looked up, surprised. "Forgave him? For what?"

"For loving someone else. It was only for a short time. It didn't make any difference to us."

"Dad had an affair?"

She nodded. "A long time ago."

"With whom?"

She shook her head. "You wouldn't remember her, love. She left Kilmanogue. You knew her son Tommy. She was a real beauty." Her eyes misted over. "But I knew he'd come back to me."

"Are you talking about Mrs O'Connor?"

She nodded. Her eyes closed.

"Tommy's mother is dead." The words were out before I could stop them.

Her eyes fluttered open. "Is she? But how do you know? Nobody in Kilmanogue knew where she went."

"I met her in London." Her eyes widened. "She often asked about you, Ma. Now I know why."

"How did you meet her? Was it through Tommy?"

Fortunately Anna chose that moment to come in with the tea. A nurse followed. "Your mother needs rest. Take that out to the corridor."

"We'll be back in a little while Ma." I bent down and kissed her.

"Remember what I said about Anna," she whispered. Her breathing was shallow. I nodded and pulled away so that Anna could move nearer. "They're lovely children, Anna. Take care of them."

"I will, Ma." Anna was close to tears again.

We went to the end of the corridor where there was an alcove with seats. After gulping down some tea, I decided to find a doctor. I went along to the nurses' station.

"The doctor's in theatre, I'm afraid."

"In that case can you tell me anything about my mother's condition?"

She shook her head. "Sorry. I've only just come on duty."

"We'll be down here or in the ward if he comes back, okay?" I pointed at the alcove. She turned back to her screen.

I flopped down onto the seat again. Anna was staring out of the darkened window. "Ma's going to die, isn't she?"

"Of course not." I hugged her. Underneath her eyes were black rings. Whatever happened to the blonde bombshell? I knew the answer to that one, of course. "Does Jonathan make you happy Anna?" Her head shot up at my question. She opened her mouth and closed it again. Then she started to cry. I put my arm around her again. "I'm sorry. I'd no right to ask that. Not with Ma being so sick."

She looked at me through the tears. "Jonathan's fine. The children are fine. I don't know why I'm crying."

"Sorry love. I'm sure he's a wonderful husband."

"Just because you can't find a husband doesn't mean that mine isn't any good."

I laughed. "That's my sister. Come on. Drink up that tea and let's get back."

When we got back Ma was asleep. She looked much calmer so I turned to Anna. "You go home to the kids. I'll stay here."

"What if she wakes up?"

"I'll call you. You'd be back in twenty minutes."

The doctor walked into the ward. "Are you the Brown sisters?" We nodded. It was a long time since I'd heard that expression. He looked at the monitor then took up a chart from the bottom of the bed. "Your mother's had a heart attack, I'm afraid. She's not responding to the treatment as well as we'd like."

"Does that mean…?"

"It could mean anything," he answered quickly. "I'm sorry to be so vague, but it's very hard to tell in these cases. She's not young and I suspect she's been ignoring the signs for some time." He made some notes on the chart and put it back at the end of the bed. "You two look exhausted. Go on home and try to get some rest. There's nothing more you can do here."

Anna looked doubtfully at him. "Are you sure?" He nodded.

"We've run some tests. We'll know more in the morning." His beeper sounded. "Sorry, I have to go."

Anna took his advice and went home. I pulled a chair up beside Ma. Her breathing was quieter now, more relaxed, so I started to relax too. The heat of the ward was making me sleepy. I closed my eyes for a minute and was about to drift off, when...

"How come you knew her so well, Maggie?" Ma's voice sounded stronger, almost normal.

"Knew who?"

"Mrs O'Connor."

"I told you Ma. I met her in London." I got up and busied myself with her pillows. "Are you comfy? Anything I can get for you?"

"Don't change the subject." Her voice had weakened again.

"Why didn't you tell us you were having pains?"

"Don't mind those doctors." She gave a little sigh. "What do they know? She was a lovely woman, Mrs. O'Connor. She didn't have an easy life."

"She was very good to me."

"When?" She looked hard at me.

"When I was pregnant."

I don't know why I chose that moment, but something in me told me it was time for the truth. There'd been too many lies. Ma gaped at me; her mouth dropped open and closed again. "Remember that time in London, the computer project?" She nodded. Her eyes never left my face. "I was due in August. She was the landlady I stayed with."

"Why didn't you tell me?" Her voice was only a whisper now.

"I didn't want you to be ashamed."

"I'm your mother, Maggie. For God's sake, how could I ever be ashamed of you?"

"That's what she said too." I smiled. "She wanted me to tell you all along."

"What happened to the baby?"

I looked away from her penetrating gaze. "He was six weeks early. He wasn't expected to make it. Up to a short while ago I thought he'd died." A tear slipped down her cheek. "Don't cry, Ma. That was a long time ago."

"I can't believe you didn't trust me. You shouldn't have had to face that on your own."

"I didn't. Mrs O'Connor looked after me." The tears were running down her face. I dabbed at them with a tissue. "Don't cry, Ma. It's over."

"Where is he now?"

"I don't know. He ran away from the orphanage. We're trying to trace him."

"We?"

"Tommy's helping me. We've been friends for years. He's away most of the time but when he comes home we see each other. He and I..." I stopped.

"Do you love him, Mags?"

I nodded miserably. "But he doesn't love me."

"How do you know?"

"Because he keeps leaving me."

Her eyes closed wearily. I sat and held her hand while she slept. I was just beginning to doze off myself when she stirred.

"Find someone else, Maggie." She gripped my hand. "Someone who can be there for you." Her voice faded again. I had to lean close to hear her. "We all need someone, no matter how strong you think you are..."

She fell into a deep sleep. Her breath seemed desperately weak, as if it was a struggle even to take the air into her lungs. I sat there, watching her chest rise and fall. Her hand lay on the bedspread. I covered it with mine, willing my energy to transfer from my fingers into hers, those same fingers that had cooked and cared for us as long as I could remember.

I could feel her pulse weakening. Her chest was still going up and down but more unevenly now. My whole world had stopped to focus on this one movement. I sat there watching, listening, and waiting. All my concentration was on her breath. Suddenly her body shuddered. There was a little sigh. Her chest stopped. I rang the bell, but knew it was too late.

I walked up and down outside the cubicle in a daze, while the doctor checked her out. I couldn't cry. Death held little fear for her. Her Faith in God and Dad would see to that. It was the living who'd suffer, the ones who were left behind.

The funeral took place two days later. Everyone in Kilmanogue, it seemed, turned out to pay their respects. Anna and I sat in the front pew close to the coffin, Jonathan, Nell and the two children beside us. It reminded me of Dad's funeral, but we'd been the children then. We'd had our mother to mind us. Now we were the adults. We were supposed to be the minders. The ceremony was over in an hour. Anna broke down several times, especially during the final prayers at the graveside. Remembering what Ma had said, I held her hand and comforted her.

Then came the moment when the coffin was lowered into the ground. I threw a single rose after it. It reminded me of the rose she used to pluck from our wilderness of a garden all those years ago. As the first shovel full of soil covered it, the action seemed to symbolise the end of hope or happiness for Anna and me. I suddenly envied Ma. We were the ones who needed to be cried for, not her. We were the lonely ones, the ones left behind. The tears welled up inside. I felt as if my heart was about to break.

Then I felt tiny warm fingers wrapping themselves around mine. "Don't cry, Auntie Maggie. I'll mind you." It was Emily. Her touch stopped me making a fool of myself.

A few days later, the solicitor read the Will. She'd made it years ago, soon after Dad's accident. There'd been some recent changes too. Her share of the business was to be divided equally between Anna and me. The house was Anna's for as long as she needed it. If sold, the proceeds were to be divided between the two of us. Knowing Jonathan, I could see the wisdom in this. The house they lived in at the moment was heavily mortgaged. With his problems, who knew when they might have to move out?

"With what you already own, this makes you the biggest shareholder, Maggie." Nell hugged me. "Congratulations, boss."

"Thanks, Auntie Nell," I said, "but it doesn't really change anything."

Jonathan left the room. Anna walked out after him.

CHAPTER 7

Back at work, people shook my hand and made little speeches of condolence. I had to stop myself from reacting to their sympathy. As the full reality began to sink in, the sadness descended on me like a weight. Childhood memories kept flooding back when I least expected them. Happier times in Kilmanogue, walking with Dad on the beach, swimming, playing tennis, coming home to the smell of baking. A wonderful carefree childhood, spent in the absolute certainty that everything would stay the same.

I buried myself in my work. Being the major shareholder in the family business, I decided to have a proper audit done on the books. I hired a Dublin firm to do it, one that was well known and respected.

"Your mother would have been proud of you," Nell said, when I told her, "that's why she left you in charge."

"Be sure to warn the others. I don't want anyone thinking I'm going behind their backs."

"They'll never think that. Jonathan's away at the moment, but I'll get Anna to tell him when he comes back."

I tried to ignore a sudden trickle of alarm. "Please make sure she tells him, Auntie Nell. Auditors don't give any warning. They just drop in out of the blue."

"Stop worrying, Maggie." She laughed. "He's hardly going to object."

"He… he might think I don't trust him."

Their preliminary report was on my desk three weeks later. It wasn't good. They'd found two new bogus accounts through which Jonathan was taking small, but regular, payments for goods that hadn't been received into stock. This time they were able to track down the cheques. The money had ended up in one of his personal accounts, in spite of the new signature system I'd set up. The only way he could have done it was by forging signatures. They promised a final report in a fortnight. It would contain full evidence of their findings.

I read the report again slowly. He obviously felt he could do what he liked. I got up and walked to the window. This time I really was on my own. I turned on my heel and walked into the outer office.

"Cancel the afternoon meeting, Maura. I have to go down to Kilmanogue."

As I drove, I prepared myself for the confrontation. I was terrified of being beaten up again, but I was far too angry to worry about it. Instead, I tried to concentrate on the facts, the bogus accounts, the goods that hadn't been received. I drove fast. Part of me was hoping he'd be there so I'd get it over with. The other part of me was dreading he would.

He was the first person I saw when I walked into the shop. He was lolling against the counter, chatting up a young woman. Anna was entering the woman's purchases in the till. She looked frazzled, as she squinted at the figures on the price tags.

"Hi there," I said cheerfully, trying to act as if nothing were amiss.

She nodded, without taking her eyes off the machine. She hit the total button and the bill popped out. "That'll be thirty-two pounds ten please?"

"You mean twenty-two?" The customer giggled coquettishly at Jonathan.

"Sorry. Twenty-two." Anna blushed and took the notes from her. She counted out the change carefully.

"Just as well I was watching." The customer smiled as she pocketed the money.

Jonathan frowned at his wife. "That's not the first time, is it?"

"I've said I'm sorry," Anna mumbled, her face scarlet.

The customer waved her goodbye to Jonathan and left the shop.

Anna closed the till with a bang. "What are you looking at?" She glared at me and ran a tired hand over her eyes. "Checking up I suppose, now you're the big boss." She turned away and started to tidy a shelf behind her.

"We need to talk," I said to Jonathan out of the corner of my mouth.

"Anna can look after you," he smirked. "I'm off duty."

"It's you I want to see. Come upstairs for a minute."

His expression tightened for a moment, then the smirk was back on his face. "Certainly, boss. After you, boss." He followed me out through the back of the shop. I could feel him uncomfortably close as I climbed the narrow stairs.

"How dare you?" I rounded angrily on him after I shut the door. "How dare you steal money from the business?"

He was speechless for a moment, then he came towards me, threateningly. "Have you forgotten what happened the last time you interfered?"

"I've just seen the preliminary report from the auditors." Inside I was shaking, but somehow I managed to keep my voice firm. "They found your bogus accounts."

"What accounts?" His eyes glittered with hatred.

"Their full report is on the way. I'll have all the evidence in a week."

Panic flitted across his face. I shuddered. Could a son inherit his father's crookedness? Was that why Johnny was always in trouble? Were these things in the genes, predestined, unavoidable? Was there nothing anyone could do to… ?

His fist caught me across the jaw.

"You don't know when to quit, do you?" He hit me again. I fell against a box and slid to the floor. "You sad bitch, you can't even keep O'Connor happy." He stood leering down at me. "The only satisfaction you get is interfering in other people's lives. Well you'll be no good to anyone after I've finished with you." He turned the key in the door and pulled off his belt.

I screamed, but I knew they'd never hear me in the shop. I hunched over trying to protect myself as the blows rained down on my shoulders. He was out of control. After a few minutes he stopped, chest heaving. I fell back against the wall. He towered over me, panting for breath, belt in hand, perspiration streaming down his face.

"That'll teach you to mind your own bloody business."

"It is my business. Anna's my sister."

"And she's my wife, so stay out of our lives."

"She doesn't realise what sort of bastard she's married to. I bet you never told her about you and me either?" I said in a flash of inspiration.

"You mean that stupid little night in Dublin?" He laughed harshly. "That meant nothing and you know it."

I struggled painfully to my feet. My shoulder was beginning to throb. I leaned against the wall trying to gather enough strength to make a run for it. I started to move but he grabbed me by the arms and pinned me back up against the wall.

"Who else knows about those accounts?"

"Only me and the auditors." I reached up to rub my eye and gasped as my hand came away covered in blood.

"Good." His voice was cold and flat. "Okay, Miss Smart Ass, here's the new deal. Stay quiet about those accounts and I won't take any more money. Talk and I'll be only too happy to tell Anna all about our little fling. She's not going to like hearing that her darling sister slept with her husband," he leered. I gasped at my stupidity. He was right. Anna would feel I'd betrayed her. The fact I'd kept silent all these years would only confirm her suspicions. "Well, is she?" He shook me, his hands digging into my arms.

"What about the auditors?" I whispered.

"You're the accountant. Make something up. This little beating is nothing to what you'll get if you tell anyone else. So your silence in exchange for your sister's peace of mind. Do we have a deal?" His fingers tightened on my arms. He had me beaten. I nodded. "And clean up that face before you come downstairs. I'll tell Anna you fell off the ladder. She probably won't even notice. She's too worried about herself at the moment," he added as if this were a normal conversation. "We're off to Dublin tomorrow to see an eye specialist. One of these days I'll have to trade her in for a younger model, I suppose," he sniggered, as he unlocked the door. He walked down the stairs whistling.

I dabbed my eye with a handkerchief. When I got down into the shop he was nowhere to be seen. Anna was serving a customer and didn't even look up. I slipped into the back kitchen and looked in the mirror at the gash. Anna walked in as I was reaching for a cloth. She looked at me concerned.

"Jonathan said you fell?"

"It's nothing." I kept my face covered with the towel. "Just a graze."

"Awkward as ever eh?" she said grabbing a roll of paper for the cash register. "When you're ready, come out. I can't do everything on my own."

"You go on. I'll be out in a minute."

She left. My upper body felt like a punch bag, but the only damage visible was the cut over the eye. God knows what I'd look like when the bruises came up. I found the First Aid box, put a plaster over the cut, and hurried out.

Early the following morning I returned to Dublin. There were several shades of purple around my eye. Just as well I didn't have to go into work for a few days. I cleaned the flat for the morning. It was somehow soothing to do ordinary things like hoovering. I had a light lunch then ran a hot bath and poured half a bottle of bubble bath into it, before sliding gingerly into the steaming bubbles. If I could just keep my mind turned off another while, I might get some inspiration as to what to do next. I was half asleep, almost submerged in bubbles when the phone rang. I ignored it. Whoever it was could ring me back later. It rang off after a few minutes and I drifted back into a doze. I was still in the bath half an hour later when the doorbell rang. I woke with a start. The water was cold. I jumped out, pulled on my dressing gown and ran over to the intercom.

"Is that Miss Brown?" A gruff male voice came through.

"Yes" I answered nervously. "Who's that?"

"The Gardai, Miss. Could you let us in please?"

I pressed the buzzer, releasing the outside door. Two Guards came upstairs to the apartment. One was so young he looked like he was just out of school.

"Margaret Brown from Kilmanogue?" the older one asked. I nodded uneasily. "Sorry to disturb you Miss. Could we come in please?" I stepped aside to let them in. "Are you on your own?" the Guard asked, looking around.

My mouth had gone dry. "Wh…. what's happened?"

"There's been an accident. The Gardai in Wexford have been trying to reach you by phone."

"It's not Anna, is it?" I grabbed him by the arm. "Tell me quick."

The two faces floated in front of me. The older man put out his arm to steady me. "I think you'd better sit down, Miss." My blood ran cold.

"She's not dead," I screamed, "please, she can't be."

He pushed me down into a chair. "No, Miss, but I'm afraid her husband is."

A surge of relief ran through my body. "Oh thank God."

He coughed. "You don't understand, Miss. He's dead."

"But she's alright? You did say she was alright?"

"No. She's badly hurt."

"How bad?"

"You know doctors, Miss. They don't really tell you anything."

"Where is she?"

"In the Regional. They weren't far from home when the accident happened."

"Thanks for letting me know. I'll go down straight away."

I threw some clothes on. The whole way down in the car I prayed as I never prayed before. I kept seeing her tired face in the shop the day before. I remembered what my mother had said about looking after her. I hadn't done a very good job. Thank God it was Jonathan who'd been killed and not her.

The nurse led me into the cubicle. Anna lay there white as a sheet, head and eyes covered in bandages. Her hand hung out from the bed. I took hold of the fingers and squeezed. There was no response. I looked up frightened at the nurse.

"Is she still unconscious?"

"Yes, but she should come round shortly."

"Why all the bandages?" I asked, "she won't be able to see anything."

"What have they told you?"

"Nothing."

"I'll get the doctor." She left the cubicle pulling the curtain behind her. I squeezed the limp fingers again.

"Anna, Anna can you hear me?" I felt a slight pressure, and called again louder.

She stirred and moaned.

"Maggie?"

"Yes love, it's me."

"Why is it so dark?" She put her hand up to her face. When she felt the bandages, she screamed. The nurse ran in and pulled her hand away.

"Leave the bandages alone please, Mrs. Good."

"What happened?"

"How much do you remember?" the nurse asked gently.

"We were in the car. Jonathan was driving. He was driving fast." Her voice began to quicken. "We were having a row about something, I can't remember what. I tried to make him slow down. Then this truck came out of nowhere... "

"Don't worry. You're safe now. The windscreen came in on top of you. You had an operation. Try not to move too much."

Anna's hands went up to the bandages again. "But why is it so dark?"

"You mustn't touch those." The nurse took her hands and put them firmly under the covers. She turned to me and whispered. "Don't let her near the bandages. The doctor will be along in a few minutes."

I took Anna's hand. "Me again, love. How d'you feel?"

"Terrible. What about Jonathan?" Anna tried to sit up. "Is he here too?"

I put a restraining hand on her shoulders. "Yes but... "

She relaxed back against the pillows. "We were having a desperate row. He wasn't paying attention to the traffic."

"Do you remember what it was about?" I asked nervously.

She shook her head. The curtain twitched. The doctor came in, gave a brief smile in my direction. "Welcome back, Anna. How do you feel?"

"Who's that?"

"The doctor who operated on you. Are you in any pain?"

"Yes."

"I'll give you something. Do you remember what happened?"

"We were in an accident. We hit a truck. The nurse said the windscreen came in on top of us."

"That's right. Your husband took most of the impact." He looked at me. I shook my head quickly. I felt she'd had enough for the moment.

"You'll need to be very quiet over the next few days. We'll have to take another look at your eye in a week or so."

"Does that mean only one of the eyes was injured?" I asked. He frowned at me and shook his head. I could have bitten off my tongue. There was an uneasy silence.

"Why don't you answer her?" Anna said petulantly.

"I'm sorry. We couldn't save the left one. There was too much damage." Anna screamed. Her nails dug into my hand as he continued. "We managed to get most of the glass out of the other one."

"How soon can you take the bandages off?"

"I'm afraid you'll have to put up with them for the moment, Anna," he replied.

"Better get my husband come to me then, if I can't go to him."

"Time enough for that," he said calmly reaching for a syringe. "I'm going to give you something for the pain." Anna flinched as he pumped some medication into her vein. "It will help you sleep too. I'll be back later."

"Thanks, Doctor," Anna sighed. "Be sure to tell Jonathan I was asking for him."

The doctor waved at me to follow him out of the cubicle. We moved out of earshot.

"I don't think she's ready to hear about her husband yet. She needs to be kept quiet if those stitches are to heal."

"But she will see again?"

To my horror, he paused before answering. "I'm not sure. The glass did enormous damage. We've got most of it out, but one of the pieces is very close to the optic nerve. I honestly don't know." He shook his head "We've a long road ahead."

I stared at him, horrified. "But with one eye already gone… "

"As I said, we'll look at her again in a few days when the stitches heal," he interrupted. "Her condition is rather unusual, actually. Any history of eye problems in the family?"

"I don't know. But recently she was having some trouble. In fact I think they were on their way to an eye specialist when the accident happened." I suddenly remembered what Jonathan had said after the beating in the shop.

"I thought so. I'm going to call in a consultant, Tim Kelly. He'll be down to have a look at her in the next few days. In the meantime, it's very important she be kept calm."

I nodded dully. The possibility that Anna might lose her sight was too horrible to contemplate.

"When should I tell her about Jonathan?"

"Leave it as long as you can." He put his hand on my arm. "She's going to need a lot of support over the next few weeks." His bleeper went off. "Sorry, I have to go."

Auntie Nell arrived just as I returned to the cubicle. She was walking slowly, leaning on her stick, her eyes red from weeping. I pulled her to one side.

"Anna hasn't been told yet about Jonathan," I whispered. "I'm so sorry. How are you coping?"

"Not too bad love." She sighed. "I didn't have him very long." She smiled sadly. "But I can't complain. I was lucky he came back into my life when he did."

"The doctor doesn't want Anna told yet."

She looked at me, horrified. "But she has to know."

"Yes, but for the moment she has to be kept calm. She's already lost one eye. They're trying to save the other…oh God Auntie Nell, what if… " I couldn't go on.

"Poor Anna, losing a husband and now this."

"Where are the children?"

"With the neighbours. They'll come in to see her after lunch. I won't tell them about Jonathan until after that." Her voice broke. "I tried to tell them this morning but couldn't."

Anna was awake when they arrived later. After a few minutes of lively chatter, Auntie Nell led them away.

"Hearing their voices was better than any medicine," Anna said cheerfully, when I leant over to kiss her. "Emily, bless her, gave me her lucky coin. You'll have to have kids of your own, Mags. You don't know what you're missing." I straightened up quickly. Perhaps it was just as well she couldn't see my face. "Maggie?" she said petulantly, her hand flailing around trying to find me. "Where are you?"

"Here, sorry." I took her hand and sat down close to the bed.

"Have you seen Jonathan yet?" The question took my breath away.

"No."

"Shame on you, Mags. Go and give him a big kiss from me." She must have sensed my hesitation. "Go on. What are you waiting for? He's bound to be worried."

"Okay." I got up reluctantly.

"Tell him I forgive him," she said gaily, "and I'm sorry about the row. I'll be in to see him as soon as I can."

"Okay."

"And tell him I love him."

I wandered out into the corridor, unsure where I was going. I bumped into the nurse who'd been with Anna the night before and told her about the visit from the children. "And now she wants me to go and see Jonathan. What'll I do?"

"Go see him and say goodbye. He'll be in the mortuary chapel. Take the lift to the basement and follow the signs."

I didn't know what else to do.

Despite all he'd done to me, I could feel nothing only pity, as I looked at him lying there. For the first time, I saw similarities between him and Auntie Nell. I started to wonder again about Johnny. He was bound to look like his father. Sister Gertrude had spoken about blue eyes. Remembering the hatred in Jonathan's eyes at our last encounter, I shivered and went home. I couldn't face Anna again that day.

She was much calmer when I went in to see her the following morning. She was able to tell me all about the accident. She only got upset when she described the row they'd been having over unpaid bills. I was horrified to hear that their power had been cut off. "Why do you think we used to go down to Ma so often for dinner, stupid? Everyone's not as organised as you are. Poor Jonathan." She smiled tolerantly. "I expect too much of him." I swallowed hard but said nothing.

She went on and on about the accident. She'd been trying to make him slow down. "He wasn't in a fit state to be driving Mags. He'd been drinking, you see. When I nagged him about the bills he got mad, roared at me to mind my own business." They'd just gone onto the dual carriageway when a truck began to overtake. She'd seen the truck coming up alongside the car and had tried to warn him. "But he was so busy giving out about how much work he'd have to do now with Ma gone, that he wasn't minding." She started to cry. "He was giving out to me for not signing the last cheque too. When I told him it was only because I didn't know what it was for, he went into a rage. The angrier he got the faster he drove. He said he didn't see why he should have to go to women to get cheques signed. He was looking at me instead of the road. There was an awful sound. The car swerved. There was a flash of lights, glass everywhere."

She cried for ages after that, but when she eventually stopped, she was much calmer. By the time I left her, she was sound asleep.

I called back to see her later. "How's the pain?"
"Not as bad. How was Jonathan when you saw him?"
"Fine," I lied, and pulled over a chair.
"Why won't they let him come and see me?"
"He...er... he probably needs to rest."
"Was he glad you'd called?"
"Yes," I mumbled. "Would you like me to read you some of the news? I got the paper on the way in."
"Come on, Mags. What did he have to say for himself? Was he sorry about the row we were having?" she giggled. I said nothing. "What's the matter with you?"
"Nothing."
"Is there something you're not telling me?"
"Of course not."
"Yes, there is. I know by your voice. Is it bad?" She knew by my silence it was. She reached out blindly, grabbed my arm. The colour drained from her face. "He's bad, isn't he?"

I took her hand and held it. "Yes."

"How bad?" I couldn't answer. My throat had gone dry. The words wouldn't come out. "Tell me." She was squeezing my hand so hard that my flow of blood was blocked. "For the love of God, Maggie," she screamed.

"I'm sorry, love. Jonathan didn't make it."

She collapsed back onto the pillow. Her voice sank to a whisper, "You mean he's… he's…"

"Yes."

I sat on the bed and held her. After a few minutes I managed to press the buzzer. Marion the night nurse had just come on duty. She came in smiling, but her expression changed when she saw the state her patient was in. "I'll get something for her."

I sat with her after she'd been sedated. She finally drifted off into a troubled sleep. Poor Anna. Bad and all as he was, life would be tough with two children to rear on her own. At least now I knew Jonathan hadn't told her about our night together. She'd never have forgiven me. As I watched her sleeping, I vowed to help her as much as I could in the years ahead. It was beginning to look as if she'd need me too. We'd need each other. It would be like the old days. My mind drifted back to childhood, when the only decision we had to make was whether to swim on the beach with the day-trippers, or walk further on to the harbour. Anna groaned in her sleep and turned over. Her husband was dead, but at least she had two wonderful children. What had I to show after all that time? I looked at my watch and wondered where Tommy was, more importantly who was he with. I stood up and stretched to ease my back.

"Time you got some rest yourself, Maggie." It was Marion, in to check her patient. "She'll be out of it for several hours. Go on home. We'll look after her."

"When will you know about her eye?"

Marion frowned. "Mr. Kelly was talking to the doctor today. They'll be meeting again tomorrow. I'm sure they'll want to speak to you then."

I kissed Anna and left the hospital.

"When are these bloody bandages coming off?" She was demanding in a high-pitched tone, as I walked into the cubicle next morning. The young nurse who was tidying the bed didn't answer.

"Making trouble as usual, Sis?"

Anna looked up in my direction. "Maggie, tell that lassie if she doesn't take these things off this minute I'll rip them off myself."

The nurse looked at me frightened.

"There'll be no ripping off, Madam," I laughed. "Enough of your ranting and raving. You heard what the doctor said."

"But I have to say goodbye to Jonathan. It's not much to ask, is it?"

"No love." I gave her a quick hug. "But you have to give the stitches a chance to heal first."

"Oh Maggie, what am I going to do without him? I know you and he didn't get on too well, but he was a good father."

I sat down beside her and took her hand. "Tell me about him."

"You don't want to know. You're only saying that to keep me quiet," she said sulkily, but when I fixed her pillows, she lay back and started to talk. She told me how he used to read to the children late at night. "They loved his English accent," she said with a smile. "They used to tease him about his pronunciation like Kink of kinks."

"What's that?" I asked, relieved she could smile about something.

"King of Kings," she explained. "The kids were forever asking him the name of that film, then they'd roll around the bed laughing, and repeating it the way he said it." Her smile faded. "Oh God, I can't believe he's gone. How am I going to manage on my own? I'm not independent and strong like you, Mags."

How come everybody thinks I'm so strong?

"But it's great having a sister all the same, isn't it?" She snuggled into me. "You'll mind me, won't you?"

"Of course I will, love. I'll always be here for you."

And who'll be here for you Mags? I heard my mother's voice in my head.

Anna gave a contented sigh. "You were always the strong one. Whether 'twas the nuns in school or the boys on the tennis court, you were able to take them all on. And you usually won too."

"Did I?"

The curtains were pulled aside.

"Good morning, ladies." The doctor walked in accompanied by an older man. "This is Mr. Kelly, the consultant. He'd like to take a look at your eye, Anna."

"I'll go," I said, and got up to leave.

"No, no, don't leave me," she shrieked.

"I'll only be outside, silly." I kissed her lightly and left.

Ten minutes later the two men came out. "That's agreed then," the doctor was saying, "we'll set it up for tomorrow morning." The consultant nodded and walked down the corridor. The doctor took my arm.

"I'm afraid the news isn't too good," he said. "It's more or less as I suspected. There's been major damage to the cornea. He's going to try to get some more of the glass out, but he's not too hopeful."

"Has she been told?"

He shook his head. "The nurse is prepping her for surgery now. We have to keep her hopes up to the end."

"Surely she could have some sort of transplant?"

"Usually yes but she has a congenital defect, which is complicating matters. We'll do our best to find a match, of course. Who knows? We might be lucky. I'm sorry. I'm afraid her troubles are only starting."

His words chilled me. I was afraid to ask the question that was on the tip of my tongue. I was too frightened to hear the answer.

That night I spent some time with Auntie Nell. Jonathan's funeral was planned for the following day. The children were staying with a neighbour. They'd reacted to the news more calmly than any of us had expected. Perhaps they were still too young to take it all in.

I don't know how Auntie Nell got through the next day. I looked at her kneeling stiffly at the edge of the pew, her face frozen like marble, staring straight ahead as if afraid to look down at the coffin. If only she could cry. But perhaps she did all her crying when she was alone. How else would she keep so calm? I thought of all the years she'd been robbed of a son, robbed by an unforgiving society that didn't allow people to make mistakes. She'd had him for only eighteen of his forty-five years. The same length I'd been without mine. But I'd had some sort of choice. Or had I? I looked sideways at the two children kneeling white-faced beside me. I prayed for them and their mother, who was at that moment on the operating table. I even said one for Jonathan. He was out of our lives now. Life was short. The accident had proved that. Tommy was right. I'd keep searching. If my son was alive, I'd go to him. If he was dead, we'd visit his grave and say goodbye. I smiled. Even here at Jonathan's funeral Tommy was on my mind. So much for independence.

CHAPTER 8

The following week I returned to work. Anna cried bitterly and begged me to stay. I promised to visit her every spare minute I had.

Over the next few weeks her progress was painfully slow. The bandages were taken off. Now she was wearing a patch over the sightless eye, and a small tape over the eye that was being treated. The children had christened her Sinbad. They were teaching her games of touch, games they'd been taught in infant class. The peals of their laughter echoed down the corridor. The doctors hadn't given up on her. Each time they removed another piece of glass, more light entered through the mists. Following each operation there was another visit from Mr. Kelly, more tests to be done, more results to be reported. But the message was the same. Damage to the cornea had been severe. The congenital deformity continued to impede the likelihood of their finding a match. With each operation, Anna's mood swung one hundred and eighty degrees. Beforehand, she'd be planning what she'd do when she got out of hospital. Afterwards, she'd sink down into despair as the results came back.

One day, she was allowed home for a couple of hours. The doctors wanted to see how she'd cope in familiar surroundings. The visit was a disaster. She wasn't ready to cope. I began to wonder if she ever would.

One Sunday night I drove back to Dublin after a particularly distressing visit. Everything seemed to be getting on Anna's nerves, even the children. They'd been particularly troublesome over the weekend, but who could blame them? They wanted to be out in the fresh air, playing with their friends, not in some dreary hospital, trying to cheer up their mother who was becoming more and more depressed as the weeks went by. I was getting depressed myself. In the last few months the bottom seemed to have fallen out of my world. Work and hospital. Hospital and work. Was this a foretaste of the rest of my life? Was it all downhill from now on?

As I turned the key in the apartment door, the phone rang, interrupting the dangerous flow of thought. I picked it up, expecting it to be Auntie Nell checking up on my journey back, but it was the English detective agency, a Mr. Wainwright. "We've found your son, Miss Brown."

I gripped the table. "Where is he?"

"In prison in Manchester."

"Prison?" I gasped.

"He's changed his name several times over the years. That's why it took us so long to track him down," he explained calmly. "He's known as Johnny Kerr now."

"Johnny Kerr but..."

"He's in a high-security wing in the prison. He's been dealing, I'm afraid."

"Dealing?"

"Drugs."

"Drugs?" I echoed dully.

"Our report is on its way," the cool tones continued, "I thought you'd like to know as soon as possible. I've been trying to get you for the last couple of days."

"I was down the country."

"Ring me if you have any questions. Good night, Miss Brown." He rang off.

I put down the receiver and sat down. I was feeling faint, couldn't think. The call repeated in my head, the words beating their way into my brain. *Prison, drugs.*

That night, I took two sleeping pills. The report arrived in the first post. Johnny had been in and out of half a dozen reform schools and had run away from each one. He'd started using drugs from the age of eleven. Soft ones first, then he'd switched to hard ones. To fund his habit, he started dealing. Three times he'd been put through a rehabilitation program, but at this stage, as far as the drug rehabilitation people were concerned, there was nothing more they could do. They'd written him off. I read the report a second time, then a third. I couldn't believe it was my son they were describing. A short handwritten note was attached to the report.

Dear Ms Brown, I'm sorry the news is not better. As per your instructions we've made no attempts to approach your son. If you want us to do anything further, please let me know. Bill for services enclosed. Yours etc. Peter Wainwright.

I rang the office, and told them I'd be late. Then I made coffee and sat down to read the report again. I should be delighted. After all, my dream had come true. The main thing was, my son was alive. I sat on the sofa staring out the window, while the coffee went cold. He was a criminal, in a high-security prison, his latest sentence twenty years. The Judge had specified that the sentence must run full-term. There'd be no reprieve, no recommendation for clemency. *He'd come out middle-aged*, the Judge had said, *Society must be protected from the likes of Johnny Kerr.*

I shuddered, and got up to make fresh coffee. This was my fault. If I hadn't given him away, if I hadn't abandoned him... The kettle steamed up the tiny kitchen, but I knew what I had to do. He was my son, my flesh and blood, my responsibility. I walked back into the sitting room and dialled the number at the top of the report.

"I'm sorry the news wasn't better, Miss Brown." I heard the sympathy in Wainwright's voice. "Is there something else you'd like us to do?"

"Yes. Make arrangements for me to visit him."

"Are you sure?"

"Yes."

"But you read the report. You know what he's like."

"He's my son, Mr. Wainwright."

"Very well. I'll get back to you."

I rang Aer Lingus and booked a seat to Manchester on Friday. Enough time had been wasted already.

It was Thursday before I heard from Wainwright again. "I'm sorry, Miss Brown. He refuses to see you."

"Did you tell him who I was?"

"Of course. Perhaps you're better off. He's a lost cause by all accounts."

"That's my son you're talking about, Mr Wainwright."

"Sorry. What do you want me to do?"

"Tell him I won't take no for an answer."

"I'll get back to you."

His call was put through to the office next day. "He's agreed to see you, but..."

"Thank God."

"Only if you make it worth his while."

"Worth his while? You mean... you mean he wants money?"

"Yes. I'm sorry Miss Brown, but I did warn you."

"How much?"

"A thousand. I offered five hundred, but he refused." My stomach churned. "I'll tell him forget it, shall I?"

"Certainly not. I'll bring the cheque with me."

"... er..." He coughed. "He said he wants cash."

"Fine. I'll bring cash then."

"Sterling. It must be sterling. I'm sorry. I'm just passing on what he said."

"Very well. Can you take me to the prison?"

"Of course. I'll get you a room at the Charlton. I'll collect you around noon tomorrow."

"Thanks."

"Miss Brown?"

"Yes, Mr Wainwright?"

"I do hope you know what you're doing."

"He's my son, Mr Wainwright," I said sharply, and slammed down the phone.

I felt like a criminal myself later, as I watched the cashier count out the bank notes. "The rate's not bad at the moment, Maggie. Are you sure you want it all in cash?" I nodded casually, trying to look as if I drew out that amount of cash every day of the week. "Doing a bit of shopping, I suppose?" I mumbled something noncommittal. "I'm sorry for all the twenties. We seem to be out of larger denominations at the moment. I've put them in bundles of two hundred," she said, wrapping rubber bands around each bundle. She put them into a large brown envelope and sealed it. "Happy shopping, and please be careful. There are lots of tricky customers around. Not that any of ours are, but you know what I mean?" she laughed. I smiled back and walked quickly out of the bank, half expecting to be accosted on the footpath.

I was bending down to get into my car when somebody tapped me on the shoulder. "Gotcha." My heart stopped. I turned to find a traffic warden waving a docket in front of me. "That'll be fifteen pounds, Miss."

"Don't be ridiculous. I've only been here five minutes."

"Twelve to be exact, and you're not supposed to be here at all." He pointed triumphantly to a sign. "It's on-the-spot, I'm afraid." He held his hand out. "Fifteen pounds, please."

"Have sense," I said, grabbing the docket out of his hand. "I don't carry that sort of money around with me." As I bent down to get into the car again he put his hand on my shoulder. I straightened up angrily. "There is such a thing as harassment you know."

"Under the new rules," he smirked, "you have to pay now."

"What new rules?"

"This area has been designated a pilot study. If it works here, it will be extended throughout the city."

"That's alright then because it won't," I snapped. "It's far too dangerous nowadays for people to carry money around with them. Your authorities should know that."

"Rules are rules, Miss."

"Stuff your stupid rules."

"I'm sorry, but you have to pay now."

"How can I, if I don't have it on me?"

We stood glaring at each other. He was the first to look away.

"You really don't have it on you?"

"No," I said, taking advantage of his hesitation to jump into the car. "Now, if you don't mind some of us have real jobs to go to." I banged the door before he could reply, threw his docket onto the dashboard and turned the key in the ignition. He rapped sharply on the window. "Don't worry, you'll get your stupid fine," I shouted, and revved up the engine. He knocked again. I turned furiously to give him a piece of my mind. He was waving a brown envelope at me. I rolled down the window, grabbed the envelope and threw it on the passenger seat. Trying desperately to keep my hand steady on the wheel, I pulled away from the kerb. There was a scream of brakes as a Range Rover stuck its tyres to the ground beside me. "Sorry about that," I shouted, and took off again.

When I was a safe distance away, I glanced in the rear-view mirror. The driver of the Range Rover was trying to fit into the space I'd vacated. The warden had his book open and was licking his pencil ready to catch his next victim. I drove back to the office shaking. How could I have been so stupid? The envelope must have slipped down between the car and the kerb when we were arguing. Suppose he'd opened it? Some fine. On-the-spot too, just like he wanted.

"You're in better form," Maura said, when I walked into the office. "I see you got your lunch?" She nodded at the envelope.

"What? Oh yes. I'll have it at the desk, make up for lost time."

Some lunch! More private hysteria.

Later, on the flight over, the questions were buzzing round and round in my head. Should I have taken Wainwright's advice? If my son really didn't want to meet me I might only make things worse. Should I wait for a while, wait until he asked to see me even? If only Tommy was here, he'd know, but I hadn't heard from him for ages, wasn't even sure where he was.

When I arrived at the Charlton I rang his sister, but she didn't know where he was either. On the odd chance he'd ring her, I left a message for him, but I knew it was probably a waste of time.

It was a waste of time going to bed early too, because I twisted and turned all night. Why didn't he want to see me? Wasn't he the tiniest bit curious? The report had made him sound like a hardened criminal, and perhaps he was. If so, who could blame him? What sort of mother would leave her baby without knowing whether he was alive or dead? It seemed inconceivable now, looking back. Why had Mrs O waited all those years before telling me? He'd be eighteen now. Who would he take after, his father or me? Oh God, what if he asked about Jonathan? How much should I tell him? I must have drifted off eventually, but if I did, it was into a nightmare filled with darkness and screams.

The phone rang shrilly. I fumbled for it. It was Tommy.

"Sorry it's so early. I'm ringing from the airport. What's wrong?"

"Which airport?"

"London. The Witch told me you were looking for me."

"They've found him, Tommy. They've found my son. I'm going to see him today."

"That's wonderful, Mags. Where does he live?"

"Here in Manchester."

"You must be dying to see him."

"You don't understand. He's... he's in prison."

There was a pause. "He must be looking forward to meeting you all the same."

I laughed harshly. "Sure. I only had to pay a thousand pounds for the privilege." I heard his sharp intake of breath. "What am I going to tell him when he asks about his father?"

"You'll find the words, love. How is the bould Jonathan anyway? Has he been behaving himself?"

I gasped. "Oh God, I forgot you wouldn't know. He was killed in a car crash two months ago. Anna was with him. She's still very bad. It's her eyes. She's had several operations, but the doctors say that she's unlikely to..."

"Slow down, love. Slow down. What happened exactly?"

"Jonathan was killed outright. The windscreen came in on top of her. The glass destroyed one eye completely."

"Poor Anna."

"The other one's nearly gone too, at this stage. She's going b...blind, Tommy. She's trying to get used to the idea, but she's terribly depressed. I've been doing my best to keep her hopes up. The children have too, but they're young. It's hard for them, especially after losing their father. "

"And how are you coping?"

"I was managing fine. At least I thought I was. Then the Agency sent this report. My son... my son's a drug-dealer, Tommy."

He gasped.

"I have to see him of course, but I don't know what I'm going to say."

"Wait. Wait. Hold everything. I'll grab a flight and come with you."

"Could you?"

"I'll be there in a couple of hours."

"Thanks. I don't think I could face this on my own."

He chuckled. "It hurts you to admit it though, doesn't it?"

"Can you make it by noon?"

"Do my best. Bye." He put down the phone.

I felt as if I'd been injected with new energy. He'd know how to deal with someone like Johnny. With him beside me I'd find the right words. I got up and had a shower. Feeling hungry for the first time since Wainwright's call, I picked up the phone and ordered a full English breakfast.

It was after eleven by the time I finally emerged from my room ready to face the world. There was a queue at Reception; obviously some group who'd booked in for the weekend. I walked out for some air. Horns beeped, as cars jostled for position. I walked along the path and turned into a side street to get away from the noise. People were coming out of a church. Instinctively, I made for the entrance and entered the dark interior.

Mass had just finished. A few elderly people were still in their seats. I looked at their faces, etched with the lines of their life, and envied them their peace. Slipping into a pew, I looked up at the altar to see if I could find the source. A young boy was quenching the candles. He genuflected and disappeared through a side door. There was a click as the main lights were switched off. The sacristy light glowed in the darkness. Was it my fault my son had turned out this way? How could I explain? How could I make him understand? I looked around for inspiration. There was a time when all my questions would be answered in a place like this. *Dear God tell me what to say. Make him forgive me.* In desperation, I tried to remember some prayers. I started the Rosary but got lost halfway through. Then I tried the prayer Ma used to recite after the Rosary. *Remember Oh most good and blessed Virgin, that never did anyone who had recourse ... never did anyone who had recourse to your aid...*' I couldn't get any further, so instead, I thanked God for sending Tommy. I hated admitting I needed him but I couldn't cope on my own, not this time.

I stood up to leave. I had no right being here. I didn't belong any more. The sound of an organ broke the silence. I sat down again, closed my eyes as the familiar notes washed over me. *Be not afraid. I go before you always.* We'd played it at Dad's funeral. Perhaps it was Dad who'd sent Tommy?

As I emerged into the harsh brightness I felt calmer. I was doing the right thing. When I'd explain what happened, Johnny would understand. In time he might even forgive me. We could start again.

When I got back to the hotel, a man was pacing up and down the lobby. I walked towards him. "Mr Wainwright?"

"Good morning, Miss Brown. It's a long drive so we might as well…"

"Can you hang on a few minutes? A friend is coming with us."

"In that case let's have coffee. It'll save time later."

Tommy arrived the same time as the coffee. He was still in combat gear, looking out of place in the hotel lobby. I jumped up and ran over. His arms folded around me.

"It's been a long time."

"Too long."

Neither of us had been inside a prison before, much less a high-security one. Over coffee Wainwright gave us a brief outline of the security measures we could expect. He took the money to give to the Warden for Johnny.

The traffic was bad. It was almost three by the time we arrived. In the large draughty reception area all of us were frisked. I gave my handbag up for inspection. Tommy and Wainwright had to empty out their pockets. Wainwright watched as the Warden counted out the money in front of him. It was put back into the envelope and sealed. The Warden wrote something and held it up for my inspection. *JOHNNY KERR—PRISONER 15496—£1,000.* I nodded, shocked, as the cold reality of the words sunk in.

We were directed unceremoniously into an inner room. The door clanged shut behind us. This room had no windows. It was divided by a counter. Wire mesh ran from floor to ceiling on the far side of the counter. It was quiet compared to the busy reception area we'd just left. All we could hear now was the whirr of security cameras. A door opened on the far side. A dark-haired young man entered and stood there, scanning the room with hard blue eyes.

Tommy nudged me. "That must be him." My heart was racing. I tried to smile, but my jaw was stiff with tension.

Wainwright waved. "Kerr. Over here"

The man frowned and came towards us. His eyes ran over us and stopped at Tommy. He looked scornfully at the combat gear. "So you're the proud father?"

I found my voice. "No, Tommy's a friend of mine. I'm Maggie. I'm your…"

"I know who you are." The hard eyes turned on me. "Did you bring the money?"

I nodded. "The Warden has it."

"You must be either very stupid or very rich." He sat down and pulled out a packet of cigarettes. "Forgive me if I don't offer these around," he smirked.

Wainwright pulled up chairs for Tommy and me. He stood by, within earshot. My son relaxed back in his chair and pulled slowly on the cigarette. He exhaled and stared at us through the cloud of smoke. Then he swung back on the chair, balancing it on the two back legs, and started to blow smoke rings at the ceiling. There was an uneasy silence.

"You were hard to find," I said.

"Yeah?"

"I… I didn't even know you were alive. I've been trying to find you ever since…"

"Sure you have."

"If I'd known, I'd have been in touch years ago."

"Sure you would," he snickered. "I'm just the sort of son any mother would be proud of." There was another long silence. "So now you've found me, what d'you want?" I stared at him, my mind so full of questions I couldn't think. "Take your time. I'm not going anywhere." He leaned back and started to swing on the chair again, backwards and forwards while he continued to blow smoke rings. Vainly, I searched his face for some resemblance, something of me or even Jonathan. The blue eyes reminded me of Anna when she was young, except his were cold and sharp. He looked around the room almost bored. Then he saw the security camera. The swinging stopped. He sat perfectly still as the camera rotated, his lips moving as if counting. He turned back and caught me watching. "What are you looking at?" he snapped, and started to swing back and forward again.

"Nothing. I'm just happy to have found you at last."

"Why?"

"Because I'm your mother, of course."

"Mother. Huh. Some mother."

He'd said it all. I bowed my head and felt the despair wash over me. He was right. As a mother I'd failed him.

Tommy put his arm around me. "Did you not want to see her?"

"Ah, it talks." Johnny turned his gaze on Tommy. "Why should I, Soldier Boy?"

"Most people like to know where they came from."

"Most people," he snorted. "Normal people, you mean."

Tommy sighed. There was silence again. The swinging continued. Backwards and forwards. Backwards and forwards. I watched my son through the clouds of smoke. To be so hard in such a short time! The clock on the wall gave a loud click as the minute hand moved on. I looked at it, horrified. We only had an hour. Already half of it was gone. I had to get through to him.

"I didn't want to give you away, Johnny. The world was different then. I had my reasons."

"Reasons?"

"Yes. I was young, not much more than a child myself…"

"There's always a reason, isn't there, mother?"

"I don't understand. What d'you mean?"

"Oh, I knew there'd be a reason, but d'you know what I thought it was?"

"What?"

The swinging stopped. "That you were dead." I gasped. The swinging resumed. "Why aren't you dead, mother? That's the only reason I'd accept."

"Come on." Tommy grabbed my hand. "We're leaving."

I pulled my hand away and leaned forward.

"Johnny, please. I've come a long way to see you."

"How thoughtful. How is the proud father by the way? Assuming you know who he is, of course."

Tommy gasped, but this was the question I'd been dreading.

"I'm sorry to have to tell you, he was killed a few months ago."

"Ah, so he was a dealer too, a dangerous business."

"Of course not. It was an accident, a car crash."

"Oh." He seemed almost disappointed. "Well in that case, motherrr," he smiled, his lips curling round the word, "you can tell me what he left me."

"But don't you want to…"

"I mean he must have left me something. I am his beloved son after all."

"I… I never told him about you."

"What? In all that time?" His eyes widened for a second. I shook my head miserably. "Nice one, mother." He pulled slowly on the cigarette. "Very nice."

"I know it sounds bad, but… " I stopped. What was the point? He'd started to swing on the chair again, backwards and forwards, eyes half-closed. This had gone horribly wrong. Wainwright had been right. I shouldn't have come. I'd only made things worse. The minute hand moved on again. There was still so much to say, so much to explain. I tried again.

"Johnny, as God is my Judge, I didn't even know you were alive until a few months ago. I thought you died as a baby." His eyebrows twitched in disbelief, but I carried on. "A friend of mine only told me a few months ago."

"Some friend." He blew another smoke ring into the air.

I looked sideways. Tommy's jaw had tightened. "She was a good friend. She was his mother."

"Mothers… huh!" He blew smoke into Tommy's face.

"Tell me about yourself," I said quickly, putting my hand out to restrain Tommy. "What made you run away from the orphanage? Please Johnny, I want to know. I want to know everything about you."

"Why? Conscience at you?" The hard blue eyes focussed on me properly for the first time. Their cold brilliance bored into me, frightening me with their intensity.

"I can't turn the clock back. God knows I would if I could. At least let me make it up to you now."

"Ah now you're talking, motherrr." His lip curled around the word again. "The lousy grand didn't hurt too much. Plenty more where that came from, I'd say, eh?"

Tommy jumped to his feet. "Don't you dare speak to her like that."

"So, it moves as well." Johnny took another drag on the cigarette and leered up through the smoke. "Want to get into her pants, soldier boy, is that it? Shouldn't be too difficult, with her history." The colour rose in Tommy's neck. His fist clenched.

"Watch your mouth, young man," Wainwright spoke up for the first time. "Your mother has been more than generous with you."

"A thousand quid, you call that generous?" He balanced the cigarette on the wire mesh and started to clap his hands slowly. "A thousand quid after almost twenty years. Fifty quid a year. Wowee." He took up the cigarette again and swung back. "So she wants to know what she can do for me? Well she can get me another stash to start with, say ten, no let's make it twenty grand this time. Then she can get me out of this kip. After that …" His voice went very quiet. "Do you know what she can do?" I held my breath. He swung the chair back balanced it for a minute then brought it forward with a clatter on the floor. "SHE CAN LEAVE ME THE FUCK ALONE." The blue eyes shone cruelly from the dark face.

I screamed as Tommy sprang forward. Wainwright's arm shot out to restrain him. Two security guards appeared from nowhere on the other side of the mesh and pulled Johnny off the chair. They dragged his arms behind him and pushed him towards the door.

"Back to the cage for you, Kerr."

"SEE WHAT YOUR LITTLE BOY HAS TO PUT UP WITH, MOTHERRR?" Johnny screamed as the guards pushed him through the door. "THIS IS ALL YOUR FAULT. IF YOU HADN'T THROWN YOUR BABY TO THE WOLVES…" The words died away as the door banged shut. There was a rattle of keys and a clang of a bolt going home.

I sat there, stunned. The sound of the bolt reverberated around the room and echoed again inside my brain. Tommy put his arm around my shoulders. I brushed it away, jumped up and ran towards the exit. My lungs were bursting. I ran out into the yard leaned against the wall until my breathing returned to normal. Wainwright followed a few minutes later. I got into the car, lay back against the upholstery and closed my eyes. The vision of my son being dragged away made them snap open again. I tried to focus on the green countryside, but instead my eyes were drawn like magnets to the barbed wire and the tall watchtowers at each corner of the prison. Who could be normal locked up in a place like this?

Tommy emerged a few minutes later. He got into the front seat beside Mr Wainwright and reached back. "You okay?"

"Fine." I closed my eyes wearily.

There was less traffic on the roads going back. The two men chatted in the front of the car. I tried to doze, but each time I closed my eyes, I relived the scene. A few times the traffic woke me and I'd drift off again, but the nightmare carried on inside my head. I wondered, if I went over it often enough, whether the pain might lessen.

Mr Wainwright dropped us off at the hotel.

"I need a drink. Come on," I said to Tommy and headed for the bar but he steered me firmly towards the lift instead.

"No. You go on up to the room. I'll get a bottle."

When I got into the room, I ripped off my clothes and stood under the shower. The water was scalding but I didn't care. I wanted to hurt. I needed to pay for what I'd done. My son was living in Hell. He blamed me and he was right.

I stayed there under the jets until I heard Tommy arrive. "Make it a large one," I shouted. Whiskey might help. If I could just get through tonight, if I could just get one night of sleep without nightmares, I might be able to blot it all out. After a few minutes, I emerged wrapped in a bathrobe. Tommy was standing at the window looking out.

He handed me a glass of whiskey. "Water?"

"Don't drown it." I let him add a few drops before pulling the glass away. I sat down on the side of the settee. "Thanks for being here, Tommy. Don't know what I'd have done…"

"I kept wanting to punch his face in."

"You don't understand what he's had to put up with…"

"He's an evil bastard, like his father," he said, interrupting me. "I was talking to the warden. They've had some beauties in that place but that guy beats the lot. They've never met anyone like him. Even the worst of the prisoners shun him apparently, and in a place like that…"

I put my hands over my ears. "Stop. I don't want to hear any more."

"Sorry, Mags."

I took a long swallow. The liquid burnt its way down my throat. I put the glass to my mouth and drained it. "Again please." He took the glass and refilled it from the bottle. He reached for the jug of water, but I grabbed the glass from his hand. I almost choked on the raw alcohol.

"Serves you right," he said, splashing some water into my glass. I took it and sat down on the couch. He sat down beside me. We sipped our drinks in silence. I turned to him.

"What am I going to do, Tommy? You'll have to tell me. I can't think any more."

"Face it, love. He's a lost cause."

"I've abandoned him before. I can't do it again." I started to cry. He got a tissue and dabbed gently at my eyes.

"He's not worth one of those tears, Mags. Forget him. Get on with your life."

"But he's my son."

"WAKE UP, MAGGIE," he shouted. "He's scum. They told me things about him I wouldn't repeat to a living soul." I looked up at him, horrified.

"What sort of things?"

He shook his head stubbornly. "Never mind. Drink up. It'll help you sleep."

I took a sip of whiskey and lay against his shoulder. "Even in my worst nightmares, I never dreamt it would be like this. God knows, I didn't expect everything to be perfect, but I was hoping we could set things right, maybe start again sometime, build some sort of a future together."

He planted a kiss on the top of my head. "Don't think about it now."

"What future could he have in that place?"

"Don't, love. You'll drive yourself mad."

"But I have to." I sat up crossly. "It's my fault he's in there. I failed him before. I can't do it again."

"Give me that glass." He got up and went over to the bottle. "There's nothing like whiskey for killing the pain."

He was right.

Some time later, something woke me. I was stretched out on the bed. Tommy was lying on the floor, his head propped up against my legs. He mumbled something.

"What you thay?" I asked.

"How 'bout thome ff...ood?" He grinned foolishly at me. I nodded eagerly. "Only I can't find the cooker." He waved his hand, forgetting he was holding a glass. I watched the whiskey make a golden arc through the air before describing a wider arc on the cream carpet.

"Cooker? What cooker?" I asked fuzzily.

"No cooker no food," he muttered, slumping defeated against the bed.

We both contemplated the profundity of that last statement for a few minutes.

"I know. Room thervith," I roared, with all the pride of a TV contestant.

"Anyone ever tell you you were brillo?" He waved his hand in a flourish again. Fortunately the glass was empty by now. "Theak and chipth for me, pleathe."

"I'll have n'omelette," I sighed and closed my eyes.

We snoozed for a while. Then Tommy tugged at my toe. I opened my eyes lazily. "What d'you want?"

"Food, Maggie, food."

I stretched. "Good. I'm hungry."

"Ith not ready yet."

"But we ordered ageth ago."

He shook his head from side to side.

"Not zackly."

"Wake me when ith ready." I turned over petulantly and settled down. He tugged my toe again. "Thop that. I want to go back to thleep."

"Thomebody hath to order it." I opened one eye. He was grinning at me and tapping his head. "Thee. You're not the only clever one."

"If you're tho clever, order it yourthelf," I said, and sank back into the pillows.

He dragged himself up and lumbered across the room to the phone. I heard him say something. There was a pause. "What room number are we?" he asked.

"God knowth," I answered without bothering to open my eyes.

"God knowth," he repeated into the phone.

There was an even longer pause, then I heard him give the order for our steak and omelette. "What d'you want to drink, Magth?"

"Whithkey what elthe?"

"Whithkey what elthe," he repeated and tried to hang up. The receiver fell on the floor. I opened one eye and watched him swoop down pick it up and try again. At the third attempt he finally settled it back into its holder. I closed my eyes and turned over. I felt him clamber up onto the bed behind me. He fell asleep at once, his snores reverberating through my spine. Peace at last.

I was dreaming of forklift trucks. I was driving a great big yellow one. Tommy was driving another. We were heading for the edge of a cliff. Fast. Too fast. I shouted at Tommy to slow down, but he couldn't hear me. Bells were ringing. I shouted again, but the ringing was louder so he couldn't hear. We were near the edge now. Nothing could stop us going over. I screamed, one last loud scream as we both catapulted into eternity.

I sat up in bed, perspiration rolling down my face. The phone was ringing. I poked Tommy. He rolled off the bed and landed on the floor.

"What d'you do that for?"

"Answer the phone, dopey."

He staggered over and picked it up. "Who? Oh yes, I think we ordered something alright… Oh! Sorry about that." He put down the phone and started to giggle.

"What's so funny?" I asked, without turning my head.

"Wait and see."

I heard him pad over to the door. I turned and watched him pick up a tray from the corridor. "They couldn't get in, so they had to ring us." He brought the tray over to the bed. Silver salvers covered two large plates. Apart from that there was a bottle of whiskey, a jug of water, two glasses, napkins and cutlery. I lifted the salvers curiously.

"Mm smells nice. Who ordered all this?"

"I did," he said proudly. "Don't you remember?"

"Clever thing." I tweaked his chin and looked into the bloodshot eyes. He picked up the bottle of whiskey and put it to one side. "Water on the rocks for both of us, I think."

In less than ten minutes the food was demolished. It took minimum effort to slide the tray onto the floor and roll ourselves back onto the bed. All I remember after that was the warmth of Tommy's body beside me and a feeling of peace. The world and its troubles were far away, outside the door. The demons were gone for the moment. The whiskey had done its work.

When I woke, daylight was pouring into the room. For a second, I wondered where I was. Then I saw my son's cold blue eyes and the previous day flooded back. Would things have been different if I hadn't given him away, or would he have turned out badly one way or another? Should I try to forget him and get on with my life, as Tommy advised? Then I saw him being dragged back into the cell, heard the hatred in his voice as the door closed, the clang of the bolt as they shut him away, and I knew I couldn't. Last night I'd had Tommy and the whiskey to help blot it all out. What would I do tonight on my own? I moved closer to his warm body and tried to relax. What would Dad have advised?

We were walking to the harbour for a swim, Anna, Dad and me. He was ahead of us telling us to walk straight, shoulders back. *"Left right left, I had a good job and I left."* The old marching song made me feel safe for a moment. Then Johnny's cold eyes with their message of hatred broke through again. I started to hum but the sound wouldn't come. *Left right left.* We were back in the dream. Dad ahead, Anna and me behind, trying to keep up. Dad turned and looked back at us, his eyes smiling. So that's where my son had got his eyes. Desperately, I kept humming, trying to keep the dream alive. *"Left right left. I had a good job and I left... left right left... I had a good job and I left"*

Tommy stirred. "What's with the army song?"

"Dad used to teach us on our way to the beach."

"I wish I'd known him. Ouch!" He held his head.

"Serves you right." I sniffed. "Where are you off to next?"

"Never mind. Tell me about your Dad."

"Don't try to change the subject."

"Speaking of changes of subject..." He trailed his finger up my arm. My skin started to tingle. I pulled my arm away impatiently.

"Stop it. Tell me where you're off to."

"You know I can't."

"This relationship is so bloody one-sided. I'm fed up with it."

He looked up at me, astonished. "What are you talking about?"

"About you and me, Tommy." He said nothing. His silence made me more angry. "Come on, know-all. What exactly is you and me?" Silence again. "There's no you and me really, is there?" I sighed. "There's just you and the Army or the Air Force or whatever band of renegades you're working for, and then there's me. But only when it suits you and them, whoever they are, to fit me in." I brushed away his protest. "Don't try and deny it. How do I know what other girls you have in whatever God-forsaken part of the world you're working at the moment?"

He put his hand under my chin and pulled my face towards him. "Mags shut up for a second and look at me. I'm here for you now, aren't I?"

I pushed his hand away. "Sure you are, and when will you have to leave again?"

He hesitated. "This evening, I'm afraid." He looked at me nervously. "I'm sorry, but there's somewhere I have to be... "

"See what I mean?" I jumped out of bed. "We have this twenty-four-hour thing. What sort of a relationship is that?" I looked down at him. "Oh, don't worry, I won't stop you. Off you go and fight your bloody wars. I won't call on you again." I turned on my heel and headed for the bathroom. "And thanks for sparing the time yesterday. I hope it wasn't too inconvenient." I stomped into the bathroom and slammed the door behind me. I sat on the side of the bath and stared at the washbasin.

I sat there for what seemed ages. Then I had a shower and sat down again wrapped in towels. I was afraid to come out. Afraid he'd still be there. Even more afraid that he wouldn't. Finally, I plucked up the courage.

He was putting the last of his gear into a roller bag. He zipped it up and turned to me. "What are you going to do, Mags?"

"What do you care?" I retorted, and plugged in the hairdryer.

He came over to me and took it out of my hand. "We never have time to talk properly. I've often wondered what would have happened if we'd…"

"If we'd what?" I snapped the hairdryer back and turned it on again.

"If we'd done the normal thing years ago."

"Normal thing?" I switched off the dryer and looked at him.

"Got married, settled down, had kids, you know." He smiled and pushed a strand of wet hair back from my forehead. "We'd have had nice kids, you and I." I turned away quickly so he wouldn't see the tears, which had sprung unbidden into my eyes. He took the hairdryer gently from me and laid it down. Then he pulled me towards him and brushed my tears away with his little finger. "You're not the only one who gets lonely, you know."

"You don't know the meaning of the word."

"You couldn't be more wrong."

"Don't give me that. You could never be tied down. You know it and I know it"

"But what if… " He stopped, then continued. "This contract will be up in a few months. What if you and I…"

"Forget it. It's too late."

"You're probably right." He bent down to pick up his bag. "You should marry someone safe like Richard."

"Maybe I will."

He stepped back as if scalded and looked at me. I stared back mutinously. "Mags, you can't." We stood there glaring at each other for a moment.

"What if…" Then he stopped and turned away. "No, you're right. I'd be the husband from Hell." He laughed, but there was no humour in it. "But you can't pin all the blame on me, Mags. I'm not the only one who likes freedom. You have power trips of your own. Your job, your career, all those computer projects." He smiled a sad slow smile. "We're a right pair, you and me. If we'd got married, we'd have ended up hating each other. I couldn't bear that." He sighed. "You're right. We have left it too late." There was a long pause. I said nothing. "Will you be okay?" he asked gently.

"Why wouldn't I be?"

"Is this it then?"

"Oh go away, Tommy. Get out of my sight."

He picked up his bag and walked towards the door. He opened it and turned around. "Are you sure? We've been through so much together."

"Oh for God's sake, go. You're only prolonging the agony." I pushed him out the door.

He turned. "But maybe if we talked more about…"

I slammed the door in his face. It had taken all my strength. I lay weakly against the back of the door and slid to the ground.

"Maggie, please." He banged on the door. "We can't leave it like this. Come on. Open the door."

"You'll miss your flight."

"Forget the flight. This is more important."

"Tommy for God's sake, go. There's nothing left to talk about."

"But I haven't said… "

"You've said all there is to say. We both have."

I knew if I opened the door I wouldn't be able to let him go. I covered my ears with my hands to block out his voice. After a few minutes I heard his footsteps going downstairs. I waited until the sound had faded before daring to move. This time he wouldn't be back.

It was only when I got back home to the apartment in Dublin and caught sight of myself in the mirror that I realised how much the weekend had taken out of me. Red eyes, grey skin, lines I'd never seen before etched out on my forehead. I looked as old as I felt. I ran a bath and sank into it. The phone rang. I ignored it. We'd said all there was to say. The truth hurt. There was no going back. Tommy and I were finished. The phone continued ringing. I pictured him standing in some airport, one eye on the flight announcements. He'd be worried when I didn't answer. Let him. Ten seconds later I was out of the bath running across the room leaving a trail of frothy bubbles. As I picked it up it rang off. Shivering, I got back into the bath but the pleasure had gone out of it now.

That night I took a sleeping pill. It was the last one. I flung the empty packet into the bin. I was getting far too dependent on them. Somehow I'd have to learn to manage without them as well.

CHAPTER 9

Over the next few weeks I learned to stop jumping every time the phone rang. Tommy had obviously taken me at my word and decided to leave well enough alone. As the time went by, I felt more in control of my life again. I even began to enjoy my weekly outings with Richard.

"Not everyone works as hard as you do, Maggie," he said one night after I'd remarked how full the restaurant was. "Most people try to enjoy life."

"I enjoy life too," I said crossly, taking another sip of wine as if to prove it.

"Do you?" He looked hard at me.

"Of course I do."

"But are you happy?"

"What sort of question is that?"

"A simple question," he sighed. "I know so little about you."

"Don't be ridiculous, Richard. We've been seeing each other for years."

"Once or twice a month, and that's subject to your job or some emergency in Kilmanogue. Don't worry. I'm well aware where I am in the pecking order."

"Poor Richard." I put out my hand to his. "I don't treat you very well, do I?"

"No." He smiled grimly. "God knows I'd happily see you every night of the week, if you'd let me."

"No way." The words were out before I could pull them back. He took a quick swallow of wine, but not before I'd seen the hurt flash across his eyes. "Oh God, Richard, I'm sorry."

"You wouldn't say that if I was O'Connor." He cut savagely into his steak.

"Tommy's out of my life. I told you."

"Really?" he said sarcastically.

"Yes, really," I snapped.

We continued the meal in silence. Richard was far more perceptive than I'd given him credit for. Why couldn't I make do with him instead of...? I wiped some Kiev sauce from my chin.

"Did I ever tell you I wanted to be the first woman on the moon?"

He choked on his steak. "What's that got to do with anything?"

I shrugged. "Just thought you'd like to know."

He put down his knife and fork and looked at me. He had a peculiar expression in his eyes. "I really don't know the first thing about you, Maggie, do I?"

"Don't be silly. Of course you do."

"Why do you come out with me?"

"Because I like you, of course."

"You *like* me?"

"Yes. We enjoy each other's company. We respect each other's work. We're fond of the same things. Isn't that enough? We're both unattached. We're both…"

"Available is the word you're looking for, I think." He signalled a passing waiter. "And no, it's not enough. Two coffees, please."

"That's not fair. There's more to us than that."

"Is there?"

"Of course there is."

There was an awkward silence. The waiter arrived with the coffee.

"You're in a funny mood tonight," I said, reaching for the pot.

"Am I?"

"Yes." I poured. "You're being very dramatic all of a sudden. Cream or milk?"

"Quit playing hostess," he shouted, "and put down that bloody pot." Surprised by his change of mood, I put it down and looked at him. He gripped my hand. "Seeing we get on so well why don't you marry me?" He was holding my hand so tight, it was hurting.

"Don't be ridiculous, Richard." Pulling my hand away, I handed him his coffee. "You know it's not like that."

"I rest my case." He sat back and glared at me.

"You're so irritating sometimes, d'you know that?" I said crossly, lifting the cup to my mouth. I quickly put it down again. "This is cold. Call the waiter."

"Call him yourself." Richard's eyes glinted dangerously.

"Never mind, it'll do."

We finished the coffee and left the restaurant without another word passing between us. We travelled home in silence. Usually a careful driver, that night he drove fast. Twice he sped through orange lights.

"Coming up?" I asked, when we arrived at the apartment.

"What for?"

We sat in silence staring out the window.

"You weren't serious, were you?" I asked after a minute.

"You must be the only woman in Ireland who responds to a proposal like that."

"Richard, I'm sorry, but you're the last man in the world I'd expect a proposal from."

He sighed. "See? There's more of it."

I picked up my bag. "Usual time, Saturday?"

"What's the point?" He turned the key in the ignition. "Goodbye, Maggie. I hope he's worth it."

I looked at his tense face, then leaned over and gave him a quick peck on the cheek.

"Goodnight, Richard. Take care."

He continued to stare straight ahead, and didn't reply.

I looked back when I got inside the hall door. His car hadn't moved. The courtesy light was on. I saw him reach into the glove compartment. Curiously I stood watching as he put a cigarette in his mouth. A lighter burst into flame. His hands were shaking as he leaned forward to light the cigarette. The courtesy light went out. I could see the glow of the cigarette in the darkness as he sat there unmoving. I closed the door puzzled. When had Richard started smoking?

I didn't hear from him the following week, so on Friday I rang him and suggested a movie. "No Maggie. I think it's better this way." His voice was cold, impersonal. "For me anyway."

"It seems a shame when we're both so… "

"Available? Let's not go over the same old ground."

"Does it have to be all or nothing? Why can't we go on the way we were?"

"Because I'm fed up having to make do with O'Connor's leavings," he burst out. "Go away Maggie. Let me get on with my life."

"If you're sure that's what you want?"

"It's not, and you know it. I hope *you* find what *you* want. Goodbye." With that he hung up.

I knew only too well what I wanted, but, unlike Richard, he was not available.

CHAPTER 10

In the months that followed, I was too taken up with work to worry about my non-existent love life. A new project had just started with a company who had branches all over Ireland and the UK. A computer analyst was working for me fulltime to design the system to the client's requirements. Despite that, I was beginning to realise that if the project was to be brought in on time, I'd need more help. The expense would exceed the current budget, so my first job was to persuade their Financial Controller to give me more funding. They gave in eventually, and the project took off. After a few months our design was approved and the software adapted accordingly. The staff training started. For weeks I worked day and night, travelling to each office to ensure that all deadlines were met.

At the weekend, I'd drive down to Kilmanogue to check on Anna's progress. Things had become more hopeful over recent months. She'd been subjected to a new battery of treatment and sight tests. Some of the veils of darkness were at last beginning to lift. The consultant was now quite hopeful that, in time, she'd hold on to a modicum of vision. She still wore a patch over her bad eye, and the children were still calling her Sinbad. Although she was becoming more tolerant of the hospital, she was still suffering severe mood swings. Sometimes, from sheer exhaustion I found it hard not to lose my temper.

One Wednesday night I got back from a long work session of staffing problems in one of the client's country offices. There were two messages on my Ansaphone. I pressed Playback reluctantly. *'Hello, hello, Jesus, Mary and Joseph, I hate these bloody machines. Maggie? Maggie? Oh sorry you're not there, are you? I hope your trip went well. Ring me when you get in. Thanks.'* I smiled. Auntie Nell hated machines of any kind. I pressed the button for the second message, wondering if it might be Tommy. It was because of him I'd bought the machine in the first place. I was still hoping that some day, out of the blue, I'd hear his voice. But it was Auntie Nell again. *'Hello? Hello? Sorry, love, I forgot to leave my name. It's your Auntie Nell. Don't forget to ring me, no matter how late.'*

A sleepy voice answered when I rang. "Maggie, thank God, I know you're busy at work, but I thought you should know that Anna's condition has deteriorated."

"But things were going so well. She told me last weekend she could make out my shape against the window. She was thrilled. We both were."

"I know, love, I know, but the new prognosis is worse than we'd expected."

"Go on," I said, fearing the worst.

"Apparently they ran some new test this week. He says the cornea is deteriorating rapidly. Normally it would take years, but in her case it's going to be very quick."

"What about a transplant?"

"You should talk to him, love. I don't understand half the words he uses."

"You're probably worrying about nothing," I said, trying to cheer her up. "I'll give him a ring first thing. How's the leg, by the way? Have you been able to sleep at all?"

"Yes, but I don't want to get hooked on those pills."

"At your age you'd be entitled to be hooked on something, Auntie Nell."

"I'm glad you're back, love. You must be exhausted with all that travelling."

"I am."

"I wish you were nearer. It's lonely here without your mother. And now with Jonathan gone too…"

"I'll be down as soon as I can," I promised. It must be hard for her losing her son, no matter how bad he was. I immediately thought of my own. I'd been trying so hard over the last few months to suppress the memory of that terrible visit. "Give Anna a big hug from me, Auntie Nell. The kids too."

"I will," she yawned. "They'll be glad you're coming down."

"You'd better go back to bed. We don't want to undo the good of those pills," I said with a laugh. "I'll ring you tomorrow."

The following morning I rang the hospital. It was almost noon by the time the consultant got back to me. It was just as Auntie Nell had said. They'd been hoping that the medication would slow down the deterioration in Anna's condition, but it wasn't working any more. I asked him about a transplant.

"We're running out of time, I'm afraid," he replied. "It's vital she starts classes at once. She'll have to learn to adjust to her condition."

"Are you telling me she's going blind, in spite of all the operations?"

"I'm afraid so, but with new technology, new skills, life doesn't have to be over, especially for someone like her. She's young. She'll learn to cope."

"With two children to look after?"

"I'm not saying it will be easy. I have to go now, I'm afraid."

"I'd like to be there when you tell her, Doctor."

"How soon can you come down?"

I looked at the pile of files on my desk. "Tomorrow afternoon?"

"Fine. I'll see you both after my rounds." He hung up.

That evening, I picked up a booklet I'd been given on coping with blindness. I hadn't looked at it properly before. I suppose I'd been hoping I wouldn't have to. There were all sorts of tips about day-to-day tasks, basic things like stapling currency notes to differentiate between notes of different value. All very well, providing you could find the stapler and know which note you had in your hand to begin with. I turned to another page about filing and using different types of covers on files to help identify them by the texture. There was more of the same for clothing to identify colours by using safety pins stuck in labels. The booklet stressed the importance of order, a place for everything and everything in its place. It didn't sound much like Anna.

Next day I worked through lunch and got on the road early. Anna was kicking up a terrible fuss when I walked into her room.
"Get out, whoever you are," she screamed in my direction. "Get out."
"Stop the racket, Sis. It's only me."
"Oh Maggie. You heard?" she cried.
"Yes, I'm sorry, love." I took her hand. "They promised to wait 'til I got down."
"The nurse let it slip, but I don't believe it. I can't be going blind, not after all the operations." I could hear the desperation in her voice. I sat down on the bed and cuddled her. "It's not fair," she sobbed. "I'll never see the children grow up."
"I'm sure it's not as bad as they say. They're probably just covering themselves."
She stopped crying. "D'you think so?"
"Of course. While there's life, there's hope eh?"
"Oh Mags. If only you were here all the time."
"I'll try and get more time off, I promise."
"The kids are too much for Auntie Nell."
"I know. I'll see what I can do," I said, giving her a quick hug. "Now dry up those tears and let's have some tea. Did you finish the fruit cake?"

I had a chat with the Financial Controller the following week. But, as I suspected, time off was out of the question for the moment. "Surely there are some clients around Wexford who need special attention?" I asked, knowing full well I was clutching at straws.
He shook his head. "Sorry, Maggie. You know the business as well as I do. I'm sorry about your sister. You can be as flexible as you like with your time, but we need you based here not in Wexford."

A few days later I came up with a compromise plan. By working from eight in the morning to eight in the evening four days a week, I could spend three days in Kilmanogue with Anna and the children. I put a rough schedule down on paper showing the clients with whom I was currently working, and how I proposed to fit in all the work. Anxious to demonstrate that they wouldn't be discommoded in any way, I listed all the meetings, visits, and backup work I intended doing. I then sent it off marked for the Financial Controller's immediate attention. His response came that afternoon by way of a phone call from his secretary.

"He's given the go-ahead, Maggie," Catherine told me.

"Are you sure?" I was surprised how quickly he had agreed.

"Between ourselves, he was quite impressed," she said with a giggle. "He hadn't realised how much time you were actually spending on the clients. On the strength of it, he's going to raise some of their fees at the next review."

"You're kidding!"

"You'll have the formal note in the morning. He had to run off to the conference," she giggled again. "You know, the *conference?*"

Some conference. The Financial Controllers had formed a new organisation. They were having a golf match out in Dun Laoghaire to celebrate the end of their first year in existence. He'd been playing well recently, and was hoping to win. I was grateful for his approval. It would be fun to be with the children, and it would give Auntie Nell a much needed break every weekend.

I didn't tell them in Kilmanogue until the following Friday. Sunday was Mothers' day. It would make a nice present for Anna.

"But I was hoping you'd get home for good, Mags."

"This was the best I could do, Sis. I'm sorry."

"Well I'm delighted." Nell beamed. "What do you think, lads?"

The children had brought in a present for their mother. They were busy unwrapping the parcel. "It'll be great, Auntie Mags," John said, pulling impatiently at a coloured tape that was wrapped around the box.

"Leave it, thicko, I'll do it." Emmy pushed his hand away, and started to pick delicately at the knot until it loosened. She pulled off the coloured tape and rolled it into a tidy ball. Then she got a nail file and split the sealing tape across the top of the box.

"Hurry up, Emily," Anna said. "What's taking so long?"

"Have patience, Mummy. You'll get your present," Emmy giggled as she finally opened the box. She lifted out a coloured clock with huge numbers on it. "Here you are."

"What is it?" Anna asked, mystified, as her fingers closed over the present.

"It's a talking clock. It's from Emmy and me," John said solemnly.

"We saw it advertised in a magazine and sent away for it." Emmy smiled proudly.

"We had to save up for weeks and weeks," John added. "Do you like it, Mummy?"

Anna was frowning as she fumbled with the knobs. "Yes, but how does it work?"

Emmy picked up Anna's fingers and held them on a knob. "You have to press this knob here." Her mother pressed. A mechanical voice answered, *'The time is a quarter past seven.'* Everybody laughed.

"Do it again, Mummy," Emmy shrieked.

Anna smiled and pressed the knob. *'The time is a quarter past seven'*.

"He sounds like a right eejit," John said grumpily, "I thought he'd be more like a spaceman."

"He's no eejit," Anna said. "I love him, and ye're so thoughtful to have found it for me. I'm always annoying the nurses, asking them what time it is."

"Do you really love him, Mummy?" Emmy asked anxiously.

"I do, darling. He's the best present I ever got." She reached out to her daughter. "Come here and let me give you a thank-you hug." Her daughter moved closer and hugged her. Anna opened her arms towards John. "John, don't you want one too?"

He shrank back against the wall. "Boys don't hug." But then he relented and moved into the waiting arms.

"Let's give him another go," Emmy said and pressed the knob. *'The time is twenty past seven,'* the voice intoned gravely. She pressed the knob again. *'The time is twenty-one minutes past seven'*. "That was quick," she giggled.

It was a happy visit. Nell went home early. Anna was in such good form that the children and I stayed on. She made us move some of the flowers from her locker to make space for the clock. She practised putting her hand out to press the knob without knocking anything over. It was late when we finally took our leave of her. The children and I were tiptoeing down the corridor when we heard *'The time is eleven o'clock.'* We ran giggling to the lift.

"What's that sound?" Matron emerged from the nurses' station.

"What sound, Matron?" I asked innocently.

'The time is eleven o'clock.' Anna must have hit the button again.

"That sound."

"Must be one of the patients," I said, pushing John and Emmy into the lift. I got in after them and quickly pressed the button. We stood there trying to keep our faces straight.

"I'd better check on Mr Robinson." Matron hurried off as the doors closed. "He must have woken again."

"Poor Mr Robinson," John giggled, "she'll probably wake him up and ask him why he's not asleep."

"And then he'll ask her what time it is," Emmy chortled.

'*The time is eleven o'clock*' they chorused, sounding just like the mechanical voice. I smiled down at their happy faces. It was good to see them laugh. They'd had more than their fair share of tears.

My new schedule started the following week. The early start took a bit of getting used to, but I got so much done in the peace and quiet of the empty building that, by the time most people arrived in, I had a head start on them. At first I was exhausted by lunchtime, but then I realised the secret was to eat a proper lunch. That way I could last all day, and it meant I only ate lightly in the evening, and that in turn, meant fewer trips to the supermarket. The only snag was, that by Thursday evening I was usually too tired to drive down to Kilmanogue, so I used to wait until early Friday morning. I got into the habit of bringing the week's newspapers down with me and reading them to Anna. That way we both kept up-to-date with what was happening in the real world, the world outside work and hospitals.

One Friday morning Anna was looking particularly depressed when I walked in.

"I'm sorry. The traffic was worse than usual." I bent down to kiss her. "How have you been?"

"Fed up."

"Why don't you ask Nutty what time it is?" The children had nicknamed the clock after the Nutty Professor. She smiled, and obediently pressed the knob. '*The time is half past nine*', the mechanical voice announced gravely.

"The other patients are starting to complain about him," she said. "They're great kids, aren't they Mags? Auntie Nell says they do all their own ironing."

"Even John?"

"Even John." She nodded emphatically. "Apparently he tried the usual boy's trick, made a complete mess of it at first, but our Emily wasn't falling for any of that. She kept showing him until he got it right. If only Ma were alive to see that." Anna lay back on her pillow. "Remember how she wouldn't let Dad near the ironing?"

"Or the washing or the cooking or the cleaning." I smiled.

"Now, now, girls." Auntie Nell was just coming in the door. "He was bringing in the wages, remember? That's all a father was meant to do in those days. Nice to see you, Maggie."

"That was before Women's Lib found it's way to Kilmanogue." I pulled a chair out for her. "They were good times though, weren't they?"

"Fabulous. Remember all the walks?" Anna smiled in my direction.

"And the swims," I added.

"And the sand castles," she retorted quickly.

"the tennis matches"

"the nuns"

"the processions"

"the prayers"

Auntie Nell looked from one to the other as we sparked off each other.

"And don't forget the hymns."

"Oh yes. Which was the one that got you into trouble?"

I started to sing in a little girl voice. *"Bring flowers of the fairest"*

She joined in *"Bring blossoms the rarest."*

We carried on together at the top of our voices, *"From garden and woodland and bollocks and blaze."*

"Girls, girls… please." Nell frowned. "Ye're supposed to be ladies."

"Those processions were great fun," Anna sighed, "though we didn't think so at the time, with Sister Dympna breathing down our necks."

"My neck you mean. You were her pet."

"I was no such thing."

"Oh yes you were."

"Oh no I wasn't."

"Oh yes you were."

"I was not."

"Girls, girls," Auntie Nell chided again, "there are other patients here too, you know."

"Sorry, Auntie Nell," Anna said. "They were great times. Weren't they, Mags?"

"Yes love, they were. We were lucky."

"We were so happy and safe then."

Nell sighed, "You two certainly have wonderful memories to look back on."

"That's all we're left with," Anna said glumly. "Still, at least I have the kids. They're my future now." She turned her head in my direction. "Hey, Mags. How come with all that dancing in Dublin you never found anyone?"

"What's with the past tense?" I retorted. "I'm still looking."

"Better hurry up then. You're not getting any younger."

"Maybe she's hiding someone up in that fancy apartment," Auntie Nell said with a smile. I laughed.

"I wish I was. The men I fall for seem to be either married or… or else they're not the marrying kind."

"Come on. There must have been someone," Anna insisted.

"One or two…"

"Why don't you tell us about them?" Auntie Nell said.

"Yes, come on, Mags."

To get them off my back, I began to tell them about Richard, how we'd met through the business, how much we had in common and how reliable he was.

"He sounds nice, dear," Nell said, but Anna wasn't as convinced.

"He doesn't sound very exciting to me."

"He's not," I agreed. I didn't tell them about the shaking hands I'd seen as he lit the cigarette after our last meeting. The vision had haunted me ever since. "He's gone now anyway, so let's change the subject."

"There must have been someone who really turned you on," Anna insisted.

"Yes there was, but… " I stopped abruptly.

"I knew it. Come on. Tell us." She sat up eagerly.

"He's gone too, I'm afraid." I laughed. "Sorry about that."

"You don't seem to have much luck with your men, Mags, do you? Jonathan was no angel but one thing I can say about him… ." Nell and I looked up as she paused dramatically. "With him I was never bored. I know he was a bit of a bollocks. Sorry Auntie Nell, he was. But at least I was never bored."

Now, that was something Anna and I could agree on.

"Who's for Madeira cake?" Nell asked, opening her bag.

"I'll get the tea," I offered quickly and headed out to the nurses' kitchen.

Because Anna had been in for so long we now had the run of it whenever we wanted. I was on my way back with a full tray when I bumped into Marion.

"Anna's in great form, isn't she?"

Marion nodded. "Support is so important at a time like this."

"No chance of a reversal of her condition?" I asked hopefully.

She shook her head. "I'm afraid not. Mr Kelly wants to talk to you both in the morning. There's a call for you, by the way."

F&F still hadn't got used to my not being there on Fridays. I went into the little office and picked up the phone.

"Is that Margaret Brown?"

"Yes."

"Sergeant Smith here. Could you call into the Station?"

"I thought I'd paid that parking ticket, Jimmy?"

"You did, but we have a message for you."

"Okay," I said, looking at the tea tray. It seemed a long time since breakfast.

After the tea and cake I headed off to the Garda Station. I'd said nothing to the others.

"You'll be more comfortable in here, Miss." The Senior Guard came out and led me into a small office off the corridor.

"Why the special treatment?" I asked nervously. "Have I another fine to pay?"

"Are you the mother of Johnny Kerr, currently serving a jail sentence in Manchester?" I nodded speechlessly. He picked up a piece of paper from the desk. "It's bad news, I'm afraid. There's been an accident, a car crash." His face swam in front of me. Someone pushed a chair under me. "We've just received this fax. He was trying to escape apparently."

"That can't be right." I found my voice. "It was a high-security prison."

"I'm sorry, Miss." He picked up the phone. "You can bring in the tea now, Mary."

"What happened?" I whispered.

He looked again at the paper in his hand. "He hijacked a laundry van, killed the driver and drove out through the gate and onto the motorway, but went in the wrong direction. When he tried to turn back, the van skidded and turned over."

"Dear God." I looked at him, horrified. The door opened. A Ban-Garda walked in with tea. She couldn't have been more than a teenager.

"Thanks, Mary. Drink some of this, Miss. It'll help." He pushed a mug over to me. "I rang the prison. It was a bad smash. His neck was broken on impact." I started to shake. He pushed the mug nearer. "Go on. Take some."

I picked up the mug. It shook so much I had to put it down again. "Are you sure it was Johnny?"

"His name was on the tag." He returned to the report. "He still had his foot chains on. I don't know how he managed to drive but apparently it wasn't the first time. High as a kite, I suppose… "

"What?"

"Sorry, Miss." He dropped his eyes again to the report. "It's hard to know what to say. We don't get many of that sort over here."

"I beg your pardon."

His face reddened. "I keep forgetting you're the lad's mother."

"It's alright," I whispered. "I only found him a few months ago, you see?" He nodded sympathetically. "He was a drug-dealer." I swallowed hard. "He blames me for everything that's gone wrong in his life." I shuddered at the memory. "Maybe he's right." He shifted uncomfortably but said nothing. "I intended to go and see him again when things had cooled down. I even started a letter. I was hoping to get him to see my point of view, I suppose, but then my sister, her eyes were damaged, she's had all these operations and…"

"I'm sorry, Miss."

"How is he? Is he bad?"

He couldn't meet my eyes. He looked down at the fax.

"Brain-dead." He said the word so softly I thought I'd imagined it. Then he repeated it. "Brain-dead. Sorry Miss. They'll… er…keep… " He coughed. "They'll keep everything turned on until you've had a chance to…" I sank back in the chair and closed my eyes. I heard him mutter "Sorry Miss," once more as he left the room.

I was glad to be on my own, to enter the swirling darkness inside my head. I saw the prison yard again, the barbed wire fence, the watchtowers. I saw a van burst through the gate and race onto the motorway. I watched as a line of traffic bore down. *Stop him, dear God, stop him*, I screamed, and opened my eyes to the empty room. My heart felt like lead. Everyone who had ever been important to me had gone. I dropped my head into my hands. The door opened.

"Is there someone I can call for you, Miss?" I shook my head.

"Another cup of tea?"

"No thanks."

He closed the door quietly. After a few minutes, I got up and left the station. I went back to the hospital. I told nobody what had happened.

That night I went over and over the months since the visit. Would Johnny have let me see him again? Would it have made any difference if he had? In my heart I knew it probably wouldn't. I remembered the way his eyes had watched the security camera, counting the seconds as it rotated around the room. He must have been planning his escape even then. That must have been why they had chains on his feet. He must have been desperate when he'd attempted to drive with them on. What must he have been thinking as he raced onto that motorway and discovered he was going the wrong way? The panic as he tried to turn the van around, the fear as it went out of control. Several times during the night, I got up and made tea. I ransacked the house for sleeping pills and found some in the back of a drawer. The nightmares had returned with a vengeance. This time I had no one to make them go away.

I was like a wet rag next morning as I left for the hospital. My bag was packed and in the boot of the car. I wasn't sure what to do next. Should I go over and say goodbye or tell them to turn off the machines now? In either case there were arrangements to make and any arrangements could be made more easily from Dublin than from Wexford.

Anna was still in good form from the previous night. "Morning, Maggie," she called brightly from the bed. "Want to know what time it is?"

"If you must. " I sat down heavily.

'The time is ten minutes to ten,' the mechanical voice answered. "Go on, Nutty. Say it again," she giggled. "Maggie didn't hear you. *The time is ten minutes to ten.* One more time, Nutty. She's a bit deaf." She pressed the knob again. *'The time is nine minutes to ten'*.

"FOR GOD'S SAKE QUIT PLAYING WITH THAT YOKE," I shouted, brushing the clock out of her hands. It fell off the locker and landed on the floor with a bang.

Anna shrank back in the bed.

"What's wrong with you?"

I reached down to pick up the clock from the floor. "Sorry. I shouldn't have taken it out on poor Nutty."

"Is he working?"

"Yes, he's fine," I said, putting the clock into her hands. I pressed the knob. *'The time is eight minutes to ten,'* Nutty said in a squeaky voice.

"You've broken him," Anna wailed.

"For God's sake Anna, grow up. It's only a bloody toy."

"It's more than that to me," she said, holding the clock close to her chest. "I'm sorry, Sis," I said guiltily. "Something's come up at work. I have to go back this evening. What time are you expecting Kelly?"

"*Mister* Kelly to you. He said around ten, but you know how busy consultants are."

"They like us to think that. I wonder what he wants to tell us?" I examined her good eye. "Look up at me." She obediently opened it wide. "It looks normal enough except for the tiny scars where the stitches were."

She sighed. "I'm so tired of all this blackness. I had a lovely dream last night. I could see again. I was waiting for you to come in. I was dying to see your face when I told you. Then I woke up and the darkness was back."

"But you told me a while ago you could make out my shape against the window."

"Everything has gone much darker since then."

"Let's hope he has something good to tell us, eh?" I said, trying to cheer us both up.

"I doubt he has."

"Would you like me to read the newspaper?"

"No. I'm not in the mood."

"Good morning, ladies." The crisp tones were unmistakable.

"Morning, Matron," we chorused, as she swept into the room. Instinctively I stood up.

"Mr Kelly's coming to see you today."

I looked at my watch. "He said ten. I hope he won't be late."

"Mr. Kelly doesn't operate to timetables, my dear."

"But I have to get back to Dublin."

"And how are we feeling this lovely morning?" she said, ignoring me as she straightened Anna's bedcovers.

"Fed up, if you must know," Anna replied grumpily.

"Good girl," Matron answered, and swept out of the room.

I laughed. "Who does she remind you of?"

Anna giggled. "Sister Dympna, of course."

"Wonder where she is now?"

"Dead, I suppose. I'll never forget those music lessons and the ruler on the knuckles when we got the notes wrong."

I laughed. "No wonder we didn't like the piano..."

The door swung open. The consultant sailed in, Matron hovering anxiously at his heels. "Good morning, Miss Brown." He nodded to me.

" 'Morning Mr. Kelly," I muttered.

"Open wide now, Anna, like a good girl." He stood over her and shone a pencil light into her eye. "Hold just for a minute," he said, as she automatically recoiled from the light. "Mmm... good, good, thank you." He put the light away into his pocket and turned to me. "You're the sister, yes?"

"Yes. I'm Maggie. We spoke a while ago."

"Oh yes, well you know about your sister's condition?"

"She's neither deaf nor stupid, you know, and she's quite capable of speaking up for herself."

"Maggie, don't be rude," Anna burst out. "He's only doing his job."

"I'm sorry, Mr Kelly," I offered contritely, "please go on."

"It's not looking good, I'm afraid," he said slowly. "Her condition is deteriorating."

"You said that the last time." The words were out before I could stop myself.

"These latest tests show we haven't as much time as we thought."

"What does that mean exactly?" I asked, trying not to look at the frightened expression on Anna's face.

"We were hoping to find a match but I'm afraid, time is running out."

"But there is still some time?" Anna whispered.

"Yes, indeed there is, and while there's time there's hope," he said briskly. "We mustn't give up hope, my dear. Must we?"

"May I see you outside?" I asked abruptly.

"Well, I am in rather a hurry. It is Sunday and…"

"Just for a minute?"

Out of the corner of my eye I saw Matron open her mouth and close it again.

"Okay then, Miss Brown. If you're quick." He hurried out of the room. Matron and I followed him. I closed the door in case Anna could hear. He was standing impatiently looking at his watch.

"We're all busy, Mr Kelly," I said. Matron's lips tightened.

He looked up, surprised. "I suppose we consultants tend to forget that sometimes." He broke into an unexpected smile. It made him look more human. "I'm sorry, Miss Brown. What was it you wanted to ask me?"

"Are you saying that soon it will be too late even for a transplant?" He nodded. "And what sort of time are you talking about? Weeks? Months?" I wasn't in the mood to mince my words.

"In another month the damage will be irreversible." My heart sank. "But don't give up yet." He put a hand on my shoulder. "We're doing all we can. We've notified all the other hospitals, but I'm afraid if nothing happens over the next couple of weeks…" He didn't need to finish the sentence. "Now I really must go, Miss Brown."

"Thanks for your time, Mr. Kelly." I shook hands with him and returned to Anna.

"I hope you weren't rude to him, Maggie."

"Why does everybody treat those fellows like gods?"

"He is God, as far as I'm concerned," she said quietly.

"I suppose so, love." There was something nagging in the back of my mind.

"And what did God have to say for himself, anyway?"

"Just that we still have some time and they're doing all they can."

"Good." Anna sank back contented. "Off you go then if you must."

I looked dubiously at her. "Will you be alright? Auntie Nell said she'd bring the kids in after lunch."

"I'll be fine. I have the radio and I have Nutty to keep me company. Off you go."

As I stood waiting for the lift I still had the niggling in the back of my mind. It was something Mr. Kelly had said. The lift arrived. I got in and pressed the ground floor button. Something about the other hospitals. The lift stopped. The doors opened. Then it came to me. I ran out of the lift over to the reception desk. "Has Mr. Kelly left yet?"

"You'll have to make an appointment." The receptionist replied crisply and returned to her computer screen.

"This can't wait. It's urgent."

"I'm sorry. Our consultants never see anyone without an appointment."

"I know he's up there. I was talking to him a few minutes ago. Please."

She looked at me, then lifted the phone and dialled. "Mary, has Mr. Kelly left yet? ... Right. Thanks." She put down the phone and leaned across the counter. "He's leaving Ward Nine at the moment," she whispered. "Don't tell Matron. Okay?"

"Thanks." I ran back to the lift and hammered on the button. The light showed it was at the top floor. I couldn't wait so I ran up the stairs. Ward Nine was behind the nurse's kitchen on the same floor as Anna's.

He was standing with Matron when I got to the top of the stairs. They stopped talking when they saw me.

"Mr. Kelly," I gasped breathlessly, "I need to ask you something."

"I've told you all I can, Miss Brown." He frowned. "There's really nothing else I can say."

"Could a sibling be a match for Anna?"

"Of course. But I don't under..."

"What about a sibling's child?"

"Possibly," he nodded. "There'd have to be tests of course. It would depend on a number of things."

"Really Miss Brown," Matron barked, "you've taken up quite enough of Mr. Kelly's time."

"In that case we might have a donor," I said, leaning back against the wall.

"A donor? Who?"

"My son."

"Your son? But I didn't know... When did he...?"

"He was in a car crash yesterday. It happened in Manchest......"

Suddenly everything started to whirl. I felt arms holding me, steering me into a chair. When things cleared again, Mr. Kelly and I were sitting in a small alcove off the corridor.

"Are you alright?" he asked anxiously. I nodded. "You were telling me about your son?"

I handed him the scrap of paper the Guards had given me. "I was going to ring them when I got back to Dublin."

"This must be hard for you," he said softly after scanning it. "Perhaps some good will come out of it." He touched my hand. "I'll follow it up straightaway."

"When will you know?"

"In a few hours. Will you be staying on here?" I nodded. "Don't say anything to your sister. Better not to raise false hopes." With that he hurried off down the corridor.

I shuddered at the memory of the blue eyes blazing their hatred through the wire mesh. Was it possible those same eyes could help Anna? What would she think if she knew? I got up and went back into her room.

I found her fretting. "What if we don't find a match, Mags?"

"Don't worry. They're still looking."

"I was sure we'd find a donor. That's why I was able to put up with all this." She waved her arms around frantically. "What will I do if…?"

"Don't love." I sat down on the bed and put my arms around her. "It's not over yet."

"Yes it is."

"Let's find something to do." I looked around desperately for a way to distract her. "What would Ma have done?"

"She'd have said another bloody rosary. Some good that'll do."

"Why don't we give it a try?"

"You can if you want to," she said grumpily. "I'm not in the mood."

I couldn't really blame her. The hours dragged by. Each one felt like two. We had numerous cups of tea and finished all the cake. I tried not to picture what was happening in Manchester. Auntie Nell brought in the children but they got too rowdy so I sent them off with her for a walk.

Around five I couldn't stand the confines of the room any longer, so I persuaded Anna to come out for some air with me. She held onto my arm tightly the whole way. We found a bench and sat down in the sun. I tried to describe everything that was going on in the park. She laughed at my attempts to describe what people were wearing. "Better stick to the day job, Mags. You'll never make it in the fashion business."

"That's why I never wanted to work in the shop. You were the one with the clothes sense." I could have kicked myself for being so tactless.

"That won't be much use when I'm blind."

"So this is where you are, girls." I looked up and saw Mr. Kelly approach. Anna jerked around at the sound of his voice. "What's he doing out here?"

"I have news for you," he said, sitting down beside us. Anna moved over nervously to give him more room. He nodded at me over her head. "We've found a match, a young man who's been in a car crash in England."

"But you said…" Anna stopped.

"You're sure it's a match?" I looked hard at him.

"Certain." He nodded emphatically. "They've run all the tests. The results are positive."

"Who is he?" Anna asked. I shook my head in warning at Mr. Kelly.

"Just another victim of the roads, I'm afraid," he replied quickly. "He was in his late teens. That's all the information we have. His mother has given her consent."

"Isn't that wonderful, Maggie?" Anna squeezed my hand. "Why are you so quiet? Aren't you glad for me?"

I gave her a quick hug. "Of course I am, love. I'm delighted." I turned to Mr. Kelly. "When will the …er… operation take place?"

"His cornea will be removed at once. The transplant is scheduled for noon tomorrow." He smiled and looked at me. "His heart and kidneys could be harvested too. That way, by dying he'll be giving new life to a number of people." I nodded, glad that Anna couldn't see my face.

She was in great form that night, insisted on my washing her hair. I kept telling her it would be tucked into a plastic cap and the surgeons would have other things on their mind, but my words fell on deaf ears.

Later, on my way home, I rang the prison. In accordance with the State custom, the remains of Johnny Kerr Prisoner Number 15496 would be cremated.

CHAPTER 11

It was morning, the day of Anna's operation, the day her life could begin again. Mr Wainwright from the agency telephoned, expressing his sympathy. I told him about the cremation and rang off quickly. I was far too concerned about Anna to spend time talking to him.

As soon as I got in to the hospital, I broke the news to her that I had to go to London; that something had gone wrong with my last project.

"But you can't leave now, Mags," she whimpered, all the anticipation and excitement of the previous night evaporated.

"I'm not going anywhere until I know you're okay. By the time I get back you'll be your old self again bossing everyone around."

"What if something goes wrong?"

"You heard Mr. Kelly. He's done this operation hundreds of times."

But she wouldn't calm down. Around eleven, Marion came into her room. "This will do the trick," she smiled, as she prepared an injection. "She won't even remember going down to theatre."

"Promise you won't leave me, Maggie." Anna sank back on the pillow. "I'm trusting you to keep an eye on them."

"Keep an eye on them?" I laughed. "When did you become a comedienne?"

"When did I become a ca...ca... ?" Her voice trailed off.

"Doesn't take long, does it?" Marion smiled at me. "Off you go."

But I wanted to stay with her to the last minute, so I sat down and picked up a copy of Woman's Way. I tried to concentrate on the magazine, but Johnny's eyes were boring into my brain. I couldn't help feeling I was betraying him all over again. I flicked over the pages, trying to obliterate the image, but every page seemed to have eyes on them, glamorous sexy ones in the ads, deep soulful ones belonging to the heroes in the stories. From time to time I checked on Anna. She'd always been able to look beautiful, even while she was asleep. Today, her arms were spread in a graceful arc above her head, her hair draped across the pillow in long golden strands. She seemed to have recovered something of the old glamour.

The door opened. An orderly walked in with a trolley followed by Marion. My heart thumped as I watched Anna's hair being tucked into a plastic cap. She was lifted and slid smoothly onto the trolley. She gave a gentle sigh as she settled onto her new bed, but remained in a deep sleep. I followed them along the corridor. Marion barred my way at the entrance to the lift. "You'll have to say goodbye here."

"Take care of her, won't you?" I leaned down to kiss Anna.

"We will. Don't worry." Marion smiled. "Why don't you go get some lunch? What's on today Paddy?"

"Roast pork," he said, pressing the button, "with crackling and roast spuds."

The doors closed. I watched the lift descend through the numbers. The light stopped at the sign for *'Theatre.'* I turned away. There was nothing more I could do for her now, so I took Paddy's advice and went to the canteen. After a couple of mouthfuls, I pushed the plate away. I couldn't remember the last time I was hungry. I toyed with a piece of apple tart. I felt sure Tommy would want to know what had happened so I went into a telephone booth in the main hall and called the emergency number. Nobody there knew where he was, but I left a message anyway. It probably wouldn't get to him, and by now he'd probably forgotten all about me and my son, so what did it matter? What did anything matter?

Thinking a spot of fresh air might revive me, I left the hospital and walked across the road to the park. A few young mothers sat around on benches, surrounded by toddlers playing in the afternoon sun. I sat down under a tree and watched them. They were trying to get a dog to fetch a stick. They kept throwing the stick and shouting at him, but the dog didn't seem interested. One of the smaller lads ran up to him, threw the stick and then ran after it to show the dog what they wanted. The others kids watched to see if it would work. The lad looked back to see if the dog was following him and tripped. He fell headlong into a puddle of mud and started to cry. His mother ran over and picked him up. The others kids started to jeer. There was a sharp whistle. The dog's ears cocked and he shot off towards an elderly man who was approaching slowly, aided by a walking stick. The dog jumped up and down barking and wagging his tail. The old man put the lead on. The toddlers looked on disappointed, as man and dog disappeared out the gate of the park. Tears all wiped away now, the little lad joined the older kids again and they went back to their game. Afternoons like these were something Johnny and I never had. He'd probably never even played football. Because of me, he'd missed out on those things. No wonder he'd hated me. A distant bell rang. Three o'clock, time to return.

Anna wasn't back from theatre, so I sat down and picked up the Woman's Way again. Then I threw it down and went to the window. The traffic was starting to build up. Soon I'd have to face into it. This waiting was getting me down. I was never blessed with patience. I took after Dad in that respect. *'For goodness sake John, stop your fidgeting and go for a walk,'* was what Ma would say. I hoped they were watching over Anna now, wherever they were. She'd need all the help she could get.

At long last the door opened and Paddy pushed in the trolley. Matron hovered behind. Anna's eyes were covered with fresh bandages. I leaned down and kissed her.

"Maggie?" she said drowsily, raising a hand to the bandages, "is it over?"

"Don't touch those bandages, Anna," Matron said sharply, "Mr. Kelly will be in to see you in a few minutes."

"How was the roast pork?" Paddy asked, as he helped Anna slide back onto her bed.

"Lovely thanks."

"Told you, didn't I?" He grinned and left the room.

"Don't go jumping around now, like a good girl," Matron said, as she tucked the blankets in tightly around her patient.

"No...won't," Anna yawned, "want... back...sleep."

The door opened. "And how's my favourite blonde?" Mr Kelly was still wearing his theatre gown.

"Sleepy." She yawned again and slipped further down in the bed.

"Did everything go okay?" I looked at him anxiously.

"Perfectly. The bandages will come off in a day or two."

"Will she... will she...?"

"Yes" he smiled.

"Thank God!"

"Shouldn't you be going over to Manchester?" he whispered.

"I wanted to make sure she was okay first."

"She's fine. Don't worry. You can ring her later tonight."

I looked at my watch. He was right. I didn't have much time if I was to make the flight.

It was dusk when the plane touched down. The Hertz car was in the appointed space. I'd been given directions to the prison. Never having been to a cremation before I had no idea what to expect. Darkness was closing in as I drove along the motorway. I felt more alone than I'd ever felt in my life. My heart sank further as the high walls of the prison loomed into view.

The yard was lit by massive spotlights. The Warden was standing framed in the doorway. As we shook hands, the strangest feeling swept over me. I felt I was in a play and somebody had just handed me a script. I was playing the part of the mother of a young man who had just died. I was grieving, of course, but it was nothing personal. It was somebody else's story. It would be a difficult role to play because I'd never had a son and even if I had, he'd never have been in prison. But I wasn't afraid. I knew I could do it. It wouldn't hurt, because it wasn't real.

The Warden stood to one side as I entered the prison. He led me towards a bench. "I've organised some tea," he said. "We have a few minutes before the … er…" His face blurred for a moment. I felt his hand on my arm. The fog cleared. He was holding out a cup to me and smiling. "Where's that young man of yours?"

"Young man?"

"The one you were with last time?"

"We're no longer together."

"I'm sorry. You shouldn't have to go through something like this on your own." He sat down beside me. "Burying a child is against the natural order." I nodded and sipped the hot liquid. "Though I have to say he was a tough one, your Johnny."

I turned to him. "Tell me about him. There's so much I need to know."

He shook his head. "Sometimes you're better off not knowing."

I caught his arm. "Don't say that. Please. What was he like?"

"A loner."

"He must have had some friends?"

He shook his head. "Not to my knowledge."

"Surely, in a place like this?" I insisted.

"No. He didn't seem to need anyone."

"What about visitors?"

"Never had any. Except for Social Workers of course, and the time you came. He was always on his own. Seemed to prefer it that way." We sat in silence for a few minutes, then he continued. "Lots of prisoners try to break out of here, you know, but they usually work in a gang. Not young Kerr. Every time he made a break for it, he was doing it by himself. Probably used the money you'd given him to buy some cooperation on the outside." He shook his head. "He didn't trust anyone in here. Independent to the last. Poor sod. Cost him dearly in the end."

Independent, that's something he got from me, I thought.

The Warden looked at his watch. "If you're ready Miss, I think we'd better go."

I followed him through a side door down a stone corridor. The ceiling was high. A single narrow window let in the only light. There was a hole in the glass through which a cold wind whistled. Somebody had tried to fix it with a piece of tape. I shivered as we passed it. Our footsteps echoed dully on the stone flags. At the end of the corridor a door opened into a tiny chapel. I paused at the entrance to let my eyes get accustomed to the darkness. I looked around and shuddered. There was a plain black coffin on a table to the side of the altar. A white candle on top of the coffin. Unlit.

The warden walked ahead of me up the aisle. I followed shakily. He stopped at the top and ushered me into a seat but I stood mesmerised staring at the coffin. I put my hand out to touch it. The wood felt cold. There was a small metal plate. *John Kerr 1964—1983.* They'd said this wasn't real, but suddenly I wasn't so sure. Confused, I looked at the Warden. He nodded and helped me into the pew. I knelt down, my gaze drawn like a magnet back to the coffin. Who was this John Kerr? Some mother's son, according to the script. Some other mother. I knew he couldn't be mine.

A young priest emerged from behind the altar and carried a lighted taper towards the candle. I could see his hands tremble as he tried to light it. After the third attempt the flame caught and the candle flickered into life. I watched it grow stronger, then quiver in a sudden draught. The light cast an orange glow across the black wood. It appeared less black now, less dead. The priest sprinkled Holy Water over the coffin and started to mumble some prayers. I couldn't hear the words. All I could hear was my own heartbeat. The priest looked over at me from time to time, as if I were part of the scene. He seemed too young, too innocent to be in a place like this. He sprinkled the water again and made the Sign of the Cross. Then he removed the candle. In the wall behind the table, curtains parted. I hadn't noticed them up to now.

The coffin started moving towards the opening. I felt a scream build inside my head. I swallowed back the bile in my throat. I must keep calm. It wasn't over. I couldn't afford to lose control, not yet, not until the end of the play.

The coffin was still moving. Only half of it was left in view now. The scream started to build again. The coffin disappeared and the curtains fell back into place. Nothing left now only the empty table. I sank back wearily against the seat. That young boy was gone to the flames, the flames of Hell. My body started to shake. I tried to stop it but couldn't.

"Miss, are you alright?"

I looked up at him. Then I knew. This wasn't a play. This was real. It was my son who had gone to Hell, not somebody else's. The room spun. I heard a door open, the sound of running footsteps. Suddenly there were strong arms around me, familiar bristle against my face. I looked up into golden flecks. It was over. It didn't matter if I broke now. Tommy would take the pain away.

For what seemed like an eternity I clung to him, sobbing my heart out. Eventually the tears stopped and I could speak.

"What took you so long?"

"Is that all the thanks I get for crossing half the world?"

"Where were you?"

"Don't ask," he said with a grin, "and if it wasn't for Wainwright I wouldn't be here."

"You are. That's all that matters." I sighed, and leant back against him. There was so much I had to tell him. "How long can you stay?" He shook his head. I stared up frightened. "Please Tommy, a few days at least. I... I..."

"Go on. Say it."

"I... I need you. Don't go away again, not yet."

"Who said anything about going away?"

"What do you mean?"

"I've decided to join the human race again, Mags." I stared at him uncomprehendingly. "So this time you're stuck with me whether you like it or not. What have you to say about that?"

"I don't believe you."

"Oh, you can believe me alright," he grinned, "Mick and I have been saving. We've put an offer on an old hangar down in Kildare. We're going to open a flying school. I'm going to be flying again. Isn't that wonderful? I'm home for good Mags. You and I can be a normal couple. I know how much you like your independence and that's all very well, but there comes a time when even you..."

"Normal?"

He chuckled. "Well, we can try."

"I've never liked that word."

"Me neither." He grinned again. "So, are you game?"

"On one condition."

"Name it."

"I'm your first pupil."

"You? Why would you want to learn to fly?"

"I've always fancied going to the moon."

The Beginning.

Anne Dunphy lives in Dublin. She started writing in 1995. Her articles have been published in the national press and magazines. Her radio plays have been produced by local and national stations. She also writes for stage and screen. One of her plays was produced by the Prairie Dog Company of Chicago in 2001.

Second Chances is her first novel

ISBN 1-4120-1386-0